The Traditional Theater of Japan

The Traditional 演劇

Theater of Japan

*by Yoshinobu Inoura
and Toshio Kawatake*

New York · WEATHERHILL · Tokyo
In collaboration with the Japan Foundation

This book was originally published in English by the Kokusai Bunka Shinkôkai in two volumes under the titles *A History of Japanese Theater I: Noh and Kyôgen* and *A History of Japanese Theater II: Bunraku and Kabuki*. The characters on the title page read *engeki* (drama).

Credits for the monochrome photographs are due Tadashi Kimura, Yutaka Umemura, Toshirô Morita, and National Research Institute of Cultural Properties.

First one-volume edition, 1981

Published by John Weatherhill, Inc., of New York and Tokyo, with editorial offices at 7-6-13 Roppongi, Minato-ku, Tokyo 106, Japan. Copyright © 1971, 1981 by the Japan Foundation, 3-6 Kioi-cho, Chiyoda-ku, Tokyo, Japan; all rights reserved. Printed in Japan.

Library of Congress Cataloging in Publication Data: Inoura, Yoshinobu, 1914– / The traditional theater of Japan. / Originally published in 1971 in 2 separate volumes: A history of Japanese theater 1: Noh and Kyôgen and A history of Japanese theater 2: Bunraku and Kabuki. / Includes index. / Theater—Japan—History. / I. Kawatake, Toshio, 1924– joint author. / II. Title. / PN2921.I67 1981 / 792′.0952 / 80-29635 / ISBN 0-8348-0161-2

CONTENTS

Editorial Note ix
Periods of Japanese History x

Part One. Noh and Kyôgen

Introduction: A Brief Perspective 3
1 The Current of Ancient and Medieval Drama 5
    Ancient Drama, 5 • Medieval Drama, 10
2 Kagura 17
    History of Kagura, 17 • Ancient Types, 19
3 Gigaku 24
    History of Gigaku, 24 • Performances of Gigaku, 26
4 Bugaku 31
    History of Bugaku, 31 • Performances of Bugaku, 34
5 New Sarugaku 40
    History of New Sarugaku, 40 • Performances of New Sarugaku, 42
6 Protoypes of Noh 46

v

At the Imperial Court, 46 • At Temples and Shrines, 48 • Among the Common People, 49

7 Ennen Noh — 52
History of Ennen Noh, 52 • Performances of Ennen Noh, 56

8 Sarugaku Noh — 62
History of Sarugaku Noh, 62 • Performances of Sarugaku Noh, 65

9 Dengaku Noh — 69
History of Dengaku Noh, 69 • Performances of Dengaku Noh, 71

10 Shugen Noh — 75
History of Shugen Noh, 75 • Performances of Shugen Noh, 77

11 The History of Nohgaku — 81
Three Periods of Development, 81 • First Stage of Consolidation: Kan'ami, 82 • Second Stage of Consolidation: Zeami, 89 • Final Stage of Consolidation: On'ami and Zenchiku, 95 • Period of Change: Nobumitsu, 100 • Period of Stabilization, 102

12 Nohgaku Today — 107
Actors, Stage, and Performance, 107 • Yôkyoku as Noh Text and Dance as Action, 111 • Noh Music, 113 • Sets, Properties, and Masks, 114 • Five Classes of Noh, 115 • Writers of Noh, 118 • Functions of the Kyôgen Actors, 119 • Kyôgen Writers and Hereditary Texts, 120 • Kinds of Kyôgen, Repertoire, 121 • Kyôgen Masks, 124

13 The Relation with Chinese Drama — 126

Gigaku, 126 • Bugaku, 127 • New Sarugaku, 128 • Ennen Noh, 128 • Nohgaku, 129

Part Two. Bunraku and Kabuki

14 Tokugawa Theater 133
The Four Great Performing Arts, 133 • Bunraku and Kabuki as Sister Arts, 134 • Their Common Characteristics, 136 • This-World Humanism of the Popular Audience, 138 • Social Restraints, 142 • Bunraku, Kabuki, and the Stratification of Japanese Theater, 144

15 The Style and Beauty of Bunraku 146
The Name Bunraku, 146 • The Three Components, 147 • Tayû and Samisen, 148 • Puppets and Puppeteers, 149 • The Aesthetics of the "Super-Puppets," 154 • Puppet Plays for Adults, 154

16 The Drama of Bunraku 156
Literary Jôruri, 156 • The Varieties of Jôruri, 157 • The Composition of Jôruri, 160 • The Dramatic Elements of Jôruri in Sewamono, 161 • The Dramatic Elements of Jôruri in Jidaimono, 166

17 The History of Bunraku 171
An Orderly Development, 171 • The Three Elements, 172 • The Origin and Development of Puppeteering, 172 • Jôruri and the Samisen, 174 • The Age of Old Jôruri, 177 • Development and Decline of Gidayû Jôruri, 178 • Present Conditions of the Bunrakuza, 182

18	**The Style and Beauty of Kabuki**	183
	An Introductory Note, 183 • The Stage and the Theater, 184 • Actors and Their Art, 188 • Style and Aesthetics, 195	
19	**The Drama of Kabuki**	205
	Classification, 205 • The Eighteen Favorites, 207 • Kizewamono, 209 • Dance Pieces, 212 • Kabuki and the Life of the People, 214	
20	**The History of Kabuki**	217
	Origin and Early Development, 217 • The Establishment of Real Drama with Dialogue, 219 • Expansion Through Adaptations from Bunraku, 219 • The Maturation of Edo Kabuki, 220 • Modernization, 221	

Appendix 1: The Repertoire of Bugaku Pieces	225
Appendix 2: The Repertoire of Noh Pieces	227
Appendix 3: The Repertoire of Kyôgen Pieces	233
Index	245

Groups of photos appear between pages 54–55, 182–83

EDITORIAL NOTE

The Hepburn system, with minor modifications, has been followed in romanizing Japanese words, the chief difference being the use of a circumflex instead of a macron to indicate long vowels, as was done in the original Kokusai Bunka Shinkôkai editions. The exception to this rule is the word Noh, which is used instead of Nô and also appears in this form in such compounds as Nohgaku, Dengaku Noh, Sarugaku Noh, and the like. Theatrical genres appear in roman with capitals—for example, Gigaku, Dengaku, Noh, Kabuki. Japanese personal names are given in Japanese style: surname followed by given name.

PERIODS OF JAPANESE HISTORY

Divisions used in this book	Other possible divisions
Primitive period: up to A.D. 600	Jômon period: up to 200 B.C.
	Yayoi period: 200 B.C. to A.D. 250
	Tomb period: 250–552
Ancient period I: 600–800	Yamato period: 300–710
	Nara period: 710–94
Ancient period II: 800–1200	Heian period: 794–1192
Medieval period I: 1200–1250	Kamakura period: 1192–1333
Medieval period II: 1250–1350	Muromachi, or Ashikaga, period: 1333–1573
Medieval period III: 1350–1450	Nambokuchō period: 1335–92
	Sengoku period: 1467–1600
Medieval period IV: 1450–1600	Azuchi-Momoyama period: 1573–1600
Tokugawa period: 1600–1868	Edo period: 1600–1868
Modern period: 1868–	Meiji period: 1868–1912
	Taishô period: 1912–26
	Shôwa period: 1926–

PART ONE

Noh and Kyôgen
by Yoshinobu Inoura

INTRODUCTION:
A BRIEF PERSPECTIVE

The history of Japanese drama is not, contrary to popular thought, anything extraordinary, isolated from the rest of the world, but is an integral part of the history of world drama. Be it ordinary drama, or masked drama, or puppet drama, all drama expresses man's spiritual and cultural life directly, impressively, and vividly by bodily action. It comforts and delights people, stimulates them to think, and purifies their minds. The world of drama becomes meaningful only when it is supported by the active participation of those who enjoy it. And it reflects man's life all the better for this.

In recent years, Nohgaku (Noh and Kyôgen) and Kabuki as representatives of Japanese drama, and the *jôruri* puppet play known by the name of Bunraku, as well as the ancient court music and dance known as Bugaku, have on a number of occasions been performed outside Japan. The special quality of Japanese drama that attaches great importance to atmosphere cannot easily be explained in writing, and therefore those people outside Japan who have had the chance to see these performances are fortunate indeed. Further, if they have the chance to see the arts in Japan, their understanding will be deeper and more accurate, because in performances abroad it is likely that items believed to be of interest to the audiences of each country will have been selected for the program, and other parts of the plays will have been cut, to avoid boring the public, or the manner of presentation will be modified to make the plays more readily understandable. All these are expediencies that can hinder proper appreciation.

In Japan today, many theatrical arts of long standing, some dating from a thousand years ago like Kagura and Bugaku, are still performed for those who appreciate them, while various forms of contemporary drama are presented for other audiences. This is a phenomenon that is not commonly found in other countries. But even here are restricting circumstances, for what can be seen on the stage today does not necessarily represent each category at its best. What we see is the result of many changes in the past. Even those forms of drama that have died were valuable in their own periods. Here I wish to present, historically, the various types of drama that flourished in different periods and to make clear as far as possible the history and present state of Japanese drama, which is unique and yet possesses universality at the same time.

On the fringe of Japanese drama are innumerable elements such as fragmentary songs, dances, narratives, and mimicry. Of these, those with clearly recognized standards and artistic values are referred to by the term *geinô* (public entertainments or theatricals). Out of the seeds of these arts germinated what may be called predramatic forms, which developed into full-fledged drama with substantial form and content. Moreover these three—*geinô* (predramatic entertainments), the predramatic forms, and full-fledged drama—always possessed close interrelationships and continue to influence each other in the present day. Only by keeping this *geinô* constantly in mind can one clearly grasp the history and reality of Japanese drama.

Roughly speaking, three attitudes are discernible in the study of the history of Japanese drama being carried out at present: orthodox study that concentrates on the drama itself, folkloric interpretation that concentrates on the relationship between drama and *geinô,* and the type of study that synthesizes these two attitudes. The third is the most difficult. But it is the latest and most productive attitude and promises the best results. My own attitude is in keeping with this. When approached in this way, the true features of the history of Japanese drama, I believe, will be revealed most clearly and in the best perspective.

CHAPTER ONE

THE CURRENT OF ANCIENT AND MEDIEVAL DRAMA

Ancient Drama

Primitive Period (up to A.D. 600) Two millenniums ago Japan emerged from the four-thousand-year Stone Age period of Jômon culture, when rope-patterned (*jômon*) earthen vessels were used, and entered the Yayoi period (350 B.C. to A.D. 250), when a new type of pottery, today called Yayoi after its place of discovery, supplanted the Jômon type. By that time, some progress had been made in agricultural techniques, and small settlements or villages had been formed where people began to cultivate the land, form communities, and lead fairly stable lives. Communities were joined to constitute many small provinces, among whose chieftains were women who practiced witchcraft.

After the third century, the process of the grouping together of these small provinces continued. People became more settled and less migratory. And in their life were to be seen the earliest instances of theatrical art. In their hearts was fear of nature and death as threatening forces, a fear that gave rise to reactions in such forms as shamanism and religious rituals. These led to the creation of crude and simple songs, dances, and imitative acts. Love and labor were also no less strong motives for such arts. The life of people at that time is amply testified to by the excavated articles used in religious ceremonies, ornaments, clay miniatures of musical instruments like the flute, koto, and hard drum, masks, and more particularly by clay figurines called *haniwa*, representing men and women, some having stern faces, some singing, or playing instruments, cheering and dancing merrily.

The period from the third century to the end of the sixth is called the Yamato period, from the place name of the cultural center of the period. This was the period when Kagura, the ancient drama, had just sprung up, and, once the basis was completed for its establishment as drama, it became the kernel of primitive drama. The myths of the Heavenly Cave (Ama no Iwato) and Luck of the Sea and Luck of the Mountain (Umi-sachi Yama-sachi) appear in the oldest histories of Japan, written in the next period—*Kojiki* or *Record of Ancient Matters* (712) and *Nihon Shoki* or *Chronicles of Japan* (720)—as events of the remote Age of the Gods, but in reality they reflect the actual aspects of Kagura as it existed in this early period. Likewise, there are many instances of close relationships between myths and Kagura. Also, large numbers of folk tales, legends, and more than two hundred songs quoted in the two history books just mentioned and in topographical works called *Fudoki* (eighth century) supplied materials for other types of ancient drama. All these theatrical arts of the primitive age, including Kagura and other secular plays, were crude and simple, but they gave frank expression to the emotions and feelings of the people of the time. Kagura, in particular, because it was an offering to the august gods, or was drama concerning gods, was created and produced with deliberate care, and so its position was maintained more securely than were the positions of other primitive dramatic arts in antiquity.

This period was far less subject to the influence of continental culture than the periods that followed. It was a period when, generally speaking, the traditional Japanese arts were guarded and fostered. Some degree of ties with the Asian continent, however—with China and India in particular and the Korean peninsula to a lesser degree—had existed since remote antiquity, and was reflected in myths and folklore. From the third century on, clear evidence of such contacts is to be found in politics, economy, and culture. Then, between 538 and 552, Buddhism was introduced to Japan, to exert an enormous and profound influence on religion, thought, learning, material civilization, and even the people's feeling and sensitivity—on both material and spiritual planes—for long periods to come. Along with this, Gigaku as a regular type of ancient drama was to some extent introduced, and part of Bugaku also, to Japan. Toward the end of this period, a new age began to unfold both for Japan and for ancient drama.

Ancient Period I (600–800) The first part of the Ancient period covers the seventh and eighth centuries. The seventh corresponds to the Asuka and Fujiwara periods and the eighth to the Nara period. In the middle of the seventh century, the sagacious and ambitious Prince Shôtoku (572–621), assisting the empress Suiko as her regent, strove with extraordinary zeal for Japan to absorb continental culture and paved the way for the rapid development of Japanese culture. The prince brought about innovations in many long-established undesirable habits and systems, protected and encouraged Buddhism, and endeavored to firmly establish the state's authority and improve the livelihood of the people. Even after his time, in broad terms, Japan continued its steady progress along the lines set down by him. The total population of Japan then exceeded three million, among whom were a large number of men from the Asian continent who, as naturalized Japanese, made great contributions to the nation's material and spiritual well-being. Written literature, which was closely related to drama, was already to be found at the beginning of this period. In addition to books of history and topographical works, ritual or ceremonial addresses, *norito,* were presented to the gods. The *Man'yôshû,* an anthology of four thousand five hundred poems (*waka*), and the *Kinkafu,* a transcription of koto music, date from the same period. Further, in sculpture, architecture, and painting, the age covers the Asuka, Hakuhô, and Tempyô periods, famous in art history for their gorgeous and dignified art styles. Ancient drama was to achieve development with this cultural background.

During the seventh century, Kagura continued to advance, as it had during the previous period. During the eighth century, with the change and development of both the concept of the gods and the manner of religious ceremonies, the elements of innocent imitation tended to dwindle and disappear. The primordial aspect of Kagura persisted only in local areas, where its progress was as free and unrestricted as it was crude. There was even created a type of Kagura in which dolls replaced actors. During the eighth century is also to be found the forerunner of Mikagura, the Kagura for court ceremonies, which was to be perfected in the latter half of the Ancient period. Again, there existed such dances accompanied by songs as Yamatomai and Tôka, developed on the basis of customs in Japanese provinces and in China, respectively, and adapted to conform to the life style of the court. Yamatomai, an ancient dance first performed before the emperor Ôjin (c. A.D. 400), was adopted for certain ceremonies like the *daijôe* and the *chinkonsai*. Tôka, a group dance introduced from China, featured a tripping of the feet on the ground.

Gigaku and Bugaku, imported on a large scale at the beginning of the seventh century, also developed with time. The body of Gigaku in particular had already gone through the stage of organization during the seventh century and produced a new style during the eighth. Organization of Bugaku, on the other hand, began during the eighth century, and it was not until the next period that further advancement occurred.

In this way, in the first half of the Ancient period, indigenous Japanese art and art of foreign origin came to exist side by side for the first time. Japanese drama entered an authentic "historical" age. Forming the background for this was the liberal supply of cultural energy from the continent and the exploration and display of Japan's own latent energy that was thereby liberated.

Ancient Period II (800–1200) The four centuries from 800 to 1200 are known as the Heian period, when the emperor, with the capital in Kyoto then called Heian-kyô, ruled the country, assisted by the Fujiwara family, a mighty aristocratic family that wielded enormous power. The T'ang dynasty of China, which exerted great influence on Japan in the first half of the Ancient period, had decayed and was followed by the Sung in the tenth century, but Japan, which had fully absorbed T'ang culture, began to create new Japanese culture on an independent basis in the middle of the ninth century, and, with the progress and prosperity of an aristocratic society that was supported by economic development, there flourished a type of culture characterized by the grace and brilliance of the court and aristocracy. At the beginning of the tenth century, the court and aristocracy had discovered a now classic beauty that put great store in emotion and intelligence, spirituality in content and expression, and harmony of form. Then, toward the end of the century, their idea of beauty was further elaborated to such an extent that it could rely on emotional and symbolic expression referred to by the highly sophisticated concepts of *aware, okashi,* and *yosei,* a beauty thick with deep but repressed, delicately unostentatious feeling. The famous novel *The Tale of Genji (Genji Monogatari)* is written with this aestheticism, and the final form of Bugaku also was supported by this sensitivity. During the twelfth century, the militarists' influence slowly rose. Intercourse between provincial culture and the culture of the capital region began, which led to transformation and confusion in cultural and aesthetic viewpoints. There also arose a new tendency in Buddhist philosophy that brought it closer to the people. Similar changes took place in various aspects of culture that marked the transition to the Middle Ages that followed.

The ancient drama of this period included, apart from what it inherited from the preceding period, an important new addition, Shin Sarugaku, and other forms, which became the direct sources of the drama of the Middle Ages.

In the lineage of Kagura, the ceremonial Kagura for the court, Mi-kagura, was first perfected; other forms of Kagura for dancers and for dolls were also created, developed, and perfected; the unique Seinô Kagura was likewise perfected. Gigaku, which had been completed in the previous age, began to decay in the tenth century because it did not match the Buddhism and the aesthetic attitude of the new age, and it soon became extinct. Bugaku, on the contrary, reflecting the general trend against the absorption of Chinese culture, thrived. There was much experimenting with many new compositions and adaptations after the middle of the ninth century. Bugaku effected a thorough reorganization and refinement in every aspect, until in the early part of the eleventh century it was perfected as a manifestation of the aesthetic ideals of the court and aristocracy.

Contemporary with this drama that continued from the previous era, there arose in the tenth century a popular new type of Sarugaku, Shin (New) Sarugaku, which thrived during the eleventh century and gradually disappeared, having been assimilated into other medieval drama. This was conceived as a uniquely Japanese art as contrasted with the older Sarugaku of foreign origin. In it many fragmentary songs, dances, and imitative acts of various kinds enjoyed by the people were utilized, while it also cultivated its own unique, droll style of imitation. It was characterized, however slightly, by the emphasis it laid on the elements of action and speech. Apart from these, there were also Dengaku, born of peasants' music and dance, as well as the arts of sorcerers (*jushi* or *shushi*), which were an attempt at the dramatization of Buddhist sorcery practiced in temples. These also developed into medieval drama. Among special instances may be mentioned the imitative arts represent-

10 • NOH AND KYÔGEN

ing court ceremonies, and original plays by courtiers, rich in the elements of action and speech, performed in the late twelfth century.

In the twelfth century, with the growth of intercourse between different classes and different regions, there arose a consciousness of the distinction between one's own culture and that of others. Interest in legends was stimulated by the growing complexity of social life. These tendencies brought about corresponding changes in drama. Plots came to have more weight, and elements of dialogue and imitation were added. Herein is to be found the beginning of transition from ancient drama to medieval drama.

MEDIEVAL DRAMA

The four centuries of this period were a time of military government (*bakufu*). The military, headed by the shogun, took the reins of government, having achieved the unification of the country by military power and shaped the framework of feudalism. The Medieval age[1] is divided into two periods, Kamakura and Muromachi, with the year 1333 as the boundary. Although it was an age constantly afflicted by natural disasters and warfare, Japan continued social and economic growth. By the end of the period the population of the country had reached twenty million. A unique national culture had been created on the basis of the traditional court culture, with the power of temples and shrines in its background and the militarists' viewpoint as its spirit. Drama also made great advances in concept, structure, and production, as well as in theory, and in every respect showed a strong medieval character, best represented by Noh and Kyôgen (Nohgaku). According to a rough dramatic-historical division, the Medieval age consists of two periods, one ending with 1350 and the other starting with 1350, each of which is subdivided in this book into two stages.

Medieval Period I (1200–1250) This was the incipient period of medieval drama. Amid the social and political chaos, the foundation of medieval

---

[1] The word is misleading, because the same word covers a different period in European history. It is, however, generally accepted in Japan to use the word Chûsei or Middle Ages for the period after the Ancient period and before the Tokugawa age. To avoid misunderstanding some use the term Middle period.

drama was laid. First to appear were Ennen Noh and Sarugaku Noh as new genres of drama.

Kagura and Bugaku continued to be performed as in the previous period, but Gigaku had almost died out. Ennen Noh had its origin in various kinds of fragmentary arts (dance, song, colloquy, etc.) performed after Buddhist services in large temples. These performances were expanded and given the form of drama. Sarugaku Noh was a development of Shin Sarugaku, but both share a common characteristic in laying emphasis on the element of legend.

Medieval Period II (1250–1350) This century was a time when natural and man-made calamities followed one after another, including attacks by the Mongol fleet, which occurred on two occasions (1274 and 1281), and the fall of the Kamakura *bakufu* in 1333. There were continuing social unrest and economic difficulties, but by overcoming these adverse conditions people managed to bring about a kind of stability in life and culture and succeeded in the formation of what was characteristically medieval.

New religions—Zen-shû (Zen), which had come from Sung China, and Jôdo-shû (Pure Land Buddhism), Ikkô-shû (Shin-shû), Ji-shû, and Nichiren-shû (Nichiren Buddhism), which were born in Japan—spread widely among the people and brought salvation and encouragement to suffering souls. Again, Japanese priests who went to Yüan and Ming China, or Chinese priests who became naturalized in Japan, through their experiences abroad and the knowledge they brought to Japan, had some influence, it is thought, on the formation and growth of Ennen Noh and other genres.

Ennen Noh continued to be enriched and in the latter part of the period arrived at a stage of certain perfection. Performers of Sarugaku Noh also, through their ties with large monasteries, attained economic stability, established companies (*za*), and, through competition between companies, increased the influence of this genre and strove for the enrichment and sophistication of the contents of the plays. Also, Sarugaku Noh played by villagers was included in services at the festivals of temples and shrines, and frequently semiprofessional players appeared. In this way Sarugaku Noh was perfected at the end of the period, which turned out to be preparation for further development, into Noh and Kyôgen, in the next period.

Dengaku Noh, which was also an important medieval drama comparable to Ennen Noh and Sarugaku Noh, was completed as drama a little later. Dengaku Noh was created by the combination of the fragmentary arts of Dengaku, but in this process received extensive influence from Sarugaku Noh. Moreover, in the latter half of the period it progressed rapidly and rose to a dramatic level as high as that of Sarugaku Noh. Besides these three, noteworthy also was Shugen Noh, though it was of smaller scale than they. This was a drama developed by itinerant Buddhist monks (*yamabushi*) of the Middle Ages for the dissemination of Shugendô, a kind of belief born of the union of primitive mountain worship and Buddhism. Its ceremonial part was shaped in the early half of this period, and its general dramatic part in the latter half. Later it was further to be enlarged, but its connection with other genres of drama deserves notice here.

Again, in this period, among the Kagura type of plays were many based on mythology. These continued to develop under the influence of various genres of contemporary drama and in character approached nearer the general medieval drama. On the other hand, their contribution to the formation of Sarugaku Noh and other kinds of drama was not a small one. Sometimes Kagura was combined with elements of other kinds of drama, or with fragmentary dramatic arts, to produce unique, quasi-dramatic art forms. Among the arts still extant in rural provinces today, there are considerable numbers of variations of Kagura like Hana Matsuri, Yuki Matsuri, Shimotsuki Matsuri, Bugaku, Dengaku, and Ennen, which belong to the types just referred to, dating from this period. Besides these, there were two types of songs, Enkyoku (Sôka) and Kusemai, that existed on the fringe of these new dramas and contributed to their enrichment in the next period.

This second period was a time when all medieval drama was shaped, and the prototype of its structure was firmly established. It was a part of the Middle Ages especially rich in antique quality, when the influence of temples and shrines (Buddhism and Shintoism) was predominant in culture and drama. Characteristic was the fact that Buddhism and Shintoism did not exert their influences separately but together, through what is called the "merger" of the two religions, or *shin-butsu shûgô*. This made possible the formation of the unique, superior quality of medieval drama, but at the same time it cannot be denied that medieval drama was thereby subjected to a limitation that caused it to remain incomplete as drama.

Medieval Period III (1350–1450) This one century saw, in its first half, the added enrichment and heightened elegance of Ennen Noh and Dengaku Noh. Although these still remained prosperous enough in the latter half, on the whole they failed to rise above the level of antique drama. Sarugaku Noh on the contrary, shaped a little later than these two and not yet completed at the beginning of this period, had the good fortune to see the advent of two great masters: Kan'ami, with his revolutionary creativity and adaptability, and his son Zeami, with his powerful hand in the enrichment, refinement, and deepening of the art. It was they who caused Sarugaku Noh to discard completely its antique style and to emerge as Nohgaku (Noh and Kyôgen), new styles of medieval drama. The process of formation of Nohgaku is a complicated one, but it lies partially in the trend of Sarugaku Noh, which had been scattered over provincial areas, toward centralization and urbanization in response to new social situations and cultural movements. This was achieved by studying and absorbing the merits of various types of drama and fragmentary songs, dances, and imitative acts. Effective use was made of the tradition of Shin Sarugaku that had lasted since the ancient period, and in its pursuit of beauty the Noh kept pace with the *bakufu's* aspiration to the ideals of the court and aristocracy, and finally the theories of *yûgen* and *hana* were established, all the while giving some deference to the tastes of the common people. This concept was perfected by Zeami, and toward the end of the third stage of the Medieval period was inherited by On'ami and Zenchiku in their respective aesthetic interpretations, the former emphasizing more beautiful and elegant performance and the latter rather solitary refined production. But it is no exaggeration to say that everything fundamental to Nohgaku was determined in the age of Zeami. By far the great majority of the more than two hundred pieces of Noh in the living repertoire of the twentieth century were either written originally or adapted from earlier works during this period by Zeami and his contemporaries and successors. Original compositions and adaptations concerned the three aspects of text, chant, and dramaturgy. The playwrights were at the same time actors. Moreover, Zeami and Zenchiku also wrote many excellent theoretical works. It should be noted, however, that chant and dramaturgy went through some degree of change in later periods. Kyôgen, until the preceding era, had been blended with Noh, or when it existed independently it was only a very simple form. In this period the separation was completed, and Kyôgen came to be treated as standing below and subordinate to Noh within the framework of Nohgaku, although more than a century was needed before it changed into the Kyôgen we know today. Shugen Noh, while it inherited pieces with the significance of rituals and prayers and pieces containing droll humor, also had a new addition, called the warrior dance, describing warriors' battles and tragic emotions.

There were other arts on the fringe of drama that influenced it in terms of subject matter, language, and music. Such were the Enkyoku and Kusemai mentioned above and what is known as Heikyoku, which was a narrative (*katarimono*) consisting of recitations of *The Tale of the Heike* (*Heike Monogatari*) to the accompaniment of the *biwa* (lute), and the common people's popular songs (*kouta*). At the end of the period the dance (*mai*) element of Kusemai attained some independence as Kôwakamai. On the other hand, the prosperity of orthodox Nohgaku stimulated the growth of Noh and Kyôgen played by women and boys. Its popularity was such that sometimes there were even performances by actors of lower grades.

Therefore this was a period when new styles and the old existed side by side, competing with each other, the former struggling hard to overwhelm the latter and gradually succeeding in the second half of the period. Arts that traditionally pertained to temples and shrines—arts religious, provincial, simple, and crude—declined, and the emphasis shifted to the urban type. Also, it was a time when the court-aristocratic style and the military style existed together in a mixed state as a successful union. Nevertheless, even within these new tendencies there lingered old patterns, and the good tradition was not wholly forgotten. It was for this reason that special flavor and rich emotion were maintained and that the art was not restricted either locally or in terms of social classes. This tendency produced palpable results only in the next period, the fourth stage, though its success was restricted to Nohgaku. In provincial areas and among common people, the antique style still continued to be preserved.

Medieval Period IV (1450–1600) This century and a half was a time when incessant battles and conflicts continued throughout Japan and violent social upheavals took place. As a result, in culture, regional and class confusion set in, and changes in drama were also radical and extensive. What was remarkable was that in the midst of this confusion the seeds of modern culture, and of modern drama, were already forming.

Ennen Noh steadily declined, as the influence of Buddhist temples was rapidly reduced. At the Myôrakuji in Yamato, creation and presentation of new plays went on actively, but the performances were not on as big a scale as in the preceding age, and toward the end of this period Ennen Noh had mostly died out. Only in some provinces were fragments of Ennen Noh retained and performed. At the Môtsuji temple in northern Hiraizumi, in particular, the old style is still retained fairly well.

Dengaku Noh, since it closely resembled Nohgaku, was the first to feel its pressure and after the middle of the period fell into obvious decay. Only its ritualistic portion and fragments of its dramatic portions remained, scattered in various districts. The main cause of decay was that it persisted too much in ceremonial performances and was too conservative in other ways.

Shugen Noh, as it was rooted chiefly in provincial areas, was in a different situation from those of the two genres mentioned above. It continued to be enriched, particularly that part of it, the warrior dance, which matched the trend of the times, and after this many new pieces were added to the repertoire.

Noh in the fourth stage had less of the style of elegance and subtlety established in the previous stage. More emphasis was put on conflict, its storytelling quality was improved, its style was given more verve, and altogether the dramatic effect in the ordinary sense of the word came to predominate. This transformation was partly due to the personalities of the playwrights Kanze Nobumitsu, Komparu Zenkyoku, Kanze Nagatoshi, and others, but partly also to the trend of the time, and it by no means deviated from the general character of medieval drama. On the other hand, its dependence on temples and shrines lessened remarkably. It was changing, with increasing speed, from the form of banquet (*kyôen*) in which people—and, to their thinking, Shinto and Buddhist deities too—watched and enjoyed it, to the form of a public performance (*kôgyô*) in which people, independent of religion, appreciated it. In a word, it was progressing in the direction of modern drama. Kyôgen reflected the feeling and mode of life of the common people, whose rise in society had been remarkable, and achieved great progress over the previous age in the delineation of manners, in satire, and in humor, thus becoming the direct source of present-day Kyôgen, though as a genre it had not yet been sufficiently consolidated. On the model of these early Noh and Kyôgen plays, there were presented in many localities and in large numbers other types of Noh and Kyôgen plays performed by women and young boys, by semiprofessional amateurs, and even by beggarlike folk.

Fragmentary pieces of acts or shows on the fringe of drama included brilliant Kusemai, performed by women and young boys, and Kôwakamai, characterized by briskness and tragic sentiment and performed by men. From the latter there developed a type of dance called Daigashiramai. Originally, Kusemai meant unorthdox dance, and the word was used in Bugaku documents. It was in the fourteenth century that women dancers came to Kyoto for the Gion festival and danced on a festival float. Kusemai declined after Noh came to the fore of theatrical arts. Kôwakamai, a pair dance that flourished after the middle of the Muromachi period (fifteenth century), was later protected by the Tokugawa government for ceremonial purposes. Daigashiramai was a fifteenth-century pair dance with dialogue, sometimes performed in trio. Also, there developed *sekkyô,* a type of narrative whose purpose was to disseminate Buddhism, and *jôruri,* a narrative of the lineage of Heikyoku. The influence of these currents of miscellaneous entertainment arts led to the rise of puppet plays (Ningyô Jôruri) and Kabuki, which became the two main streams of modern Japanese drama in the Tokugawa period.

CHAPTER TWO

KAGURA

History of Kagura

Kagura, the origin of which is tied to that of Shinto rites, became differentiated into various types under the influence of the changing views of the deities and of the *geinô,* a term that refers to drama and such fragmentary arts on its fringe as songs, dances, and mimicry.

Kagura, which was the representative "theatrical art" of the period when people's life was centered round Shinto rites, remained representative of Japanese drama even in the seventh century and later. The myth of the Heavenly Cave cited below contains vestiges of the Kagura of the time and is indicative of the most basic of the Kagura with a highly shamanistic nature. The myth of the Luck of the Sea and Luck of the Mountain suggests a similar origin but is more concerned with men than with deities and has a greater significance as a reproduction of the world of myths. Attempts to intensify this tendency become more frequent in later times. Kagura that started in the first half of the Ancient period saw the development of such types as were combined with the customs and events of the year and with the progress of life and culture. Sometimes, stimulated by drama of foreign origin, there grew up popular folk dances (Fuzokumai) related to deities, such as the gods of Hachiman, Kashima, and Sumiyoshi, in which the elements of mimicry and realism were elaborated. To the same group belongs the Seinô dance pertaining to the Amabe, a maritime tribe.

Dating from the ninth century was the Mikagura, performed at the ceremonies in the imperial court. This was a serious type of play, originating in the Kagura offered to the god Hachiman and then adapted to court use. In its earlier days it contained in a subordinate section the droll actions of *zae no onoko*. As yet not formalized or given fixed form, it seems to have been a lively art. The *zae no onoko*, it should be explained, were the musicians and dancers of Mikagura, although the term, found in records of the middle Heian period, sometimes denotes only the one who specialized in Sarugaku. The dance was often accompanied by improvised dialogue.

Parallel with this Mikagura held in the imperial palace, there was the Kagura performed among the common people, called Satokagura or "village kagura," which consisted of imitations of *tanemaki*, or seed sowing, and other farming activities as a sort of incantatory magic, and the dance of *Okina*, in which the god appeared in the figure of an old man connected with a prayer for longevity. The anthology of popular songs *Ryôjin Hishô*, dating from the twelfth century, contains many songs about Shinto shrines and festivals that enable one to infer that there was in wide existence among the people the Kagura in close affinity with life.

During the thirteenth century, which was already the age of medieval drama, the dramatic quality of Kagura increased, and, while preserving traditional elements, through adoption of new dramatic techniques and making use of various novel "theatrical arts" a different kind of Kagura was introduced, one dealing with the myths and mystic doings of divine spirits. Especially noticeable was the syncretism of Shinto and Buddhism. Of the plays called by the name of Kagura existing even today in various localities, those of the archaic style mostly date from this period.

In the seventeenth century and later, the influence of the gay and urban "entertainments" and drama, and of the colorful customs and events that accompanied economic prosperity, caused the representation of myths to be more dramatic and enjoyable. It even gave rise to a comic type of Kagura called Daikagura. This proclivity to entertainment is to be ascribed to the decay and degeneration of the concept of deity. In outlying provinces, however, people usually disapproved of divergence from traditional ways. In cities, Shintoism and Buddhism were again separated. Even at present, besides the Mikagura, various other austere types of Kagura, based on miscellaneous concepts, are being performed at Ise Shrine and shrines elsewhere. Will there come the day when the Japanese nation becomes oblivious of *kami* (sometimes identified with *hotoke* or Buddhas) who are either their ancestors or protectors of their life or sometimes evil spirits to be conquered? The life of Kagura is not likely to come to an end soon.

Ancient Types

The Kagura of the Heavenly Cave Amaterasu, the sun goddess, who was considered the ancestor of the emperors, the ruler of the Heavenly Plain (Takamagahara), the highest, absolute deity, comparable to Zeus, was exasperated at the misbehavior of her brother Susano-o and hid herself in the Heavenly Cave (Ama no Iwato), plunging the world into utter darkness. The gods, horrified, met together, made offering to the goddess, and cried out to her. The goddess Ame no Uzume, half-naked, danced a humorous dance on top of an inverted tub to appease the anger of the sun goddess, who was finally mollified, made her appearance, and restored light to the Heavenly Plain. This story, built upon the concepts of the nature god, the god impersonated and the god absolute, evinces the combination of the primitive death concept with the underlying belief in resurrection and the ceremonial practice of funeral rites, deriving suggestions from natural phenomena such as the solar eclipse. Needless to say, it was no event of the Age of Gods. It was based on the events of the world of mortals but had been moved back in time to the mythological scene and handed down as such. The *Record of Ancient Matters* (*Kojiki*), compiled in 712, records that all the gods laughed heartily to see Ame no Uzume dance. The *Chronicles of Japan* (*Nihon Shoki*), completed in 720, even uses the term *wazaogi*, which means "imitative gesture," to refer to it. (Later the term came to mean "actor.") This is an interpretation a little more advanced than that of the former and attaches a far clearer significance to the event as a dramatic performance than does the former. Perhaps it was a consciousness only possible in the latter part of the Ancient period. The account in the *Record of Ancient Matters*, however, contains simple dialogue and also refers to the trick of using a mirror to produce a reflection of the sun goddess, which would show that the event was already something more than a mere rite, incantation, or prayer. In other words the myth of the Heavenly Cave indicates that the basic structural form of Kagura, complete with the ritual formality and with *modoki* (mimicry or a simplified and in a sense vulgar explanation of a rite), had already been established in the prehistoric period.

Tradition has it that the descendants of Ame no Uzume were the family of Sarume no Kimi, a family who by profession had been shamans (*miko*) at the imperial court in the early period. Probably, on the basis of the tradition coming down from the primitive period, they performed the dance of their ancestors, representing in the Kagura the myth of the Heavenly Cave. *Miko* dances were shamanistic, and in their nature are considered as belonging to the primitive Kagura. Kagura of this category has since come to be called Kagura of the Heavenly Cave (Iwato Kagura) or Kagura of ancient times (Jindai Kagura).

The Kagura of Luck of the Sea and Luck of the Mountain The younger god Hoho Hikodemi, the man of Yama-sachi (literally, "what the mountain yields"), was at variance with his elder brother Hono Susori, the man of Umi-sachi ("what the sea yields"), because he had lost the fishhook he had borrowed from the latter. He was tormented relentlessly by his brother until he obtained from the sea god's daughter two precious balls, called *kanju* and *manju,* by means of which he could cause the tides to rise and ebb at will. Using these magic balls, he chastised the cantankerous Umi-sachi, who finally surrendered and swore that he would for all time be a guardian of his brother and be a man of *wazaogi,* or mimicry. Historical sources contain accounts of the actions he performed, particularly imitations of a man being drowned in the sea. When we remember that the actions were preceded by the two gods' conversation, that two magic balls were used as props, and that some attempts were made at facial makeup, such as applying pigments to the skin, it may be inferred that the actions already had the basic elements of a public performance and that attention had been given to the manner of presentation.

This myth is the story of the oath of submission, based on the tradition of the mountaineers having conquered the maritime tribes. The account that Umi-sachi swore to become a man of *wazaogi* and that his descendants are held to have been *hayato,* a small primitive tribe in the southern district that served the emperor with "entertainment arts," makes one imagine that it was a description with an obviously dramatic intention, based on a far earlier tradition, with much consideration paid to what had prevailed prior to primitive times. This is an ancient drama concerning the pledge of submission that was different from the rites of the Heavenly Cave or from shamanism, but a primitive oath was at the same time an oath to the god. Moreover, considering that the period treated was the Age of the Gods, the piece might well be called Kagura.

What, then, was the significance of the Kagura of Umi-sachi and Yama-sachi in the history of drama, when compared with the Kagura of the Heavenly Cave? In its authenticity as Kagura it was obviously less definite than the latter and was of a lower level, but at the same time its significance as the progenitor of general dramatic art free from religious connotations was far richer.

Mikagura Mikagura (Court Kagura) is for ceremonies at the Imperial Palace, and therefore it is extremely serious and highly dignified. Originally it appears to have contained some comical actions performed by *zae no onoko*, but these have since been lost, and now it consists only of songs and dances in which dramatic qualities are rather scarce. Mikagura was formerly performed in the garden of the Naishidokoro Hall (now Kashikodokoro Hall) at midnight, illuminated by burning torches, every December, and also on such occasions as ancestral festivals. The performers are those who ordinarily perform Bugaku. The program consists of, first, *Niwabi*, a song, followed by the dances of the *ninjô*, or leader, entitled *Torimono*[1] and *Karakami*,[2] to the accompaniment of songs and instrumental music. Third, there is *Achime*, a shamanistic ritual that may possibly be derived from the legend of Isora. Then follows a section with a leaning to *modoki* parody or imitative art independent of rituals, and here the *sainô* makes his appearance. Last, there are songs—*Saibari, Senzai, Haya-uta,* and *Hoshi*—the exact meanings of which are unknown but which may be used for religious occasions like requiem masses. In the ancient period these songs numbered about eighty, and the performance lasted for two

---

[1] The imperial Kagura consists of *Niwabisahô, Achimesahô, Torimono, Ôsaibari* (not performed today), *Kosaibari,* and miscellaneous songs. *Torimono* are ritual tools, including *sakaki, mitegura, tsue, sasa, yumi, tsurugi, hoko, hisago,* and *kazura,* which provide the subject matter of nine songs, with an appendix of *Karakami*.

[2] Korean god.

or three days, but nowadays the Mikagura takes only four hours. The Kagura at the *daijôe,* the enthronement ceremony of the emperor, belongs to this category.

Kagura of Seinô Isora, a vassal of the sea god, dances, holding high the magic balls, *kanju* and *manju,* in order to assist the naval forces of the empress Jingû in her expedition to Korea. Isora is the ancestor of the Azumi family of the Amabe tribe in Chikuzen Province. According to tradition the empress Jingû lived in about the third century, but there appears in the Kagura a character of the Age of the Gods who corresponds to Toyotama-hime, the daughter of the sea god who gave Yama-sachi the two magic balls. Thus the story has assumed the appearance of a story of the mythical age, which gives it the quality of a Kagura. It has been associated with the name Seinô. Originating in the Azumi family's tradition, it is still performed with the words that have come down from the late Ancient period, by simple, rustic dolls at the Usa Hachiman Shrine and by dancers wearing white cloth masks like the *zômen* of a Bugaku dance at the Kasuga Wakamiya Shrine.

Masked Kagura Kagura dancers sometimes wore masks and sometimes, as in the Mikagura, did not. The unmasked type of Kagura was generally more archaic and more ritualistic in nature; the masked Kagura, more modern and more dramatic. Masks had existed since primitive times, but under the influence of Gigaku and Bugaku, which were advanced masked plays, and more especially of Noh plays of various kinds, most of the Kagura in the Middle Ages, whether in central or provincial shrines, came to be performed as masked plays. The use of masks was extremely effective in expressing the spirituality of myths and divinities and moreover accorded well with the growing tendency toward realism and the added dramatic effect that characterized the development from ancient drama to medieval drama. Basically the archaic type of Kagura was in the form of pantomime, accompanied by music (*hayashi*) or song (*hayashi-uta*), but in the Tokugawa period, under the influence of Nohgaku and Edo dramas, there was added the form in which the dancers sang and spoke as well. This was an attempt to bring the world of the immortals down to the world of mortals, but in becoming mundane it lost the mystic atmosphere peculiar to

Kagura. Kagura still in existence in local areas includes, apart from those mentioned above, the Kagura of Togakushi (in Nagano Prefecture), Takachiho (in Miyazaki Prefecture), Sada (in Shimane Prefecture), Chichibu (in Saitama Prefecture), Taga (in Shiga Prefecture), Bitchû (in Okayama Prefecture), Tsugaru (in Aomori Prefecture), and many others.

The Kagura stage is set in the garden in front of the shrine or in the Kagura Hall (*kagura-den*) or the Worship Hall (*haiden*). As the performance is stylized, the space used for the dance is small, two by three meters being the minimum, three by five meters medium, and six by eight meters the maximum. In most cases the small or middle size is considered large enough.

CHAPTER THREE

GIGAKU

History of Gigaku

The Introduction of Gigaku The term Gigaku (伎楽, sometimes written 妓楽) originally meant music for religious services at Buddhist temples. Because it was imported from the South China state of Wu (Japanese pronunciation, Kure), it is also called Kuregaku. Tradition has it that around 550 Chih-tung, or Chisô, a relative of the king of Wu, came to Japan, bringing with him books on Buddhism and Buddha statues. He also brought Gigaku masks, instruments, and costumes. This was the first time that Gigaku was introduced into Japan. The dance itself, however, was not included.

It was in 612, when Mimashi (Japanese pronunciation), a dancer of Paekche (Kudara) in Korea, came to Japan, that the dance of Gigaku was first made known to the nation. Prince Shôtoku, then regent, with a view to disseminating Buddhism, invited him to live at Sakurai near Nara and teach Gigaku to Japanese boys. He ordered that one set each of the props Mimashi had brought be preserved at Tachibana-dera, Uzumasa-dera, and Tennôji temples. The masks brought over by Chisô are not extant today, but those brought by Mimashi still exist at Hôryûji temple, serving as actual proof to support evidence of the introduction of Gigaku to Japan.

Origin of Gigaku The fact that Gigaku was not born in the state of Paekche but had its origin in Wu can be inferred from its alternative name Kuregaku (Wu music) and the name of an instrument, *kure no tsuzumi* (Wu drum), as well as from the fact that in several Gigaku pieces, as listed below, there appear Wu kings and Wu women. Evidence in the masks and contents of the pieces, however, indicates that a fairly large number of pieces had come from Hsi-liang (in Japanese, Seiryô), Ch'iu-tzu (Kiji), India (Tenjiku), and other places.

Gigaku is conventionally classified into four groupings:

1. *Kojin* (barbarian) group: *Chidô, Baramon, Suiko-ô, Suiko-ju*. From the masks it is assumed that *kojin* denoted an Aryan race from the western region of China. Here, of course, "barbarian" is to be construed as "foreigner." The title *Chidô* literally means one who prepares the way, while *Baramon* means Brahman. *Suiko-ô* portrayed a drunken barbarian king and *Suiko-ju* a drunken barbarian retainer.

2. *Gojin* (people of Wu) group: *Gokô* (king of Wu), *Gojo* (Wu princess), *Kongô* (Japanese version of the Sanskrit *vajra*, or diamond, symbolizing firmness and used as an attribute of a Buddha or a Bodhisattva), *Rikishi* (wrestler), *Taikofu* (old man or old woman accompanied by two children, *taikoshi*, who visit a Buddhist temple), *Taikoshi* (children on a pilgrimage).

3. *Nankaijin* (native from the southern sea): *Konron* or *Kuromu* (here representing a villain).

4. *Irui* (beast and bird) group: *Shishi* (lion), *Karora* or *Karura* (king of birds in Indian mythology).

It is not likely that in Wu and Paekche Gigaku was used solely as the formal drama for Buddhist services at temples. In all probability Prince Shôtoku undertook some alterations in the pieces to make them serve purely such purposes, but at the same time his intention was to make Buddhist services merrier and to familiarize people with Buddhism.

Traces of Change The changes that Gigaku underwent are known from books of history; records at numerous large temples; the *Kyôkunshô*, a book on music (especially Gagaku) dating from 1233; other literature; and masks. From the inventories of treasures at various temples we know that there were eleven masks at the Hôryûji in 748, fourteen at Saidaiji in 780, twelve at Kôryûji in 886, and thirteen at Kanzeonji in Chikuzen Province in 905. Masks that have survived now number about two hundred and fifty and may be divided into four groups as given above. Of these, the thirty-two masks existing in Hôryûji mostly date from the seventh century, including those brought by Mimashi himself. There are one hundred and sixty-four masks at the Shôsôin repository in Nara, mostly from the eighth century but with some earlier ones. The thirty-three masks at Tôdaiji are of the eighth century or later. Some are preserved at other temples and museums. By far the greatest majority of the masks are "old masks" (seventh and eighth centuries), but Tôdaiji has five "new masks" made in the Middle Ages, with more embellishments, a type also represented by other specimens elsewhere. These "new masks" are not without historical significance as showing the process of decline of Gigaku. It can be inferred that temples possessing these masks held Gigaku performances frequently. The ages of the masks are determined from the signatures of the carvers on the masks, records of their history, and their style. These and other sources of information enable us to identify several changes that divide the history of Gigaku.

From Ancient Glory to Medieval Extinction   The history of Gigaku may be divided into the following four periods: (1) the seventh century, the period of systematization, when it retained the old rules of the alien countries and unfolded the remote traditional beauty; (2) the eighth and ninth centuries, the period when the art prospered; (3) the tenth to the twelfth century, the period when it decayed; and (4) the thirteenth to the sixteenth century, the period when it died out. The second period may be divided into two: the time of ascendancy and the time of security, when new styles were added, the body of the art was enlarged, and, by means of the opportunity presented by the famous ceremony of the Great Buddha image of the Tôdaiji temple in the Tempyô era (752), its grandeur and luxury were elevated to unprecedented heights. In the twelfth century both the music and the acting rapidly decayed. After the middle of the thirteenth century the art was transformed and came to be looked upon as identical to *gyôdô*, a rite in which monks and believers walked round the Buddha statue, chanting prayers all the while.

Performances of Gigaku

Basic Aspects   Gigaku was performed in large temples in the metropolis and in local provinces on the *busshôe* (meeting on the Buddha's birthday, the eighth day of the fourth month) and on the *gigakue* (the fifteenth of the seventh month) every year to add grandeur to the ceremonies and on other occasions of special importance. In 606, six years before the introduction of Gigaku to Japan, it was officially decided that two days of *saie* (an assembly of monks for chanting sutras accompanied by feasts) should be observed each year in Buddhist temples. It is to be inferred that Gigaku, introduced soon thereafter, was quickly adopted to add color to the assembly. The front court of the temple served as the stage. It was surrounded by thousands of monks and worshipers. There was no stage setting or curtain. Only a minimum number of props appeared. Every performer except the musicians wore a mask, which, like the mask of Greek drama, was large and covered the whole face. The masks were of high artistic quality and gave an emphasized rendering of the inner character of the person and his facial expression at the climax of the drama. Four kinds of instruments were used: the flute, cymbals (*dobyôshi*), a pair of small gongs, and the Wu drum, which was worn in front. As to how Gigaku was performed, the account in the *Kyôkunshô* is the most explicit. The author, Koma Chikazane (1172–1242), belonged to an old family of Bugaku musicians. Although the dances of Gigaku had all but died out by his time, he made his account on the basis of old books of music and reliable traditions, so that it can be considered to be faithful to the original. If one uses it carefully, comparing it with other old materials, it is possible to reproduce a vivid picture of Gigaku in the Ancient period.

The Procession of Actors In the *Kyôkunshô,* reference is made to "ten Gigaku," and in inventories of treasures of the above-mentioned temples more than ten different Gigaku masks are listed, so it is not to be doubted that there were at least several Gigaku pieces. First, masks were carried in a procession, as in the Dionysian festival, to a musical accompaniment, round and round, heightening the atmosphere. Then, on the stage, a series of dramatic pieces were performed. Finally, music would be played again to conclude the whole affair. This composite program coincides with the famous procession at the festival of the Kasuga Wakamiya Shrine and the offering of the many performances, such as Seinô, Dengaku Noh, Sarugaku Noh, and Bugaku at the temporary shrine (*o-tabisho*), which date from the late Ancient period and still survive today.

The procession proper was preceded by the music *netori,* a purely ritualistic musical prelude, and *gyôdô,* a procession of monks who recited sutras, going around Buddhist chapels and statues. The proper procession of Gigaku, which then began, was led by *chidô,* who wore a long-nosed mask, followed by a flutist, a cymbal player, and ten Wu drummers. Then came a lion, performed by two men, followed by two lion cubs, each wearing the mask of a child. They performed the dance "The Lions of the Five Directions" (*Gohô-jishi:* a dance of Chinese origin, so called from the five directions, east, west, south, north, and center, to which the lions turn and offer prayers), accompanied by songs. To this point the performance was ritualistic. What followed was *modoki,*[1] lighter and more familiar in content, and intended to impart Buddhist or practical wisdom. The central piece, with the largest scale, was the play *Konron* (or *Kuromu*), which was followed by three short pantomimes.

The Play Konron The play *Konron* had six characters. On special occasions and in later periods there were more than ten. First, Gokô, the king of Wu, enters, wearing a dignified mask and a precious crown. He gives a sign to the greenroom and orders the flute to be blown to announce the commencement of the main program. As he takes a seat at the side, the program begins in a grave atmosphere. With musical accompaniment, Kongô, wearing a fierce-looking mask, enters, and seats himself beside the king. Next Karora, or Karura, wearing a mask looking like a weird bird, enters and dances an energetic dance to fitting music, giving an adumbration of the atmosphere of Konron's original home shown in a later scene. Karora may have been Garuda in Sanskrit, king of birds in Indian mythology, or may have been the fire-eating bird or the monster bird who eats poisonous snakes—there is no proof for any of the theories. The character who enters next is Gojo, the daughter of the king Gokô, who wears a lovely girl's mask and takes up a conspicuous position on the stage. Each character's entry is always accompanied by music in the greenroom.

[1] Secondary player or clown who often appears in Japanese performing arts. The verb form *modoki* means "to imitate" or "to modify" some action. Thus *modoki* became a kind of comic parody, performed after more serious pieces. *Sambasô* after *Okina* in Noh and *Ninomai* after *Ama* in Bugaku are examples.

Finally enters Konron, the villain, wearing the mask of a horrible demon, to the accompaniment of music. He introduces himself in an impetuous dance. While dancing, he focuses his eyes on Gojo and is enchanted by the girl. With a fan he beats the *marakata,* a phallus-shaped stick, and dances a violent, impulsive lovemaking dance to the accompaniment of dynamic music. Finally he catches hold of Princess Gojo.

Whereupon enters Kongô, wearing a mask suggestive of strength. A wrestler (Rikishi) opens the gate, and Kongô, with the music, walks to the stage, clapping his hands vigorously and performing the dance of entrance. With the assistance of the wrestler he grapples fiercely with Konron and finally suppresses him, rescuing Gojo from her predicament. Putting a rope on Konron's *marakata,* he swings it about, bending it and knocking it around, in what was known as the waving-the-*mara* dance (*marafurimai*). The music accompanying it is quick, as is fitting to a dance of final victory. The piece, dramatic as it is, had a religious meaning. That is, it was a commandment against lust. *Mara* in Sanskrit also means "obstacle." Konron is the incarnation of lust, the obstacle to enlightenment; Gojo, the medium for enlightenment; Rikishi and Kongô, primarily guardians of Buddhism. This is a play of admonition against concupiscence as an obstacle to Buddhahood, exciting the interest of the audience with its ingenious presentation.

Three Plays of Mimicry Next are presented the three pieces of mimicry. Baramon (Brahman), in the play of the same name, is a monk and a member of the highest caste in India but becomes the father of a child, and in order to bring him up suffers the humiliation of washing his swaddling clothes, which act is comically parodied on the stage. At a time when strict commandments were enforced by ancient Buddhism, the play was a warning to both monks and laymen, showing how a monk who broke the rule against lust had to repent and redeem himself. The second play, *Taiko,* though in later years several variations of it appeared, originally concerned an old man who, with his orphaned grandchild, bows reverentially before the Buddha image. The ancient mask has a melancholy look. The piece also had significance as a lesson on how to hold rites for the dead. The finale was *Suiko,* a humorous mimicry of the drunkenness of the king of Hu (Ko, northern barbarian in China) and his followers. The piece probably had something to do with the commandment against intoxication. As it was the concluding piece, it was remarkable for its dramatic elements and for its gay and boisterous scenes.

Finale   When the above pieces are ended, gay parades of dancers are staged as a finale. The whole Gigaku program ends with a procession of joyous music, consisting as before of two flutists, two cymbalists, and twenty Wu drummers. Gigaku was a theatrical art highly appropriate to adorn ancient times, but, as we have seen, it was doomed to extinction.

CHAPTER FOUR

BUGAKU

History of Bugaku

The history of Bugaku is even longer than that of Gigaku, and it is also a far more richly documented subject. Materials that serve to show its historical changes are history books; official and private diaries; stories, tales, and other literary works; books of secret teachings in the families of hereditary Bugaku artists; ancient masks, implements, and costumes; practical actions and performances that were imported; and provincial Bugaku, which still exists in local provinces in more or less distorted forms. In particular, Koma Chikazane's *Kyôkunshô* (1233), Koma Tomokazu's *Zoku Kyôkunshô* (1270), Toyohara Muneaki's *Taigenshô* (1515), Abe Suehisa's *Gakkaroku* (1690), and other books are of primary importance, while the genealogical tables called *Kechimyaku,* showing the lineages of masters and students, are most practical and valuable, being the records left by those who were actually engaged in the art. Such books as well as other literary works, however, may sometimes contain legendary or fictitious accounts and require discreet treatment. The examination of all these evidences will show that the history of Bugaku from A.D. 600 may be divided into several periods.

From Chaos to Order: Importation and the Music Bureau In the seventh century (first half of the Ancient period), although this was the initial stage, selection of foreign and vernacular music and dances was already in progress. The eighth century (second half of the Ancient period) was the period of reorganization. In 701, the Imperial Music Bureau

(Gagakuryô; also known as Utaryô) was first established within the imperial court, consisting of two divisions for Chinese music, or Tôgaku (T'ang music), and Korean music, or Komagaku (Koguryô music), including Shiragigaku (Silla music) and Kudaragaku (Paekche music), each with a fixed number (seventy-two) of music-and-dance masters and students.

From this time on, positive reorganization and adjustment proceeded until the position of Gagaku[1] was officially confirmed as the music and dance of the imperial court, as opposed to Gigaku as the music and dance of Buddhist temples. In practice the reorganization had not yet been sufficiently advanced. According to the official system of the Gagakuryô, the fixed staff for the Chôtengaku, Japanese music and dance proper that accompanied rites and ceremonies at the imperial court, was two hundred and fifty-five, including the singers, dancers, and flutists. In 736 eight music-and-dance pieces of Lin-i (Rin'yû Hachigaku)[2] were introduced to Japan from the southern part of the Asiatic continent by Bodai Senna, a Brahman of South India, and Fattriet (or Buttetsu), a Rin'yû priest.

Bugaku Given Its Final Form The ninth century was the time when Bugaku took a long step forward, to be substantially established in a form that has come down to the present. The credit for having made this quick development possible goes in the first place to Owari no Hamanushi (733–?) and in the second to Ôto no Kiyokami (?–834). The honor of having supported them goes to the emperor Nimmyô (reigned 833–49). Hamanushi, continuing from the preceding era, was active over a long period and came to be looked upon by later musicians as the virtual founder of Bugaku. He went to T'ang China to investigate the old style and corrected the confusion that had existed in Bugaku up to his time with respect both to the dance and to the music. He also composed new pieces of vernacular dance and music. He was himself a dancer. His original compositions and adaptations number several dozen, many of high artistic value. According to the record of the Koma family, Moroyuki, an ancestor of the family, was the

---

[1] Gagaku consists of Kangen (music) and Bugaku (dance).
[2] Rin'yû was an old country in the present Vietnam. But a recent study tells us that the music originated in India.

husband of Hamanushi's daughter. The other man, Ôto no Kiyokami, was the leading figure in adaptation and original composition of music, his works also including many masterpieces. This period, at the middle of which was the emperor Nimmyô's reign, was the period when Bugaku underwent a big change. It ceased to be a foreign art and became a Japanese art.

The first half of the tenth century was a continuation of the previous period. Production of new compositions and adaptation went on. The emperor Murakami (reigned 946–67) was called the "sacred king of music" in recognition of his patronage of Bugaku. As a result, a high degree of refinement was achieved in its musical aspect. Also, the rapid advancement in court and aristocratic culture added more grace and delicacy to every aspect of Bugaku. Dancing even became a pastime for aristocrats.

At the beginning of the eleventh century, it was officially decided that the Koma family should represent the "Left" group (T'ang music and dance) and the Ôno family the "Right" group (Koguryô, P'ohai,[1] and Japanese music and dances) in order that the two families should compete for better refinement. In the early part of this period the subtle sentiment born in the previous century was more highly developed. In the middle of the period, at the suggestion and with the support of Fujiwara no Yorimichi, the *kampaku* (chief adviser to the emperor), painstaking efforts were made by musicians to express this concept, which ultimately found fruition in making Bugaku the property of the court aristocracy.

After 1086, the system of the "retired emperor" taking the reins of government was introduced and succeeded in curbing, as intended, the political power of the Fujiwara family. The emperor Horikawa (reigned 1086–1107) subjected the music and dance of Gagaku to strict criticism, so that the musicians, according to the judgment passed on them, had either their merits or their defects intensified, and on the whole the free, vigorous quality was lost. No longer did the nobles dance as a pastime. The musical families treasured their secret theories and methods, and this gradually led to the decline of Bugaku in general. But soon the times changed. The military class was steadily on the rise,

---

[1] P'ohai (Bokkai) was a country in Manchuria that flourished from the late seventh to the early tenth century.

and political power was shifting to their hands. The imperial court became too impoverished to maintain its support of Bugaku, which then had to rely on large temples and shrines for subsistence. In the early Medieval period, that is, the thirteenth and fourteenth centuries, there was a remarkable loss of dances; many pieces were retained only in the provinces; and there was a general preference for the virile dance, Hashirimono, with its jumping motions. The late Medieval period, the fifteenth and sixteenth centuries, was a time of continued decay.

Revival of Bugaku and Changes in the Music Bureau In the Tokugawa period, as a result of the decay, there were only fifty families of musicians, who totaled few more than ninety-odd persons. The Tokugawa government assembled musicians from the Sampô Gakusho, or the three groups of musicians in Kyoto, Nara, and Tennôji in Osaka, with their tradition dating from the Medieval period, for its own ceremonial music and founded the Momijiyama Music Bureau (Momijiyama Gakusho) in Edo Castle. After the Meiji Restoration, in 1890 the four music centers were united into the Gagaku Bureau (Gagaku Kyoku), which later became the present Music Department of the Imperial Household Agency (Kunaichô Gakubu). However, there are still today musicians at the temples and shrines in Nara and Tennôji temple in Osaka and in other local areas. In some provinces the classic style is still retained.

Since old times the musicians at Tennôji, being the descendants of Hata no Kôkatsu, a naturalized Chinese, bear the surname Hata and are divided into four families: Sono, Hayashi, Oka, and Tôgi. The musicians at Nara, who are said to be descended from Furen-ô, king of Koma in Korea, bear the surname Koma and were divided into seven families: Hayashi, Ue, Shiba, Oku, Tsuji, Kubo (窪), and Kubo (久保). In the music department of Kyoto there were such families of musicians as Ono, Toyohara (now called Bunno), Abe, and Oga (called Yamanoi since recent times).

PERFORMANCES OF BUGAKU

Purpose, Masks, Implements, Stage Bugaku has always been regarded as the dance of the imperial court, from the time of the ancient Bureau of Music to the present Music Department. It was principally performed by professional dancers who were officials of the Headquarters of the Imperial Guards (Konoe-fu) and sometimes also by young members of the aristocracy, as part of the rituals and to entertain guests at banquets. In *The Tale of Genji* we find descriptions of such dance pieces as *Seigaiha, Shunnōden,* and the like danced by the young prince, Hikaru Genji, and others on such official occasions as the festival of flowers in spring and of red maple leaves in autumn. The special women's dance (*jogaku*) was performed by dancers at the office of female dancers, singers, and musicians in the imperial court (Naikyôbô). Large temples and shrines were protected by the imperial court, and they generally sustained the same cultural tradition. They used Bugaku in their prayers for rain in times of drought, in the entertainment of Ennen Noh, and also as religious music dedicated to the Buddha or the Shinto deities. Similar types of Bugaku also found their way to provincial areas. After decay and then revival, it came to be treated as ceremonial music and dance, but very recently there has arisen the tendency to enjoy it as a type of classic dance and music.

Of old masks of Bugaku, fewer than one hundred and fifty of those for the principal roles now exist in the Tôdaiji and other temples and shrines as well as in museums. So few have survived probably because they were frequently used and damaged. Apart from these there are a fairly large number of new masks dating from more recent periods. Bugaku masks are of wood, colored with lacquer, and show a more advanced technique than do Gigaku masks. Because of the diversity of the origin of Bugaku dances and because of their large number, the masks also exhibit many different facial expressions and shapes, but, except for two, all the masks are male. The exceptions are the mask of a young woman, used in *Ayakiri,* and that of an old woman, used in *Ninomai,* a Rin'yû piece performed after the dance of *Ama.* Unlike Gigaku masks, Bugaku masks are intended to give a somewhat stylized presentation of the persons' characters and their general movements. They are a bit smaller in size than Gigaku masks and have less volume, which perhaps is due to the difference in the nature of the dance and the construction of the stage. There are some very special types of masks, known as *zômen,* made of cloth or paper, which show a high degree of stylization.

The Bugaku pieces were silent plays except for some recitations in the old-style pieces, but they all excelled in the quality of the accompanying music. The Left music was used for the Left dance, represented chiefly by pieces originating in T'ang China, the instruments being *ryûteki* (horizontal flute), *hichiriki* (*flûte à bec*), *shô* (mouth organ), *kakko* (drum), *shôko* (gong), and *taiko* (flat drum). The Right music was used for the Right dance, represented chiefly by the Komagaku or Kôraigaku, the instruments being *hichiriki, komabue* (horizontal flute), *sannoko* (side drum), *shôko,* and *taiko.* The Left dance was more cheerful than the Right. The costume differed from piece to piece and from bureau to bureau, but on the whole red was the basic color of the costume for the Left group, and green that for the Right, corresponding to the gay and quiet characters of the two types of dance and music. There was nothing by way of stage setting, but occasionally such accessories (*torimono*) as a halberd, drumstick, bamboo twigs, crown, and flower ornaments were used, and in a few pieces the figure of a serpent and similar props (*tsukurimono*) were also used. Of the stage, there is a record that the one used at the installation ceremonies of the Great Buddha statue of the Tôdaiji in 752 and again in 861 was a huge one, twenty by twenty meters, on which dozens of people could dance at a time. Another record mentions a slightly smaller one used for official rituals at the court. But after the usage became fairly well established, the stage normally was about seven by seven meters and raised about one meter above ground. This was set in the garden or in the palace, and on it a maximum of six dancers (often four or two, and occasionally one) performed. In the rear the greenroom was constructed.

Classification of Bugaku: "Warbling" and "Recitation" Bugaku admits of several ways of classification. To divide it into *samai* or *sabu* (Left dance, of T'ang origin) and *umai* or *ubu* (Right dance, of Korean origin), according to the origin, is one way. One may also distinguish between old and new pieces according to the time of derivation, or again between large, medium, and small pieces according to the scale. The most practical way of classification, however, is by the contents and the modes of the dance. According to this, Bunnomai (civil dance), or Hiramai, is a graceful, elegant dance in which the dancers wear the costume of civil servants (*tsune no shôzoku*). A typical dance of this kind was *Katen.* Bunomai (martial dance) is a heroic, virile dance, the dancer carrying a sword or halberd in hand (example: *Taiheiraku*).

Hashirimono or Hashirimai (running dance) is a brisk dance with jumping motions similar to the gallopade (example: *Ryôô*). Tôbu is a children's dance (example: *Kochô,* or *Butterflies*). The type Jogaku, represented by only a few pieces, is exceptional in that it uses masks of women (example: *Ayakiri*). Originally there were words that went with the dance, technically called "warbling" *(ten)* and "recitation" *(ei),* so that the meanings and contents of the pieces were clearly understood by the audience of that time. Their rearrangement in the Middle Ages, however, caused the primordial storytelling and dramatic elements to recede, and the emphasis came to be placed mostly on the pursuit of symbolism and stylized beauty, owing to the current popular preference. The overall decay further caused the loss of whatever had remained of "warbling" and "recitation." After the Medieval age the original meanings of most of the pieces were lost. Fortunately, the *Kyôkunshô* and other classic books on music contain descriptions of old traditions and theories. Also, the current comparative studies in music and dances of China, Central and West Asia, India, and other regions have led to the suggestion of new interpretations.

Deserving especial notice from the point of view of dramatic quality are the Bunomai, Hashirimai, and part of the Bunnomai, which retain old styles. Typical of the Bunomai, the *Shinnô Hajin Raku* is said to depict a brave king of the Ch'in dynasty of China trampling the enemy's camp. The martial feat of the general is beautifully stylized by a dancer wearing a helmet and carrying a halberd and a sword.

Hashirimai (running dance) is characterized by a unique jumping style of dancing called "piece with running motion" (*hashiride*). The mask has an extremely grotesque expression. *Ryôô,* the representative piece of this class, is remarkable for the many puzzling accounts of it in old books of Bugaku. According to one old document, it is based on the legend that Ch'ang-kung (Chôkyô), king of Lan-ling (Ranryô), went into battle wearing an awful-looking mask to scare the enemy and won the day. The mystery of the legend, together with the record that a unique, secret technique of somersault was used by the dancer, adds to the interest this piece holds. *Genjôraku,* classified by the author of *Kyôkunshô* as T'ang music, is in reality a dramatization of an old Indian legend of a hero's fight with a poisonous serpent, his victory, and his return to his castle. A small snake figure is placed on the stage. This dance retains much of the storytelling element in the presentation and has the alternative name of *Kendaraku* (*Snake-watching Dance*). *Batô* is also of Indian mythological origin, portraying King Pedu mounted on a white horse going to kill a poisonous serpent. The serpent again appears in the companion dance (Tsugaimai), *Korohase,* in which it is eaten by a monster bird. Also of the running-dance class are *Nasori, Konju, Kitoku,* and *Sanju,* all having been frequently performed after the Middle Ages in the Ennen Noh and Bugaku in local provinces because of their dramatic interest and their extraordinary dynamic power.

Some of the Bunnomai (civil dances) are plays of mimicry resembling the archaic Gigaku. *Konju,* for example, is a piece of comic mimicry like *Suiko* of Gigaku. *Kotokuraku* presents several wild youths and two men who invite them to partake of wine. They all get intoxicated. The masks are so made that performers can even move the noses. *Saisôrô* shows man's change from youth to old age and contains a "warbling" section to depict the transiency of life. *Kanampo* is comic mimicry of a man fishing at the water's edge. Of this class, many pieces existed until the twelfth century and were performed together with the pieces whose keynote was grace and elegance, to serve as entertainment. They were performed at the imperial court together with many other old acrobatic pieces, from which they were not much distinguished as in later years. But after the twelfth century they were quickly forgotten. Now only a few pieces remain extant, performed in shrines and temples in provincial areas.

Integral Composition of Plays: Jo-ha-kyû and Hana Bugaku was closely associated with the life of the highest cultured classes of people, so that it was refined in every aspect. It was characterized by remarkable achievements even on its theoretical side. The *Kyôkunshô* contains many minute discussions, including descriptions of the movements of dancers, entitled "Tablature of Dance" (*mai no fu*). Its theory of *jo-ha-kyû*,[1] or the three stages of gradually rising force, has established, both in music and in dance, the canon of the form of composition. The composition of the program ranging from ritual to parody (*modoki*)

---

[1] In its complete form Gagaku is composed of the three movements *jo* (prelude), *ha* (climax), and *kyû* (finale). But some pieces have only two movements: *jo* and *ha* or *ha* and *kyû*.

was determined as follows: *Embu*[1] (*Furihoko*) to pacify heaven and earth, civil dance, martial dance, and running dance, with auspicious finale. One dance each from the Left and Right groups constituted the pair dance. In this way the rules of composition for individual pieces and for the whole program were established in detail. This idea still lives in the actual performance. In *Ryôô,* for instance, the performer is required to dance slowly at the beginning and then briskly and jerkily, "as if breaking the boughs of trees." The idea of heightening the dramatic effect by means of variety has something in common with the theories of *hana* (flower, or highest stage effect) of Nohgaku by the actor Zeami.

Bugaku lost its primitive dramatic quality by alienating itself from the original legends and by discarding realism, but it acquired a new dramatic quality of high value from the point of view of archaic drama by being endowed with a perfect aristocratic quality, an advanced theory, refined expression, and rich tradition. Moreover, in view of the great influence it exerted on later drama, the merit of Bugaku in the dramatic history of Japan is greater than is usually estimated.

---

[1] A short dance that usually opens the program of Bugaku. The dancers of Sahô (Left) and Uhô (Right), one by one, appear on the stage and wave their wooden halberds in three directions for purification of the court.

CHAPTER FIVE

NEW SARUGAKU

History of New Sarugaku

The Name The new type of Sarugaku performances known by the name of Shin Sarugaku rose in the latter half of the tenth century and lasted until the end of the thirteenth century. The name is a well-established one and appears in the title of a book about this type of performance called *Account of the New Sarugaku (Shin Sarugaku Ki)*, written in the early eleventh century. In contrast, we will call the older type of Sarugaku by the name of Ko Sarugaku (Old Sarugaku)—the type centered around the Sangaku 散楽 ("miscellaneous performances"), which was the precursor of New Sarugaku. In the tenth century, Sangaku gradually came to be called Sarugaku. This change was not merely due to the similarity in pronunciation but also reflected the change in the contents and the clarification of the idea. By phonetic change Sarugaku 猿楽 was sometimes pronounced Sarugô, and the characters 散更 (Sangô) were often used. New Sarugaku was generally called simply Sarugaku.

Sangaku as Old Sarugaku Sangaku, which constituted the principal part of Old Sarugaku, consisted of the Pai-hsi (百戲 Hundred Arts), Tsa-hsi (雜技 Miscellaneous Arts), and the like that had arisen in China on the basis of what had been imported there from Central Asia before the Christian era and had been collectively known as Sangaku (Sanyüeh)[1]

[1] A wall painting in Tunhuang (敦煌) and the stone images at Hsiaot'ang Shan (孝堂山) in China give some pictures of acrobatic performances. Also in the *Book of*

after the sixth century. In the eighth century these began to be absorbed by the Japanese. Their contents were, as described in the section on Sangaku in *T'anghuiyao*,[1] theatrical art, song and dance, acrobatics, magic, conjuring, and so forth. The picture of Sangaku on the arch of a bow in the Shôsôin repository dating from the mid-eighth century is valuable, showing the acrobatic arts, including juggling balls. *Shinzei Kogaku Zu*, dating from the end of the twelfth century, is a picture of Sangaku then surviving. Though the picture is supposed to depend partially on oral tradition, it is still valuable. In the *Kyôkunshô* and other books on Gagaku, there are comments about Old Sarugaku pieces like *Chien-ch'i K'un-t'uo*,[2] the music for a Sangaku piece of Central Asian origin, said to have been popular in T'ang China. From these evidences it appears that Sangaku, although gradually decaying, held its own as a part of Bugaku or its equivalent, thriving on the protection given it by the imperial court, and maintained its position as the so-called Tô Sangaku (T'ang Sanyüeh). At that time, at the banquet following the Sumai no Sechie (Festival of Wrestling), one of the annual events of the imperial court, Sangaku (called Sarugaku) was always performed. Also, at more relaxed banquets, it was performed for entertainment, often with improvised shows to amuse the people. The extemporized shows stimulated the growth of the "theatrical art" of the common people, which, grafted on the basis of the primordial art inherited from antiquity, gave birth to a type of Sarugaku independent of the Sangaku explained above. Such was the situation in the latter half of the tenth century.

Birth of New Sarugaku   The New Sarugaku developed on the basis of the entire body of Sarugaku, with Sangaku at the center. What is to be called "Sarugaku among the people" had a close bearing on the formation of the elements of mimicry in New Sarugaku. The fact that New

---

Chou (周書) compiled in T'ang China, the term 散楽雑戯 is found. In contrast to the aristocratic Gagaku, Sanyüeh was widely performed as entertainment for the general populace.

[1] 唐会要 (*Tôkaiyô* in Japanese) was compiled by Wang P'u during the Sung period in China, giving accounts of T'ang China.

[2] 剱気褌脱 (*Kenkikodatsu* in Japanese). One of the Gagaku pieces derived from Sanyüeh of T'ang. In China it was a kind of juggling with swords. In the mid-eighth century it was introduced in Japan, but the art of juggling was put in the category of Dengaku, and only the music was taken into Gagaku repertoire.

Sarugaku was plebeian in nature would seem to suggest its plebeian origin, but this was not necessarily so. It appears more probable that Sangaku and its closely attached elements constituted the basis, to which plebeian elements were added later. (This will be further clarified in the next section.) In the early eleventh century, there were fairly refined players who performed different varieties of Sarugaku, each introducing his original ideas based on his own view of New Sarugaku. In their hands, various new elements were assembled to create New Sarugaku. Characteristic of New Sarugaku were its urbanity and its emphasis on mimicry and comic gestures. Refinement was demanded of it, and large audiences from both high and low strata of society crowded to see it. In the introductory part of the *Account of the New Sarugaku*, published around 1030, the author, Fujiwara no Akihira (?–1066), who had been given the title of distinction Monjô Hakase (Master of Learning), says that, of all the New Sarugaku pieces he had seen in the preceding twenty years, the ones performed on a certain evening at the festival on the outskirts of Kyoto were the best. He proceeds to mention the contents of the pieces (listed below) and gives his comments on the players. Besides this important work, he has to his credit some other writings, including the *Unshû Shôsoko*,[1] which contain references to contemporary folk arts. New Sarugaku continued to be performed until later, but in the meantime those elements that had lent themselves to its development achieved their own growth independently, while New Sarugaku itself cultivated its most strongly characteristic features, and in the latter half of the twelfth century it gradually developed into the Sarugaku Noh of the Middle Ages.

Performances of New Sarugaku

The *Account of the New Sarugaku* mentions twenty-eight pieces of this form of art. From the contents and lineage, these may be divided into four groups.

[1] Also called *Unshû Shôsoku*, *Unshû Ôrai*, and *Meigô Ôrai*. A collection of excellent letters written by Fujiwara no Akihira, a noble. Valuable source material for studies in the daily life of the court people as well as in the folk arts and beliefs observed during the period of festivals.

1. Sarugaku pieces found in other contemporary popular entertainment arts.
2. Sarugaku of Old Sarugaku origin.
3. Miscellaneous fragmentary predramatic Sarugaku such as the one-man show of mimicry.
4. Sarugaku of dramatic mimicry.

The first group comprises four pieces: *Noronji*, a performance concerning witchcraft; *Hikihito no Mai*, a dance of a dwarf; *Dengaku*, a dance and song originating in the rites of rice planting; and *Kugutsu*, performed by dancers or puppets.

The second comprises four: *Tôjutsu*, T'ang tricks; *Shinadama*, jackstones; *Ringo*, diabolo; and *Yatsudama*, jugglery with eight balls—acrobatic and conjuring arts of Sangaku origin.

The third comprises four: *Hitori Sumai*, solo wrestling; *Hitori Sugoroku*, solo backgammon, both being mimicry performed by one man; and two lion dances called *Mukotsu* and *Ukotsu*.

The fourth comprises sixteen pieces, which might be called "dramatic sketches," showing well the characteristics of New Sarugaku. They form the main body of the art. Pieces in this group show:

1. The mock-important gait and posture of an aged local magistrate (*tairyô*);
2. The humorous movements of the arms and legs of a low-class official (*toneri*), to the comical tunes of a song, by the side of a lake where he is fishing for small prawns;
3. A monk in an important post in a mountain temple near Kyoto who, frightened at something, tucks up his long loose trousers and runs in consternation;
4. A woman of considerable age, of a respectable home somewhere in Kyoto, who despite her age blushingly covers her face with a fan;
5. A wandering blind man who chants tales to the accompaniment of the *biwa* (lute);
6. The professional wishers of good fortune, called *senju manzai*, a kind of beggar, who pray for the success of wine brewing;
7. One who, having eaten so much that his sides ache, strikes his belly and moves his breastbone;
8. The humorous movement of the neck muscles of the dancer of *Ibojirimai*, a mimicry of the acts of a mantis;

9. A reverend monk who, forgetful of his relinquishment of worldly ties, covets a gay-colored stole;

10. A respected nun who, having become pregnant, seeks the gift of swaddling clothes for the baby shortly to be born;

11. A high-ranking court lady (*kôtô*), who usually has her face covered with a veil, seen one day exposed, having forgotten to conceal her face with a fan;

12. An official (*kurôdo*), believed to be a serious man, who one day whistles unintentionally the tune of a flute;

13. The humor of a young low-ranked official impersonating an old man in the dance *Sakammai*;

14. The humor of the thickly painted face of a young girl in the service of a shrine (*miko*), coquettish like a courtesan;

15. A man of Kyoto, as befits a man about town, enjoying easy jokes;

16. Lastly a country man, in Kyoto for the time, standing embarrassed in unfamiliar streets, this so as to be connected with the preceding piece.

Of the sixteen pieces belonging to the fourth group, those in the latter half of the listing seem to be rich in dramatic elements, potential for further elaboration as drama.

All the pieces, from group 1 to group 4, were probably made more effective by ingenious facial makeup and props. It is to be imagined that, while the interest was focused on the principal themes listed above, there were introductory and concluding portions before and after the central parts. Perhaps dialogues, monologues, songs, and dances were liberally interspersed, and music was used when necessary. Judging by the subject matter, Akihira's description of the audience as consisting of people from different walks of life seems well grounded. From this it will be known that there thrived at that time a colorful kind of "entertainment" and that efforts were made to make active use of such entertainment in the creation of original art works. The men concerned with New Sarugaku tried to find humor and comic effects in the haphazard surprises, satires, and jokes that diversified the life of town dwellers, and they succeeded. This was why New Sarugaku prospered. The New Sarugaku programs were made up of an assortment of plays of different kinds, with consideration being given to the better effect of the program as a whole. The leaders of New Sarugaku took care to control the progress of the program skillfully and effectively, and the musical accompanists performed in keeping with the acts. New Sarugaku was in every respect a fully articulated drama.

Fujiwara no Akihira attempted critical remarks on the style and merit of ten famous contemporary New Sarugaku performers. Among the ten, two are noted only for their shortcomings, and four are especially eulogized as real masters. These four are Hakuta, Jinnan, Jôen, and Keinô, whose names also appear in a fourteenth-century dictionary, the *Nichûreki*, which lists master artists in different fields. Akihira speaks of them as "exquisite beyond all description," "saints," "divine," and goes on to describe their facial looks and appearance. The account is simple, but it is suggestive enough to indicate the ideals at which their performance aimed and the high artistic consciousness they maintained. Granting that Akihira is not free from occasional exaggerations and that he was prone to favor art of the popular type, it must still be admitted that New Sarugaku had enough intrinsic value to win comments from the pen of a man who was an instructor in literature at the imperial court.

CHAPTER SIX

PROTOTYPES OF NOH

AT THE IMPERIAL COURT

It was only natural that at the imperial court, where dignity and grace were considered most important, a theatrical art that relied heavily on conversation could not prosper. But pieces accompanied by small-scale dialogues were often enjoyed. For instance, those who were losers in the competitions, such as the poetry contest (*uta-awase*) or the flower contest (*kusabana-awase*), were required to do something as punishment, and they often imitated the acts of *zae no onoko* of Mikagura and miscellaneous old popular arts. Such were also frequently performed for entertainment at the relaxed drinking parties that were then in vogue. In the twelfth century, when the formality of the imperial court was being weakened, at the rehearsals (*shurai*) of the more important annual events (*sechie*) sometimes excessive freedom was taken in the name of imitation—for instance, the subject seating himself on the emperor's throne and the master and retainer exchanging positions in the families of lords. Even where such extreme turnabouts were not perpetrated, the rehearsals had usually become opportunities for recreation, and people delighted in improvising novelties in costumes and in other devices. In a nobleman's diary dating from 1280, it is recorded that while on a journey he was the loser in the "cuckoo contest" and was made to perform a piece of the Sarugaku Noh named *Go* (*Chess*) and *Inquest in the Court of the Local Governor* (*Honjo no Monjaku*), a Furyû piece.

The Furyû was a kind of drama performed in fancy dress and accompanied by *hayashi* music. The performance probably consisted of simple imitative acts, but the original pieces were, as described below, plays of highly dramatic nature, with much dialogue, solid in structure, and rich in variety of content, particularly conflict.

Originally the word *furyû* meant something urbane and elegant. After the Heian period it was also applied to some aesthetic products such as robes that conveyed the feeling inherent in the legends and poems of old, and finally it came to indicate luxurious parades, fancy-dress processions, and group dancing. Such festivity of Furyû became very popular from the end of the Heian into the Kamakura period, and often orders prohibiting Furyû were enacted by the court. The Furyû of Ennen emerged from the tradition to become a special religious art of the temples. Some of the Furyû dances are still extant in various provincial performances.

The play *Inquest in the Court of the Local Governor* was performed by Bugaku dancers at Narasaka on the occasion of the visit of the emperor's messenger as he traveled back to Kyoto after attending a festival at the Kasuga Shrine in Nara. It is a mock representation of the trial of a robber by the police. A detailed account of the play is extant and is found in the *Gyokuyô,* a nobleman's diary dating from 1178. There are six characters in the play: the magistrate (*hôgan*), the chief inquisitor (*kado no osa*), who handles most of the inquest, his two assistants, the robber, and the robber's wife. It is a one-act, one-scene play; the scene is the room of the police office (*kebiishi-chô*). In view of the characters and the contents, it is divided into four parts. (1) The magistrate and the chief inquisitor enter and introduce themselves, and the magistrate takes his seat opposite the imperial messenger. (2) The inquisitor's two assistants bring in the robber and place him in the center. The inquisitor asks many questions of the robber, who answers, pleading not guilty. (3) The robber's wife is brought in and examined, but she asserts ignorance and asks the policemen to question her husband. (4) They question the robber again, but since his answer is the same as before, they subject him to torture. Then, to the marvel of all present, he discloses the appalling news that both the former governor of the province of Izumi and the magistrate now seated in front of him are well acquainted with the whereabouts of the missing treasure. Finally the robber is sent to jail and the play ends.

This play is remarkable for the technique of gradually leading up to the climax, and the use of an unexpected development, as well as for the sharpness of its social satire. It is also remarkable that the players were professional Bugaku dancers and that the contents of the play admitted of comical treatment as well as psychological analysis. Moreover, the magistrate was not a dancer but the real official. Although it was plain that he was not the actual villain, his presence there added to the effect of surprise. In a sense it was a highly effective entertainment provided by the magistrate for his superior, the imperial messenger. Although in all probability it was performed in the style almost of a medieval drama, this play contained within it the potentiality of surpassing medieval drama and of developing into modern drama.

At Temples and Shrines

In the ninth century the sorcerer (*jushi;* also called *shushi, sushi, zushi,* or *noronji*), who practiced incantation at temples and shrines, came to participate in the show as part of the program of the Tsuina Festival ceremony of exorcism at New Year's, impersonating the role of Ryûten or Bishamon, guardian deities of Buddhahood, and conquering demons (*oni*) as symbols of obstacles to enlightenment, whose roles were played by low-ranking sextons called Sarugaku *hôshi*. Similar shows were also presented in the second and fourth lunar months. As time went on, they gradually lost their serious religious significance. In the twelfth century the sorcerer was often replaced by the sexton in the role of the guardian deity. There were more than a dozen pieces, including the *Mañjuśrī in T'ang* piece (*Daitô Monju-te,* in which the Bodhisattva Monju—Mañjuśrī in Sanskrit—appeared on the back of a lion), warrior piece (*musha-te*), and sword piece (*ken-te*), performed as *modoki* or parodies. In many of them, gorgeous costumes were used to make the plays deserving of the appreciation of courtiers, to compete with the position and movements of Sarugaku players. The orthodox sorcerer was sometimes called *hô-noronji*. The actions of both *hô-noronji* and *jushi* consisted of gallop-like movements called *jushi-hashiri* and brisk running acts called *hashiride*. This type of play still exists in some parts of the country. The temples, in order to spread Buddhism, produced primitive plays based on traditions and legends, telling of the Buddha's rescuing the dead from hell and sending them to paradise. Sometimes they told such stories in simple doll plays and caused people affiliated with the temple to perform them, expecting that ultimately the villagers themselves would begin performing them. The Buddhists' attention had been shifted from the upper class to the middle and lower strata of society, and such plays were useful instruments by which to propagate the religion to remote provinces and to the lowest class of people. A special branch of Buddhism, Shugendô, also adopted the same policy with good success. The cause of the success of the plays at Buddhist temples was that entertainment was added to the solemn rites in the entire construction of the program to give people a sense of familiarity and to add variety to the plays.

At Shinto shrines there were few developments to speak of except Kagura. There were some ceremonies in which songs, dances, and conversation were effectively used, like the ceremony of Okina, which embodied the prayer for longevity and rich bountiful harvests; or Onda, which was a prayer offered for, and also in celebration and anticipation of, the farmers' luck in the new year; or the ceremony of praying for and celebrating good fortune in life at sea and in the mountains. Onda, also called Taasobi or Harutauchi, consisted of magical incantations carried out in the precincts of Shinto shrines, which were taken for rice fields, where a series of sketches representing farmers' life from sowing to harvest was performed. Most of these ceremonies, however, had largely grown out of the life of the people and can hardly be regarded as creations of the shrines themselves. Be that as it may, shrines had the Kagura, whose importance as something above mere drama was to increase with time.

Among the Common People

The predecessors of Noh among the common people, which thrived chiefly among farming and fishing communities, were mostly plays at temples and shrines transformed and inherited over the years, but there were also pieces that had developed independently, including among others the types called Taasobi and Dengaku. Deserving especial attention were the imitations of sexual acts, connoting prayers for harvests; the prototype of *Okina* used for rituals and for prayers in Dengaku Noh, Sarugaku Noh, and Shugen Noh; and the unique acts calling for performing on cross-shaped stilts called *taka-ashi* (literally, "high legs") and *hitotsu-ashi* (literally, "one leg"), which, symbolic of the manner of cultivation and containing acrobatic elements, were prayers for rich harvests. The latter two continued to be performed until after Dengaku came to be played by professional artists and were inherited by Dengaku Noh. One of the prototypes of *Okina* was incorporated in the *daijôe*, the emperor's enthronement ceremony, and came to be known as *Okina of the Rice Crop* (*Inanomi no Okina*). When transferred to temples and shrines, the *Okina* was given Buddhist or Shintoist interpretations, and the role of *modoki* was added to it. *Okina* was thus enriched, but basically it was a product of the common people.

From the tenth century, when New Sarugaku was born, professionals of ancient drama and of miscellaneous related dances and music began to be active even among the common people, and the art of the professionals began to diverge from that of the people both in content and in expression. In the Middle Ages, the divergence grew wider. People imitated the acts of the professionals who were active in the court and in temples and shrines, learned lessons in doing so, and gradually began producing, on the strength of that experience, new pieces that were directly associated with their daily life. The force that worked to bring this about was the will of the people to make beautiful, pleasant, and meaningful offerings to the gods. This will was expressed as *hôraku*, meaning the pleasure of a pious and virtuous life. People, however, were also possessed of high sensitivity; they not only revered the deities but also regarded them with such a sense of proximity that they longed to rejoice with them in a spirit of merrymaking. The Hana Matsuri (made up of numerous dances, songs, and imitative acts), which from the Middle Ages to the present has continued to be performed in remote mountainous areas, especially Mikawa Province, now Aichi Prefecture, is a product of this spirit. This type has been preserved in many parts of the country in various different forms, and among them are often to be found specimens belonging to the category of medieval plays or predecessors of Noh.

The people affiliated with temples, who were engaged in drama and allied arts, including the New Sarugaku players, had mostly come from the lower classes. It was from the latter part of the Middle Ages to the early Tokugawa period that they left temples and shrines, came under the protection of the military class, and then became completely independent. During this process they acquired an infinite potentiality for the creation of drama.

CHAPTER SEVEN

ENNEN NOH

History of Ennen Noh

The Formation of Ennen and Ennen Noh Ennen Noh is a result of the development of Ennen—which word connotes the prayer for longevity—as a dramatic art. Probably it was thought at the time this play was created that it would bring about a harmonious atmosphere and promote the welfare of the audience. Ennen originated quite a long time ago. At first it was a ritualistic banquet following Buddhist services and Shinto ceremonies in temples and shrines, to which some improvised songs, dances, and imitative acts were added for entertainment. Gradually the entertainment elements came to predominate as the object of appreciation. New ideas were introduced, other dramatic arts were assimilated, and its enlargement and enrichment went on. In the first half of the twelfth century, there were produced some pieces of Ennen particularly rich in dramatic quality, and thus the prototype of Ennen Noh became established. In the early part of the twelfth century, the Ennen at the Kôfukuji temple in Nara had already become so overly gay and luxurious that it was suppressed by the government. One would have to admit, however, that, in view of the enormous economic and social influence exerted by the large monastery of Yamato Province, this great development was only a natural outcome. Moreover, the allied arts that surrounded Ennen and the movements of the dramatic world at that time supplied a strong and favorable background. In 1199, the songs and dances of altar boys (*chigo*) and the Sarugaku of priests (*daishû*) were performed at the Tôdaiji monastery as an Ennen program. The *chigo* were the good-looking boys who were the objects of the love of priests in temples and performed temple dances combined with popular dances (Rambyôshi[1] and Shirabyôshi[2]) and children's dances (*warabemai*). The *daishû* were lower-class priests, some of whom were semiprofessionals and were responsible for the performances ranging from songs-and-dances to acts and conversation.

Establishment In the early thirteenth century, besides simple songs and dances, there was the recitation called *kaikô* (prologue), which consisted of sentences in praise of ritual services. Comic elements were added to *kaikô* from time to time. Further, witty repartee that parodied it completed a form of amusing dialogue. In the half century that followed, there were established different types of dramatized legends, combined with Shirabyôshi, Bugaku and its music, or pieces with legendary plots with emphasis on the song elements. The first record to be found in literature of such a performance of Ennen Noh refers to the Ennen of *yuimae*[3] (annual meeting for the study of the *Vimalakīrti Sūtra*) at the Kôfukuji temple in 1247, when, according to the account in the *San'e Jôitsuki*,[4] two dance pieces, *A Buddhist Novice at Mount Konron* (*Konron Shugakusha*) and *Blind Priest* (*Mekura Hôshi*), were performed together with Dengaku pieces. These two are both smaller in scale than pieces of Ennen Noh in its period of perfection. They rather belonged to Furyû, with some makeup and ornamental setting, simple song, dance, acts, and speech, accompanied by music. *A Buddhist Novice at Mount Konron* has the same theme as Renji (a type of Ennen

---

[1] A type of tramping dance. Probably derived from incantation in which a sorcerer tramps upon the ground to overwhelm the underground devils.

[2] The name of professional female dancers and their dances, which were in vogue from the end of the twelfth to the early thirteenth century. Exceptionally the dance was performed by male dancers. But in most cases it was done by girls wearing white robes (*suikan*) and *eboshi* hats and carrying short swords. It was accompanied by the rhythms of the beating of a wooden mace or fan with the occasional addition of small drum, flute, and cymbals.

[3] One of the three Buddhist assemblies, held at Kôfukuji temple in Nara on October 10, originated by Fujiwara Kamatari in 658.

[4] According to *Genkô Shakusho,* Emperor Nimmyô institutionalized three lecture meetings of Buddhism in 834, namely, *gosaie* in the palace, *saishôe* at Yakushiji temple, and *yuimae* at Kôfukuji temple. *San'e Jôitsuki* gives a biographical list of the lecturers and main events.

Noh rich in the exchange of dialogues in songs) of a later period, while *Blind Priest* is of the same class as the New Sarugaku piece *Biwa-playing Priest (Biwa Hôshi)*. Both had Buddhist significance. There are several documents of the time that mention performances of Sarugaku and Furyû given as part of a program of Ennen, but the reference to Sarugaku here probably does not mean that real Sarugaku Noh was introduced into the Ennen performance. It reflects, rather, the common idea of the time that conversation, mimicry, and comic acts constituted the peculiar features of Sarugaku. Only those persons associated with the temples and shrines were well acquainted with the legends and myths of the three countries India, China, and Japan, so that Sarugaku players could learn only from them. Ennen Noh, by dint of its advantage in point of subject matter and plot, was established slightly earlier than Sarugaku Noh, but each developed its own unique way of presentation and composition.

Among each of the dramatic forms of this time, there existed considerable variety. Of Furyû, there exist specimens at various stages of development. The above-mentioned *Inquest in the Court of the Local Governor,* played by courtiers in 1280, was also called a Furyû play, but it belonged to a type that depended more on dialogue. Of Ennen Noh, there was the dance type, known as Grand Furyû (Daifuryû) and Small Furyû (Shôfuryû), and the type with more song elements, namely Renji. The priests of lower class, who were the performers, are referred to as Sarugakushû and sometimes as Furyûshû, Yusô, and Kyôsô. The *yu* (literally, "play") in *yusô* means song and dance, and *kyô* (literally, "mad" or "insane") in *kyôsô* connotes that, although the play was not Buddhist, it was an entertainment that would eventually lead to religious enlightenment.

Period of Perfection The fourteenth century was the period of perfection in Ennen Noh. A Tôdaiji document of 1327 mentions the number of the artists scheduled to go to Kyoto to perform Ennen Noh as follows: four actors, five singers, two flutists, two *hichiriki* players, three *shô* players, two *biwa* players—eighteen in total. Because of their excellent art in the performance of Ennen Noh, these eighteen artists had been invited from Nara by a major temple in Kyoto to display their art for appreciation by the dignitaries. One century later, such trips of musicians to Kyoto became more frequent, and their art was

Haniwa: man and woman dancing. Seventh century.

Haniwa: woman with drum. Sixth to seventh century.

Mikagura: *ninjômai* from *Sonokoma*. Imperial Palace, Tokyo.

Seinô Kagura. Kasuga Wakamiya Shrine, Nara Prefecture.

Takachiho Kagura (Iwato Kagura). Miyazaki Prefecture.

Great Buddha Hall, Tôdaiji, Nara. A grand performance of Gigaku took place in front of this hall in 752 in honor of the newly made image of the Great Buddha.

Gigaku mask: Gokô or Kure no Kimi.

Gigaku mask: Konron or Kuromu.

Gigaku mask: Gojo or Kure Onna.

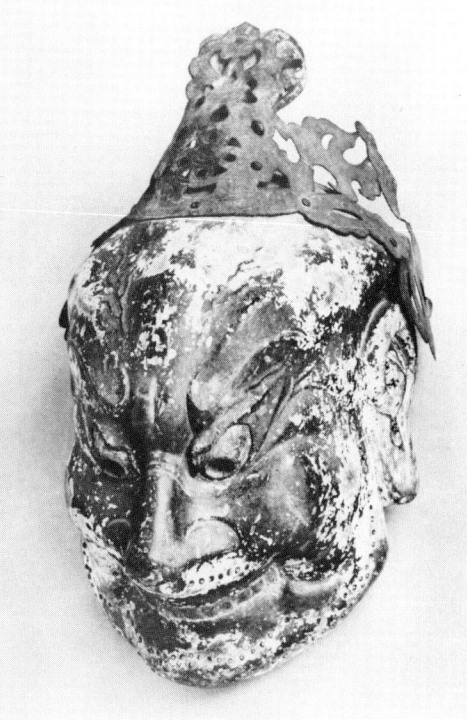
Gigaku mask: Kongô.

Ryôô.

Embu.

Genjôraku.

Nasori.

Soriko.

Tagyûraku.

Manzairaku.

Gagaku ensemble (Kangen).

Bugaku mask: Chikyû.

Bugaku mask: Ayakiri.

Bugaku mask: Waraimen.

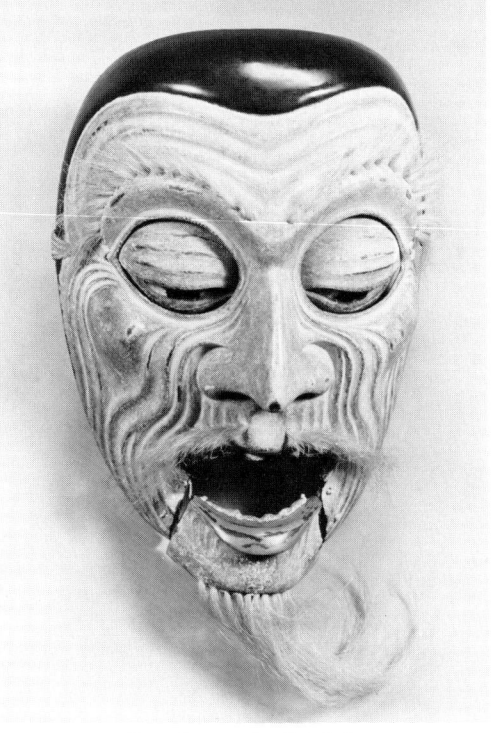
Bugaku mask: Saisôrô.

Ennen Noh: *Rôjo* (old woman's dance). Môtsuji temple, Hiraizumi, Iwate Prefecture.

Kurokawa Noh. Kasuga Shrine, Kurokawa, Yamagata Prefecture.

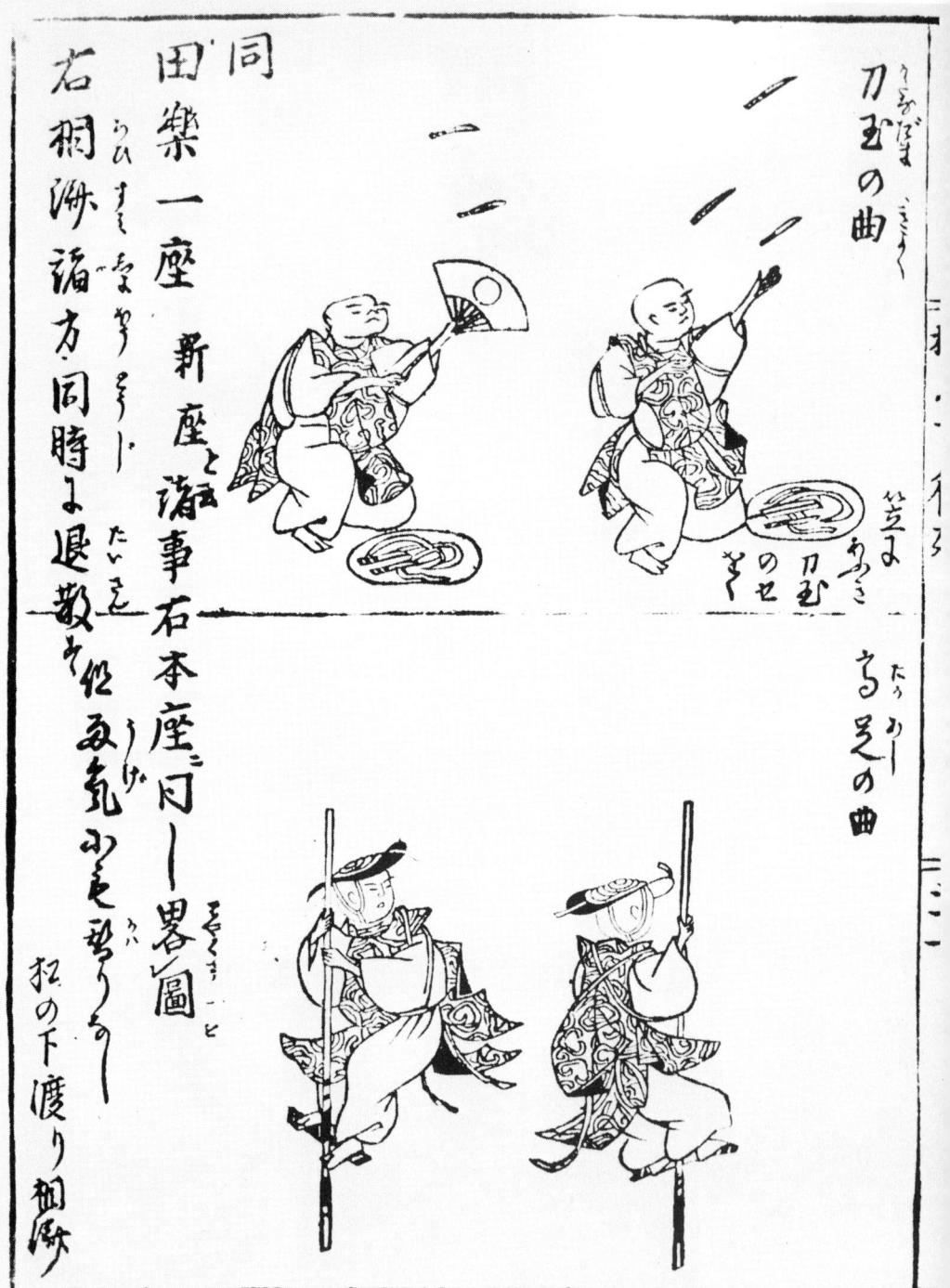

Performances by Dengaku priests: art of sword throwing and art of stilts.

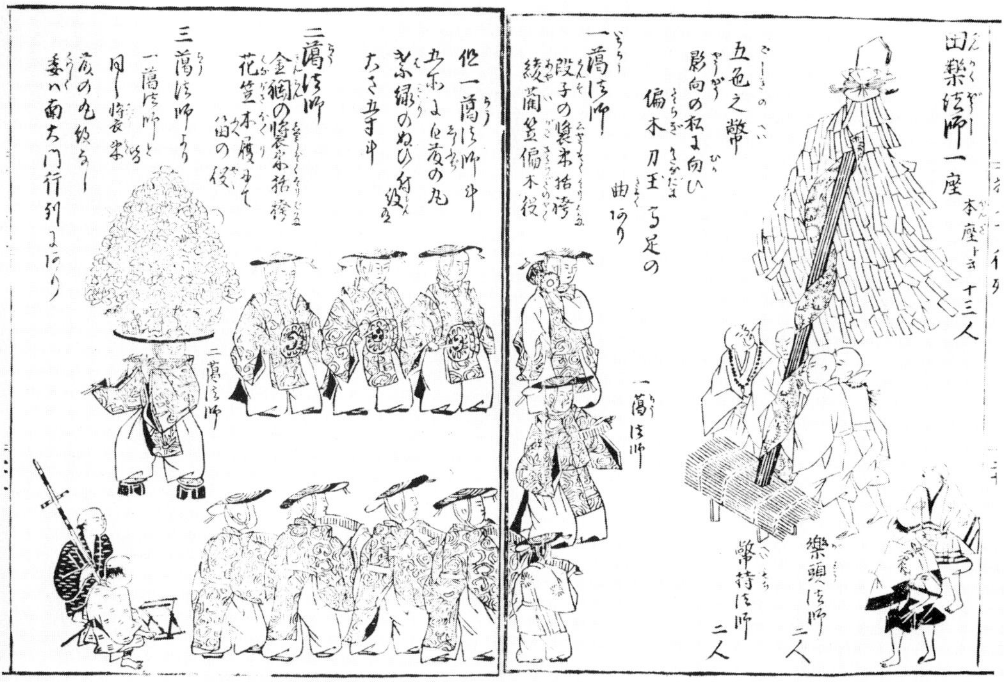

Troupe of Dengaku priests.

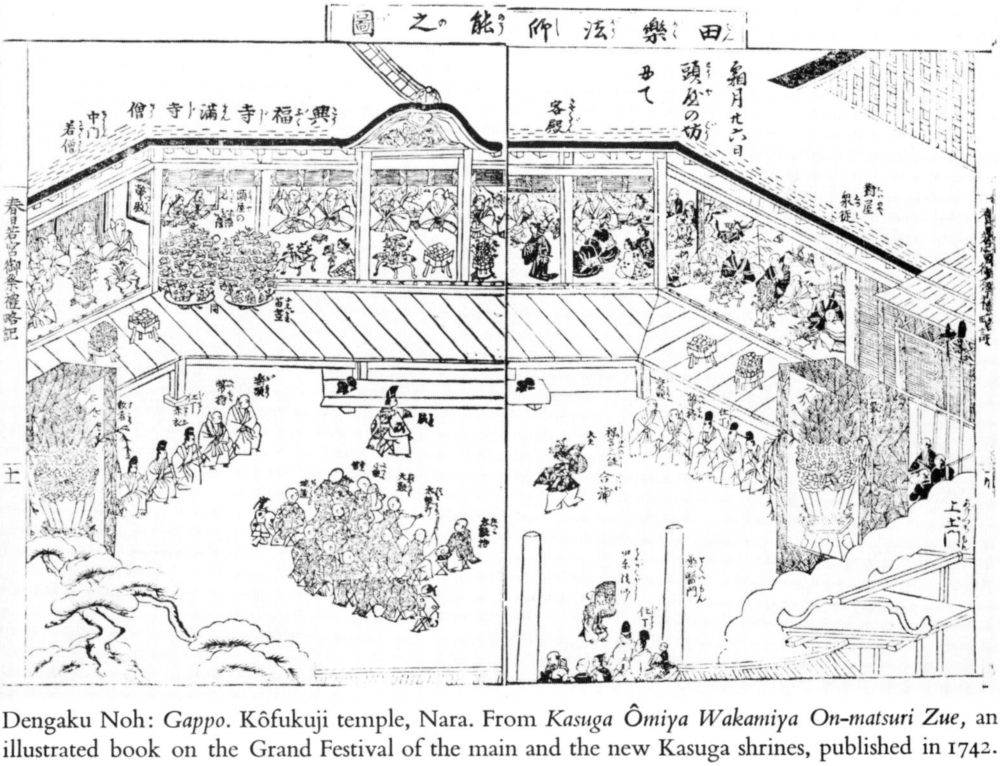

Dengaku Noh: *Gappo*. Kôfukuji temple, Nara. From *Kasuga Ômiya Wakamiya On-matsuri Zue*, an illustrated book on the Grand Festival of the main and the new Kasuga shrines, published in 1742.

Shugen Noh: Bushimai (warrior's dance), *Suzuki no Saburô*. Aomori Prefecture.

Shugen Noh: Kitômai (prayer dance), *Kanemaki,* dealing with the same subject as the Noh play *Dôjôji*. Aomori Prefecture.

Shugen Noh: Dôkemai (clown's dance), *Warabiori* (Picking Bracken Sprouts). Iwate Prefecture.

Kôwakamai: *Ôe*. Fukuoka Prefecture.

Noh stage, Nishi Honganji temple, Kyoto. Constructed in 1598, it is the oldest type of the present Noh stage.

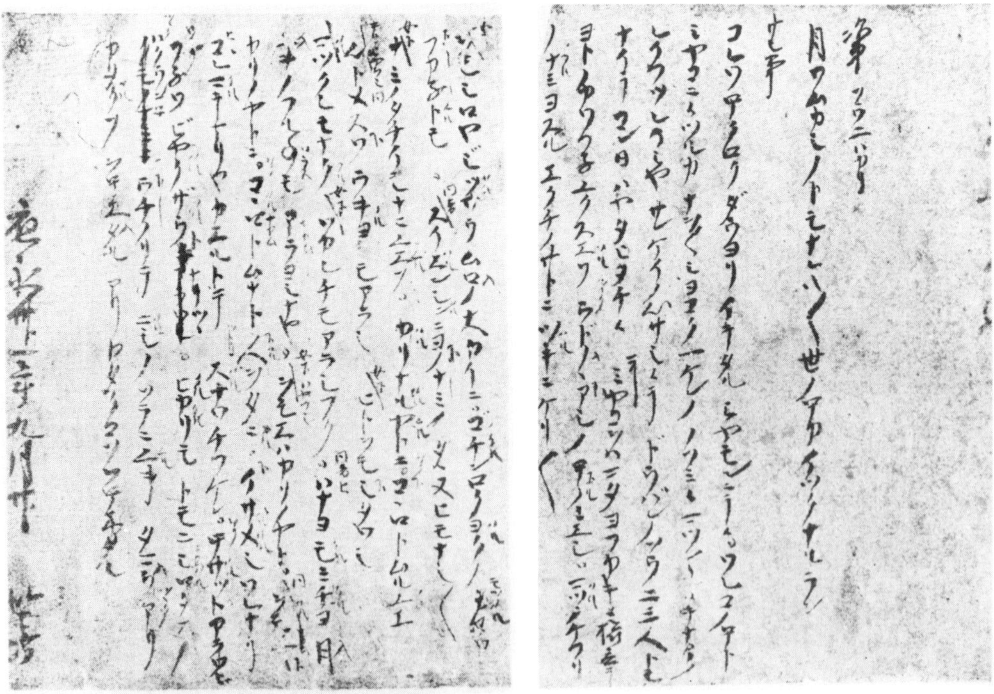

Original manuscript of Noh play *Eguchi,* by Zeami.

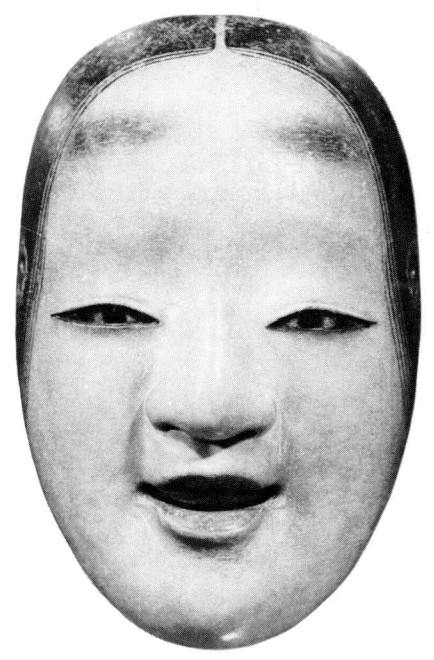

Noh mask: Ko Omote.

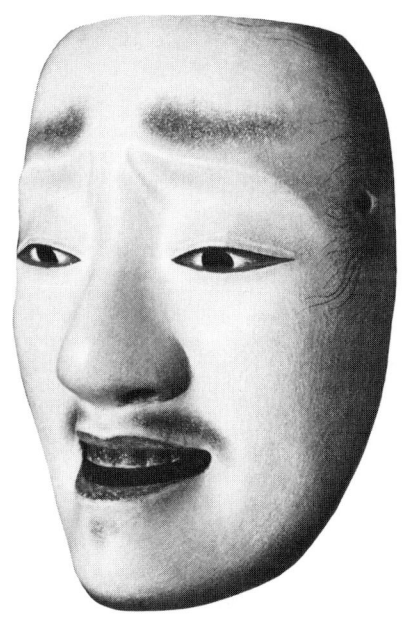

Noh mask: Chûjô.

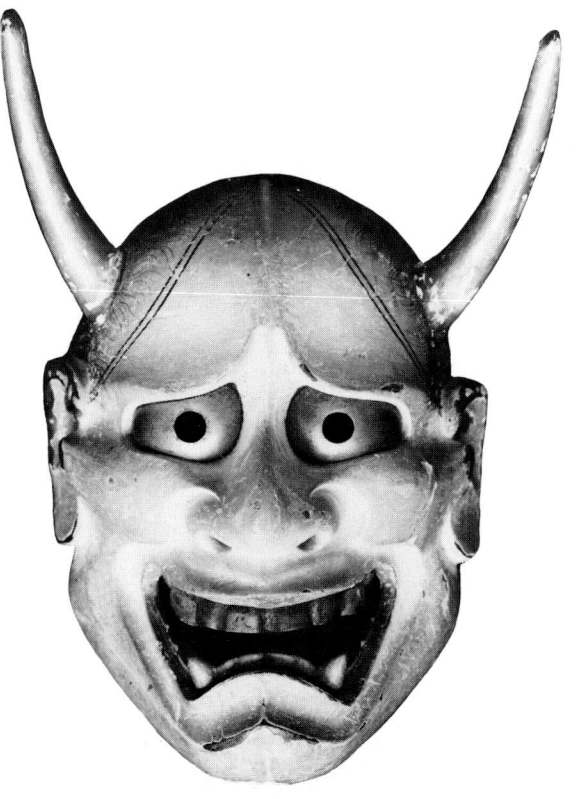

Noh mask: Hannya.

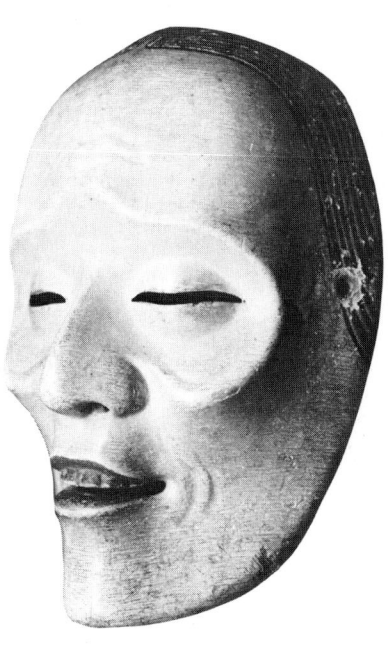

Noh mask: Uba.

Momijigari.

Sumidagawa.

Yashima.

Yuya.

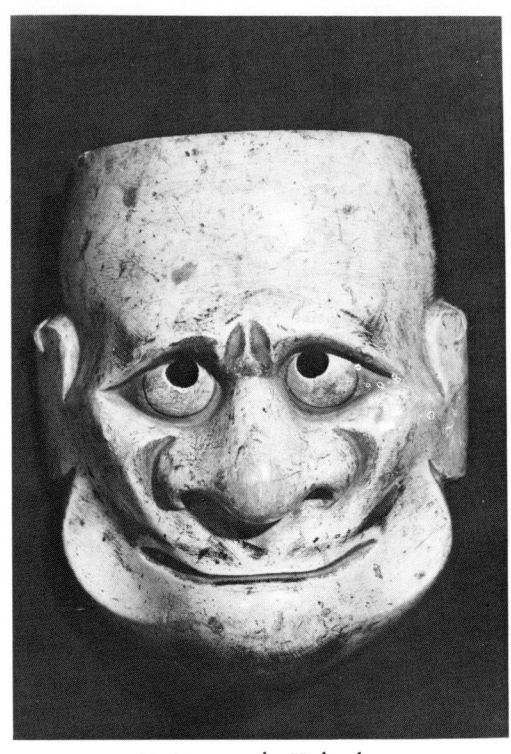

Kyôgen mask: Kobuaku.

Kyôgen mask: Ebisu.

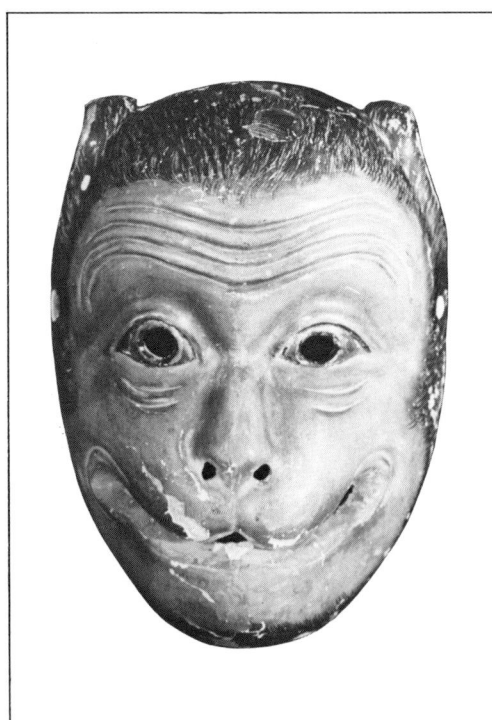

Kyôgen mask: Saru.

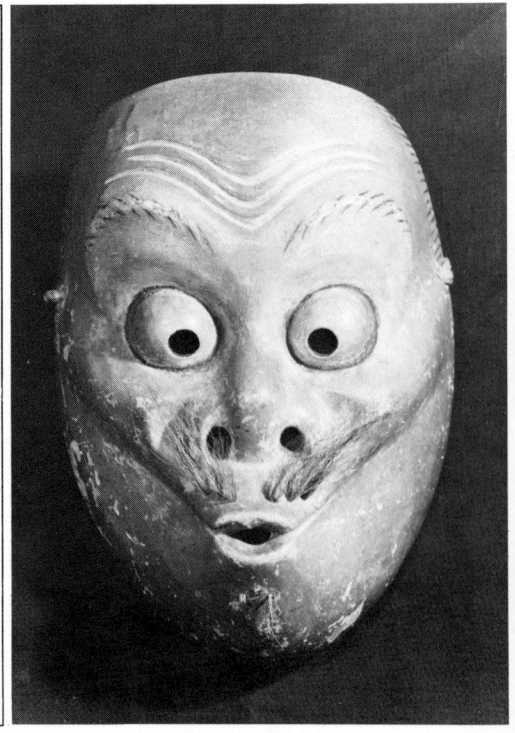

Kyôgen mask: Usobuki.

Bôshibari.

Kani Yamabushi.

Tsurigitsune.

enjoyed by the shogun in Kyoto and by other important people. The above-mentioned case shows that Ennen Noh had made substantial progress at that early date.

In the record of the Ennen held at Hôryûji in 1340 to pray for rain, we read that four pieces were performed for the occasion, namely, *The Renji Concerning the Visit to the Fountainhead of the River Tatsutagawa, Visit to Mount Konron and the Meeting with Eight Hermits, Eight Great Rivers of the Dragon King,* and *Dance, Snail, Dance!* The first is Renji and the remaining three are Furyû. All the four pieces had contents fit for performance in a ritual program of praying for rain. In addition to these, the program contained a prologue with a novel, humorous touch. Thus the Ennen on this occasion had a full program, with a prologue, a dialogue, and a gay finale although it was just to pray for rain. The Ennen for grand occasions like the regular *kegon'e* (Avataṃsaka festival), *yuimae* (festival devoted to expounding the *Vimalakīrti Sūtra*), and *seshinkô* (meeting devoted to Vasubandhu) must have had a grander construction.

Period of Inheritance The fifteenth century and the first half of the sixteenth century were a period when the perfected art of the preceding period was inherited. During the first half of the period the art flourished under the warm support of the Ashikaga shogun, and a notable point about this was the extreme luxury and brilliance referred to as "Ennen, the August Pastime of the Lord of Muromachi" (*Muromachi-dono Onmoteasobi Ennen*), Muromachi being the site of the shogunate residence in 1429. However, notwithstanding the added splendor and refinement, no great essential change was made in this period.

In the early sixteenth century, there was the remarkable activity of Son'ei and Ei'in, priests of the Myôrakuji temple on Mount Tônomine, who produced eighteen new pieces. These, however, were in the pattern of earlier works and were new only in the subjects treated. Nevertheless, while Ennen of the Kôfukuji, Tôdaiji, and Hôryûji had already started to decline because of warfare, that of the Myôrakuji continued to be performed because the temple had the advantage of being located in isolated mountains. The temple rearranged the surviving plays, added new pieces, and compiled the textbook of Ennen called *Versions of the Temmon Era* (*Temmon-bon*), which contains fifty-two pieces. This book is the most valuable standard work for the study of Ennen Noh.

Urban Decline and Provincial Survival In the early Tokugawa period, Ennen disappeared from the central district on account of the weakening of the power of temples and the general changes in the manners of the times. It survived in many cases only in isolated provincial temples and shrines in distorted forms or in fragments of songs and dialogues. What is now called Ennen is often actually fragments of Dengaku, retaining none of the features of real Ennen. Only the Môtsuji temple in the Tôhoku district preserves the old-style Ennen of the early Medieval period, and every year, on the twentieth night of January (the lunar calendar), a performance of selected pieces is given at Jôgyôdô, a temple dedicated to Mātela (Madarajin), the guardian deity of the Tendai sect of Buddhism. The program consists of children's dances and a few of the Noh plays whose texts are still in existence: *Hana-ori, Tome-dori, Komachi, Ominaeshi, Obasute-yama,* and *Ôbo ga Mukashi.* It also contains the *chokushi-mai,* a piece with comic elements. The style is different from that performed in the Yamato district as described below, but there are some features common to both, and the songs of the chorus (*ji-utai*) are in the style of Buddhist chant (*shômyô*).

Performances of Ennen Noh

Construction of Ennen Program Ennen Noh was performed at the very end of the whole Ennen program, of which it was considered the most important part. Ennen had brought to perfection the traditional composite construction—one most appropriate as the "banquet form" —and evolved from ritual to comic, from fragmentary to unified, from song-and-dance and dialogue to drama. The songs were the songs of young boys and Buddhist chant. The dances were Shirabyôshi, Rambyôshi, and Yusôbyôshi danced by *chigo* and *yusô*. Yusôbyôshi were pieces prepared for the performance of the *yusô,* or monks specializing in the Buddhist performing arts. The words used on these occasions were known as *kaikô, tôben, rongi,* and *kyôgen* (comic words) and were recited by *yusô*. The three dramatic types of Ennen Noh were arranged in the order of their scale as Renji, Shôfuryû, and Daifuryû. Hence the Ennen program consisted of Ennen Kabu—(1) songs, (2) dances, (3) conversational recitation—and Ennen Noh—(4) Renji,

(5) Shôfuryû, (6) Daifuryû. This style of arrangement enriched the effect of the whole program and, at the same time, of each of its components.

Masks, Setting, and Stage   For the presentation of Ennen Noh, masks of other forms of drama were appropriated, or new ones made on their pattern, for roles such as those of ghosts. It does not appear that any original style of mask was created. Generally such was the usage in Noh at the early stage. In costume, props, and settings also, the gorgeous decorative manners of Furyû were followed, but wherever possible simplification was done, and effort was made to follow symbolic, stylized production and treatment. The stage, which measured about six by eight meters, was in the garden, with the greenroom in the rear. On either side (left and right) of the stage was constructed a good-sized hill, which was supposed to be the abode of ghosts. The hills were also the place where the Bugaku music and Rambyôshi were played. The instruments, in addition to those mentioned previously, included large and small drums.

Source Materials and Composition of the Plays   The subject matter of the plays was taken from old traditions and historical stories of the three countries India, China, and Japan. The Japanese sources included *Record of Ancient Matters* (*Kojiki*) and other histories; *Tales of Long Ago* (*Konjaku Monogatari*) and other books of tales; *Anthology of Chinese and Japanese Verse* (*Wakan Rôeishû*), *Tales of the Heike* (*Heikyoku*), and other books of poetry (*waka,* poems in Chinese, popular songs, and narratives). Among Chinese sources were *Hanshu* (*Kansho*)*, Shih Chi* (*Shiki*)*, Meng Chu* (*Mokyû*)*, Lieh-hsien-chuan* (*Ressenden*), and other books of history and romance. Indian sources included Buddhist tales. Japanese tales often told the same stories as those of other countries. In most cases stories familiar to both the authors and the audience were used. Contemporary stories were avoided and historical tales preferred. Also, many of the tales were transformed and adapted by the authors' imagination. The construction of the program of each part of Ennen Noh (Renji, Shôfuryû, and Daifuryû) consisted of two divisions in six sections as follows: first half: (1) *kaikô,* (2) *mondô,* (3) *michiyuki;* second half: (4) *okotsuri,* (5) ghosts, (6) finale.

Renji Of the three parts of Ennen Noh, Renji is the richest in song elements. A monk of the temple sponsoring Ennen makes his appearance. He starts on a trip, praying for the prosperity of his temple, looking for treasures to adorn Buddhist services, or seeking an abode for contented living. He finally finds what he longs for. In the course of his travel he meets a ghostlike person who dances Shirabyôshi and Rambyôshi. The songs and dances inserted here are nearer in nature to Shôfuryû, since the performances are not meant for private individuals but as prayers for miracles for the sake of the prosperity of Buddhism and of the temple he belongs to. What he longs for may be mythical treasures like the elixir of life, the gem of Mount Konron, the sacred luna tree (*katsura*), or the lotus flower in three layers. Or he may long to meet the Hassen (Eight Saintly Hermits) or the Shôzan no Shikô (Four Recluses of Mount Shôzan), to visit their abodes, or to find some cool place in summer and to listen to Kangen music.

1. *Kaikô* provides the prologue or introduction to the performance.
2. *Mondô* (questions and answers) is a colloquy on the thing searched for and on the possibility of its being found.
3. *Michiyuki* (journey) is important as a means of transferring the scene to a remote place. A Shirabyôshi of a noble tone is sung and explains the itinerary. *Michiyuki* is thus one of the highlights of Renji. The poem is in the style called *imayô,* consisting of several verses employing the 7-5 or 8-5 system of syllables, in the tone of Chinese poetry—for example,

> Ame no Kawara[1] ni yukikurete,
> Tanabata-tsume[2] ni yado karan.
>
> Benighted by the side of the Heavenly River.
> I will seek a lodging at the Weaver Girl's.

4. *Okotsuri* is an incantation to conjure up ghosts. This is the section with the strongest stage effect among the six sections.
5. Appearance of ghosts in the latter half, although of lesser importance, has such characters as Sarasvatī (Benzaiten, goddess of music), dragon god (Ryûjin), page of the Palace in the Moon (Gekkyû *dôji*), four recluses (*shikô*), and others.

[1] The Milky Way.
[2] The Weaver Girl Star, Vega.

6. The finale in most cases begins with a plain speech of introduction and then proceeds to songs that delineate the scenes and lead to the conclusion, as in *Tazunuru Tsuki no Kazura Renji,* where, after the appearance of the page of the Palace in the Moon, a series of the songs *furyû-goe, okina-goe,* and *haya-uta* close the piece. This section also, introducing various novel ideas, is very impressive. There are instances in which Shirabyôshi and *Etenraku* (a Gagaku piece) were used.

Renji, in this way, has its emphasis on the array of interesting songs in *michiyuki, okotsuri,* and the finale. To these is added the introductory part, consisting of *mondô* and the like, with characters and stage settings that might add color to the play. The play as a whole was so constructed as to show progressive development and was so produced as to heighten the dramatic effect. Special attention was paid to the verse making and the singing.

Shôfuryû In Shôfuryû, the sections 1, 2, and 3 consisted of simple conversations. The characters were travelers or Confucian scholars rather than monks and were in secondary roles, not primary ones. The colloquy took place between persons facing each other. *Michiyuki* consisted of movements indicating "walking round." The remote destination, when reached, was shown by setting an artificial flower and other things on the floor. Section 4, *okotsuri,* small in scale, was short songs in the form of Shirabyôshi or *waka* poems. Sometimes words of Buddhist prayers were used. Section 5 in the latter half usually consisted of two parts, namely songs and speech. Stage settings were used. For instance, in *The Traveler and the Confucian Reach the Milky Way (Yûkaku Jusha Tô Ginga no Koto),* the Weaver Girl (Vega) appears carrying a distaff and the Herdsman (Altair) leading a cow. The Weaver Girl sings: "To whom shall I give a night's lodging but to you who come only once a year?" Then the two declare, "We are Altair and Vega. Now tell us whence you have come." This is obviously based on the famous Chinese romance of the Weaver Star (*tanabata* in Japanese), in which the two stars, in love with each other, are permitted by the god of heaven to meet just once a year, on the seventh night of the seventh month, crossing the Milky Way.

In section 6, the introduction is followed by music and dance. For example, in *Singer of Buddhist Songs Pays a Visit to Mount Shôryôzan (Shômyôshi Shôryôzan ni Môzuru Koto),* the player, together with two companions, dances *Monju* and then the dances *Chuang-tzu* (*Sôshi*), *Sarasvatī* (*Benzaiten*), *Heavenly Being* (*Tennin*), *Dragon* (*Ryû*), *Hermit* (*Sennin*), *Seven Wise Men* (*Shichiken*), and others, all the dances being interesting in their own ways. The dance *Dragon* (*Ryû*) is to be found in *The Poet Drinks the Wine of a Hermit's House* (*Shijin Senka no Sake o Nomu Koto*), in which Fei Ch'ang-fang (Hi Chôbô) throws a fresh bamboo stick into a pot, out of which a boy emerges and dances. Shôfuryû, like this, consisted chiefly of words, with occasional songs. Its effectiveness, however, was largely dependent on the interest of the dances. Its stage settings were more elaborate than those of Renji. On the whole it employed a way of production more or less similar to that of Noh. The dance was not large in scale like Bugaku but moderate like Shirabyôshi and other minor dance pieces. The choreography was arranged with care so as to reflect the personality of the characters, and even their costumes enhanced the effect to a great extent.

Daifuryû Daifuryû was not much different from Shôfuryû, but the subject matter with which it dealt always concerned the exalted society of kings and nobles, so that in every way it tended to be grand and luxurious. First the king or noble appears. (The role is taken by a child, so the speech is spoken by his vassals.) He tells his name and explains in some detail his objective in life, which his vassals approve. The sections 2 and 3 are lacking. Of section 4, two ways of presentation were possible: that of calling actual persons to the scene or that of invoking (the verb is *okotsuru*) ghosts. Ghosts are sometimes human beings transcending time and space, but no distinction is made as far as the words of invocation are concerned, for even ghosts are summoned by the same realistic address.

Section 5 in the latter half usually contains the speech of ghostlike characters who introduce themselves. In the presentation of this part, tools and stage settings far more elaborate than those in Shôfuryû are used. In the piece entitled *The White Fish That Jumped into the King of Chou's Ship* (*Shûô no Fune ni Iru Hakugyo no Koto*), the player walks a little distance, reaches a big river, and beats the drum, whereupon the god of the river appears and pushes the boat forward. The river runs high, and the king orders the god to quiet the river. The river calms down, and people rejoice that the king's good luck is certain, when a white fish jumps into the boat. Various other fishes also appear and run about on the stage. In other plays the "running things" (*hashirimono*) may be wild geese or other birds, toads or reptiles, or even mighty gods like Koreijin,[1] who not only runs about in fearful headgear and costume but also crushes mountains. *Susano-o no Mikoto Conquers the Serpent* (*Susano-o no Mikoto Daija o Shitagaeru Koto*), of which a different version is to be found in a Kagura play, has a scene where the serpent drinks wine from the barrels and Susano-o mutilates the body of the serpent and saves the distressed old couple. In *The Story of the Ball of Rising Tides and the Ball of Ebbing Tides* (*Kanju Manju Ryôka no Koto*), a prince, Isora, beats the drum and leaps into the sea, whereupon two dragons appear, each holding a magic ball, which one of his vassals transmits to the ministers of right and left. In *Lien Ch'eng-wu and the Biwa Music* (*Ren Shôbu Biwa-kyoku no Koto*), the emperor plays the *biwa* in the Seiryôden palace (of which the set is placed on the stage), whereupon the ghost of Lien Ch'eng-wu appears. A retainer tells the emperor that someone like a ghost has come. Lien says to the emperor that he has come to teach him secret music. The maestro goes on to the palace and plays the *biwa*. In these portions the plot, production, and setting are all extremely well constructed. The alternation of speeches and scenes, so inevitably connected together, heightens the dramatic effect.

The dance frequently contained "running pieces," as seen in the program *A Wise Man* (*Chieh-hsien*) *Debates with a Pagan* (*Kaiken Gedô to Rongi*), at Kôfukuji in 1429, which consisted of the four pieces of Gagaku *Taiheiraku, Komaboko, Batô,* and *Nasori*. Children's dances were also favored. These evinced love for young boys and a liking for virile jumping motions. The *Karakami* of Kagura that was sometimes added was an exception. Otherwise all the dances were grand and gorgeous ones fit for the society of sovereigns and nobles.

---

[1] God of mountain and river.

CHAPTER EIGHT

SARUGAKU NOH

History of Sarugaku Noh

Early Development: Amateur and Professional Troupes The history of Sarugaku Noh, running over a century and a half from the beginning of the thirteenth century, constituted the prelude to the subsequent history of Nohgaku. Regarding the early Sarugaku, we have records of "Sarugaku priests" in Nara and also know that among the priests and lower-class employees of the Kôfukuji and Tôdaiji temples there were specialists in Sarugaku. These facts suggest that New Sarugaku had developed fairly well by that time. It should be noted, however, that for Dengaku there is evidence suggesting the existence of two companies (*za*), Honza and Shinza, seventy years previously—that is, about 1130—although Dengaku was not yet of high dramatic quality. Similarly, it would be rash to assume that Sarugaku Noh had become an advanced dramatic art only because of its sustained history. The first forty years were a period when, absorbing the new-style songs and dances of Shirabyôshi, the contents of the art were gradually organized. This was the period of its separation from New Sarugaku.

There is a record dating from 1246 to the effect that Sarugaku Noh was complete with dance, song, and musical accompaniment. Although these elements must have existed since earlier times, that such a definite statement was made suggests the growth of Sarugaku Noh as a dramatic art. Sarugaku Noh was in many ways influenced by Ennen Noh, which thrived on the same scene—temples and shrines—and moreover had by this time been firmly established. But, since the temples and shrines accorded Sarugaku Noh only a lower rank in comparison to Dengaku Noh until later times, it could not easily ascend to the level of prominence where grace was to be sought. Still, a positive effort was being made to heighten the quality of comic mimicry that had constituted the nucleus of New Sarugaku from the point of view of songs and dances.

There is a document of 1288 that seems to suggest the existence of a company or troupe attached to the Kôfukuji monastery. More significant is the record two years later stating that the chief musician (*gakutô*) at Eikyûji, a branch of the monastery, identified himself by the title Nyoi Dayû. One might assume that the title *tayû* (*dayû* in combination), indicative of the post of a chief, shows that a company was in existence. In 1284 the play entitled *Go* (a game of chess imported from China) was performed by the loser in a game as the "loser's show" (*makewaza*) at the imperial court. This *Go* is said to have been the original of a later play (of the same title) ascribed to Dôa or Zeami. About this time there were, apart from the general or ordinary companies, the Sarugaku Noh Za of the *noronji* (incantation sorcerer) group—that is, Honza, Shinza, and the Hôjôji Za. It is reported that the Honza finally took the leadership of the three companies. In the *noronji* group there was another company called the Ise Sarugaku Za. One can easily imagine that there was hot competition among these companies. The competition, however, became even more serious somewhat later, in the period when Sarugaku Noh was perfected. Again, in a record of 1270 a certain *tayû* of the Sakôdo Za, the original home of today's Kongô Za, is mentioned as belonging to the Hôryûji temple. The Emmai Za, cradle of the Komparu Za, belonging to the Kôfukuji temple, had a still older history. The staff members of these companies, with the *tayû* at the top, were assigned to the posts of chief musician (*gakutô shoku*) or "shrine *tayû*" (*shinji tayû shoku*) in temples and shrines. By this means the companies contrived to maintain economic stability and strove to improve their art. Those who were professionals were the nucleus that was soon instrumental in the completion of Nohgaku.

At its foundation, however, the "Sarugaku of the low classes of people" (Semmin Sarugaku) had existed in many places for some time under the command of temples and shrines or independently; "village folk's Sarugaku" (Gômin Sarugaku) was also performed, on a voluntary basis, by villagers at the festivals of temples and shrines. Professional

Sarugaku in most cases had developed from the Sarugaku of low-class people and villagers and received stimulus from this for its development. Independently there was, at the imperial court and in the houses of members of the military class, Samurai Sarugaku, performed by warriors who were amateurs. Each had its own peculiar features, but none made specific effort to emerge from the set patterns of Sarugaku Noh for the respective occasions.

Moreover, although the performers were laymen, most of them were accustomed to serve regularly at festivals and rites, so that they soon came to have some understanding of the play or developed the will to satisfy the artistic desires of the people. They were therefore never remiss in refining and enriching their art. Sometimes from among the laymen there appeared players who surpassed the professionals and who indeed later became professionals.

The sixty years from 1240 were the period when the foundation of Sarugaku Noh was consolidated.

Period of Perfection: Enrichment, Style, Artistic Level The first half of the fourteenth century saw the perfection of Sarugaku Noh. The preceding period consisted of two parts, one differing considerably from the other. During the latter part, the basis of Sarugaku Noh was consolidated, whereas in the period of perfection efforts were made for its enrichment and refinement. By that time Ennen Noh, Dengaku Noh, and Shugen Noh had all been perfected, or their footing had been set; a new style of songs known as Enkyoku (宴曲) had become fashionable, as had also Kusemai (曲舞), which was accompanied by dance. The popular song, Kouta (小歌), was gradually coming into vogue. Thus, under the influence of medieval drama and allied arts, Sarugaku Noh was steadily paving the way for the advent of Nohgaku. The performers were similar to those in the previous period, but the difference of influences became noticeable between the companies that were largely conservative and those that were more progressive in using the new style.

About Sarugaku Noh during the period of perfection, there is no better factual account than that of the Sarugaku Noh performed by virgins in the service of shrines (Miko Sarugaku Noh), as noted in the description of the Kasuga Shrine performances given below. It should be noted that the central figure of the period was Bishaô Gonnokami, who was the direct ancestor of the present Komparu school. He was born toward the end of the preceding period, and throughout the period under discussion he endeavored, successfully, to create the Komparu style. His Emmai Za was attached to Kôfukuji temple. With the support of this large temple his company wielded, it is to be imagined, great influence on others. About the "action of a demon" by his eldest son, Mitsutarô, Zeami writes in his *Talks on Sarugaku* (*Sarugaku Dangi*) that, while his contemporary Uma no Shirô represented the demon—or the apparition in which the dead person made his transformation—as a mighty figure swaying about in a huge presence, Mitsutarô's demon acted delicately, disappearing quietly and appearing again just as quietly. Shirô belonged to the Emmai Za, and his style was considered the "rough" (*rikidô*) style, whereas Bishaô's style was the subtle (*saidô*) style. It was this latter style that Zeami regarded as standard. About another son, Komparu Gonnokami, the author of the *Sarugaku Dangi* is rather disparaging, saying that his art was boorish, but Komparu Zenchiku, on the contrary, in his *The Quintessence of Performing Arts* (*Kabu Zuinôki*), praises him as retaining the antique style and as resembling an ink painting in transcending the vulgar in taste. These two critical views, perhaps, were not as opposed to each other as would appear. His art style, probably, had already struck Zeami as antique. It is to be surmised that the art style and art level of the father Bishaô, in his last years of life, were reflected in those of the two sons, and Bishaô had created those qualities in the period under consideration.

Performances of Sarugaku Noh

Program Composition Sarugaku Noh of the classic type consisted of several genres, one of which, for example, was Kamakura-period Sarugaku, which even in the period of perfection contained tricks like sleight of hand. Sarugaku Noh of the new type, however, saw its varieties revised and the foundation completed for the general unity of the composition of the program in Nohgaku of the later period. The program was to begin with the ceremonial *Okina,* which was a prayer and celebration for a rich crop and longevity. There followed several kinds of Noh, and in between were performed fragmentary pieces of allied arts. The inserted pieces later came to be exclusively

Kyôgen, but in the period under consideration no such restriction had yet arisen. There was also the dance of exorcism, *hôgatame,* which purported to be a prayer to subdue the evil spirits in the four directions on the occasions of divine rites and the dedication of new houses. According to the *Document of the Suzuka Family (Suzuka Monjo),* an actual example of this is to be found in the Kasuga Miko Sarugaku of 1349, taught by professionals.

Kasuga Miko Sarugaku Noh The shrine virgins (*miko*) in the service of Kasuga Shrine were all skilled in general dance and song in addition to Sarugaku Noh. One of their tasks was to dance the Kagura of Shirabyôshi, unique with long verses, to the accompaniment of the small hand drum (*kotsuzumi*). For a performance in 1349, the dancers took lessons for four months from Tôdayû, a professional, for *Okina* and three other pieces.

Since, of all the instruments, the horizontal flute was the most important, being responsible for melody, and most effective in creating atmosphere for the dance, the lessons for this instrument were given with the greatest care. The Worship Pavilion (Hainoya) of the shrine served as the stage. In the Worship Hall (Haiden) nearby sat the musicians (*hayashi*), consisting of one flute player, one hand-drum player, two players of cymbals (one of whom was sometimes replaced by the player of the large drum), and several singing *miko* girls.

The program consisted of the *Okina,* a Noh play, Rambyôshi (popular song with dance), and another Noh play and lasted for about three hours. However, since the progress of the program was not continuous, it is to be surmised that each Noh play in it actually took less than forty minutes.

The ceremonial piece, *Okina,* was in the antique or classic style. There were five roles: Tsui Harai (a young harbinger), Okina Omoto (a bearer of the mask of a holy old man, Okina), Samba Sarugô (interpreter of Okina's dance), Kaja no Kimi (a young man), and Chichi no Jô (another old man). At that time this was the usual form, and it remained basically the same in later times.

The two Noh plays will be referred to here as *Norikiyo* and *Izumi Shikibu.*

The setting of *Norikiyo* is the court of Toba-in, the ex-emperor. Including the hero, Norikiyo, there are six roles. Satô Norikiyo, a warrior in the service of the ex-emperor, later in life became a Buddhist priest and was renamed Saigyô. The story is to be found in the *Saigyô Monogatari Ekotoba,* an illustrated scroll of the *Tales of Saigyô,* which appeared a century earlier. Many legends and traditions had grown up around Saigyô, who was respected as an excellent poet. In particular, the story told in the *Tales of Saigyô (Saigyô Monogatari)* of 1480 is the closest to this play. The time of the play is 1127. The play is divided into two parts, as follows:

1. The ex-emperor and the ex-empress sit in the Toba Palace, attended by two followers, one man and one lady. Norikiyo makes his appearance, accompanied by a follower. The ex-emperor orders him to compose a poem to be written on the painting of a sliding door. Norikiyo thereupon composes ten poems and recites them to the ex-emperor. One of the poems is

> The deep snow
> On the high mountain
> That had fallen thick has melted.
> The water of the river Kiyotaki
> Has risen and flows in white ripples.

2. The ex-emperor, struck by the excellence of the poems, orders the lady-in-waiting to dance an auspicious dance in a flamboyant manner.

The play *Izumi Shikibu* is set in the house of the court lady whose name provides its title. There are five characters, including Izumi Shikibu. Izumi Shikibu was a contemporary of Murasaki Shikibu, author of *The Tale of Genji* and, like the latter, was in court service around the year 1000. In the literature of the Middle Ages, however, Murasaki Shikibu was frequently represented as the mother of Izumi to make an interesting story. The fifteenth-century story of Koshikibu is an example of this bold assumption, and *Izumi Shikibu* is based on this curious tradition. From the point of view of the contents, the play is divided into two parts.

1. Murasaki Shikibu pays a visit to her daughter, Izumi Shikibu, who is in bed with a serious illness. She comforts her, and together the two lament their hapless lot. Izumi Shikibu, now breathing with difficulty, composes a *waka* poem about her sadness on having to depart, before her mother, to the other world.

2. On hearing this poem, Ubusuna-gami, the *genius loci,* makes his appearance, says that he was touched by the poem, and predicts that she will soon recover and be summoned again to court service. Then a boy whom he has brought with him, beautifully adorned with flowers, dances an auspicious dance of flowers.

The two plays cited above have many things in common. Both Norikiyo and Izumi Shikibu were people respected as poets of the highest order. Both of the plays evolve around themes that, though legendary, were well known. Both are concerned with the merit of good *waka* poetry and naturally, being tales of Japanese origin, deal with contemporary events. Moreover, through the introduction of brilliant auspicious dances, variety is sought and higher dramatic effect is contrived. This technique of composition and presentation was in its essence inherited by the Nohgaku that followed.

CHAPTER NINE

DENGAKU NOH

History of Dengaku Noh

Formation and Establishment: Honza, Shinza, Celebrated Actors Dengaku, with its localized, conservative tendency, was slower in developing from archaic drama to medieval drama than the urbane and progressive Sarugaku. The grand Dengaku performance of 1096 caused a furor even among the courtiers, to the extent that it stimulated Ôe no Masafusa, holder of the title of doctor of literature, to write the *Account of the Dengaku in Kyoto* (*Rakuyô Dengaku Ki*). But Dengaku neglected to cultivate its dramatic quality. There is a record of a troupe of fifteen persons having given a skillful performance of humorous exchange of dialogues in 1270. In imitation of Sarugaku Noh, Dengaku then began to emphasize the enrichment of the element of medieval drama, which it soon accomplished.

The half century beginning with the year 1300 was the period of establishment. The *Entairyaku*, the diary of Tôin Kinkata (1291–1360), the chancellor (*dajô daijin*), under the date third month of 1311, records that the ex-emperor saw Dengaku and that in those years entertainment of this kind was enjoying an almost alarming popularity in many places. Its extraordinary vogue even led to the habit of calling by the name of "Dengaku disease" the epidemic that started soon afterward. Hôjô Takatoki, who became the regent (*shikken*) of the Kamakura *bakufu* (military government) in 1316, was a fanatic patron and connoisseur of Dengaku Noh in the last seventeen years of his life. He was not satisfied with the art of the Dengaku players of Kamakura and brought the players of Honza and Shinza from Kyoto. In the *Taiheiki,* a war chronicle, there is a record of how master artists performed Dengaku Noh at the Sannô Shrine in Hie and of the grand view of the Dengaku Noh performance for soliciting contributions on the Shijô banks of the Kamogawa river in Kyoto, watched by an audience of several thousand people. This enormous vogue shows that Dengaku Noh had developed into a well-organized art. The popularity was also due to the activities of talented artists who established it and gave it refinement. Dôren and Kôren, belonging to Honza company, are mentioned in *Sarugaku Dangi* by Zeami, and though a bit inferior to them, there were also Hana Yasha and Fuji Yasha, belonging to the Shinza company. Itchû of Honza, whom Kan'ami respected as an orthodox artist, had studied under Dôren and others and was a master who was active immediately after Dôren and exerted great influence over the early period of Nohgaku. A good account of the actual state of Dengaku Noh at the end of this period is to be found in the record of the Kasuga Shrine for the year 1349, explained below.

Perfection and Decay The latter half of the fourteenth century was the period of perfection of Dengaku Noh, which was followed by the period of decay. Itchû continued to be active from the previous period, giving dignified performances. Somewhat later appeared Kia, who excelled in music and exerted influence on Nohgaku, and also the master artist Zôa. These persons, each in his own way, contributed to the enrichment and polish of the art. Dengaku Noh was thus perfected and was in no way inferior to—indeed it often far surpassed—the new styles of Nohgaku, such as the Yamato Sarugaku school of Kan'ami and Zeami, which thrived in the metropolis and made great progress, and the Ômi Sarugaku of Dôa. After 1333, when the Kamakura *bakufu* was replaced by the Muromachi *bakufu,* Dengaku Noh was favored by the shogun Ashikaga Takauji and others. An almost similar situation continued for some time. Also, as a result of the efforts of the masters mentioned above, Dengaku Noh was given urbane refinement and, while retaining some of its rustic simplicity, achieved a tasteful style like that of Nohgaku, or sometimes better than that of Nohgaku, which was one reason for its popularity. Its perfection in this period, however, meant at the same time that Dengaku Noh came to resemble Nohgaku and that some of its unique quality was lost. Moreover, it lacked the spirit of further improvement, as is to be gathered from the fact that it could not discard the performance of an act on stilts, which had been used in agricultural rituals since old times. It did not dare to go beyond a certain point, and consequently it was finally overwhelmed by the rapid development of Nohgaku.

As will be explained below, the performance of Dengaku Noh in 1446 was the last big event in its history. After that, it decayed quickly in many places, not excepting Kôfukuji temple and Kasuga Shrine, which had been its most powerful supporters, and was generally superseded by Nohgaku. Only the Grand Festival (On-matsuri) of Kasuga Shrine retained the ancient tradition. In the Tokugawa period, out of the thirteen once-established repertory plays, only such pieces as *Kikusui*, *Jisei*, and *Gappo* were being performed. According to the *History of Dengaku Priests* (*Dengaku Hôshi Yurai no Koto*), a report to the Tokugawa *bakufu* in 1755, of all the pieces of Dengaku Noh, which had numbered three hundred, only a little more than a dozen were extant, and no dance piece survived. On the other hand, most of those that were preserved in local provinces had been modified, but there are a few that retain their ancient forms today. These include the Dengaku of the Kasuga Wakamiya Shrine in Nara, the Nachi Dengaku in Shingû (Wakayama Prefecture), and the Ôji Dengaku in Tokyo.

Performances of Dengaku Noh

Rites, Instruments, Masks, Stage Dengaku Noh consisted basically of ritualistic arts like *Chûmonguchi* (a piece played at the gate) and *taka-ashi* (an act on stilts), which dated back to the time of Dengaku. Compared to these, drama was placed in a secondary position. In the former a unique instrument called *binzasara* was used and, in the latter, flute, small hand drum, and large drum. Masks were used occasionally, although their use was more restricted than in Nohgaku. The stage was considered large enough if it measured five or six meters square. Like the Nohgaku stage, it had a bridgelike passageway (*hashi-gakari*) leading to it.

Kasuga Priests and Dengaku Noh: Ren Shôbu, Hanzoku Taishi On the tenth day of the second month in 1349, according to *Documents of the*

Suzuka Family, a performance of Dengaku Noh was offered the deity by the priests (*negi*) of Kasuga Shrine at the Worship Hall. After the ritual and contest of dance (*Tachiai*), in which four persons competed in a performance in homage of bamboo, there were presented two plays: *Ren Shôbu* and *Hanzoku Taishi*. The Shinto priests performed after receiving instruction from professional Dengaku Noh players.

Ren Shôbu had five characters, of which the dragon king of the sea and the dragon god wore masks. The play was divided into four scenes, the first and fourth representing the imperial court of Japan; the second, T'ang China; and the third, a scene on the sea. The story goes as follows:

1. Emperor Murakami orders his vassal Fujiwara no Teibin (or Sadatoshi) to go to China (of the T'ang dynasty) to learn a secret piece of *biwa* music.

2. Teibin meets Lien Ch'eng-wu (Ren Shôbu), *biwa* master of T'ang China, who initiates Teibin in three secret pieces of *biwa* music and gives him three famous instruments.

3. On his way back to Japan, Teibin is attacked by the dragon king and two sea gods, has to throw one of the instruments into the sea, and narrowly escapes.

4. Emperor Murakami plays on the treasured instrument named Genjô at the Seiryôden Palace. The spirit of Lien Ch'eng-wu appears and gives him the instrument that had been lost at sea and teaches him a secret piece.

Hanzoku Taishi had seven persons appearing on the stage. The play was based on the story that Prince Hanzoku captured a hundred kings to thwart the spread of Buddhism. It is divided into two parts. The king who appears in it is accompanied by two ministers.

1. Prince Hanzoku captures King Fumyô.

2. The priest offers prayers, and two Go Dairiki Bosatsu, the guardians of Buddhahood, assist the king in suppressing the prince.

Ren Shôbu was based on an old Japanese legend. The story closely resembles an episode in *The Tale of the Heike*. *Hanzoku Taishi* was based on *Fumyô-ô Kyô* and *Ninnô Kyô* and is related to the stories appearing in *The Collection of Buddhist Tales* (*Hôbutsushû*) by Taira no Yasuyori and other works. *Ren Shôbu* is a musical story and a story of Japan. *Hanzoku Taishi* is a Buddhist story set in India. Thus they differ in contents and in origin, but both emphasize an atmosphere of weirdness, which is chiefly responsible for their dramatic effect. When compared with the Sarugaku Noh performed by *miko* maidens at the same time, these had more of a supernatural inclination. Even when some earlier and later examples are added to them for consideration, this difference is still noticeable. In Sarugaku Noh there were also elements of weirdness, but they did not go beyond a moderate degree. Therein is to be found one of the causes for the future rise and fall of the two kinds of Noh.

The second cause was still more important. As shown in the writings of Zeami, in the presentation of Noh, songs and dances had not yet been fully united with speech and action. The subject of *Ren Shôbu* had already been dealt with in a play of Ennen Noh. It was a subject close to the liking of the people of the time and was probably based on an actual event of thirty years before, when the precious musical instrument Genjô was lost. Like *The Four Goblins* (*Shihiki no Oni*), which was performed as Kanjin Noh—that is, Noh presented for the purpose of raising funds for a temple—and dealt with an incident that occurred some years after *Ren Shôbu* appeared, the latter concerned a topic of the day and was indicative of the vigorous creative urge that produced this type of play.

Bun'an Dengaku Noh   Dengaku Noh was performed on the seventeenth and eighteenth of the third month in 1446 at the Jûshin'in temple in Nara. The *Record of Noh in the Bun'an Era* (*Bun'an Noh Ki*) gives an account of it. On the seventeenth, Prince Sadatsune was invited to the performance, and, after Kangen music and other offerings, Dengaku Noh was performed. The program began with the ceremonial pieces *Chûmonguchi, Binzasara* (in which the special instrument *binzasara* was used), *Tachiai,* and *Katana-dama* (juggling with several swords), after which the following ten Noh plays were presented: *The Shunkô Gate at Atsuta* (*Atsuta no Shunkô-mon*), *Trial of Women* (*Onna-zata*), *A Lunatic at Kitano* (*Kitano Monogurui*), *Bamboo Flute* (*Shakuhachi*), *Bird Chaser* or *Clapper* (*Naruko*), *Scribe* (*Shosha*), *Saint Hônen* (*Hônen Shônin*), *Ono no Komachi, Folding Screen* (*Byôbu*), *Sanekata.*

On the eighteenth, Shogun Ashikaga Yoshimasa's younger brother Yoshimi was invited, and the ceremonial pieces were followed by the eight Noh pieces *Drawing of Water* (*Mizukumi*), *Atsumori*, *Woman's Revenge* (*Onna no Adauchi*), *Sekihara Yoichi*, *Buddhist Invocation in the Night* (*Yonembutsu*), *Haraka*, *Genji*, and *Wakamizu*.

The troupe consisted first of seventeen and then eighteen players, two of whom were Kyôgen players. Between Noh pieces in the program, some Kyôgen plays were presented. According to the *Picture of the Festival of the Ômiya and Wakamiya of the Kasuga Shrine* (*Kasuga Ômiya Wakamiya Gosairei no Zu*), which records the practices of the time, the Dengaku Noh of the Grand Festival comprised thirteen pieces: *Kikusui, Matsudomoe, Tsunemasa, Furugôri, Shinobu, Gappo, Hakozaki, Yuki Oni, Kashiwa, Hitsuji, Jisei, Tamatsushima,* and *Ayai*. From these titles it will be noted that there were more pieces based on Japanese legends and traditions than in the period of establishment. The change reflected the rising interest of the public in its daily life in and after the period of perfection and the desire to compete with the plays of Nohgaku, the rival art. However, because of the inferiority in composition and manner of production, Dengaku Noh was ultimately to be overwhelmed by its rival.

CHAPTER TEN

SHUGEN NOH

History of Shugen Noh

The Formation of Shugen Noh   Shugen Noh is entertainment produced by priests of Shugendô, a religion that developed in the climate of mountainous Japan. The nation's primordial cult of mountains had combined with Buddhism, Shinto, and Taoism and had already taken this form of religion in the Nara period. Professing En no Ozunu as its founder, it imposed severe training, in the mountains, on its followers, who made trips about the whole country and established bases on the eminent peaks in many localities. In the Middle Ages, reflecting the trend toward the eclectic union of Shinto and Buddhism, itinerant monks (*yamabushi*) of Kumano, Haguro, and other regions traveled to remote areas, where they practiced austerities. As a means of propagating their faith, they created their unique Noh, on the basis of the knowledge and training they had obtained in music, Noh, and allied arts, probably in central districts like Yamato. This they performed themselves in addition to ritual ceremonies and dances, and soon villagers began to participate in the performances.

The Old Style   Shugen Noh was firmly established in the middle of the thirteenth century, but, compared with that of later periods, it had an antique style. Because of the situation of its growth, ceremonial ritual and dance were the first elements to be formed and were to continue longest in importance. The contents of this Shugen Noh of the old style began with ascetic training, consisting of rigorous practices of incantation accompanied by *yudate* (in which boiling water is used) and *hibuse* (in which fire is used). The second element was the Gongen-mai, a dance performed with the head of a lion to which the spirit of Gongen, a god of Shinto and Buddhism as well, was believed to be transferred. This dance probably had its origin in the lion dance of Gigaku and later became a ritual of the *jushi*.[1] *Yudate* is to be found also in Shinto Kagura of various localities and in Hana Matsuri.[2] *Okina*, which is a dance of prayer for the happy life of villagers, was also used. Next, as dances of prayer that had entertainment elements for propaganda purposes, those telling the history of mountain gods and Buddhist deities and those showing the spiritual powers of Shugendô priests were performed in an attempt to initiate the villagers in the faith while making them feel at home with it.

These dances, as a principle, were performed by Shugendô priests themselves, who did not always stay at their retreats in the mountains. They gathered from many places at such principal headquarters as Haguro, Kumano, and Ômine for training. They also settled down in a small villages remote from the center, were active as leaders in cultural matters in each locality, and were respected by the local people. Under such favorable conditions, the contents of Shugen Noh were enriched, until, in the fourteenth century, the archaic dance Dôkemai was perfected, increasing the comic quality.

The New Style In the fifteenth century, on the pattern of composition that had been established by the prayer dance (Kitômai) and the comic dance, there developed the warriors' dances (Bushimai), which were chiefly concerned with depicting the valor of warriors in battle. Especially, toward the end of the century, the influence of the Kôwa-

---

[1] *Jushi* (also *jukonshi* or *noronji*). Originally a group of monks attached to temples, whose duty it was to perform special incantation. Later their practice developed into a kind of theatrical performance and became the origin of Sarugaku, called Jushi Sarugaku.

[2] Hana Matsuri (Flower Festival). A kind of Kagura held at night in the severe winter months of December and January in the mountainous districts of Aichi, Shizuoka, and Nagano prefectures. "Flower" in this case seems to refer to the flower of the rice plant. The festival was thus a prayer for the healthy growth of rice, suppression of evil demons, and a rich crop. It existed as early as the end of the Muromachi period in mountain villages of Mikawa Province, where it survived chiefly among the *yamabushi* of the locality.

kamai of the Daigashira school then in vogue—a narrative art with a small element of dance—resulted in increasing the heroism in the plays. Many adaptations were made from the plays of Nohgaku that thrived concurrently with it. Some were very elegant in taste.

The primary characteristic of warriors' dances was naturally in the treatment of heroic or tragic subject matter. Reflecting the phases of a world torn by battles, and taking into account the fancy of the people in remote mountainous districts, this type of drama thrived. The plays of the archaic period also, in all of their variety, were recast in new fashion and enriched. The comic dance had something suggestive of the old-style Kyôgen of Nohgaku. In the time of the new style, there were more and more chances for villagers to participate in events other than ceremonies and ritual dances, and this led to the creation of the forms of banquet entertainment. These forms had the special quality of constantly absorbing new elements, so that, even in the early Tokugawa period, some influence of modern dramatic art was exerted on warriors' dances and clowns' dances and brought about a modernization of the manner of presentation that made it fairly different from the medieval style. Still, the rules of composition remained basically unchanged to the end, in both the program construction and individual plays. One may call by the term "Shugen Noh of the new style" those plays in which the modernization was conspicuous.

Shugen Noh decayed quickly after the issuance in 1868 of the government order that Shinto and Buddhism should be separated, but it still survives in dozens of places. Shugen Noh of the new style has survived prominently in the Tôhoku district. In several cases the medieval style is well preserved, while in a larger number it is only partially preserved. Very frequently, even where the art has died out, the documents, masks, and properties have been preserved. The plays are differently designated according to the origin and localities: Yamabushi Kagura, Hôin Kagura, Shishimai, Nohmai, Kumanomai, Bangaku, Hiyama, Daijô Kagura, and Nambu Kagura.

Performances of Shugen Noh

Masks, Instruments, Stage In Shugen Noh, usually various masks of the Kagura, Dengaku, and Kyôgen types were used. The singers sang the words. The dancers were silent except for meaningless interjections, unless the dances were clown dances or special kinds of warriors' dances. The instruments were the flute, cymbals, large drum, and occasionally the *sasara*. There was no stage setting in the ordinary sense. Properties and tools were kept to the minimum. A big temple bell, for example, would be shown symbolically by a miniature replica. The makeup was simple, though some attempt at realism is discernible. The stage was the worship hall of the shrine or the parlor of the house of the *tôya* (the man on duty), temporarily covered for the purpose. A space of two by three meters was considered large enough for the stage.

Program Composition The program was made up of the ceremonial dance, warrior's dance, and comic dance in this order, and a prayer dance was sometimes added before or after the warrior's dance. Sometimes Gongen-mai was added at the end. In every case the pieces were so arranged as to shift the emphasis from grave ritualistic acts to light *modoki* parody, from songs and dances to conversation and mimicry, as the program progressed. The dramatic effect as a whole was well calculated.

The composition of a single play was one unique to Shugen Noh, although the influence of *jushi-hashiri* (gallop-like movements) may possibly be detected. The typical sequence would be: prelude (*shinka*), entrance (*makude*), introduction (*jimai*), delineation (*samadate*), and finale (*jimai*). After the prelude, with the song of *makude,* the middle of the curtain at the back of the stage is lifted, and from behind it the dancer emerges. The dancer dances to music that serves to introduce him. Then, accompanied by a song (*samadate*) that describes the central theme of the play, he dances and acts. It ends in the finale called *jimai*. The performance of a play in most cases took more than half an hour. It was customary to present more than ten plays from early evening to midnight.

Four Types of Dance The first of these is the ritual dance (Gireimai). Of this category the Gongen-mai was a kind of lion dance. Sometimes the celebration of the completion of a new house, known as *hôgatame* and *moutari,* or the *haka-jishi*, a Buddhist service, was performed. *Okina* of the Shugen Noh was a piece in which Buddhist elements were strong. The figure of the dancer, showing the changes of a man from youth to age, retains the old style.

To the second type, the prayer dance (Kitômai), belong *Nenji, Tenri, Sambon-ken* (*Three-Swords Dance*, a piece belonging to the *ken-te* group performed by *jushi*), and *Yamagami* (*Mountain God*). Especially noteworthy is *Kanemaki*, dealing with the same subject as *Dôjôji*, a play of Nohgaku. Whereas *Dôjôji* is centrally concerned with the transformation of a girl into a serpent, this dance shows the Shugen priest suppressing with the power of his ardent prayer the girl who clings to the temple bell and tries to break it. Its focus is on a commandment against women's obsession with love and on the power of the Shugen priest's prayer, thereby showing people the holy merits of Shugendô. It has precisely appropriate contents and presentation as a play for Shugendô. The mask of the praying dancer is skillfully made, giving the impression of strong magical power and at the same time heightening the dramatic effect.

The third type, the warrior's dance (Bushimai), is also called "rough dance" (*aramai*) because of its violent movements. Most of the pieces in this category deal with such subjects as the combats between Genji and Heike warriors, the vendetta of the Soga brothers, and the like, as in *Shinobu, Yashima,* and *Soga Kyôdai*. At one time there were more graceful pieces, from different sources. These were mostly adaptations from plays of Nohgaku, on the model of the pieces just mentioned. One of the pieces of this type deserving attention is *Tomoe* (also *Kiso*), dealing with a well-known woman warrior. Another is *Suzuki no Saburô,* a piece remarkable for its complicated story and its taste, containing in the latter half the scene of the hero Saburô's valorous combat to protect his master Yoshitsune at Takadate, and in the former half a pathetic scene of his parting from his mother before going to battle.

The fourth type is the comic dance (Dôkemai). Also called Kyôgenmai, this is a type of satire. Rich in rural taste, it is also conversational. The type comprises a large number of varieties: the fox hunter's dance, the rice planter's dance, and others, all more or less connected with the life of rural people. Because the plays admit of extemporized speeches, the villagers enjoy them all the more, responding with cheers and hurrahs.

Among the pieces of this kind the classic-style *Warabiori* is the most noteworthy. The play consists of three scenes. In scene 1 a beautiful young girl enters. She has come to pick *warabi* (bracken sprout, delicious type of food in spring) in the mountains for her parents. On her way home she has to cross a river. She approaches an old boatman who happens to be there, saying, "Pray carry me across, and I will do whatever favor you may ask." The old man complies but after reaching the other side asks her to stay at his house. The girl wishes that he would give her a few days' time, as she has to bring the freshly picked *warabi* home to her parents. In scene 2 a woodcutter, wearing an object in the shape of an ox head (a phallic symbol), appears, performs many antics and dances, and exchanges droll conversation with the girl. In scene 3 the old man, looking fearful because he is angry with the woodcutter, appears and grapples with the latter. There are two endings to the play. According to one, a happy ending in the style of a Shugen Noh, the girl flees away unharmed. The other ending is tragic, the girl being snatched away by a demon.

Scene 1 of this play has a tranquil, elegant tone, resembling the first half of a Noh play in conception and composition, whereas scene 3 resembles its latter half. Scene 2 is comical and is suggestive of the simplicity of Kyôgen.

As a whole, *Warabiori* is an excellent work of art, rich in variety and dramatic effect. Clown-dance plays not only are characterized by their humorous touches, but also, when at their best, often have a wealth of medieval romanticism and something that reminds one of the archaic composition before the differentiation of Noh and Kyôgen had yet taken place.

CHAPTER ELEVEN

THE HISTORY OF NOHGAKU

Three Periods of Development

Sarugaku Noh, which had achieved a certain degree of perfection, entered into a second stage of rapid development after the middle of the fourteenth century, and remarkable changes were made both in content and in form. Although the structure of its theater (notably the stage), stage setting, masks, and costume remained basically the same, basic changes in the words, music production, and theories were quite significant. Parallel to these changes were conspicuous enlargement in the type and scope and improvement in the style and level of the performance. The term Sarugaku Noh continued to be used until two centuries later, but 't is now common to refer to the art after it underwent these essential changes by the term Nohgaku, to distinguish it from Sarugaku Noh in its earlier stages. There was never a break in the continuity between Sarugaku and Nohgaku, but they differ greatly in quality.

The term Nohgaku is a general term that covers both Noh and Kyôgen. But several appellations are generally used. The term Nohgaku is frequently used to refer to Noh alone. Kyôgen is sometimes called Noh Kyôgen to distinguish it from the same term used in Kabuki, where Kabuki Kyôgen or simply Kyôgen signifies a Kabuki play of that genre. Here the term Nohgaku should be understood to refer to Noh and Kyôgen inclusively.

What may be called, in the history of Japanese drama, the Age of Nohgaku started in the middle of the fourteenth century and extends through the present day, spanning six centuries. Its history may be roughly divided into three periods according to the phases of development: the period of consolidation, the period of change, and the period of stabilization. The first covers the rather brief span from 1351 to 1470. It was a rich period and the most significant in the history of Nohgaku. It is also one of the most brilliant periods in the history of Japanese drama as a whole. This period may further be divided into three stages of development. The second period lasted until the end of the sixteenth century. It was a time of progress in anomalous forms. The third period covers the Tokugawa age and also Japan's modern age, when Nohgaku, by the process of inner replenishment, was given its present aspect.

Nohgaku has thus changed greatly from its early days to the present. From the point of view of Kyôgen, however, the above periodical division is, strictly speaking, not wholly valid. Nevertheless, in essential respects it may be used for Kyôgen as well. Also, in view of the subordinate position accorded Kyôgen in Nohgaku, the above division of periods is adequate.

Nohgaku, although it was completed in most of its basic and essential aspects by the activities of Kanze Zeami Motokiyo in the period of consolidation, still required a long time and the serious efforts of many people for its true perfection.

First Stage of Consolidation: Kan'ami

This particularly important period, which marked the transition from Sarugaku Noh to Nohgaku, began in 1351 and lasted until 1384, the year of Kan'ami's death, or, according to some scholars, until several years later, when Zeami was thirty years old. Kanze Kan'ami Kiyotsugu, born in 1333, was in his twenties during this first stage and was still in his apprenticeship. At that time, in Yamato Province, there were many *za* (companies), with the Emmai Za (later known as the Komparu Za) foremost among them. In provinces nearby—Ise, Kii, Iga, Settsu, Yamashiro, Tamba, Ômi, Mino, Echizen—and even in more remote provinces, there were also *za* or similar groups, which, while maintaining close relations with shrines and temples as they did in previous ages, took more and more interest in performing Noh for the general public. Most of them, however, merely performed what they saw and learned and had no active desire for innovation. Such ambition was shown by only a few *za,* including the Komparu Za. By their efforts the way was paved for future progress. Dengaku Noh, in which there had been increasingly severe competition since the previous period, prospered all the more under the warm protection offered by the new Ashikaga *bakufu* and saw the appearance of several men of great talent, including Itchû, who influenced Zeami. Politically, in this period, the imperial court was divided into the Southern (Yoshino) and the Northern (Kyoto) factions, which fought each other. The Ashikaga *bakufu* supported the Northern Court, so that Kyoto was the central seat of power, and despite the general unrest due to minor struggles in local provinces, there was a kind of stability in the city, where drama and other entertainments prospered even more than before. Also, the birth of the new *bakufu* in Kyoto, the old metropolis, after the fall of the Kamakura *bakufu* in the remote Kanto district in 1333, was an event that, with respect to culture, caused provincialism to be dismissed in favor of urban elegance, and the old style to be discarded in favor of the new. Reflecting this cultural tendency, Nohgaku emerged from Sarugaku Noh, making great progress and being consolidated in its new form. In this process, the leading person was Kan'ami.

Kanze Kan'ami Kiyotsugu, whose infant name was Kanze, was born the second son of Kamishima Kagemori, lord of the small fief of Asoda in Iga Province, according to existing records. For some reason, as a boy he was adopted by a family of Sarugaku Noh performers in Yamato Province. After receiving training for some time, he founded a *za* at Obata, Iga Province, and a short while later moved it to Yûsaki, Yamato Province. He was then in his twenties. This Yûsaki Za was the forerunner of the later Kanze Za. He returned to Yamato probably because he could have more chances for study there and also because he had the ambition of going to metropolitan Kyoto to join in the greater activity there. For more than ten years after this, he set his creative mind to elaborating *monomane* (literally, "imitation"—that is, the realistic presentation of characters), in which the Yamato Sarugaku excelled. At the same time he absorbed the essence of *yûgen* (a simplified, elegant expression of phantasm), in which the Ômi Sarugaku excelled, from the master artist Inuô Dôa, to heighten the artistic quality of his art. All the while he revered the noted master Itchû of Dengaku Noh as his teacher and learned from him the art of harmoniously combining *yûgen* and *monomane,* as well as the high artistic level born out of practice. This conscious synthesis was something unknown in the old-style Sarugaku Noh, while at the same time it matched the general tendency toward urban elegance.

Kan'ami, in 1369 or 1370, when he was nearly forty, held a seven-day performance at the Daigoji temple, near Kyoto, which proved successful with the city people. It is to be imagined that even before that he had given performances in Kyoto. These must have been occasions for him to acquire the refined manners of the townspeople. Even according to his own theory, a man in his thirties was in an important period for training, when he could make the best progress in life and when the shaping of his unique style was to begin. Some years later, in 1374, when he performed Noh at Imagumano, Higashiyama, in Kyoto, Ashikaga Yoshimitsu, the third shogun, following the recommendation of Ebina Nan'ami, one of his close retainers, went to see it and first had a chance to witness Kan'ami's art. Yoshimitsu had already been shogun for six years but was still only seventeen. He was, however, surrounded by many men of rich cultural attainment. Moreover, the young shogun had by birth been endowed with keen aesthetic sense and at once recognized the excellence of Kan'ami's performance. He was also attracted by the talent of the twelve-year-old Tôwaka (sometimes called Fujiwaka or Fujiwakamaru; later Zeami), who performed at the same time. He acted as patron to both the father and the son and often commissioned their performances of Noh. He even let Tôwaka wait on him constantly like a page. Yoshimitsu's rich culture, keen connoisseurship, and warm protection benefited not only the father and son but also Nohgaku itself, which owes a great deal to him for its secure establishment.

Kan'ami, availing himself of the opportunity, made up his mind to accomplish the transformation of Nohgaku. From a drama associated with shrines and temples, he wanted to change it to a drama supported by the *bakufu* and the military men who longed for the cultured life at court. But he did not proceed with this transformation as radically as did Zeami. He still did not make light of the appreciation by provincial and ordinary people. This was not solely because of the close and longstanding connection of Nohgaku with these people. It was also partly because of Kan'ami's personal temperament, for he was a man who could not completely rid himself of the rustic manners he shared with the people of Iga and Yamato and become completely urbanized. Even after his success in the capital he continued to go to the provinces. In 1384, soon after performing Noh at the Sengen Shrine in the remote province of Suruga, he died there. It was a death that fitted him very well. He was then at his best in displaying the vigor of performing that he had always considered important. He could not have been more glad than to die during a tour of the provinces while performing for the masses, whom he had continued to love even when he was leaning more and more to the urban style. But his son, Zeami, was still a young man of twenty, and the future of the Kanze Za thus did not admit of optimistic outlook. The future of Nohgaku itself looked uncertain. That this fear turned out to be groundless was the result of hard work and support by a large number of people.

Kan'ami's achievements included, in connection with performance, the development of the theories of *yûgen* and *monomane* mentioned above and the establishment of the concept of *hana* (charm of performance) that went with them. All these were inherited and elaborated on a higher level by Zeami. *Hana* (flower), it should be noted, is the aesthetic effect of charm and interest characterized by novelty and grace (*yûgen*).

But Kan'ami's contributions were not restricted to the realm of action. It is desirable that the words and music of Noh, because it is a combination of song and dance, be written by the same person, and this was what Kan'ami did. He not only wrote original texts for Noh but also rewrote old pieces of Sarugaku Noh and Dengaku Noh and made adaptations from other categories of drama and entertainment. His works numbered at least several dozen. Some are known to have existed from the writings of Zeami. Some were rewritten by Zeami, and others and have come down to this day, including the famous pieces *Saga Monogurui* (*Madwoman at Saga*), *Shizuka ga Mai no Noh* (*Shizuka's Dance*), *Shii no Shôshô* (*The Ghost of Ono no Komachi*), and *Jinen Koji* (*Priest Jinen Koji*), the first three of which were renamed when rewritten and are now known as *Hyakuman*, *Yoshino Shizuka*, and *Kayoi Komachi*.

In writing the text, Kan'ami, while on the whole following the earlier way of using legendary materials, carried out various experiments to introduce a new style. He also took interest in events of real life. Even when he dealt with classical subjects, he did not forget their significance in contemporary life. He also frequently took up current events, to which he gave lively treatment, adding witty, clever conversations, and he succeeded in creating vivid scenes through a keen observation of the movements of characters and the progression and nature of events.

In his texts, he achieved greater success by the clever use of the kinds of songs and dances in vogue at his time, Kusemai and Kouta. Yamato Sarugaku, in its melody, had always been characterized by the style of Kouta. Kan'ami, just before going to Kyoto, studied Kusemai with Otozuru, an accomplished artist of women's Kusemai of the school of Hyakuman, an expert of women's Kusemai in Nara. Kan'ami used the knowledge thus gained to introduce Kusemai into Noh. In doing this, he sometimes used the original wording of Kusemai, unchanged, for Noh, or a wording close to the original, and sometimes created new words in imitation of it. The melody was basically what was called Kouta-bushi Kusemai—that is, Kusemai with the Kouta style added. It is not clear whether anyone preceding him had done this, but it is to be imagined that there was a precedent. Still, it was he who, by giving it a thorough development and appropriate treatment, achieved success and enjoyed the accolades given to a pioneer. His first attempt was the Kusemai in *Shirahige (White Beard)*. Zeami's comment that it was very near the original Kusemai shows that it had still been only insufficiently digested in Noh.

Kusemai is a kind of song consisting of long series of tasteful observations and phrases, and picturesque descriptions of events, expressed in prose with some rhythmic effects and set to music with the rhythm given by the beating of the hand drum. Since it was an art in the tradition of Shirabyôshi, which emphasizes dance, it was ordinarily accompanied by simple dance, but dance was sometimes omitted because often the words were so full of meaning and the melody was also very attractive. Even in Noh, the presence and absence of dance distinguished the two styles of *kuse*, *mai-guse* (sung while dancing) and *i-guse* (sung while sitting). In Noh, that part called *kuse*, originally traceable to Kusemai, is placed as a rule in the most important part of a piece. By the introduction of Kusemai, Noh gained dignity and solemnity and an added overall richness of variety. It also remarkably enhanced its epic quality. This technique dates from Kan'ami and was inherited by Zeami and others.

Kan'ami foresaw the changes of the times and the general trends in theater and drama and made very effort to study the direction to be taken by Nohgaku, its performance, its words, and its melodies, with respect to their principle and practice. He overcame many difficulties by dint of critical acumen, broad understanding, and sheer decision making and succeeded in establishing a new style before others did. While Inuô Dôa, Komparu Mitsutarô, Komparu Gonnokami, and also Itchû and Kia of Dengaku Noh, enjoying the fame of master artists, nevertheless devoted themselves solely to technical improvement, Kan'ami attempted innovations and enrichment in all the aspects, including the theoretical and practical sides of the play, the music, and the performance. Experts were not lacking in those days, but he had the eagerness for advancement and a keen insight, which were but rare in others.

The Nohgaku that sprang up from the old-style Sarugaku Noh and was established as a new art is true only with respect to Noh, which is only a part—if the more important—of Nohgaku. The other part, Kyôgen, had not yet emerged from the crude state of its initial period. Documents on Kyôgen in this period are very scarce. We read in Zeami's *Shûdôsho* (*Directions for the Participant in Noh*: a book meant as basic instruction for those taking up the art) that there was a Kyôgen master named Tsuchidayû, and in his *Sarugaku Dangi* (*Talks on Sarugaku*) of masters Ozuchi and Kiku of the Shinza, and it may thus be inferred that the performance of Kyôgen had advanced to the extent that it deserved some comments on the style and level of its art.

Kiku, mentioned above, was a player of Dengaku Noh. Also, the program of Ennen performed in 1352 at the Nimpeiji temple in the remote Suô Province included *Yamabushi Seppô* (*Sermon by the Itinerant Priest*), probably of the category of "Yamabushi pieces" of later Kyôgen. This may have been a loan from the repertoire of contemporary Sarugaku or Dengaku rather than an original Ennen piece. It is to be noticed, however, that there existed original comic *mondô* (dialogues) and short comic sketches in Ennen. For example, in a piece called *Kyôdono* in the Ennen program held at Môtsuji temple at Hiraizumi a comic character named Ariyoshi appears. The Kyôgen in Shugen Noh was also of the comic type. Comic acts are indispensable in a play meant for the general populace, and even Nohgaku of the consolidation period could not do without them.

The relation between Noh and Kyôgen was not simple, but basically it was not much different from what it is today. The actors of Noh and those of Kyôgen were rigorously distinguished from each other with respect to their functions, and no interchange could be permitted. The Kyôgen actors stood lower in rank and were responsible for playing semi-ceremonial pieces in which the role of *hogaibito* was adopted. This role, portraying a kind of beggar who went from door to door and offered felicitous remarks or performances, appeared in plays like *Matsutake Furyû*, in which the spirits of pine and bamboo felicitate longevity, and in *Tsurukame Furyû*, in which the spirits of crane and tortoise perform a similar function. Kyôgen players appeared in such dances as *Sambasô* (the latter half of *Okina*) and in Ai Kyôgen, the interludes between the first and second halves of Noh plays. They were also called upon for Noh roles when some special meaning was acknowledged in the action or status of the character portrayed. In addition to these duties, they performed Kyôgen as completely independent plays. The factor in which Kyôgen of the time differed most from the fixed Kyôgen of later periods was that Kyôgen actors mingled with Noh actors more liberally than one would imagine from the situation prevailing today, not only playing the roles of comic characters but also sometimes playing realistic and prosaic parts. The status of Kyôgen actors in Nohgaku was something like that of lower-rank acolytes of temples and shrines in relation to the dancers in Bugaku.

As in the medieval farce of western Europe, the wording of Kyôgen plays before the Tokugawa period was not prescribed minutely. Only the broad outlines, plots, and highlights were determined before the performance was begun. The actors were left free to improvise. Accordingly, we have nothing in black and white that records what actually transpired on the stage.

Such being the case, one cannot give ready credence to the tradition that Gen'e, who died in 1350 at the age of eighty-three, first wrote fifty-nine Kyôgen plays, as the histories of Kyôgen families tell us. However, as Gen'e was an esteemed and learned priest of Kyoto and had such keen interest in worldly affairs that he once took part in a reform project, it appears probable that he helped the growth of Kyôgen by providing materials and making critical comments. Gen'e is held to be the founder of Ôkura, the oldest school of Kyôgen, and it is not improbable that he was at least in some way connected with it, but in more practical terms the actual founder of the school was Hie Yahei of the line of Ômi Sarugaku.

The contents of Kyôgen of the time, judging from the popular tales and lampoons that were then current, were not mere jokes and buffoonery but had more poignant, sarcastic elements. It is also likely that Kyôgen sometimes contained dances and song elements inserted in the conversation. In other words, it was almost like what we see on the Kyôgen stage today. Acting, however, was mostly of a crude character, showing as yet but few traces of symbolism or stylization. Those people mentioned in Zeami's writings, and also Roami of the succeeding period—people whom Zeami extolled—were all rather exceptional. By extolling them Zeami was trying to adapt Kyôgen and harmonize it with Noh. The process of development of Kyôgen thus remains vague in many respects, but it kept gradually on the rise until the end of the fifteenth century. Because of Kyôgen's character, its creators had far greater liberty in utilizing current events and phenomena to enrich the contents of the plays. Still, no such rapid progress as in Noh could be hoped for until the period of change.

Second Stage of Consolidation: Zeami

The second stage was a time when, upon the legacy of the previous age, the process of enrichment and deepening was advanced and the consolidation of Noh was almost completed. The central character was Zeami Motokiyo, who, after his most brilliant achievements, was to be exiled to Sado Island in 1434. The second stage covers the half century up to that year.

Kanze Zeami Motokiyo (1363–1443) at the age of twenty-one (1384) lost his father and assumed the responsible position as the young Kanze Dayû the Second. Taking the leadership of his company, he lived through more than ten years of training full of hardship and hope. His famous work *Fûshi Kaden* (or *Kadensho*)[1] was written for the most part in 1401 and 1402. The book was the first—and the most representative—

---

[1] An excellent English translation is available: Zeami, *Kadensho,* translated by Chûichi Sakurai, Shûseki Hayashi, Rokurô Satoi, and Bin Miyai (Kyoto: Sumiya-Shinobe Foundation, 1968).

book of principles of his art, as well as of Nohgaku in general. It is the consummation of the results attained in the first stage of the consolidation period—the stage that preceded his and also marked the starting point for his own future activity. It makes it possible to assess the achievements of the previous age, with Kan'ami as the chief figure. The book as a whole is not free from crudeness and is sometimes faulty in the arrangement of materials. It is not readily to be discerned in what parts and to what extent Zeami's own views are expounded, but it is not to be doubted that in many points it contains elements that were in later years to develop into his mature theories and writings. The main object of the book consists in explaining how the beauties of Noh might be so displayed as would best fit the time, place, and people, and how this might be maintained constantly throughout a lifetime. In the chapter "Nenrai Keiko Jôjô" (Ages of Training), the relation between the performer's age ranging from seven to over fifty and the beauty and training of Noh is discussed. The chapter "Monomane Jôjô" concerns the technique of representation with reference to different characters: women, old men, characters not using masks, mad people, monks, warriors, deities, demons, and Chinese roles. There are chapters discussing various other problems. The author expounds his principles and makes comments always with reference to practical needs, as is usual with many comparable theoretical treatises in Japan.

Ashikaga Yoshimitsu, who was Noh's greatest patron, retired from active life in 1397 and lived in the Kinkaku (Golden Pavilion) in Kyoto, but even after relinquishing the post of shogun he wielded enormous practical power and had virtual control of politics until he died eleven years later. While he was clever enough to consolidate the foundation of the *bakufu* and successfully unite the Southern and the Northern courts, he was also enthusiastic in his cultural policies. His nearest retainers were men of rich culture: he was intimate with Gidô Shûshin, the learned Zen priest who excelled in poetry; he constructed the Shôkokuji monastery, from which emerged priests who were excellent poets and painters; he inaugurated the system of Kamakura Gozan (the Five Zen Monasteries of Kamakura)—in a word he warmly protected and nurtured Buddhism and culture, taught the importance of the spiritual, and, with yearning for the ancient court culture, brought about the period historians call that of Kitayama culture. This was the outcome of the amalgamation of the military culture and the court culture. Later Komparu Zenchiku extolled Yoshimitsu and said that he was endowed with high aesthetic sense, with which he valued *yûgen* and loved beauty. Zenchiku himself was keen enough to appreciate his aesthetic temperament and connoisseurship. The emperor Gokomatsu also had a deep understanding of Nohgaku and other types of plays and entertainments and even after abdication, on the strength of his great influence at court, remained a powerful patron of plays.

Both Zeami and Nohgaku enjoyed infinite advantage from the appreciative and understanding support of these powerful people. In 1408, the year Yoshimitsu died, Zeami was forty-five. Zeami himself writes in his *Fûshi Kaden* that he was then at the peak of his ability. He appeared in numerous performances in the metropolis and became affluent. He steadily broadened his scope of art in performance, enriched his art style, and improved his art level, while in the creation and adaptation of wording and melodies, as well as in theoretical aspects, he achieved further depth. Under Zeami, the Kanze Za was more influential than other troupes. It absorbed several *za,* so that its power almost overwhelmed Dengaku Noh.

Zeami longed for the art style of Kan'ami and Itchû and also analyzed the art of—and elicited profound lessons from—such renowned performers as Dôa, with his elegant style based on *yûgen;* Kia of Dengaku Noh, with his superb chanting; and Komparu Gonnokami, who, although subject to some criticism, also was renowned for this unique style.

What Zeami had learned from these people must have been far broader in scope and far larger in quantity than what he committed to writing. It was Zeami's genius and extraordinary devotion that raised Nohgaku to the high artistic level it now occupies, but in his background was also the accumulation of the genius and effort of a great many people. Even the people of Dengaku Noh were closely involved.

But with Yoshimitsu's death in 1408, the fortunes of Zeami declined quickly. His performances for the *bakufu* and the ex-emperor's court rapidly became fewer. This was a great blow to the management of his Kanze troupe, as it was to his private life, but the spiritual blow was even more serious. Dengaku Noh seized this moment to revive its influence, and Zôa's activities suddenly obtained more impetus. Zeami, however, was not one to lie idle deploring his misfortune. He made use of the leisure that was now granted him and, on the basis of what he had been able to learn by then, established principles that even surpassed those he had set down in *Kadensho*. He also systematized what he had not previously dealt with and tried to write as much as he could for posterity. He thus converted misfortune to good fortune. Apart from the hours he now had at his disposal, the philosophy he had cultivated in his hapless circumstances served to give profundity to his principles and helped the formation of theories rich in nuance and delicacy of meaning.

After about ten years during which he had not written, he produced a series of noteworthy writings, each one either a further development, an extension, or a companion of its predecessor, all being tied together in an organic relation. Some are not systematic enough, but a general survey of them all places in clear perspective the process of growth of Zeami's ideas. Some may insist that all his assertions were a development from *Fûshi Kaden*, but assuredly those of a higher dimension were totally new and were arrived at independently. The flower theory (*hana*) in *Kadensho* was amplified in *The Way to Flower* (*Shikadô*) of 1420 and the *The Flower Mirror* (*Kakyô*) of about the same time. Somewhat later was written *The Ninefold Graduation of the Learning Process* (*Kyûi Shidai* or *Kyûi Shûdô Shidai*), in which were discussed three levels of art—high, middle, and low—each of which was again to be divided into three finer sublevels. Of writings on music, *Oral Instruction on Music and Recitation* (*Ongyoku Kowadashi Kuden*) of 1419, a dissertation on articulation, was followed several years later by *Tuning* (*Fushizuke*), a dissertation on composition, and by *Vocalization* (*Fûkyokushû*), a thesis on vocal training. Some years later again, in about 1430, *Five Melodies* (*Goin*) was written, in which he expounded the theory of beauty and interest of Noh based on a penetrating analysis of its musical aspect. Also, in 1423 he wrote *The Playwriting of Noh* (*Noh Sakusho*), a systematic and minute study of the basic structure of Noh verse and the art of its composition. This book was preceded by *Two Arts and Three Forms with Illustrations* (*Nikyoku Santai Ezu*), an illustrated book on the art of mimicry. *Nikyoku* (two arts) refers to "song and dance" and *santai* (three forms) means "three types" of characters—that is, old men, women, and warriors. In 1430 he wrote *Shûdôsho* (*A Book of Instructions on the Training of Noh*) addressed to the people of the Kanze Za. From about this time he began the compilation of *Talks on Saruga-*

ku by Zeami at over Sixty Years of Age (*Seishi Rokujû Igo Sarugaku Dangi,* or *Sarugaku Dangi* for short), a collection of Zeami's talks put down rather unsystematically by his second son, Motoyoshi, but containing many items of great importance. The book is remarkable for its exposition giving concrete examples of facets of the history of drama and allied arts, more especially the Noh of Zeami's and earlier times. Nearly all of the theoretical treatises of Zeami were written during the ten years that started with the *Fûshi Kaden* mentioned above. During this period Zeami wrote many Noh plays. Three of these, including the *Matsura no Noh* and *Furu no Noh,* have been preserved to this day in his own handwriting, as have also been seven plays copied later by Zeami on Sado Island and a list of thirty-odd Noh plays copied by him. Those copied on Sado include *Eguchi* and *Yoroboshi,* although, strictly speaking, one of the seven is a hand-copied replica produced during the Edo period.

In 1429, when Ashikaga Yoshinori became shogun, Zeami and his first son, the skilled Motomasa, were forbidden access to both the *bakufu* and the retired emperor's court, and in their place On'ami Motoshige, Zeami's nephew, enjoyed the shogun's favors. This incident, it appears, occurred because Yoshinori liked On'ami's personality and his bright art style, but there were also some political reasons. Motomasa moved to Yamato Province and died there three years later, to the great grief of his father. Shogun Yoshinori had recommended On'ami as the next leader of the Kanze Za, to which Zeami had expressed opposition. He also grudged giving him access to the *Secret Records of the Art* (*Hidensho*). Perhaps his situation was aggravated by some political involvement, and two years later, at the advanced age of seventy-one, Zeami was exiled to the remote Sado Island. This was the end of the greater part of his achievement. The rest of his life extended into the final consolidation period, but, for convenience' sake, it will be described here.

Zeami accepted his bad fortune philosophically, and, thinking of the future of Nohgaku, spent his time rewriting his earlier works, writing new pieces, and hand-copying Noh books, until he was allowed to return to Kyoto three years later. He lived with Komparu Zenchiku Ujinobu, his daughter's husband, in whose future Zeami placed great store, until he died in 1443, ending a long, eventful life. Posthumously called Shiô Zemmon, he was buried at the Fuganji temple in Yamato Province. His fall from the life of glory to the ignominy of exile was tragic, but in a way this literally dramatic catastrophe had the effect of enriching his life as a man of the stage.

Spiritually, Zeami was very much influenced by Buddhism. While associating closely with the Ji-shû sect, which was fairly mundane and lenient, he also immersed himself deeply in Zen, which was transcendental, rigorous, and profound, and continued to train and develop his mind. At the same time, as he was in close contact with Shinto shrines, he had intimate knowledge of Yoshida Shinto.[1] Further, he cultivated the sense of the immense and infinite out of the eternal metempsychosis of this world and of the life of man. His unique, exalted ideas of *yûgen, hana,* and *kurai* all are derived form his own spiritual experiences or the entirety of his life in this world.

Zeami, in comparison to Kan'ami, did not highly value mimic elements and restricted the use of dramatic elements because he attached importance to song and dance. Especially he valued song and dance proper, not song and dance as imitative arts. He even tried to interpret mimicry from the standpoint of song and dance. This, ultimately, was the position that led him to establish *yûgen* as the basic idea of Noh, which transcends simple beauty and elegance. He spoke of *nikyoku* and *santai*. *Nikyoku* (song and dance) are the two fundamental accomplishments, and *santai* (old men, women, and warriors) refers to the three stock characters of Noh.

Both are controlled by this idea of *yûgen*. It was with the same purport that he regarded, in *Two Arts and Three Forms with Illustrations* (*Nikyoku Santai Ezu*), dances in forms of children (*chigo sugata no yûfû*) as *nikyoku no hompû* (proper shape of *nikyoku*) and dances in forms of women (*nyotai onna-mai*) as *santai no hajime* (the beginning of *santai*). In the development of the idea of *hana* and in the theory of beauty in Noh in his old age the deep significance of *yûgen* is well expressed, and it is united with the idea of *kurai*. The most developed idea of *kurai* is clearly exhibited in *Kyûi Shidai*. The highest, ideal art level is the unspeakable, exquisite *myôka-fû*, which it is even impossible to praise, and yet,

---

[1] Also called Yuiitsu Shinto, it was taught in the middle of the Muromachi period by Yoshida Kanetomo (1435–1511). Contrary to the older doctrine based on the theory that Shinto gods were only other forms of Buddhas and Bodhisattvas (*honchi-suijaku* theory), Yoshida held that Shinto was the foundation not only of Buddhism but also of Confucianism.

on occasion, it has to descend to the lowest rank, wherein the broad and deep outlook witnessed also in *waka* poetry is manifested. From this standpoint the order of training is shown as *chûsho, jôchû,* and *gego.* These mean that one has to start from the middle stage, *chûsanka* (middle three flowers), where one has learned the basic, general *yûgen,* and then rise to the upper stage, *jôsanka* (upper three flowers), and then descend to the lower stage, *gesanka* (lower three flowers). Then only can one reach the highest level. This is at the same time a very matter-of-fact contention and contains a thoroughgoing pursuit of the essential truth. These theories of ideas, of dance and song, of imitation, and the like are also worked out under the direct and indirect influences of the principles of poetry, drama, and entertainment, such as *waka,* Chinese poems and other literature, and Bugaku.

These principles of Zeami's were important not only as the highest achievement in this period but also because they were to determine the future progress of Nohgaku, especially Noh. They were to become valuable assets not of Japanese drama alone but of world drama as well.

It should be noted, however, that these theories were only rarely practiced faithfully in Nohgaku during Zeami's own time. Zeami's ideals, after long neglect, finally won appreciation in the Tokugawa period, and there dawned the chance of their realization. Although there were but few problems in his opinions about the wording, there were many still unsolved at that period in point of melody, tools, and music, and one can only imagine that Zeami had supplemented what he left unwritten by his own performance.

Final Stage of Consolidation: On'ami and Zenchiku

This period, while inheriting the legacy of the preceding period, had as its leaders Kanze On'ami and Komparu Zenchiku, who, although their standpoints were almost antipodal, devoted their lives to making the performance and principles of Nohgaku greater in scale and depth. The period lasted for about a third of a century from the last years of Zeami to 1470, when Zenchiku died.

Kanze On'ami Motoshige (1398–1467) was the son of Zeami's younger brother. In 1434, when Zeami was exiled, he was thirty-six, and his acting was gaining power. Considering that he had enjoyed unusual evaluation and favor for five years from Ashikaga Yoshinori, who had then not yet become shogun, he must have been an extraordinary man both in his performance and in his personality. Although he was in close blood relation with Zeami and his son, he is regarded as having been involved in the downfall of Zeami, which is rather puzzling. Perhaps his connection with the irascible Yoshinori, who was explicit in stating his likes and dislikes, had a great deal to do with bringing about this tragedy. Also, his gay and brilliant art style caught the fancy of the shogun. It was the exact opposite of the plain style of Zeami and Motomasa, who set store by *yûgen*. Herein one might find the root of all the trouble that involved them. It accords with the fact that On'ami's contemporaries have recorded that his art style remained as youthful and flamboyant in his old age as it had been in his early years. Also, the Noh text *Makiginu (Silk Drapery)*, handwritten by him, contains tablature (*bokufu*), or instructions as to the melody, remarkably more detailed than those written by Zeami and Zenchiku in their Noh texts and meant to indicate even the delicate changes of tone. This shows that he introduced fine new devices in melody and successfully devised commonly acceptable symbols to record them. It cannot have failed to be reflected in the performance itself. On'ami did not attempt any creation of new texts, having contented himself with partial changes, if any, but it is to be conjectured from the above facts that in melody he accomplished fairly extensive changes. For Noh, which mainly relies on song and dance, this change in melody meant a great deal, and naturally it required a performance that was at once delicate and gay. On'ami's historical importance lies in the innovations that reflected the new trend of the time when, a century having elapsed since the foundation of the Ashikaga *bakufu*, the world was turning over a new leaf. To Zeami and his son, these innovations might have looked like retrogression or degeneration from contemplative appreciation of profound taste to sensual enjoyment of superficial beauty. Seen from another angle, however, they heralded the trend of the next period of change and were an advancement.

In the middle stage of the period of consolidation, it became the standard form of a day's program of Noh in shrines and temples, as is written in the *Shûdôsho,* to begin with the ceremonial *Okina,* which was followed by three Noh plays, with a Kyôgen play after the first and another after the second. The number, however, was subject to change according to the occasion. It was common to increase the number in order to attract larger audiences, from which the sponsors expected to collect donations to finance the construction of temple buildings and major bridges or to carry out other projects. Soon there were cases of Noh performed to help the management of Sarugaku and Dengaku troupes. Usually the so-called Kanjin Noh (Noh performance given to raise funds for pious purposes) lasted for days, with more plays than usual in a day's program, but for some time, ordinarily, not more than four or five Noh plays were performed at one time in shrines and temples, and not more than six in the ex-emperor's court and military men's residences. The reason was that both the actors and the audience thought of sincere appreciation in the first place.

However, immediately before the beginning of the last stage of the period of consolidation the number of plays in a program increased rapidly. Among the performances for which On'ami was chiefly responsible, the Noh at the Daikômyôji temple in 1432 had eleven plays; two years later, there were two instances of fifteen plays each, and one instance is recorded as having had as many as sixteen. In the latter three cases, On'ami appeared in six plays in one case, in seven in another, and in nine in the third case, but this included two "half plays" (*han noh*), which were plays shortened to their latter parts. This surprisingly large number of plays performed by a single actor was without precedent and was On'ami's own idea. In later years practices more or less like it occasionally took place.

The average time needed for a single play was somewhat shorter than in the previous period. In terms of the Noh plays we see today in the forms that have since become fixed, the time allocated in those days was shorter by at least one-third. This short performance time remained unchanged during the next period, the period of change, but the changes in the tempo of performance corresponded to the changes of art style. If what Zeami established is to be accepted as orthodox, the practice started by On'ami and retained in the following period was heterodox. But this heterodox style best appealed to people at a time when violent changes were taking place and men sought stimulation. The performance of many pieces by a single actor and the adoption of the half-play form had the same significance.

Komparu Zenchiku Ujinobu (1405–70) was the husband of Zeami's daughter. It was for him that, next to Motomasa, Zeami had entertained greatest hopes. At that time the Kanze Za, with its headquarters in Kyoto, flourished in the metropolis, while the Komparu Za, as a company attached to the Kôfukuji temple in Nara, had its headquarters in Yamato Province. Zenchiku was the leader of the Komparu Za, but because of his close relation to Zeami his activity in Kyoto was also remarkable. Unlike On'ami, he followed the orthodox tradition of Zeami, inheriting the style of *yûgen* and *monomane,* and exhibited special ability in theoretical studies and in the creation and adaptation of texts and melodies. His work, however, was slightly different from Zeami's achievements. When compared with On'ami, he was obviously more conservative, but, having studied Zen with Ikkyû, the great Zen monk of the time, and reflecting the general trend to spiritual depth as seen in the *waka* poetry of the time, he developed theories of *yûgen* and "artistic level" that were even more profound and metaphysical than those of Zeami. He too wrote on the musical side of Noh and on *za,* but his *Kabu Zuinôki (Quintessence of Dance and Music),* written in 1456, contains relatively more in the way of concrete discussions. His *Rikurin Ichiro (Six Blossoms and One Drop of Dew),* from the same year or somewhat later, is a dissertation of a Buddhist and purely philosophical nature. These two books naturally lend themselves in many ways to comparison with the theories exposed in Zeami's *Kyûi Shidai,* but the second is especially noteworthy as a development from Zeami. In the *Rikurin Ichiro* he divided the art of the Noh into six stages (six blossoms) and united them by "absolute" truth (one drop of dew). His thesis is supported by an extremely abstruse philosophy, and although the book is interesting theoretically, its value in relation to concrete matters such as performance is doubtful. Still, even while lacking in concrete suggestion, Zenchiku's claim that the merit of Noh and Nohgaku should be sought in the highest realm imaginable gave precious pointers for its fixation in later years. In his *Shidô Yôshô (Résumé of Introductions on the Training of Noh),* written about the same time, he criticized the general art style of the time and lamented that, with confusion prevailing in the world, aristocrats and people of high rank had had their connoisseurship addled by doubts and that only crude and wild art styles were now valued as interesting. It was a time when culture thrived under the patronage of Shogun Yoshimasa, to the extent that it is known as the Higashiyama period, a distinct cultural epoch. Zenchiku had the unusual good luck of enjoying the favor of Ichijô Kanera, who was an influential, well-learned man in a high position. Men like Kanera, however, were few at a time that marked the beginning of the Age of Civil Wars. Kyoto had been devastated by warfare and reduced to ashes. But in the midst of this ubiquitous unrest there were some highly cultured men who knew the value of Zenchiku's art style and principles, so tranquil and subtle. His original plays such as *Bashô* (*The Spirit of the Plantain Tree*) and *Ugetsu* (*Rain or Moon*) were accepted warmly by these people and have continued to be played to the present day.

The Kanze Za, continuing from the previous period, was rapidly growing in influence, and the Komparu Za, by dint of its force of tradition, its intercourse with the Kanze Za, and in particular the advent of Zenchiku, who cultivated a new style, overwhelmed other companies in Yamato. Besides these two there were others: the Hôshô Za, the theater of Kan'ami's elder brother, the Kongô Za, and the troupes of the Hase district, the Hie, and several others in Ômi Province, and still others, each with a long history. However, with the passage of time, more and more of them dropped out, having been absorbed by the Kanze Za, Komparu Za, and other powerful troupes because they failed to keep up with the Nohgaku reforms or because they were divided and scattered into minor institutions. This process of selection encouraged the spread of the developments in the central district to local areas. Those troupes that survived the process had their management strengthened and also tried to improve and enrich their repertoire.

The last stage of this period of consolidation saw the vogue of Nyôbô Sarugaku (Noh) and Nyôbô Kyôgen, in which women played the roles that were originally for men, and Chigo Sarugaku (Noh) played by boys. This vogue lasted until the period of change. There also thrived the Te Sarugaku, played by amateurs who had become semiprofessionals, and plays by *shômonji,* lay felicitators who begged for money from door to door and were among the lowest classes of men. The growth and vogue of these plays had been encouraged by the flourishing of orthodox companies. Of other kinds of drama, Ennen Noh and Dengaku Noh had gone into decay, and Shugen Noh was restricted to some remote provinces, so that Nohgaku, in its consolidation period, practically monopolized the dramatic scene.

Period of Change: Nobumitsu

Nohgaku, in the century of this period, in the middle of the Age of Civil Wars, chiefly inherited On'ami's heterodoxy as opposed to the orthodoxy that had arisen in the previous period, and attempted its new enrichment. There were no developments on the theoretical side, but in practice many innovations were attempted both in song and in dance, and many courses of development were followed. In point of melody, cardinal patterns were being set, and more distinctions according to schools than in the past were made by the troupes. On the whole the melody was constantly changing. Amid all the complexity of the changes that were not easy to grasp, there appeared the new tendency to take up in the text incidents with high dramatic effect, such as conflicts, and render them in appropriate expressions. This tendency lasted until the end of the period, after which the custom of writing new pieces for performance on stage almost ceased. In other words, this was the last period when original texts were written.

Kanze Kojirô Nobumitsu (1435–1518) was the *waki-shi* (actor who exclusively took the part of the partner for the main actor) of the Kanze Za and was also a master player of the *ôtsuzumi* (a knee drum). Being a son of On'ami, he inherited much of his father's heterodoxy. He also tried to write plays in which the *waki-shi* would be given more prominent roles. Further, in response to the demand of the times, he wrote *Ataka* (*Benkei at the Barrier of Ataka*) and *Funa Benkei* (*Benkei in the Boat*), belonging to the genre of Earthly Pieces (Genzai Noh or Genzai Mono), which dealt with contemporary events with emphasis on conflict, and *Momijigari* (*The Maple Viewing*), which also concerns conflict and in which a demon participates. These plays contain songs and dances that, though lacking in the taste of *yûgen*, have an extraordinarily captivating stage effect. Other contributions to this tendency include *Youchi Soga* (*The Soga Brothers' Night Attack*), a vendetta play, and *Kurama Tengu* (*The Hobgoblin of Mount Kurama*), a demon play, both by Miyamasu. Komparu Zempô Motoyasu, grandson of Zenchiku, and Kanze Yajirô Nagatoshi, On'ami's son, also wrote plays with strong stage effects, dealing with the theme of conflict. Zempô is the author of *Sarugaku Dangi,* in which he stated his theories and described the current situation. In the field of practical performance, there were several leaders of troupes, including Kanze Sôsetsu, who achieved unique technical improvements, while a number of skilled musicians attempted many novel ideas in the musical accompaniment. These achievements toward the end of the period are recorded in *Tôbushô (Résumé of Children's Dance)* by Shimotsuma Shôshin of the Komparu school, which relates to performance, and *Tomechô,* a record of Noh programs. The Noh performed by women, children, beggars, and amateurs continued to thrive from the preceding period, but there were ups and downs toward the end of the period.

In those days, not only at the imperial court, in military homes, shrines, and temples but also among the common people, there were many persons who found pleasure in chanting Yôkyoku (Noh texts), singing Kyôgen songs, and even performing Noh and Kyôgen plays. Nohgaku, in the period of change, came to be favored and appreciated by the whole nation, and it became customary for people to accept it as a drama to be enjoyed for itself, independent of shrines and temples.

Court aristocrats Sanjônishi Sanetaka and Yamashina Tokitsugu have recorded in their diaries that they personally copied by hand Noh books and chanted the verses. This clearly shows the situation of Noh at that time. These aristocrats, because of warfare that had deprived their houses of their former privileges, had been forced to associate more closely with the common people. At the end of the period *Utaishô,* a book of comments on Noh texts, was compiled.

Kyôgen, in the latter part of the consolidation period, was developing in step with Noh itself. It was becoming more independent and richer in content. In the period of change, the changes of the times stimulated further developments, and remarkable enrichment steadily continued. In the Ôkura school, the Hie family (a family of Kyôgen players of the Ômi Sarugaku line) became attached to the Komparu Za in Nara, adopted as a son Shirojirô, son of Zenchiku, and finally named the family Ôkura, after the name of a branch of the Komparu house. The Sagi school was founded by Roami in the days of Shogun Ashikaga

Yoshimitsu and was attached to the Kanze Za. The name was adopted for the house when Rodayû appeared in the days of Yoshimasa (*sagi* being another reading for the character *ro* in Rodayû). The Izumi school originated with Sasaki Gakurakuken, of Sakamoto in Ômi Province, when he transmitted the art to Gengorô, his nephew, from whose infant name comes the family name Izumi. Generally speaking, the schools of Kyôgen mostly originated with people related to Dengaku and Sarugaku of Ômi Province.

In this period all the three schools of later years were consolidated and competed with each other in artistic excellence and composition of new pieces, thus laying the foundation for the period of stabilization in the Tokugawa age. In the period of change, because of the confused state of society, vigorous interchanges among social classes and geographical areas were going on; common people were rising economically and socially; the spirit of the so-called *ge-koku-jô* (arrogation of the lower) and the critical spirit were prevailing; and there came into vogue literature of sarcasm and irony, bright and crude humor, piquant and naive imitation, short songs and dances. Such plebeian arts were created to be juxtaposed with Noh, which was characterized by loftiness of quality, with the military class and higher classes in its background. Such arts were also sometimes meant as parodies (*modoki*) of Noh and were performed as such. It was not until the Tokugawa period that these arts were given their settled form, but their foundation was nearly completed during the period of change. In this sense, the practical establishment of Kyôgen was accomplished in the Tokugawa period.

Period of Stabilization

Nohgaku (Noh and Kyôgen inclusive) came to assume the form in which we see it today only as a result of the efforts made in the Tokugawa period. The achievements of the previous periods in both genres were inherited in the new era and were indeed held in high respect. The arts were subjected to a process of purification and deepening from the standpoint of the military classes during the Tokugawa period and given greater dignity. Since, however, scarcely any of their component parts were newly created either in wording, melody, or various other aspects, the process is to be accepted as "stabilization."

What accelerated and finalized the fixation of Nohgaku was the recognition by the Tokugawa *bakufu,* which had become its new patron, of Nohgaku for its ceremonial activities, a recognition arising from its policy of emphasizing formalism and ceremonial dignity (*kakushiki*). The shoguns of the Ashikaga *bakufu,* with a few exceptions, treated the Kanze Za as the most important company, but later Toyotomi Hideyoshi (1536–98) gave precedence to Zenchiku of the Komparu Za and Shimotsuma Shôshin of the same school. The Hôshô Za and the Kongô Za were both overshadowed by these two major companies, and only the advent of master artists from time to time enabled them rise to prominence. Kokusetsu, a leader of the Kanze Za, had early approached Tokugawa Ieyasu (1542–1616) and enjoyed his protection. Shortly after Ieyasu became shogun, he went to Edo in 1606 and had the Kanze Za recognized as the top member of the Four Troupes and One School (*shiza ichiryû*) officially nominated by the *bakufu*—namely, the two Kamigakari Za (Kanze and Hôshô) and the two Shimogakari Za (Komparu and Kongô), which had existed for many years, and the newly established Kita school of the Shimogakari group. Kanze today is still the most influential school of Noh.

All these *za* had many followers, who were attached to daimyo and were engaged in activities in local provinces. For example, there were actors of the Hôshô school in the service of Lord Maeda in Kaga Province and of the Komparu school serving Lord Hosokawa in Higo Province. Kyôgen actors, in principle, were attached to some *za* of Noh, but in practice they were more at liberty to serve whoever called for them, serving the central government and local daimyo alike. Both in Noh and in Kyôgen, there was the *sôke* or leading family, the house of the senior or chieftain of the *za,* and each of the *sôke* had its branches. Their disciples also belonged to some group or school. This framework became more and more fixed with time and was transmitted from generation to generation by inheritance, so that it was out of the question for outsiders to join it and achieve prominence. Since, however, the *bakufu* and daimyo, while demanding that old tradition should be strictly maintained in acting, also demanded refinement almost relentlessly from the actors, the system was in no small degree conducive to the improvement of artistic quality. On the other hand, numerous minor *za,* if fortunate, managed to affiliate themselves with some recognized *za;* otherwise they disbanded or changed to other occupations.

A considerable number of them turned to Ningyô Jôruri and Kabuki and stimulated the progress of these two forms of drama. These changes had taken place mostly by the middle of the seventeenth century and had been completed at the end of the century.

For information about Noh and Kyôgen actors, including musicians of Noh, ranging from the period of change to this period, the directories entitled *Shiza Yakusha Mokuroku,* which lists earlier actors of the four main troupes, and *Kindai Shiza Yakusha Mokuroku,* which lists "modern" actors of the same troupes, are extremely useful. These works, published between 1646 and 1653, are by Kanze Shôemon Motonobu and are based on the works of Jiga Yozaemon Kunihiro, enlarged and supplemented by Motonobu. Performances of Noh took place not only in the mansions of military houses, such as the *bakufu* and daimyo, and shrines and temples but were also given as Kanjin Noh by the actors of some *za* and as Townsfolk Noh (Machi-iri Noh) for the citizens of Edo, so that even common people had at least some chances to see Nohgaku.

Noh, even after the official recognition of the Four Troupes and One School, for some time retained a certain degree of mutual adaptability in the mode of acting among its schools, but in the middle of the seventeenth century each school came to stick strictly to its own repertoire and modes of production, which came to differ from those of other schools. After that the principal efforts were directed toward the added refinement and purity with which each school was to maintain its own tradition. The acting itself was determined chiefly from what had been accomplished in the period of change and was sometimes newly created, but the ideas and objectives, in effect, were those expounded by Zeami in *Kadensho* and other works. When these were pursued by the militarists of the Tokugawa period, with their extraordinary emphasis on formality and dignity (*kakushiki*), Noh gradually lost the freedom and vigor of the Middle Ages but at the same time acquired gravity, solemnity, dignity, grace, gorgeousness, valor, a celebratory quality, and other aesthetic characteristics purified and decorated with the ideas of *yûgen* and *hana* and was perfected as the supreme symbolic drama form. Over three thousand plays had been written by the end of the Middle Ages, but many were discarded in a process of natural selection and also through deliberate, rigorous selection later on and sometimes through the loss of hereditary tradition of the Noh families. From the eighteenth century on, each different school had a repertory of about two hundred pieces, and about half the number were being frequently staged. It should be noted that plays originally written or adapted by Zeami were the most numerous, occupying nearly half of the total number.

Books of Kyôgen at the end of the previous period—books like *Tenshôbon Kyôgen Shû (Collection of Kyôgen Plays, Tenshô Edition)*—had contained only the synopses of the plays. The state continued the same in the first half century in the Tokugawa period. This shows that the system of preliminary half-extemporized oral arrangement (*kuchidate*) persisted in the training of Kyôgen players. It also shows, however, that by that time Kyôgen had achieved that degree of development in which certain set patterns of presentation and speech had been established. Even in acting, up till the early stage it had been considered masterly practice to introduce extemporized ideas according to the time, place, and audience, but about the time the text had become fixed, action also became fixed and unchangeable. Moreover, in production, care was taken to show some kind of noble dignity in keeping with the current inclination of Noh, and effort was made to show each player at his best within the pattern of the fixed action. The different schools were fired by the sense of competition, and each tried to show its special excellence in text and presentation. From this resulted the interest in smart humor, sarcasm, and imitation. As opposed to Noh, the keynote of which was rhythm, Kyôgen emphasized the prosaic and was completed as an art that harmonized with Noh. This happened in the latter half of the seventeenth century. The repertory contained about one hundred and fifty plays, but because of the nature of the text, they differed from school to school more widely than in the case of Noh. In 1651 Ôkura Toraakira wrote *Warambegusa,* a book of instructions on Kyôgen, in which he stressed the need to introduce to some extent new styles, while taking care to preserve the old. The acting of his father, Torakiyo, who was a master actor, and Toraakira's own theories, became landmarks in the fixation of Kyôgen. The book entitled *Kyôgenki (Book of Kyôgen)*, which appeared about this time, is a collection of texts, undeterminable as to school, that served to augment the popularity of Kyôgen. There were many minor schools, such as the Nanto Negiryû in Nara and others, in the early years of the Tokugawa period, which prospered fairly well.

With the collapse of the Tokugawa *bakufu* in 1867, Nohgaku lost its source of patronage and was on the verge of extinction. It was at this time that Umewaka Minoru, belonging to the Kanze line, rose to the occasion and desperately guarded the tradition. He was followed by gifted artists like Kanze Kiyokado, Hôshô Kurô, and Sakurama Bamba (of the Komparu school), and Noh was resuscitated. In Kyôgen, though the Sagi school died out, the Ôkura and Izumi schools produced many excellent players. There appeared masters of accompaniment music (*hayashi*) also, but in recent years the art seems somewhat to have stagnated. However, both Noh and Kyôgen are winning high public appreciation of their unique dramatic quality, such as the exquisiteness of their symbolic expression. Overseas they have secured the understanding and approbation of more and more people, and within Japan they are beginning to actively influence other forms of drama, music, and dance. These influences are by no means due solely to classic or antiquarian interest but rather to the significance of Noh and Kyôgen for contemporary and even avant-garde arts.

CHAPTER TWELVE

NOHGAKU TODAY

Many introductory books have been written regarding Nohgaku today. Moreover, the essential part of Nohgaku became established and fixed a long time ago. Hence it will not be necessary here to present more than an outline of what has by now been perfected and is to be seen on the stage. First, some of the important changes since the outset will be explained briefly.

Actors, Stage, and Performance

As a theatrical art the combination of Noh and Kyôgen into Nohgaku is highly significant. Noh and Kyôgen differ antipodally in idea, subject matter, and expression, the relation being that of elegance versus vulgarity, classic versus realistic, dance-centered versus conversational, poetic versus prosaic. The two arts of opposite qualities enhance the effect of each other by their very contrast. Sometimes there may be programs made up exclusively of either Noh or Kyôgen plays, but this is rather exceptional. Since the consolidation period the practice has been for the standard program to consist primarily of Noh plays, with Kyôgen plays performed in between. The program was considered complete as an entirety only with the combination of the two.

The performers of Nohgaku are of three kinds: the actors (*mai-kata*), the musicians (*hayashi-kata*), and the Kyôgen players. Of the actors, there are, first, *shite-kata*, who take the principal roles; *tsure-kata*, who take the subordinate roles; and *ji-utai-kata*, who sing the chorus. Formerly these were rigorously distinguished from one another, but now they sometimes exchange roles for convenience' sake. There are five schools of *shite-kata* (protagonists): Kanze, including Umewaka; Hôshô; Komparu; Kongô; and Kita. Next, there are the *waki-kata* (deuteragonists), who play the roles of opponents in struggles against the *shite-kata* or the subordinate characters. Two schools, Shundô and Shindô, have disappeared, and there are now three schools: Shimogakari Hôshô, Fukuô, and Takayasu. Noh musicians are of four groups: *fue-kata* (wind instrumentalists), *kotsuzumi-kata* (small-drum players), *ôtsuzumi-kata* (knee-drum players) and *taiko-kata* (floor-drum players). They take part in some of the Kyôgen pieces and play simplified *hayashi* music. Of *hayashi-kata* also there are many schools. Of *fue*, there are Isso, Morita, Fujita, and other schools; of *kotsuzumi*, the two Kô houses, Kanze, Ôkura, and others; of *ôtsuzumi*, Ôkura, Takayasu, Kadono, Hôshô, and others; of *taiko*, the Komparu and Kanze schools.

The conventional Nohgaku stage, since about 1700, measures six by six meters and eighty-five centimeters high. In the rear is the *atoza* (rear seat), three meters wide (including the space for musicians). On the right is the seat for *ji-utai* (chorus), one meter wide. On the left, leading more or less obliquely from the main stage, is the bridgeway (*hashi-gakari*), about two and one-half meters wide and about ten meters long, at the end of which is the mirror room (*kagami-no-ma*) on the side of the stage behind the curtain. Behind the stage is the greenroom (*gakuya*). Every part of the stage and the adjoining rooms is made of unpainted *hinoki* wood (Japanese cypress). On the panel at the back of the stage is painted a solemn old pine tree, with some bamboos. This panel, unchanging, serves as the backdrop for all the plays. The square stage jutting into the audience has pillars at the corners, but it has no curtains or other devices to hide it between scenes. The stage, in this way, looks very simple in construction, but in reality it is constructed with scrupulous care in every detail. For example, under the stage, in several important places, large earthenware pots are half buried in the ground to increase the resonance of the songs sung on the stage, the sound of the actors' steps, and the music.

The dancers, musicians, and Kyôgen players appear from the mirror room, the curtain (*agemaku*) being raised by a stagehand. They go to the stage by way of the bridgeway. Their exiting is just the reverse of

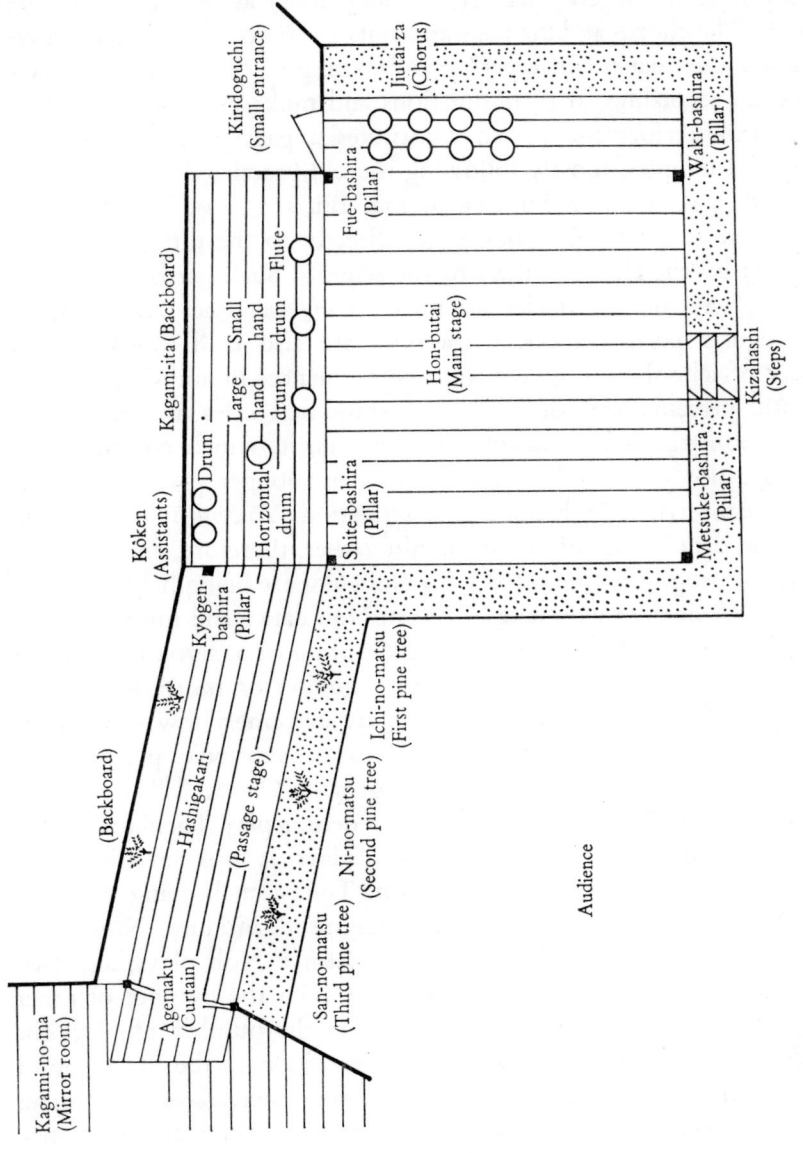

NOH STAGE

this. Sometimes they may make their exit by way of the small entrance called *kiridoguchi* (where there is a sliding door) at the right back of the stage. The chorus and the stage assistants always come and go through this door. The manner of entering and exiting of these people follows strict rules according to their functions and ranks.

Nohgaku performance often constitutes a part of the festivals at shrines and temples, mostly following the old practice dating from the Middle Ages and the Tokugawa period. But the most important are those given at the theaters belonging directly to the different schools or owned by the rich members of the schools. Such performances are held regularly, once or twice monthly, or several times yearly. Apart from regular performances, extra ones are also held. Sometimes a number of schools will give a joint performance. In addition to these authentic presentations of Nohgaku, simplified ones are given frequently, sometimes by students or amateurs, in which costumes and masks are not used, and only excerpts from longer plays are given. Further, concerts of Noh singing or recitation (Yôkyoku) without the acting and dancing are often given. Altogether, therefore, an enormous number of programs connected with Nohgaku are being held throughout Japan. Amateurs who take lessons in Noh dance and music number in the thousands. Those who study the chanting of Yôkyoku, including those of short duration, may number a million or more, but people who habitually go to see performances are extremely few in number.

Until about 1940, the program for a conventional performance consisted of five Noh plays—beginning with *Okina,* followed by a deity play (Kami Noh), and ending with a demon play (Kichiku Noh)— and four Kyôgen plays between the Noh plays. It took seven or eight hours to conclude this regular program. Today, in keeping with the changing world, performances of this magnitude are rare. Nowadays, at most one program will contain *Okina,* three Noh plays, and two Kyôgen. Sometimes *Okina* is omitted, and even the number of other plays is reduced. This extreme reduction in the number of plays for a performance would seem to suggest a reversion to the old usage of Zeami's time. After that time, there was a rapid increase of the number to more than a dozen, but plays took less time then, this was exceptional, and, after the second period, the number returned to the more reasonable standard of seven or eight. After that, as Noh plays came to have added dignity and solemnity, the number was slightly reduced.

In the light of these changes, the current usage can only be called unorthodox. When one remembers that only by the sequence of the five kinds of Noh—god, man, woman, lunatic, and demon—can the world of Noh conceived of by Zeami be complete, one might wish that the old usage would soon be restored, though at present there are too many adverse conditions for this.

YÔKYOKU AS NOH TEXT AND DANCE AS ACTION

Regarding how Noh texts should be written, Zeami laid down detailed instructions in his treatise *Noh Sakusho,* in which he divided the process into the three stages of subject matter, sources, and expression, including composition. He gave precedence to literary classics such as the *Ise Monogatari* (*Tales of Ise,* ninth century), the *Genji Monogatari* (*The Tale of Genji,* eleventh century), the *Heike Monogatari* (*The Tale of the Heike,* thirteenth century), and *waka* poetry, but he also used legends and folklore as well. Other writers of Noh have frequently paid more attention than he did to stories of contemporary origin. The depth of the *yûgen* mood has differed from writer to writer according to the point of view. In order to match the production that places emphasis on song and dance, rhythmic elements predominate over the prosaic.

In Zeami's idea of the construction of a play, each play consisted of five movements (*dan*), the first being the introduction (*jo*), the middle three the development (*ha*), and the last the climax (*kyû*). In the first movement, for example, the *waki* (companion; literally. one-who-stands-beside; the deuteragonist) appears on the stage: he may be a traveling monk or a minister just arriving at his destination. In the second movement (the first *ha* movement), the *shite* (*mae-jite;* the protagonist of the first part) enters and explains his situation. The third (the second *ha* movement) contains the conversation between the *waki* and the *shite*. The fourth (the third *ha* movement) is the most important part of a play, containing the song of the *shite* and the *kuse* part. The fifth movement, *kyû,* is the scene wherein the *nochi-jite* (protagonist appearing in the latter part) discloses his identity, which he has so far concealed, and dances.

What is stated above is the standard construction. In practice, there are plays in which the *shite* does not change in the latter part, so that there is no division of the play into parts. And there are plays in which the *shite* in the latter part will be an entirely different person from the one he represented in the first part. Some plays have a simplified general construction, others a more complicated one. Zeami's account goes into further detail, showing the standard length (number of words and phrases) of the passages in each movement, such as music indicating the order of the play (*shidai*), travel song (*michiyuki*), and music indicating the subject of the play (*issei*). Basically, works of later writers also largely conform to the standard.

The Noh texts are chanted by the actors (*mai-kata*) and the chorus. The musical quality is somewhere between singing and narrating. Consequently Yôkyoku contains, from the point of view of literature, many different forms ranging from pure prose to songs that are perfect poetry and, from the musical point of view, lines that go with the rhythm and lines that do not and many of intermediate qualities.

By chanting Yôkyoku, the actor describes his thoughts and explains his behavior. The chorus comments on his thoughts and behavior and frequently, on behalf of the actor, conveys his emotions and transmits his statements. Both the actor and the chorus describe the scenes and sketch the physical aspects of the surrounding locale. The words of Noh, since they are meant to be chanted, are always written from the poetic point of view. The movements that correspond to them—from simple actions to pure dances—are all referred to as *mai* (dance). "To perform Noh" is *Noh o mau* (to dance Noh) in Japanese. In other words, though Noh actually contains speeches or conversational elements, these have been embraced in the two categories of *bu-ka* (song and dance), wherein lies the idea of *yûgen* expanded to the extremities of possibility. This concept already existed in the time of Kan'ami, but it was first consolidated by Zeami. In the fixed period all efforts were made for its fullest realization.

From the time the actor puts on the mask in the mirror room, the performance always proceeds in accordance with strict manners. The faithful observance of rules, however, does not keep master players from achieving their artistic flavor and displaying their technique. The fixation of styles and patterns will promote the centripetal high polish and purification and at the same time urge the display of intense, free, and original personality. All elements of Noh—song, dance, music, the Ai Kyôgen that appears in the connecting part between the first and second halves, the part known as *naka-iri,* placed before the *kyû* movement—all have to correspond to the *kurai,* which is the level of dignity of the play. The rank of the play, as already stressed by Zeami, is determined by the subject matter, the dramatis personae, and their expression and sometimes by the history and origin of the plays.

The dance as action is regulated by various set procedures, first by *dekata* (the entrance on the bridgeway), followed by the actor's announcing his name in the play, travel songs, and dialogues. Crying is expressed by inclining the mask slightly forward and holding one hand or both hands in front of it. There are other specified mannerisms to express anger, joy, and such movements as carrying water from the sea or wrestling. Even of pure dances there are many kinds, depending on the role and the scene: the elegant female dance (*jo no mai*), ordinary female dance (*chû no mai*), a more brisk dance (*kyû no mai*), a muscular male dance (*otokomai*), a divine dance (*kamimai*), an angel's dance (*tennyo no mai*), a dance of the dragon god (*ryûjin no mai*), and others. There are also a running dance (*kakeri*), which expresses insanity, and a war dance (*hataraki*), which is a quasi-dance expressive of wild conflicts. In every case, performance should first conform to the dignity of the play, with due respect to such relevant elements and conditions as characters and scenes and sometimes to the kinds and significance of masks, following prescribed patterns yet without being restricted or hampered by them.

Noh Music

Hayashi music made rapid progress in the period of change. The flute (*fue*), as an instrument for melody, has a solemn sound, which is particularly effective when it accompanies the entrances and exits of the actors and pure dances. The small hand drum (*kotsuzumi*) and large hand drum (*ôtsuzumi*), held on the right shoulder and at the left side respectively, are rhythm instruments beaten with the right hand. These three instruments are indispensable in almost all the plays. The two drums have very different qualities, one being soft and the other sturdy. They are in remarkable contrast yet harmonize with each other. By the combination of tone, slight alteration in pitch and stress, the arrangement of pauses, and vocal ejaculations to mark time, they produce a surprisingly large variety of effects. The large regular drum (*taiko*) is a rhythm instrument used in addition to the above three in special dances and in the *kyū* movement (finale). It is not used for dances of extreme delicacy assigned chiefly to female roles or for dances of similar quality but is used with good effect in dances and scenes of gorgeousness, heroism, valor, and weirdness. It is placed on the floor, beaten with sticks held in both hands, and accompanied by short cries.

Sets, Properties, and Masks

The setting of the Noh stage, unlike that of ordinary drama, is symbolic and has a simple construction. Even a palace is represented as only about six feet tall. Ships and ox carts in which people travel are represented by stark skeletons of the objects, wrapped in white cloth. As a whole, the stage practices have something in common with those of Bugaku and Ennen Noh.

In Noh, the mask is called *omote*. Nothing shows the exquisite quality of Noh better than the masks, in which are combined the features of many kinds of earlier masks: those of Gigaku, Bugaku, Kagura, Ennen Noh, Dengaku Noh, and *jushi* plays. It was in the latter half of the Sarugaku Noh period that really original, unique masks were first made. In the consolidation period, in parallel with the enrichment in the contents of Noh, there were conspicuous qualitative improvements and the differentiation of kinds. In the period of change there was further diversification of masks. In the stabilization period, although mask making mostly consisted of imitating earlier works, the art had added refinement. Zeami, in *Sarugaku Dangi,* specifically mentions the artists Nikkô and Miroku, who made the mask of Okina; Shakuzuru of Ômi, who made the mask of the Goblin; Zazen'in of Uji (evidence: Echi of Ômi), who made the mask of the Woman; Chigusa, who made the mask of the Man; and other makers of miscellaneous masks including Ishiô-hyôe, Tatsuemon, Yasha, Bunzô, Koushi, and Tokuwaka, all of whom lived in Echizen. Among other names known to us are Himi, Echi (Ochi), Zôami, and Fukurai. Sankôbô, who was active at the end of the consolidation period and the beginning of the period of change, was the first specialized mask maker, unlike the earlier makers, who were at the same time either sculptors of Buddha statues or Noh players. His successors, the so-called Three Deme Houses—Ômi Izeki, Echizen Deme, and Ôno Deme—produced excellent makers in the early half of the stabilization period, such as Kawachi of Izeki, Mitsuteru of Echizen, and Zekan of Ôno.

Noh masks have always been regarded as something more than mere equivalents of makeup and have been credited with spiritual, mystic significance. The mask of Okina in particular is considered divine. Masks are worn by all actors except *waki*. Also *shite* and *tsure,* when they are in the roles of living men, and boy actors (*kokata*) do not wear them. Masks naturally have the intention of imitation. It is remarkable that even the masks that were taken from the Gigaku and are mainly exaggerated portrayals of a momentary emotion are still capable of an infinite variety of expression and conceal a phase of eternity. Existing at present are about 450 kinds of masks, which may be classified as follows according to their use and function ("men" here means "mask"):

1. Okina-men (holy old man): Hakushiki-jô, Kokushiki-jô, Chichino-jô
2. Jinki-men (supernatural being): Ôbeshimi, Kobeshimi, Ôtobide, Kotobide, Tenjin, Shikami, Kurohige, Hannya, Shishiguchi
3. Jô-men (old man): Koushi-jô, Warai-jô, Asakura-jô, Shiwa-jô, Ishiô-jô, Aku-jô
4. Otoko-men (man): Heita, Chûjo, Kantan Otoko, Ayakashi, Mikazuki, Yase Otoko, Arai Otoko, Kawazu
5. Chigo-men (boy): Kasshiki, Dôji, Imawaka, Atsumori, Jidô, Shôjô
6. Onna-men (woman): Waka Onna, Ko Omote, Zô Onna, Magojirô, Ômi Onna, Shakumi, Fukai, Yase Onna, Rei Onna, Masukami, Hashi-hime, Deigan
7. Uba-men (old woman): Uba, Rôjo
8. Special masks: Yorimasa, Shunkan, Yoroboshi, Semimaru, Kagekiyo, Yamauba.

Five Classes of Noh

At the end of the sixteenth century, Noh plays came to be classified into the five groups of god, man, woman, lunatic, and demon (*shin, nan, nyo, kyô,* and *ki*) according to the nature of the *shite*, or protagonist. Five plays in sequence, one from each of these five classes, make up the program. Only *Okina* is not included in any of the classes. It stands by itself as the most divine piece and is always presented at the beginning of a program.

Plays of the first group are called Kami Noh, or divine pieces, since the principal role is often a deity (*kami*). That is, in the first half the deity appears in the shape of a living man and in the latter half reveals his identity and dances an auspicious dance for the peace of the land and richness of crops. The whole play has a well-balanced construction and is as a whole characterized by dignity. To this class belong *Takasago, Yumi Yawata, Yôrô, Tsurukame, Chikubushima,* and others.

The second group is also called Shura Noh, or battle pieces. The Shuradô (realm of Shura) is the place to which, in Buddhist teaching, those who engaged themselves in battles in this world fall after death, to be condemned to eternal fighting. In most pieces of this group, the ghosts of warriors meet traveling monks, relate to them the circumstances of their deaths and their present sufferings in the Shuradô, and are finally set at peace by the power of the monks' prayers. The story in most cases is taken from either the *Heike Monogatari* or the *Gempei Seisuiki*. Belonging to this group are *Yashima, Ebira, Tadanori, Kiyotsune, Kanehira, Michimori, Tsunemasa, Shunzei Tadamori, Atsumori,* and others.

The plays of the third group, called woman pieces, are literally called "wig pieces" (Kazura Noh), as wigs are often used for women's roles. The roles for women (sometimes the spirits of trees or plants) as the central figures of the play are usually culled from classic works like *Ise Monogatari* and *Genji Monogatari*. The women tell of their obsession by love and dance elegant dances. This type of Noh is the richest in lyrical quality and in the taste of *yûgen*. Examples: *Nonomiya, Yûgao, Sekidera Komachi, Izutsu, Hajitomi, Eguchi, Matsukaze, Kakitsubata, Senju, Bashô, Uneme, Ôhara Gokô, Sôshi Arai Komachi, Hagoromo, Yuya.*

The fourth group includes present-life pieces (Genzai Mono), lunatic pieces (Kyôran Mono), obsession pieces (Shûshin Mono), and others. To this class belong so many pieces, so manifold in type, that some people prefer to call them miscellaneous Noh (Zatsu Noh) collectively.

The present-life pieces deal with events of real life, and their principal characters are neither ghosts nor assumed figures. That is why, when compared with other Noh pieces, they are more in the nature of real drama than musical plays. Plays belonging to this class include *Kan'yôkyû, Ataka, Kosode Soga, Morihisa, Shichiki-ochi, Shôson, Tadanobu, Hashi Benkei, Kagekiyo,* and *Mochizuki.*

The lunatic pieces have as principal characters people, especially women, who are temporarily deranged because of separation (by death or otherwise) from their lovers or children. Of this class are *Sumidagawa, Yoroboshi, Hyakuman, Sakuragawa, Semimaru, Hibariyama, Tamakazura, Hanagatami, Miidera,* and others.

The obsession pieces show the attachment of ghosts and spirits to earthly objects, as in *Akogi, Utô, Kinuta, Koi no Omoni, Aoi no Ue, Kanawa, Aya no Tsuzumi,* and *Dôjôji.*

The fifth group, also called final pieces (Kiri Noh Mono) or goblin and animal pieces (Kichiku Noh), is centered round superhuman beings such as devils or goblins, from legends and literary works, who perform quick and enthralling dances. Some of these ghosts, malicious and harmful, are subjugated by heroes or pacified by sagacious monks. Others, friendly to man, bring beatitude to humanity. In either case the plays have a happy ending, as in *Kokaji, Sesshô Seki, Zegai, Nue, Momijigari, Ôeyama, Kurozuka,* and others.

The above classification and the order of plays in a program are both in accordance with the principle of *jo-ha-kyû* regulating the presentation of Noh. The five-level construction of each single play explained above also applies to the construction of the whole program. Thus the divine pieces that come first correspond to *jo* (prelude). They are serious and straightforward. The goblin pieces at the end are quick and full of conflict. The woman pieces in the middle correspond to the second part of *ha* (development) and are characterized by delicacy and *yûgen*. The Shura plays and the fourth group are both parts of the *ha* portion but have leanings to *jo* (prelude) and *kyû* (finale) respectively.

The repertoires of the five schools of Noh at present, put together, including the plays that are seldom performed nowadays and the plays of which only the texts have survived, will add up to 252 plays. Here are the categories.

First group (divine pieces), 42 plays; second group (battle pieces), 16 plays; third group (woman pieces), 47 plays; fourth group (present-life pieces, lunatic pieces, obsession pieces), 97 plays; fifth group (final pieces: goblin and animal pieces), 50 plays.

Zeami regarded woman pieces as the most important. From the period of change on, however, the audiences came to accept with greater enthusiasm the plays with strong dramatic character, so that the fourth group, the present-life group, came to predominate, as it does in the existing Noh repertoire. The Shura Noh is the smallest group, but in actual program construction certain plays in other groups (usually the goblin and animal plays) may be borrowed to make up for the lack of variety.

Writers of Noh

Only several dozen Noh plays can be ascribed to known authors with certainty on the evidence of Zeami's writings and other sources, but from various angles it is also possible to determine the authorship of most of the remaining plays now in existence. The oldest list of Noh playwrights (*Nôhon Sakusha Chûmon*), made in 1524, mentions the titles of 352 plays, of which those ascribed to Zeami include 25 in the first group (*Aioi* or *Takasago* and others), 18 in the Shura group (*Sanemori* and others), 51 woman plays (*Matsukaze* and others), and 62 in the fourth group (*Yokoyama* and others). The list also mentions 32 plays written by Nobumitsu, 25 by Nagatoshi, 10 by Kyûzô, and 88 by anonymous writers. At that time there were already different opinions as to authorship, and there were many plays regarded as anonymous. Written evidence, traditions, and studies by scholars fall short of establishing the authorship of a large number. Still, most of the plays in the current repertoire are works of known authorship. The most important of them are the following (figure in parentheses shows the group to which the play belongs):

Plays based on original works of Kan'ami: *Jinen Koji* (4), *Sotoba Komachi* (4), etc—about 15 in all.

Plays by Zeami: *Takasago* (1), *Tamura* (2), *Yashima* (2), *Izutsu* (3), *Hagoromo* (3), *Nonomiya* (3), *Sekidera Komachi* (3), *Hyakuman* (4), *Aoi no Ue* (4), *Miidera* (4), *Koi no Omoni* (4), etc.—100 odd in all.

Plays by Motomasa: *Yoroboshi* (4), *Sumidagawa* (4), etc.

Plays by Zenchiku: *Bashô* (3), *Ugetsu* (4), *Tamakazura* (4), etc.—20 odd.

Plays by Nobumitsu: *Ataka* (4), *Funa Benkei* (5), etc.—30 odd.
Plays by Nagatoshi: *Enoshima* (1), *Shôzon* (4), *Katsuragi Tengu* (5), etc.—20 odd.
Plays by Zempô: *Arashiyama* (1), *Ikkaku Sennin* (5), etc.—several.
Plays by Kyûzô: *Himuro* (1), *Kosode Soga* (4), *Kurama Tengu* (5), etc.—about 15 in all.

Besides the above, more than ten playwrights are known to have written Noh plays. In most cases writers of Noh plays were at the same time composers, but in some cases they were only one or the other. Moreover, besides writing original plays they frequently rewrote or adapted earlier works. Such being the case, it is often hard to know how things actually stood, which is especially the case with plays that have been lost.

Functions of the Kyôgen Actors

The primary function of the Kyôgen actor, as previously noted, is to perform independent Kyôgen plays called Hon Kyôgen, but he also has various other functions. In the latter half of *Okina,* he takes the role of Sambasô, who performs the brisk *modoki* parody of Okina, wearing a black mask. Second, he performs Furyû, an antique, auspicious dance, when this is inserted in *Okina*. Third, in general Noh plays, he mixes with proper Noh actors in the capacity of the so-called *ashirai-ai* to take some specific role such as a retainer, or the boatman in *Funa Benkei*. Fourth, in the *nakairi,* or interval in a Noh play of the two-part construction, he acts as *katari-ai,* a role to fill the gap while the *mae-jite* (protagonist in the first part of a piece) changes costume to become *nochi-jite* (protagonist in the second part of the same piece), with explanations of the scenes and events before and after. The role may sometimes be *massha-ai,* which is a similar role but assumes the figure of the god of the locality, as in *Momijigari,* or again it may be *haya-uchi-ai,* who runs to carry the news of the battle. Fifth, there is the *kuchiake-ai,* who appears at the beginning of the Noh play and tells what serves as an introduction to the story. In the old performances the second and third functions were regarded as important, but with the passage of time, in the stabilization period, the first and fourth functions came to preponderate. Needless to say, the independent Kyôgen proper was the field in which Kyôgen players put forth the greatest effort, for it was there that they could display their talent to the full.

The music of Kyôgen, including that of *ai*, is of the simplified type specially called *ashirai* because of the difference in rank between Noh and Kyôgen actors. Not many of proper Kyôgen plays, however, require *ashirai*, and anyway *ashirai* is not indispensable to Kyôgen. On the other hand, because it is only rarely used, it can be effective. Stage setting is quite sparing, and the space on the stage is employed with great freedom. A considerable variety of properties and costumes are used, about half of them also used in Noh. Those for Kyôgen are generally simpler, and properties are mostly articles once in daily use. As 'n Noh, there are certain fixed rules as to the kinds used by particular classes of people. Fans and hamperlike stools are made to serve a large variety of purposes. Thus the techniques of transformation and simplification are employed with great liberty. Masks will be treated below. In the performance, a great many devices are made to introduce originality while remaining faithful to patterns. Humor runs unobtrusively through all the performance. The performance of Kyôgen must be in contrast to, and yet properly in harmony with, Noh. Kyôgen also has to have a certain measure of dignity.

Kyôgen Writers and Hereditary Texts

Currently, the Ôkura school recognizes 180 plays, and the Izumi school 254 plays, as their living repertories. The Sagi school, now defunct, had 200 odd plays. The plays, as has been said, are anonymous. According to the report made by Ôkura Torazumi to the *bakufu* in 1721, there were 59 plays written by the priest Gen'e, including *Fuku no Kami;* 78 plays by Komparu Shirojirô and Uji Yatarô, including *Bôshibari;* and 22 anonymous plays, including *Daikoku Renga.* The reliability of these figures, however, is very slight. It may be said that by the end of the Middle Ages basic plots and manners of presentation of the greater part of the plays had been formed. Their enrichment and purification went on in parallel with their fixation in the Tokugawa period, and the result materalized in the books of texts, called *Densho*— Ôkura Toraakira's text and the Izumi school's old text—in the mid-seventeenth century. In the Izumi school they are also called *Rikugi*. The *Kyôgen Ki,* a book with illustrations, and its three supplements—four books in twenty volumes—contain two hundred Kyôgen plays, but the school to which they belong has not yet been determined. It is scarcely a book of primary importance for the study of Kyôgen, but it is deserving of notice for having brought Kyôgen to the attention of the public and for the great influence it has exerted on drama and literature in general. Unlike the books of Yôkyoku (texts of Noh), of which a large number were printed, the *Densho* of Kyôgen plays were always kept away from public knowledge and were never printed in the Tokugawa period. This was because the texts of Kyôgen consisted chiefly of conversation, most of which was in such simple language that they could easily be imitated, should the text be circulated, and there was a fear of deviation from the tradition of the art.

Kinds of Kyôgen, Repertoire

Kyôgen plays may be differently classified according to several considerations.

1. Seen from the nature and subject of fun, there are such types as: plays stressing a joke or jokes (especially puns through the clever use of the Japanese language, in which there are many homophones); plays of humor in the life of the lower classes of society; plays of humor and satire resulting from the difference of manners between the higher and lower classes of society; plays of humor and satire resulting from the geographical difference of habits in the central and local provinces; plays of the bittersweet flavor of life; plays of the joy of life; plays of felicitation; plays as sketches of interesting manners.

2. According to the kinds of characters, there are plays of real human beings, of unreal persons (ghosts), of supernatural persons, and of weird creatures. Other classifications are also possible—for example, according to social classes, places of domicile, and occupations. In most cases the most important of the two or more characters usually determines the classification of the play. The classification of the Ôkura schools given below follows this principle.

3. According to the number of persons appearing in the play, it may be a one-man Kyôgen like *Kembutsuzaemon* and *Nasu no Yoichi;* or a

two-man Kyôgen, like *Kakiuri,* in which appear a deputy governor and a persimmon peddler; or a three-man Kyôgen, like *Suehirogari,* in which appear the daimyo, Tarô-kaja (the daimyo's manservant), and the thief; or others with four or more characters. The one-man type is exceptional, but two or three characters (*shite* or *omo,* the main character, and *ado,* the secondary actor, etc.) are sufficient to make a full, authentic Kyôgen play.

4. Of the three elements of speech (*serifu*), song (*kouta*), and dance (*mai*) that make up a Kyôgen play, the first usually predominates. The other two are totally absent in some plays, but in others they occupy prominent places. This makes possible the classification of Kyôgen into three: Serifu Kyôgen, Kayô (song) Kyôgen, and Mai Kyôgen.

5. In most cases the Kyôgen has its own story and composition, but some Kyôgen plays are parodies of Noh, like *Tsûen,* which is an adaptation of the Noh play *Yorimasa.* There are some, also, in parts of which Noh and Yôkyoku are used to good effect. Hence one may distinguish between pure Kyôgen and Noh-based Kyôgen and possibly identify a third somewhere between the two.

6. There are masked and unmasked Kyôgen plays. Further, the masked type may be classified into several kinds by the masks used.

7. Classes may be established according to the degree of practice required, beginning with the *hiramono* (plain piece for the novice), followed by *ko-narai* (slight-practice piece), *ô-narai* (much-practice piece), *omo-narai* (heavy-practice piece), and *goku-omo-narai* (very-heavy-practice piece) in the order of difficulty.

As a typical example, below will be explained the classification based on the type of *shite* in the Ôkura school.

1. Waki Kyôgen

This is comparable to Waki Noh and refers to that group of plays placed first in the regular program. As an introduction it has auspicious, peaceful contents that would induce the smile of the audience. Examples: *Fuku no Kami* (*The God of Wealth*), *Suehirogari* (*Fan*), *Takara no Tsuchi* (*A Mallet of Treasure*), *Sadogitsune* (*The Fox of Sado Island*).

2. Daimyo Kyôgen

The story of this type of play concerns a haughty and domineering daimyo revealed to be in reality a foolish and powerless character, bested by his subordinates. Examples: *Hagi Daimyô* (*Bush-Clover Daimyô*), *Futari Daimyô* (*Two Daimyo*), *Kombuuri* (*Vendor of Seaweed*),

Irumagawa (*The River Iruma*), *Kazumô* (*The Mosquito Wrestler*), *Bunzô, Awataguchi* (*Sword Contest*), *Utsubozaru* (*The Quiver Monkey*).

3. Shômyô Kyôgen

This is called Tarô-kaja Mono in the Izumi school. As the name indicates, this type is one in which Tarô-kaja, the secondary role, is the most active throughout the play. Tarô-kaja is a role resembling the clown in classic Western drama, and his character has the two sides of cunning and stupidity, smartness and squeamishness. The play concerns comic clashes between him and the primary role, Shômyô (chieftain of warriors, or local leader). Examples: *Akagari* (*Chapped Feet*), *Neongyoku, Nawanai* (*Twisting a Rope*), *Busu* (*Poison*), *Bôshibari* (*Pinioned*), *Suô Otoshi* (*The Lost Dress Coat*), *Tachi Ubai* (*Sword Stealing*).

4. Muko-Onna Kyôgen

A term referring to Muko (bridegroom) Kyôgen and Onna (woman) Kyôgen together. The former deals with the blunders committed by a young bridegroom who is not yet used to the ways of society. Examples: *Sai no Me* (*Counting Dice Spots*), *Kakusui, Kuchimane Muko* (*The Mimic Bridegroom*), *Futaribakama, Funawatashi Muko* (*The Boatman's Son-in-Law*), *Mizukake Muko* (*The Family Quarrel*). The latter concerns the humor arising from the abnormal combination of a plain-looking and aggressive woman and a weak husband who is fickle, timorous, and ignorant. Examples: *Kamabara* (*Sickle and Belly*), *Chigirigi* (*All Are Brave When the Enemy Flees*), *Hige Yagura, Hanago, Dontarô, Oba ga Sake* (*Aunty's Wine*).

5. Oni-Yamabushi Kyôgen

Both ogres (*oni*) and itinerant monks (*yamabushi*) are ordinarily credited with fearful weird powers. Kyôgen of this class is intended for hearty laughs by disclosing, on some occasion, that these beings are in reality poor imbecile things. Examples with ogres: *Yao, Narukami* (*Thunder God*), *Asaina, Setsubun* (*The Eve of Spring*). Examples with monks: *Kaki Yamabushi* (*The Persimmon Priest*), *Kani Yamabushi* (*The Crab and the Yamabushi*), *Negi Yamabushi* (*The Shinto Priest and the Yamabushi*), *Kagyû* (*The Snail*), *Fukurô Yamabushi* (*The Yamabushi and the Owl*).

6. Shukke-Zatô Kyôgen

A general term for plays dealing with the loose morals of priests (*shukke*) and the miserable lot of blind men (*zatô*) and other cripples and deformed men. Examples: *Shûron, Tsûen, Rakuami* (*The Ghost of Raku-*

ami), *Jizômai* (*The Dance of Jizô*), *Ocha no Mizu*, *Haratatezu* (*The Priest Who Would Not Get Angry*), *Tsukimi Zatô* (*The Moon-viewing Blind Man*), *Dobu Katchiri* (*A Shoal and a Depth*), *Honekawa* (*Skin and Bones*), *Uozeppô* (*A Sermon on Fish*).

7. Atsume Kyôgen

A general term for plays that do not belong to other groups. Called Atsume Kyôgen in the Izumi school. Examples: *Uri Nusubito* (*The Melon Thief*), *Fumi Yamadachi* (*Testaments of Two Bandits*), *Jishaku* (*The Magnet*), *Kôyaku Neri* (*The Ointment Vendor*), *Niô* (*The Deva King*), *Sannin Katawa* (*Three Deformed Persons*), *Takenoko* (*Bamboo Shoots*), *Iroha* (*A-B-C*).

Kyôgen Masks

Kyôgen plays of all types make liberal use of masks. Apart from many archaic masks used for Kokushiki-jô of *Sambasô* and other Furyû pieces, Nobori-hige is used for *massha-ai* in Noh, and the Tobi mask is used for a long-nosed goblin (*tengu*) and, as occasion demands, with good effect. Often the same masks are used for several plays. Apart from masks exclusively used for Kyôgen, there are some adapted from Noh masks, which have been so modified as to fit the bright and comic Kyôgen atmosphere. Kyôgen masks currently in existence include more than one hundred kinds. They are classified by their use and function as follows:

1. Masks of Shinto and Buddhist deities: Bishamon, Daikoku, Ebisu, Fuku no Kami
2. Masks of spirits: Buaku, Nobori-hige, Hana-hiki, Kentoku
3. Masks of human beings: Usobuki, Oyaji, Oto, Ama
4. Masks of animals: fox, badger, monkey, dog, ox, kite

Personification of nonhuman creatures and objects is a common practice in Kyôgen, which holds true with Kyôgen masks. Except for the masks representing animals realistically, masks for animals even have humanized features.

Kyôgen masks, although they do not have as high an artistic value as Noh masks, have something more than crude simplicity and have skillfully turned to active use what Noh masks discarded as undeserving.

In Nohgaku, the entire medieval Japanese drama found its culmination. Embodying the lofty and profound medieval mind, Nohgaku represented its final complete form. From the Tokugawa period on, Nohgaku, as a combined art of Noh and Kyôgen, went through still more severe purification and refinement and has come down to us in this form. In this way, Nohgaku has in itself a long history and rich tradition. In order to understand and enjoy this properly, we should know its background, watch both Noh and Kyôgen at one sitting, and refrain from analyzing a single play. We should grasp Nohgaku as a composite theatrical art in which all varieties are united and appreciate that part of it which expresses the noble and elegant taste of *yûgen* as well as that which imparts a sophisticated humor.

CHAPTER THIRTEEN

THE RELATION WITH CHINESE DRAMA

When we compare Japanese drama with Chinese drama, we notice several points of resemblance. This is particularly true of drama in ancient and medieval times, and to a lesser degree even modern drama, so that altogether it would be impossible to deny the relation between the dramas of the two countries. However, regarding the extent to which they were actually related, it is not easy to say anything definite. Scholars of Chinese drama tend to exaggerate, and scholars of Japanese drama to belittle, the influence from China. There is no doubt that Gigaku and Bugaku, as well as the Sangaku that went with them, came chiefly from China, but regarding the drama of later periods, it is often difficult to determine how far Japan is indebted to China. In this chapter, only the more conspicuous points of resemblance will be studied as a help in surmising the influence exerted. It should be borne in mind that proofs of the existence of direct relations are extremely scarce.

GIGAKU

Gigaku derived from the drama that flourished in the royal court and among the people in the Kure, or Go (Wu), district and in areas nearby in South China. The influence of areas west and south of China was manifest in the masks and contents of this drama. This reached Japan by way of Kudara, a kingdom in Korea. The play of *Konron* has something in common with what is called "God and Goblin Drama" (*shinki-geki*;

shen-kuei in Chinese), a drama of exorcism against evil spirits, which the Chinese drama had long since inherited. Of the same type was the drama in which the exorcist (*hôsôshi*; *fang-hsiang-shih* in Chinese) called Ko Kôtô (Hu Kung-t'ou) had an active role along with Kongô and the wrestler. *Konron* was probably one of the plays of this kind adapted to serve the purpose of Buddhism. Originally China had no noteworthy masks. Chinese masks are said mostly to derive from those introduced from other lands such as Central Asia and India. It is probably for this reason that many of the Gigaku masks have apparently no traces of the features of China nor those of the tribes living in the north of China.

Bugaku

A large portion of Bugaku had Chinese origins. Most of the pieces of the so-called Tôgaku (T'ang music), which occupy more than half of Bugaku, came from China. The category Tôgaku also covers a fairly large number of pieces of other origin adapted in the T'ang style. Again, Komagaku, considered to be of a different type, includes many pieces that had originally come from China, having traveled to Koma (the ancient Korean kingdom Koguryô) and undergone transformation. Moreover, in the adaptation of imported pieces and in the creation of new pieces, Japanese musicians seem to have followed the examples of China. Even Komagaku and Rin'yûgaku underwent such changes and when completed looked very much like proper T'ang music. Bugaku of proper Chinese origin was of two kinds, courtly and popular, both of which, after being introduced to Japan, were gradually adapted to the Japanese style, with the result that the original Chinese look became so obscured that only some exotic traits remaining in masks and costumes indicated that they were not primordially Japanese. Of the origin and performance of *Ryôô* and *Batô*, accounts are to be found in the "Description of Music" in *Kyû Tôsho* (*Chiu T'ang-shu*) and in *Gafu Zatsuroku* (*Yüehfu Tsalu*), but the performance itself no longer survives in China today. Of the history of the pieces, accounts similar to those in the Chinese books are found in Japanese books of music. It should be noted that some people believe *Batô* to be Tenjiku, or Indian, music.

New Sarugaku

Of New Sarugaku, the arts known as *tôjutsu* (jugglery), *shinadama* (tricks with balls), *ryûgo* (diabolo), and *yatsudama* (knucklebones) of the second group, derived from Old Sarugaku, had Chinese origins. The Sangaku of T'ang China had developed out of the acrobatic art named *zatsugi*. Of the first group, of the parallel Sarugaku class, *noronji* (magic), *hikihito no mai* (dwarf dance), and *kugutsu* (puppet show) can ultimately be traced to Chinese origins. In Dengaku also, some influence from China will have to be admitted, but this was acclimatized in Japan to such an extent that it could only be called a proper Japanese art. The exorcism ceremony and sword dance usually performed by the temple sorcerers had what looked like their antecedents in China; the former especially can be regarded as Chinese. The Sarugaku portrayed in *Shinzei Kogaku Zu* was of course Chinese in origin.

Ennen Noh

There were in China, from the T'ang period on, as mentioned in *Shin Tôsho* (*Hsin T'angshu*) and *I-ken-shi* (*I-chien-chih*), *gôsei* (*ho-sheng*) and *shômei* (*shang-mi*), the former consisting of announcements of what was going to be performed, the subjects being chanted; the latter consisting of riddles. These correspond to portions of the text of Ennen Noh called *kaikô* and *tôben*. But *kaikô* and *tôben* should be regarded as having grown up independently in Japan as ritual and *modoki* parodies. The *nanori* (announcing of one's own name by actors) found commonly in Renji, Shôfuryû, and Daifuryû, is similar to the *t'ung-ming* found in the drama of the Sung and Yüan periods. The actions of *michiyuki*, the liberal use of *hashirimono*, and the technique of making characters appear out of settings all find earlier or contemporaneous counterparts in the drama of Sung and Yüan. The use of speech at the entering of characters is also similar to both. In this way, many points of similarity are to be found between Ennen Noh and Chinese drama, which one may be sure are not accidental. On that ground, scholars of Chinese drama assert strongly the indebtedness of Japanese drama to the Chinese, for which, however, there is no clear evidence. But in the period when Ennen Noh developed, many Japanese priests went to China and traveled widely in the country for study and observation. Chinese priests and laymen also came to Japan in large numbers and many stayed a long time or became naturalized. Since many priests in those days took great interest in drama, it is probable enough that through them came the influence of the thriving Kabu-gi (Ko-hsi) and Zatsugeki (Tsa-chü) of Sung and Genkyoku (Yüan-ch'ü). However, as to precisely in what respects the influence was exerted there is no knowing. For the most part the influence did not go beyond suggestions. Original techniques were devised, and songs such as those of Shirabyôshi, dances such as Bugaku, materials, ideas—all reflected the likings of the Japanese of the time. What resulted, to be sure, contained to some extent Chinese style, answering the contemporary taste for things Chinese, but on the whole the style was uniquely Japanese. *Kaikô, tôben, nanori, michiyuki* actions—all were born spontaneously in Japan. The *hashirimono* is no extraordinary development in Japan when one remembers the taste for the grotesque and weird exhibited in the famous picture scrolls *Chôjû Giga (Scroll of Frolicking Animals)* and *Hyakki Yakô Zu (Picture of Pandemonium)* and tales and stories of the time. Therefore, even if the influence received by Ennen Noh from Chinese drama must be admitted on makeup, setting, subject matter, and plot to a certain extent, in most cases it did no more than give stimulus and suggestion to what was spontaneous. The most important influence, to my mind, was in the fact that Chinese drama showed, by concrete examples, that there had existed a drama in which song and dance were united and stories were told, although in Japan there had already been born dramas in which, as in the *Monjaku* play at the imperial court, speech and movement were sufficiently valued to show the possibility of development beyond plays of simple songs and dances. It may be stated with fair certainty that even without any influence from the drama of Sung and Yüan, Ennen Noh would have grown and developed nearly exactly as it did. The influence from China perhaps somewhat expedited the progress of its formation and shortened the time of its completion.

Nohgaku

Sarugaku Noh also had many points of resemblance to the drama of Sung and Yüan, and these were inherited by Nohgaku. But whether this is a case of influence from China one can never know for certain. The self-announcement made by the characters on entering had a precedent in Ennen Noh. The appearance of the main character's companion first on the stage to explain the story is similar to *fukumatsu kaiwa* (*fumō k'aiho*) in Chinese drama, but this is a practice that could be spontaneously started in any drama. The influence on makeup and setting, if any, may have come through Ennen Noh, but of direct influence there was none that would count. Zeami himself said of the manner of makeup as a Chinese that it would be enough if one could look like a Chinese. From his writings one cannot detect any trace of his having deliberately learned from Chinese drama. It should be noted, however, that his writings did not always tell the whole truth. Especially in regard to derivation, they sometimes contain doubtful statements. Again, some people, because the Nohgaku troupe of Yamato made much of the play of demons from the time of Sarugaku Noh, try to see in it influence from Chinese drama, which made much of "drama of demons," imagining that the latter entered the dramatic art of temple sorcerers and became the basis upon which Sarugaku Noh was built up as drama. Also, as to the formation of Noh and Kyôgen, some people hold that Noh corresponds to the Zatsugeki that is the serious and authentic Seizatsugeki (Ch'eng-tsa-chü), and Kyôgen to the comic and intimate Zappun (Tsapan); and that the practice of performing Zappun at the end of the first part of Zatsugeki, when two parts thereof were to be staged, to soften the mood, corresponds to the Japanese practice of placing a short Kyôgen between the two halves of a Noh play. The completed Kyôgen is a development of this Ai Kyôgen, but Kyôgen should all the same be considered to stand on the tradition dating from Shin Sarugaku. The demon play is considered by some to be a prototype of general plays even in China. In Japan, too, drama of demons is recognized as an important type of drama, but one need not see here any direct relation between Noh and Chinese drama. To sum up, beyond the slight influence Noh received indirectly, as may be inferred, in the Sarugaku Noh days, there has been no influence to speak of. In the era of Nohgaku the Japanese people cultivated spiritual depth and valued the qualities of profundity and elegance expressed as *yûgen* and *hana*, and Nohgaku became a dramatic art entirely different from Chinese drama.

PART TWO

Bunraku and Kabuki
by Toshio Kawatake

CHAPTER FOURTEEN

TOKUGAWA THEATER

The Four Great Performing Arts

Bunraku and Kabuki are the theatrical arts that developed during the Tokugawa, or Edo, period (1600–1868) as historical successors to Bugaku of the Nara and Heian periods (eighth to twelfth century) and Noh and Kyôgen of the Kamakura and Muromachi periods (thirteenth to fifteenth century).

Together with Bugaku, Noh, and Kyôgen (the latter two taken together), Bunraku and Kabuki are often called the four great performing arts of Japan. Of course, these are not the only Japanese performing arts. Subsequent to the Meiji Restoration of 1868, new forms of theater that drew upon modern subjects were created under the influence of Western theater. They include Shimpa (literally: new school), Shingeki (literally: new theater), operas, operettas, and, particularly since World War II, musicals, and others. However, because of the nature of Japanese culture and society prior to the advent of Western influence, and because these modern theatrical forms have been introduced from and based upon Western theater, they may not be considered uniquely Japanese. Thus, when we speak of Japanese theater, we are usually speaking of the four performing arts mentioned above. More accurately, it would be better to consider them as "Japan's traditional stage arts."

To be sure, in the course of well over a thousand years, there were influences from China, Korea, Southeast Asia, and even as far as India. But owing to the fact that in the Edo period—that is, during the 250 years prior to 1868 (Meiji Restoration)—Japan was virtually isolated from the rest of the world, Kabuki and Bunraku were born of, nurtured by, and perfected by the Japanese on their islands in the Far East.

There are some common characteristics in these performing arts of the Edo period, such as the father-to-son form of transmitting one's art that was followed by performers and musicians, the placing of heavy emphasis on musical and dance qualities—a nature comparable to the *Gesamtkunstwerk* of Richard Wagner—and so forth. These characteristics are key points particularly in comparing these Japanese art forms with Western forms and considering the uniqueness of Japanese theater in general.

A more detailed analysis of style and content will disclose that Bunraku and Kabuki are extremely different from Bugaku and Noh. Although the nature and history of both Bunraku and Kabuki will be discussed later, first I would like to touch upon a few points concerning the comparison of the two with other stage arts and concerning their position within Japanese theater in general.

Bunraku and Kabuki as Sister Arts

As is quite well known, Kabuki plays are performed by actors and Bunraku plays by a combination of narrators and puppeteers. By nature, a play performed by real actors differs from one acted by puppets with regard to the medium of expression. Despite this, since Bunraku and Kabuki were created in the same period for the same stratum of theatergoers, and since they shared deep interrelationships during the process of their development, they can be considered together and looked at as having identical elements with respect to subjects, dramaturgy, techniques of expression, and aesthetics. One cannot be discussed in isolation from the other.

The depth of this interrelationship may be understood by taking up even just one Kabuki play: the old reliable *Chûshingura* (full title, *Kanadehon Chûshingura, The Treasury of Loyal Retainers*), which still plays to sellout audiences. The play's "old reliable" reputation originated long ago when it was found that whenever admissions were declining, losses could always be recovered and popularity regained by presenting *Chûshingura*. The play was first adapted into English in 1915 by John

Masefield as *The Faithful*. It has come to be widely known in the West as the drama of the Forty-seven Rônin and has been warmly received in overseas presentations in the United States, Germany, France, and other countries. The international acclaim it has won has resulted from profound dramatic experiences on the part of Western audiences of both the form and content of the play.

However, although *Chûshingura* is now widely known as a Kabuki masterpiece, it was not originally written for the Kabuki theater but for Bunraku, as a narrative, poetic drama. Today, *Chûshingura* is also offered as a Bunraku play. But the more gorgeous *Chûshingura* that we see as a Kabuki play, while taking over in its entirety the work itself and performing techniques from Bunraku, has benefited by the study and improvement made by generations of actors.

This is only one example. One could also cite the play popularly known as *Terakoya* (an act from *Sugawara Denju Tenarai Kagami, The Secret of Sugawara's Calligraphy*) or *Yoshitsune Sembonzakura (A Thousand Cherry Trees)* or *Kumagai Jinya (Kumagai's Camp,* an act from *Ichinotani Futaba Gunki, The Chronicle of the Battle of Ichinotani)* or the tragedy of common folk, *Sonezaki Shinjû (The Love Suicide at Sonezaki)*. All of these were originally written for the Bunraku theater and adapted for or adopted by Kabuki. If the plays derived from Bunraku were to be eliminated, the Kabuki repertory would probably be halved.

On the contrary, Kabuki plays that have been adapted into Bunraku plays are few. But there are not a few Bunraku plays in which the Kabuki theatrical style has been closely copied. Examples of the latter are *Honchô Nijûshikô (Twenty-four Dutiful Sons)* and *Meiboku Sendai Hagi (The Disputed Succession)*.

From the plays, let us turn to the man who has been called the Shakespeare of Japan, Chikamatsu Monzaemon (1653–1724). From a youthful age he wrote many plays meant as vehicles for the Kabuki actor Sakata Tôjûrô (1647–1709). Chikamatsu exploited the experience thereby gained when he later became a specialist in writing puppet plays and went on to elevate the puppet drama from the level of miracle plays, folk tales, and accounts of heroes to a refined human drama. I will take up the achievements of Chikamatsu later in this volume, but at least it should be stated that *Chûshingura* and *Terakoya* would not have seen the light in Bunraku if this effort had not been made by Chikamatsu.

Thus Kabuki and Bunraku have met intimately and have influenced each other, to the great advantage of both. Further, the validity of thinking of the two as one may be understood.

Their Common Characteristics

Let us consider some of the characteristics that Kabuki and Bunraku share in common.

First, what is immediately evident is the rich visual and chromatic attraction of the two. As anyone may easily see at either a Bunraku or a Kabuki performance, the magnificence of the stage settings, the beauty of the costumes and coiffures, and the ornamentation abound with richness in their variety. In *Chûshingura*, for example, the stage, when the curtain opens, is filled with stone walls and a stone staircase, and to the rear at stage center is depicted a large vermilion Shinto *torii*, which is flanked by rows of evergreens receding into the distance. There the people—daimyo—wear the stately black headgear of the nobility and long-sleeved garments of black, yellow, and blue. Then a young and beautiful woman takes the stage—the *onnagata,* or female impersonator—in her sparkling deep-red robes, and everyone recognizes her as the wife of the young daimyo Enya Hangan, who, in the leading role, is to commit suicide. In the next act, beyond the new tatami mats is seen a splendid gold screen on which are painted pine trees. Then, from this palace room, the scene is changed to outside a castle in the dark night. And the scenes continue to change, to spring fields of yellow flowers spreading before a distant view of Mount Fuji, to the depths of night in the mountains when two murders occur, to a farmer's house, and to the lively streets of Kyoto's Gion district—one and then another scene and another. Appearing in the gay Gion scene is a woman, Okaru, whose elaborate coiffure is festooned with long ornamental hairpins in the classic style of the courtesan.

This magnificent presence and sense of beauty is completely lacking in the earlier Bugaku, Noh, and Kyôgen. To be sure, Bugaku is not wholly deficient in its use of color; the stage is bounded by low vermilion railings tipped with gold-colored ornamental fittings and is covered by a rich green cloth upon which the dancers, clad in exotic garb of primarily reds, blues, and greens and with strange masks concealing their faces, perform. But Bugaku, which originally was for outdoor performance, lacks dramatic development, the stage is not provided with sets, and there are consequently no changes of sets in keeping with the performance, whereas in Kabuki and Bunraku the stage is changed in accordance with the changes in the content of the play. For Noh and Kyôgen, a colorful stage was deliberately avoided; they are performed on a stage essentially colorless, or the color of wood itself. As its background, the Noh stage boasts but a single aged pine, which is never changed. Noh audiences need only listen to the literary *utai* chant to imagine the pine plains of Miho during *Hagoromo* (*The Robe of Feathers*), the battlefield at Ichinotani during *Atsumori,* and the temple deep in mountain recesses during *Dôjôji* (*The Dôjôji Temple*).

Such a purely symbolic exercise would not suffice for the sights and players of Kabuki and Bunraku, where the colorful and real are desired. If a castle is called for, there must be a castle. If the sea is to be seen, there must be the sea. For gay quarters there must be gay quarters, and for farmhouses there must be farmhouses. All must be recognizable at a glance, and the spectators must be able to feel as if they themselves are on the very spot. Even though Bunraku is dramatized by dolls, the very dolls must appear real, to the extent that their costumes and hair styles are identifiable with the ages, social status, and occupations of the persons they represent.

Although masks are not used, here too it may be said that the same type of characteristic is present. In Noh, masks are used to represent the beauty of young women, or the ferocity of one crazed by jealousy, as well as to represent gods, devils, and spirits. And it is said that during Noh performances the expression of the carved wooden mask may be seen to change. But for Kabuki this is not enough. In Kabuki one is invited to see in the faces of the actors joy and anger, grief and gladness, as well as love and jealousy, sorrow and shyness, vividly drawn from life, down to the minute details of the eyes, mouth, and cheeks, as real as possible.

This is even true for the manner of weeping. Weeping in Noh is represented by turning the masked face slightly downward and by bringing one or both hands to just before and below the eyes. Both Kabuki and Bunraku use more realistic action and vocal expression for weeping.

And yet the sets, costumes, and even the speech and motions, of course, are not exactly the same as in daily life. Speech has a somewhat musical rhythm and melody, and motions and gestures are modified in various fashions. Kabuki actors also show emotional expressions or have their faces made up in ways that often appear grotesque to non-Japanese. Although these characteristics stand out to some observers, they are by no means the whole of Kabuki. What I wish to emphasize here is that although these expressions are quite different from the realism or naturalism of Western drama, yet they are much more real than in Noh, and their reality is rooted in the experience of daily life.

This-World Humanism of the Popular Audience

The rich sensuality of color and the realism mentioned in the preceding section were what the audiences that nurtured Kabuki and Bunraku desired, and those audiences were composed of townsmen of the Edo period. They were the ordinary citizens, predominantly of the merchant class, of Edo, Osaka, and Kyoto. The imperial family and nobility had been the class that supported Bugaku, and the ruling class of the Middle Ages—that is, higher samurai and shogun-related families—had been those who supported Noh and Kyôgen. After the beginning of the Edo period, warfare was ended and peace was secured. In the cash economy that developed, the locus of power passed into the hands of the merchants, and this new class made its own culture. Ukiyoe, haiku, novels, Kabuki, and Bunraku were their property. To the merchants, the cult of tea, stone-and-sand gardens, monochrome landscape paintings, and linked verse, which had been derived from the aristocratic and Buddhist sentiments of the samurai class of the preceding age, were so excessively refined and so elegant as to be unattractive. The merchants sought entertainment that reflected their own lives with stark reality. What they thereupon created was the sensual world of the gay quarters, inebriated with color; the brilliantly colored ukiyoe; musical compositions of delicate tone for the samisen; and the real and colorful stages of Bunraku and Kabuki.

Thus the keynote of the cultural forms of the Edo period was, as is evident, the this-world thinking and realistic sense of the merchant townsmen. This realism is reflected in the subject that interested them. In a word, even though at times Shinto and Buddhist deities appear in Kabuki and Bunraku, in the plays it is the human beings first and foremost. It is humanity that is eulogized while the religious content is most sparse.

Let us look at an example: *Narukami* (*Abbot Narukami*), one of Kabuki's *jûhachiban,* or Eighteen Favorites. Narukami is a monk of high virtue, but for some reason he has become embittered against the emperor and, standing at the foot of a waterfall deep in the mountains, stops the rain from falling by confining a dragon deity, who has the power to make rain, within the waterfall by suspending a sacred Shinto rope in front of it. The drought wears on, the crops wither, and the people begin to hunger. Then the most beautiful woman at the imperial court, Princess Kumo no Taema, is sent to persuade Narukami to desist. The princess conceives of the strategem of using her wiles to entice Narukami to seduce her and then to get him drunk on ceremonial sakè. Then she will cut the rope and free the deity. (To be enslaved by lust and surrender to alcoholic drink would be two transgressions that would render Narukami powerless.) The princess succeeds. With the rope cut, the dragon deity ascends to the skies, and at once a great downpour begins. Narukami, wakened from stupor by his disciples, flies into a rage and tries to catch the princess, but it is too late. This is the plot of the play.

Thus there is a dragon deity and a display of divine power, which are supernatural and superhuman, but the monk, despite his vows to follow the path of Buddhism, is defeated by the charms of a woman. We can see here quite clearly a reflection of how human powers take precedence over the saving power of Buddhism. In 1928, after the Soviet Revolution, Ichikawa Sadanji II played this role during a Russian tour, when the play was viewed as a lesson on the negation of religion. It was the best received of all the plays presented. This is not a correct appraisal of the play as a whole, but in the emphasis that the existence of man is greater than that of the gods, I think that it was a meaningful episode.

Let us examine another sampling from Kabuki: this time, a borrowing from the puppet theater, unlike *Narukami,* which belongs to Kabuki proper. It is the scene called *Tomomori and the Anchor,* from *Yoshitsune Sembonzakura,* and is based on the Noh play *Funa Benkei* (*Benkei in the Boat*) but in both feeling and content differs considerably from the original. To discern the difference between the theater of the pre-Tokugawa ages and that of Tokugawa times, it is most appropriate to take up Noh and Bunraku or Kabuki plays that deal with the same material, as do these two.

Let us take up only religious aspects out of several points of difference. There is a scene in *Funa Benkei* in which Minamoto no Yoshitsune, one of the greatest warriors in Japanese history, is at sea in a boat with Benkei and several other retainers, at night, when many spirits approach them from the direction of the shore and threaten to envelop the boat. They are the spirits of the members of the rival Heike clan slain by Yoshitsune, rising from the bottom of the sea. When the spirit of Taira no Tomomori is about to thrust his lance into Yoshitsune, Benkei, who is a Buddhist priest, interposes himself between the two and, while rubbing together the beads of a Buddhist rosary, recites a Buddhist invocation. The spirit, which could not be vanquished by the sword, cannot withstand the power of the Buddhist Law and has no recourse but to fade away.

But in *Tomomori and the Anchor* of Bunraku and Kabuki, Tomomori is still alive and, as master of the boat's captain, lives near the shore, secretly seeking a chance for revenge. The desire of the ordinary folk to see the vivid depiction of ill-starred heroes and historical personages was thus satisfied on the Bunraku and Kabuki stages. Herein too lies the essence of these as the dramatic forms of the townsmen.

Seeing his chance, Tomomori bravely starts after Yoshitsune's boat, which has just left shore, to engage him in a final battle. But Yoshitsune has found Tomomori out and turns his attempt against him. Inflicted with wounds, Tomomori reels toward the shore, and then Benkei appears before him to say that his life will not be spared. Benkei tells him that if he at least recites sutras, he may become a Buddha and places a large Buddhist rosary around Tomomori's neck. But Tomomori, saying that this is disgusting, abruptly snatches the rosary from his neck and, summoning up the last of his strength, clambers atop a rock jutting from the sea and ties an iron anchor to his body with rope. Then, before the eyes of Yoshitsune and Benkei, he throws the anchor into the sea and, drawn down by its weight, plunges headfirst into the waters, dying by his own hand.

The Tomomori of Kabuki and Bunraku differs fundamentally from the Tomomori of Noh, who is driven off by the power of Buddhism; the difference is one of faith in man and praise for his powers.

Those who emphasize the religious nature of Kabuki and Bunraku—

they include many ethnologists—interpret the *aragoto* ("rough stuff," meaning bravura) style of acting as representing the incarnation of the Arakami deity, which drives off witches and demons. It is true that folk beliefs were involved in the origin of this acting style. Further, it is true that this *aragoto*, in performances at the time of festivals or other auspicious events, was welcomed by the Edo townsmen on the basis of latent folk beliefs. But by no means did the Edo audience call their actors gods or deities or worship them. When they exuberantly shouted the nicknames of actors, it was nothing more than an expression of patrons' love for their favorites. Their admiration was for the actor only, not for any god or deity he might happen to play, and the paeans they sang were for him as a human being. The religion of the Edo townsmen placed greater emphasis on enjoying the present, the world of the living, than on believing in salvation in the next world, and therefore tended to be sybaritic.

Worldliness and the realism of humanistic themes—these, then, are the heart of the Bunraku and Kabuki of the Edo-period townsmen. It was like the Renaissance of the West in its freeing of man from the religious sorcery and spells and the ascetic restraints that prevailed through the Middle Ages. And, by chance, this flowering of Edo culture corresponded in time to the Renaissance. Bunraku and Kabuki may be considered to have been perfected at about the same time, but in the case of Kabuki the origin is said to have been the Kabuki dance performed in Kyoto in 1603 by Okuni, a woman of Izumo Province. This same year, 1603, was the year of the death of Queen Elizabeth I and marked the peak of the theater of the Elizabethan court. It was also one year (or two years) after Shakespeare wrote *Hamlet*. On the European continent, the waves of the Renaissance had spread from Italy to France; the foundations were laid for premodern theater with the construction of the Teatro Olimpico and Teatro Farnese; actresses began to appear on the stage; popular theaters like the commedia dell'arte and Spanish theater were at their peak; and the shift began from the religious drama of the Middle Ages to drama that spoke of man. It was also the period when the popular theater was established in various countries. I believe that through comparison with those European theaters we can assign a position to Kabuki and Bunraku, among the dramatic forms of the world, as marking the conclusion of the Middle Ages and the start of an age of the theater being made to the measure of man. In fact, I think,

Bunraku and Kabuki closely approach Shakespearean and Spanish drama and the others forming the totality of Renaissance spirit and baroque expression.

Social Restraints

In addition to the humanism that is such an outstanding feature of Tokugawa theater, one more point that must be noted here is the social restraint, if not repression, experienced by Bunraku and Kabuki during the formative stages.

As has been explained, these two great theatrical forms of the Edo period were not born of and brought up by the nobility or samurai class but by the ordinary residents of the cities. While the city dwellers held power economically and in actuality were dominant, their society was by no means similar to the democratic middle-class society we know today. They lived under Tokugawa feudalism, by which system the Tokugawa shoguns, as the highest of the samurai, and those below them—the daimyo—ruled. The culture of the townsfolk, including their drama, did not have the power to resist the controls imposed by the armed strength of the upper stratum that ruled society.

Therefore, in Kabuki and Bunraku, even though there was what we may call humanitarian praise of the emancipation of man, this social restriction could not be eluded, and it led to various distortions in Kabuki and Bunraku as well as to the creation of types of the beauty of perversion that are unique to them.

For example, the existence of the *onnagata,* or female impersonator, in Kabuki was one of the products of distortion by those in power, that is to say, by the military regime. As a result of the restriction against women appearing on stage, Kabuki performers went on to devise highly exaggerated expressions of feminine beauty, such as women themselves were not capable of expressing, in their perfection of the art of the *onnagata* performed by male actors.

Another example may be found in the structure of the world of would-be historical fiction in the plays. In the case of the story of *Chūshingura,* for example, the real story belongs to the years 1701–2 in the Genroku era of the Edo period. The unfortunate hero who was forced to commit suicide was Lord Asano, or Asano Takuminokami

Naganori. The faithful retainer who led the band of revengeful samurai was Ôishi Kuranosuke, and his rival was the old samurai Lord Kira Kôzukenosuke Yoshinaka. But in the play the time is changed to the middle of the fourteenth century, and the daimyo are named Enya Hangan Takasada, Ôboshi Yuranosuke, and Kôno Moronao. They are people taken from the *Taiheiki* (*Chronicle of the Great Peace*), a fourteenth-century book of annals. In other words, the play was presented as depicting a historical event of more than two hundred years in the past. This was done because the Tokugawa shogunate—that is, the government—would not permit the documentary dramatization of events from either the world of the samurai or the society of the daimyo. The reason for the prohibition was that such dramatization might excite the general populace and lead to social upheaval or even a *coup d'état* attempt.

It would not be correct, however, to say that *Chûshingura* is a historical play only because it was presented as being based on a historical event of the fourteenth century. It was written as a contemporary play for the Edo period. Therein lies one of the complicated characteristics of Bunraku and Kabuki. As may be easily imagined, if it had been presented purely as a historical play, the average townsman, who did not have a particularly strong intellectual interest in history, would not have been as interested in the play. Even if we say that it was superficially made to take place in the distant past in order to evade suppression, the human feelings that welled up in the play and the customs seen in the principal scenes were stark realities of the Edo period. For example, when the curtain opens, the daimyo on stage should be in fourteenth-century dress and deport themselves in the manner of the past, but in the quarrel between the two daimyo—Hangan and Moronao—in the palace and also in the scene where Hangan commits suicide, the dress worn and the speech used are just as in the Edo period. Further, the scenes of the gay quarters in Kyoto and the farmhouse in the mountains are purely those of the Edo period. The play therefore depicts the time. It is a contemporary drama.

Thus, if one looks at *Chûshingura* according to the rational measure of modern times, there is no historical consistency as different periods and different customs appear to be muddled in a single play. Accordingly, intellectuals since Meiji times have criticized this point, and there even have been individuals who have belittled Bunraku and Kabuki as being boisterous nonsense and negated them as educational media because they distorted historical facts.

These contradictions were the inevitable result of the special social and political conditions that prevailed. The writers of Bunraku and Kabuki plays, rather than merely accepting those conditions, turned them to advantage in creating a world with the appeal of fiction. Within the world they fabricated on the stage they vividly portrayed the comic and tragic in the lives of the Edo masses—that is, in their own lives. Therefore, even though the plays deal with historical materials, they are by no means historical but are contemporary dramas reflecting the world around the playwrights and theatergoers, a world in which even "historical" persons have the same human feelings and are much the same as ordinary persons of the times.

Bunraku, Kabuki, and the Stratification of Japanese Theater

In the preceding sections I have shown something of the nature of premodern Japanese theater—taking Kabuki and Bunraku together—or, in other words, of the nature of the popular theater of the Edo period. It is well understood that while they are traditionally dramatic forms created by the Japanese people, they differ considerably from the dramatic forms that preceded them. The differences arose because Kabuki and Bunraku were the theatrical forms patronized by the urban classes, particularly the merchant townsmen, under the feudal regime of the Tokugawa shoguns.

In addition to this, attention must be given to whether Bunraku and Kabuki were modifications of the Noh and Kyôgen of the preceding age. True, some subjects were taken from Noh, and some plays and performing techniques were adapted from Kyôgen. But Bunraku and Kabuki grew from an entirely different rootstock. And therein lies one major characteristic of Japanese traditions. Bugaku, created in antiquity, over the span of more than a millennium, came to be transmitted as a part of aristocratic society. Even during the Kamakura and Muromachi periods and the ascendancy of the samurai-centered society, Bugaku neither perished nor was transformed and remains to this day as the ceremonial dances performed at festivals (*shikigaku*) of grand shrines and temples. The samurai took no heed of Bugaku but supported and perfected Noh and Kyôgen, which were more to their liking. In the Edo period's townsman-centered society, Noh and Kyôgen became the ceremonious drama of the upper strata of society, the shogun and the daimyo, and, along with Bugaku, continued to be transmitted intact while the townsmen, on the basis of their own society, created Kabuki and Bunraku.

Japanese tradition thus absorbs that of the past as an ingredient in forming what is to follow but, rather than merely surpassing or transforming that of the past, goes on to create new genres that stand abreast of those of old. Japanese tradition may thus be described as having multiple strata, one superimposed on another. Herein is a great difference from Western drama, where, following the decline of Greece and Rome, medieval religious drama emerged, to be displaced in its last moments by Renaissance drama, and where, moreover, classic theater gave way to the Enlightenment and Romanticism, to be superseded by modern realistic drama, which in turn has been supplanted by antirealism in this century. In the drama of the West, development has been through criticism and negation of what had preceded. A quite different process is to be found in Japan, one that is profoundly related to historic and philosophic matters and is one of the characteristics of Japanese culture.

Kabuki and Bunraku may thus be said to be dramatic forms that, in the multilayered traditional theater of Japan, were innovations by the general populace deeply imbued with qualities of human nature and closely related to actual life.

What kinds of drama, then, are Kabuki and Bunraku? Let us now turn to the theater itself and to the history of the two.

CHAPTER FIFTEEN

THE STYLE AND BEAUTY OF BUNRAKU

The Name Bunraku

First, we must look at the name of this dramatic form. What we call Bunraku is a general term for typical classic puppet plays of Japan. But originally this was a personal name, and strictly speaking we should use the term Ningyô Jôruri. This refers to a puppet play (*ningyô* means doll and, by extension, puppet) given to the accompaniment of a type of recitation or narration called *jôruri*.

Only since the middle of the Meiji era, some eighty or ninety years ago, has the term Bunraku been used. It is derived from the name of a man, Uemura Bunrakuken (1737–1810), who established a small theater for Ningyô Jôruri in Osaka in 1805, about a half century after Ningyô Jôruri had flourished at its zenith. Moreover, the name was selected for a theater, the Bunrakuza (*za* being a suffix indicating an enterprise), in 1872. The word Bunraku, taken from the name of Bunrakuken, was used to indicate both the theater and the troupe. In a short time, a rival theater, the Hikorokuza, was forced to close because of financial difficulties, leaving the Bunrakuza as the sole professional theater of its kind in the country. (Then, as now, there were similar puppet performers in the provinces, but they were amateurs, and the level of their art was low.) Ningyô Jôruri and the Bunrakuza became synonymous, until Bunraku came to be used for the drama itself, as it is used today. This in brief is how Bunraku came to be the name of this dramatic form.

The Three Components

Bunraku's three components are the narrative singing called *gidayû-bushi*, which carries the story line; the playing of the samisen; and the manipulation of the puppets.

The narrator uses a *gidayû* text, kept open in front of him, which has both the words and the intonation. This book, which contains the entire narrative for the play, is called a *maruhon*.

The stage is about as long as the Kabuki stage but differs from it in that there is neither *hanamichi* nor revolving stage. Also, as the puppets are smaller than life, the stage settings are correspondingly scaled down. The stage, which may be thought of as a space in which the puppets are to move, is so contrived that the puppets will appear to be on a level floor or the ground, when seen by the spectators.

At the part of the stage nearest the audience is a low balustrade (*tesuri*), or "third railing," indicating that it was meant to be seen and counted from the rear. About two paces back is the somewhat higher "second railing"; ordinarily, the puppets move about inside this railing. The area between this and the deeper "first railing" is called *funazoko*—the bottom of the ship—and is used as a road or street, or a garden in front of a house. Behind the first railing are placed the sets for interior scenes.

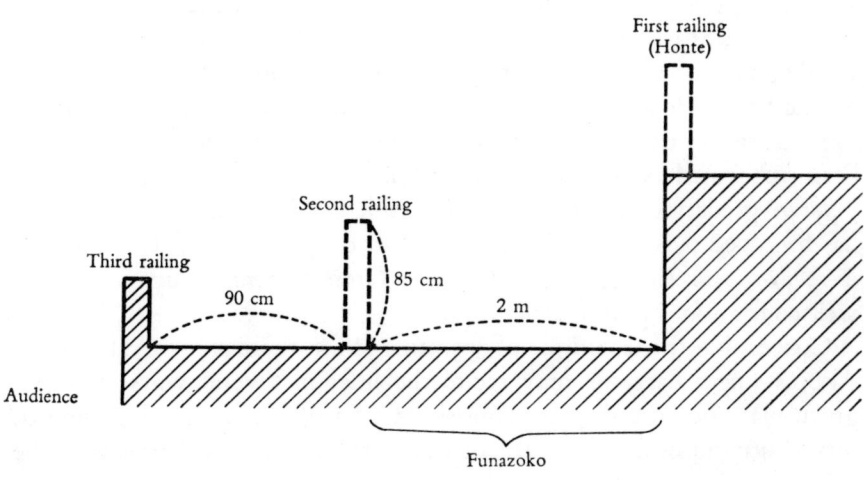

Both first railing and second railing are hinged to facilitate movement by the puppeteers.

To the right of the audience, at the side of the stage, is the dais (*yuka*) for the *gidayû* narrators (who sit to the left) and the samisen players (who sit to the right). Narrators and musicians alike wear a formal garment (*kamishimo*), and in front of the principal narrator (*tayû*) there is a heavy wooden stand (*kendai*) on which the *maruhon* rests. While listening to the narration and music emanating from the right, the spectators watch the actions of the puppets on the stage and through this combination appreciate the drama. The technique often used in other forms of puppet plays whereby the puppeteers themselves recite the lines is not used in Bunraku. There is a complete division of labor into visual and aural elements. The three—the narrator, the musician, and the puppeteer—are collectively referred to as the "three arts" (*sangyô*).

Tayû and Samisen

The *tayû*, who recites the *gidayû-bushi*, is a narrator of a type of dramatic and descriptive poetry. There are also some other types that belong to the category of the *jôruri*—and these are still extant—such as *katô-bushi*, *itchû-bushi*, *ogie-bushi*, *sonohachi-bushi*, *shinnai-bushi*, and *bunya-bushi*, as well as *tokiwazu-bushi* and *kiyomoto-bushi*, which are the necessary components of Kabuki and traditional Japanese dancing (an offshoot of Kabuki). In Bunraku's early days, there was considerable variety, and the names of narrators were made into the names of styles of the texts. However, since the first Takemoto Gidayû (1651–1714) opened his theater, the Takemotoza, in Osaka in 1685, Bunraku has been performed exclusively in the *gidayû* style.

Jôruri predating the *gidayû-bushi* is called old *jôruri*, and that which has followed it is called either new *jôruri* or *gidayû jôruri*. *Chûshingura*, *Terakoya*, and *Kokusenya Kassen* (*The Great General's Battle*) were all written for *gidayû* performance.

Concerning the technique of narrating *jôruri*, there are several schools. Also, a single narrator may recite the lines in several ways during a given play, because the text consists of two types: (1) the depiction of lyrical situations, development of the story, and the explanation of the underlying psychology (the section called *ji* or a kind of recitative), which is depicted in the third person, and (2) the words (*serifu*) of the characters, expressed in the first person.

This resembles the situation in Greek drama, where the *choros* portion is distinguished from that of the three actors, and different rhythms are to be given to the lines of *choros* and to the words of the actors, respectively, as Aristotle noted in his *Poetics*. But the *ji* section of Bunraku is marked by considerable poetic embellishment, and the recitation is done quite vigorously, while the words are closer to those used in ordinary daily life. This corresponds to the difference between the choral portion and the recitations of the protagonist and deuteragonist of the Noh play. However, because of the close ties with the realities of the Edo people, *gidayû* resembles ordinary conversation to a greater extent. Since conversational Japanese has not fundamentally changed very much since the Edo period, modern audiences experience almost no difficulty in understanding *gidayû*.

Playing the samisen provides the melody, but rather than being mere accompaniment, the samisen's music must also have and impart emotional and psychological nuances. The samisen musician is sometimes a composer as well as a performer and also plays a vital role in the transmission of the art. He must not only train apprentices but must also rigorously train and discipline the narrators with whom he shares the dais. The musicians are accompanists, in the background, of the puppets and narrators, but they are essential for the continued transmission of the dramatic form.

The samisen used for *gidayû* differs from that for *tokiwazu, kiyomoto, nagauta,* or other styles in that it is larger and has a thicker neck (called *futozao*). The profound musical strength residing in this instrument serves to make even more effective the voice of the narrator, which he first projects from his diaphragm.

Puppets and Puppeteers

The two characteristics of Bunraku that have no parallel elsewhere in the world are the puppets and the techniques whereby they are manipulated.

A puppet consists of a head, body, arms, and legs. However, since in the past women's kimonos were so long as to entirely conceal their legs, puppets representing women are made without legs.

Head, arms, and legs are detachable, and the pole on which the head rests is inserted through the puppet's torso. More than anything else, it is the delicate, precise construction of the head that gives a Bunraku puppet its life. A more complicated puppet is capable of opening or closing its eyes, rolling them, raising or lowering its eyebrows, and opening or closing its mouth, at the discretion of the puppeteer. Kiyohime, a "female" puppet used in the play *Hidakagawa Iriaizakura* (*The River Hidaka*), is so overcome with fury at being spurned by the attractive priest whom she loves that she is transformed into a serpent, and at that moment her princess' robes change to a scaly skin, her eyes snap open to larger-than-human size, a split tongue spits from her mouth, and from her now-disheveled hair emerge two golden horns (made of stiff paper)—all of which can be accomplished with one movement by the puppeteer. Impossible for a real actor to do, this is accomplished by the unique mechanism of the puppet.

This versatile change in expression and appearance is accomplished by a network of strings embedded in the torso and by mechanisms implanted in the head. When they should be frightened, the puppets look frightened; when they should be angry, they look angry. This is indicative of a strong everyday kind of realism, in contrast to the immobile expression of a Noh mask. To add another example, a small pin can be made to protrude from the mouth of a female puppet, and when mortification or sadness is called for, the end of a sleeve is caught on the pin, by means of the appropriate motion by the puppeteer. The sleeve appears to be bitten by the puppet, in a most lifelike depiction of the traditional Japanese feminine action in attempting to repress inner feelings.

We can see in these examples how the Edo townsmen sought realism in their theatrical fare. And yet all this is accomplished mainly by the use of the puppeteer's left hand, for such is the division of work in Bunraku puppetry.

However, one person would not suffice to manipulate such a precisely devised puppet. Because of this, Bunraku uses the technique of having three men work in unison to operate one puppet—something found nowhere else in traditional puppetry.

The mainstay of the three is called the chief puppeteer (*omozukai*).

He inserts his left hand through the clothing on the puppet's back in order to grasp the body from within and thus hold up both head and body, while controlling the posture of the puppet and the direction or inclination of the head as well as the expressions of the puppet's face. The life of a puppet depends upon the puppeteer's left hand. The puppeteer's right hand controls the puppet's right arm and hand.

The second puppeteer handles only the left arm and hand of the puppet, while the third puppeteer handles only the legs. Although female puppets lack legs, since it is necessary for it to appear as if there are legs within the kimono, even here the third puppeteer cannot be eliminated.

Of course, not all of the puppets appearing on stage are manipulated by three men. Puppets such as ladies-in-waiting, guards, store clerks, or passersby have faces with simple, immovable expressions and are a bit small. If these bit players overacted, they would distract attention from the starring players, so their movements are kept as simple as the puppets' construction, and one person is sufficient to handle a puppet. The puppets are called *tsume ningyô* or simply *tsume*.

But the puppets used for the main roles are all handled by three men. In the case of puppets such as those representing courtesans, they sport combs and hair ornaments that are no different from actual ones, except in size, and, clothed in many layers of extravagant robes, they may weigh as much as twenty kilograms. That this entire weight must be borne by the left hand of the chief puppeteer for a long duration at a spell is alone sufficient reason for his hard training. However, no matter how masterly the chief puppeteer may be, if the other two men are not also fully experienced, failure is certain. That the three men must even breathe in unison is the most vital point in Bunraku. The puppeteer responsible for moving the left arm and the one responsible for moving the legs must of course fully know not only the narrative and the character of the role of their puppet but also the technique used by the chief puppeteer. Thus it has been said since many years ago that training must extend to as long as ten years of manipulating the legs and ten years of manipulating the left arm. Before someone can become a chief puppeteer, twenty years of training are required. Today, with everything about us changing at such a rapid tempo, men interested in learning the art are no longer as interested as men once were in going through such prolonged rigors.

One more point that must be noted in relation to the puppeteers is that, differing from those in other Japanese forms of puppet theater or in foreign forms, they move in full view of the spectators, concealed neither by stage nor by curtain. Herein is an important point related to the beauty of Bunraku.

At the time of Chikamatsu Monzaemon, when Bunraku had first been devised, just one person manipulated each puppet by holding it up while standing behind the partition at the front of the stage, and it was only the puppet that was seen by the audience.

If only the puppets are visible, it would be proper to call it a puppet play. However, in 1734 the three-man system was perfected, and since it was felt necessary to make the puppets appear larger in keeping with that change, their size was standardized at about half human scale. It was also decided that the upper half of the puppets would be held solidly and the lower part would float in the air.

Therefore, strictly speaking, even today all the puppeteers should be clothed entirely in black with gauze-like hoods that cover their heads. In both Bunraku and Kabuki black is taken to represent "nothingness" or "absence," and this choice of color was made because black is less eye-catching than any other color. Now, however, in order to show respect for the chief puppeteer, and also because it is considered desirable and fitting to enable the spectators to see the faces of outstanding masters of the art, in his case only, the black hood is ordinarily not worn, and at times he may appear in the traditional *kamishimo* dress. But since it was proper in the past for all puppeteers to be clad entirely in black, today when a chief puppeteer is to perform without a black hood, the following announcement is usually made before the curtain is opened, preceded by the announcement of the title of the play and the names of the narrators and samisen players: "Ladies and gentlemen! Today the chief puppeteer performs without a hood."

Further, although today it is the exception, for certain scenes the puppeteer must be entirely in black. In the fourth act of *Chūshingura*, after his lord has committed suicide, the loyal Oboshi Yuranosuke, standing outside the gate of the castle now turned over to the shogunate, vows revenge and then silently leaves the stage. This grief-filled scene, taking place in the darkness of the night, would be spoiled if the puppeteer's face was visible, or if he wore anything but black.

In Japan the audience, which is used to this convention, takes no notice of the puppeteer, having mentally accepted the notion that black is to be ignored, and can appreciate Bunraku without any impediment. But among those Japanese and non-Japanese who see Bunraku for the first time there are many people who feel something strange in this practice. This is undoubtedly a natural reaction. It is true that the chief puppeteer, although his face is exposed, remains expressionless. The sight may be awesome and even unpleasant to some of the foreigners who are accustomed to the more dynamic acting of the West. But this is the technical achievement of the puppeteers who are to be exposed on the stage. If the chief puppeteer were to show even the slightest trace of the emotions ascribed to the puppet, he would attract the attention of the spectators, and it would be destructive to the fundamental principle that it is the puppets who make the play. Of course, the chief puppeteer, at one with the role he plays, should feel joyous or sad or angry as he manipulates his puppet. One of the greatest puppeteers said, "Because of the audience watching me, I am obliged not to express my feeling in tears. It is difficult to conceal my emotions." It is the same for an ordinary actor; if the heart of the character is not brought to life in the heart of the actor, a vivid performance is impossible. But the puppeteer is, after all, a puppeteer. The emotions that well up in his own heart must be utterly expressed in the puppet's expressions alone; they must be completely transferred to the puppet.

The more complete this transference of emotions to the puppet, the less expression is shown by the puppeteer. Not only is it annoying to see a puppeteer who turns his head with the puppet's head or raises his eyebrows with the puppet's eyebrows; it is also a sure sign that the puppet has not been fully brought to life. If the audience watches plays keeping this fact in mind, the lack of expression will be immediately understood. And magically enough, after one has settled into the Bunraku atmosphere, the puppeteers fade into the background.

Puppeteers, by leaving human expressions entirely to the narrators, whose words and manner reflect emotions, and to the puppets, negate themselves. Here is the primary requisite in terms of the beauty of Bunraku. An outstanding puppeteer seems to disappear before our eyes as he performs, and we find ourselves enthralled by the puppet's vivid portrayal of man—and nothing else.

The Aesthetics of the "Super-Puppets"

What comes to my mind at this point is the word super-puppets, employed by the great British stage director Gordon Craig (1872–1966), who strictly opposed any realistic performance that lapsed into unrestrained actions, and maintained that real actors should leave everything up to the director, who would handle them as if they were puppets. He called these actors made into puppets "super-puppets" (*Übermarionetten*). I think that Bunraku puppets, while they are puppets, approach the plane that Craig conceived for the super-puppets. Or, from the opposite viewpoint, they may be called superhuman (*Übermensch*).

Something that might be called either super-puppets or superhuman—this is the unique world of Bunraku.

Puppet Plays for Adults

Another characteristic without equal is the fact that these puppet plays have been created for adults and depict the world of adults.

The puppets used in modern Western-influenced puppet plays in Japan, as well as those used in puppet plays in the West, have in most instances heads that are too large for their bodies. This is the proportion of a child's body and is based on the same approach as is similarly used in children's stories and cartoon comics. Material meant for children dominates, and fantasies and fairylands are common. Even if not meant for children, undoubtedly there are many plays that, in their fantasies and their disregard for the commonplace and the real, bear a resemblance to something like *Doktor Faustus,* or the German *Puppenspiel* that influenced young Goethe in his writing of *Faust*. Thus it may be said that the special *raison d'être* of puppet plays compared to those performed by real actors lies in their being set in a world of fantasies.

But this is not the case with Bunraku. First of all, the size of the head in comparison to the torso is considerably smaller than in the average proportion among Japanese people. This may come from the intent that a puppet which is half the size of a human being appear to be an adult.

Second, the plays take place in the adult world, and their dramatic content, scale, subjects, and literary content are fully equal to those of plays that might be performed by real actors. (In this connection, one might for example consider *Chûshingura* or *Terakoya*.) The puppets display emotion with the same reality as would human actors. In overall terms, one may say that herein lies the *élan vital* of Bunraku.

Particularly because of this, Bunraku, together with Kabuki, attracted the urban audiences of the Edo period, exerted considerable influence on them, and formed a most important portion of Japanese theater. In a sense, Bunraku overcomes both the childishness traditional to puppet plays and their world of fantastic simplicity. After it had advanced into the realm of adult drama, however, it soon passed its peak, lost most of its fans to Kabuki, and fell upon distressed times.

CHAPTER SIXTEEN

THE DRAMA OF BUNRAKU

Literary Jōruri

Bunraku's literary content is that of *jōruri*. Historically speaking, Takemoto Gidayū I opened the Takemotoza in Osaka, where Chikamatsu Monzaemon, under contract to the theatrical company, wrote *Shusse Kagekiyo* (*The Success of Kagekiyo*) in 1685. All works after that are considered *jōruri* works.

Jōruri was adopted almost completely by Kabuki, to Kabuki's great advantage. In general, it may be said that it was through the introduction of *jōruri* that Kabuki was perfected in terms of dramatic literature. That is, more than the writers of Kabuki plays, the writers of Bunraku plays were a step advanced with respect to the literary quality of their work. There is a reason for this. In Kabuki, the actor is foremost, and the playwrights therefore wrote to exploit the talents of the actors. Moreover, the plays were even modified at the command of the actors. In contrast to this, in Bunraku, plays were written for performance by puppets and narrators who performed virtually just as the playwright intended. The playwright was thus free to express and develop his abilities as poet and dramatist. Chikamatsu Monzaemon wrote Kabuki plays when he was young. But after the death of the young actor Sakata Tōjūrō, whom Chikamatsu esteemed very highly, he no longer felt inclined to write for other actors, and he turned to Bunraku, where he could see performances given just as he had written.

At the hands of Chikamatsu, puppet plays were made to accurately reflect Edo society and were elevated to a popular theater representative of the sentiments of the Edo people. Let us look briefly at the main plays and varieties of *jôruri,* the foundations of which were laid and elaborated by Chikamatsu.

The Varieties of Jôruri

Gidayû jôruri is broadly divided into two categories according to the "world" to which the hero belongs and the type of society that forms the basis for the development of the play: (1) historical plays (*jidai jôruri*) dealing with the brave deeds of warriors and aristocrats (cf. *chansons de geste*) and (2) sewa plays (*sewa jôruri*) depicting the life of the general public, especially of the merchant class and farmers. They are also called *jidaimono* and *sewamono,* which are the terms used in Kabuki as well.

The *jidai* (period) of *jidaimono* (period play) refers to a period in the past, and almost all the plays draw upon narrative and other early literary works already well known. These stories may be categorized into (1) the Sugawara cycle, dealing with the story of the exile of Sugawara no Michizane (845–903), as in Chikamatsu Monzaemon's *Tenjinki* or *The Story of Lord Sugawara;* (2) the Ise cycle, dealing with the romantic adventures of a hero poet, generally attributed to Ariwara no Narihira (825–880); (3) the Genji and Heike cycle, represented by several epic stories such as *Heike Monogatari* (*The Tale of the Heike,* c. 1202, dealing with the downfall of the Taira family, attributed to Hamuro Tokinaga), *Gempei Seisuiki* (*The Rise and Fall of the Genji and Heike Families,* c. 1202, a historical work in forty-eight volumes, from 1160 to 1185, attributed to Hamuro Tokinaga), *Gikeiki* (*A Life of Yoshitsune,* c. 1400), and *Taiheiki* (*Chronicle of the Great Peace,* a historical work in forty-one volumes attributed to the monk Kojima—d. 1374—of the Enryakuji covering the period from 1318 to 1368); and (4) the Taikô cycle, generally called *Taikôki* or *A Life of the Taikô* (Toyotomi Hideyoshi; 1536–98). Among several editions of the last of these, those that are historically highly evaluated are the one by Oze Hoan in twenty volumes and the one by Nishigawara Kakuzaemon, both published c. 1661. The leading characters of the *jidaimono* were therefore persons of historical or literary fame and persons close to them.

Sewa, on the other hand, indicates linguistically the popular subjects of conversation of the time—that is, the stories of actual events that circulated among the people, corresponding to many of the local news and feature items in our daily newspapers. For example, such topics as love affairs, double suicides, robbery and murder, success, gang wars, demonstrations and riots by farmers, and the like are typical. The plays were thus dramatized versions of actual recent events and were as a body a form of living theater or people's theater.

Jidaimono are further subdivided into *ôchômono* (court plays or dynasty plays), *jidaimono* proper, and *oiemono* (family feuds).

Court plays feature incidents at the imperial court and deal with the nobles of the Nara and Heian periods, when the imperial court was the de facto center of government. Characteristic of this subdivision is *Sugawara Denju Tenarai Kagami* (*The Secret of Sugawara's Calligraphy*). This is based on the life story of the Heian-period minister Sugawara no Michizane, the Japanese patron saint of calligraphy immortalized in shrines as Tenjinsama. The main plot is the loyalty, at the risk of their lives, of the triplets Umeômaru, Matsuômaru, and Sakuramaru, on behalf of Michizane, who died at the frontier after being banished to Kyushu by the power-thirsty minister Fujiwara Jihei, and on behalf of Michizane's survivors. If another characteristic play is to be named, a good choice would be the story of the overthrow of the minister Soga no Iruka, *Imoseyama Onna Teikin* (*An Example of Noble Womanhood*). This well-known play, in which a son and a daughter of two feuding aristocratic families die with the resolve of meeting in the next world is a tragedy somewhat resembling *Romeo and Juliet*.

Jidaimono, in the narrow sense, consist mostly of plays that deal with warriors and wars of the Middle Ages, from the time of the Gempei wars (late twelfth century) through the age of Oda Nobunaga and Toyotomi Hideyoshi (sixteenth century), when Japan was being unified and the Tokugawa period was ushered in. Among plays dealing with the feud between the Taira and the Minamoto families, there is *Yoshitsune Sembonzakura,* which contains many famous scenes and is full of romanticism. This play, along with *Chûshingura* and *Sugawara,* is one of the three major plays of both Bunraku and Kabuki. At the battle of Ichinotani, Kumagai Naozane, famed warrior of the Minamoto family, kills at the seashore his sixteen-year-old enemy, the warrior Taira no Atsumori. But having realized the inhuman nature of war, Naozane becomes a monk to hold memorial services for Atsumori. This episode has been dramatized in the play *Ichinotani Futaba Gunki* (*The Chronicle of the Battle of Ichinotani*), of which one act is *Kumagai Jinya*. There are also the tragedies of the general of the Taira, Taira no Kagekiyo, who was defeated in battle and covered his tracks: *Musume Kagekiyo Yashima Nikki* (*Kagekiyo's Daughter,* of which the third act, *Hyûgajima,* is most frequently performed); *Dannoura Kabuto Gunki* (*The War Chronicle of Dannoura,* of which the third act, *Akoya no Kotozeme,* is frequently performed); and *Heike Nyogo ga Shima* (*The Island of Heike Women,* of which *Shunkan* is most frequently performed), in which the starring role is that of the monk Shunkan, who has been discovered to be the schemer behind the overthrow of Taira no Kiyomori and has therefore been banished to a desolate island. All these are masterpieces that have utilized the Gempei wars and personages. Further, there is the play based upon the battles between commanders Takeda and Uesugi, *Honchô Nijûshikô;* the play that recounts the adventures of the half-Chinese, half-Japanese hero Watônai on the Chinese continent, *Kokusenya Kassen;* and the play *Ehon Taikôki* (*The Picture Book of the Taikô*), in which the hero, Akechi Mitsuhide, kills his master, Oda Nobunaga, on account of the latter's ill treatment of him.

In the third category, *oiemono,* are dramatizations of family feuds. These were incidents rooted in the struggles for control of territory, waged within the castles of feudal lords. Themes similar to those in this category are found in Western plays such as Shakespeare's *Macbeth* and *Hamlet.* While these struggles were a manifestation of the strivings for revenge and for authority on the part of some unjustly ostracized retainers, they were also an outlet for the bottled-up energy of the samurai, who, under the absolute dictatorship and rigidly enforced peace of the Tokugawa shoguns, were thwarted from venting their energy in endeavors for success. The *oiemono* plays that dealt with such struggles were actually contemporary in theme. However, since there was fear that plays of this type might agitate the populace and incite an attempt at a *coup d'état,* the dramatization of these struggles was severely forbidden. To counter this prohibition the playwrights changed the time of the plays from the present to the past and disguised the personalities by changing the names of the casts. For example, in *Meiboku Sendai Hagi* (*The Disputed Succession*) is depicted an incident that had taken place in the mansion of Prince Datè, lord of the Sendai area, in 1671, but the time as given in the play itself is the end of the fourteenth century—a time long before the start of the Tokugawa period. The real person who appears in history, Harada Kai, was renamed Nikki Danjô in the play. The names of the members of the imperial court in *ôchômono* plays and persons figuring in the Gempei wars were used without alteration. This is a major difference between the two. As another example of *oiemono* there is *Kagamiyama Kokyô no Nishikie* (*Mirror Mountain*), which is a dramatization of an incident that took place in Kaga Province. *Kanadehon Chûshingura* is yet another example of this sort of play.

All of Bunraku's *sewamono* are set in Osaka or Kyoto or their environs —that is, in the Kansai region. In later days many Edo-style *sewamono* plays were made for Kabuki and played in Edo, but there are no Edo-style *sewamono* among Bunraku pieces. This is because Bunraku was virtually the exclusive property of the Kansai district, and almost all of its growth, and decline, took place there, not in Edo.

Among Bunraku's *sewamono,* Chikamatsu's plays hold a predominant position. In particular, high value is accorded to his double-suicide plays such as *Sonezaki Shinjû, Meido no Hikyaku* (*The Messenger from Hell*), and *Shinjû Ten no Amijima* (*The Love Suicide at Amijima*); adultery plays such as *Horikawa Nami no Tsuzumi* (*The Echo of a Drum near the Hori River*); and plays such as *Onnagoroshi Abura no Jigoku* (*The Woman-Killer and the Hell of Oil*) dealing with murder by lawless young men in contemporary settings. Also, he later wrote of the tragic love of such couples as Osome and Hisamatsu in *Shimpan Utazaimon* (*Osome and Hisamatsu,* or *Nozakimura*); of the young wife of a sakè merchant who sacrifices her own life for her husband, who has fallen in love with a dancer, in *Hadesugata Onna Maiginu* (*The Love of Hanshichi and Sankatsu,* or *Sakaya*); and of a broad-daylight murder in midsummer, in *Natsu Matsuri Naniwa Kagami* (*Summer Festival*). In all of these *sewamono* masterpieces, he depicted the pathos in the plight of the masses.

The Composition of Jôruri

Concerning the composition of *jôruri* as a basic common feature of Bunraku and Kabuki, first we should mention the characteristic that these plays are made up of numerous acts and scenes. For example, in the case of long pieces like *Chūshingura, Sugawara,* and *Sembonzakura,* for a complete performance fourteen or fifteen hours are required. Therefore today these plays are presented in two- or three-part installments. Further, many scenes are cut entirely, but the plays are written in such fashion that even a single act may be appreciated independently.

However, if one watches a play from beginning to end, he will notice that even the longest play has some sort of consistency. *Jidaimono* plays are customarily divided by their authors into five parts and *sewamono* plays into three. The plays are thus naturally given a pyramidal form of development: beginning, dramatic climax, and denouement. This may have been greatly influenced by the concepts of the *jo-ha-kyū* (introduction, development, resolution) and the five-part program of Noh plays. Bunraku's five- and three-part pattern somewhat predates the appearance of Chikamatsu, but it was he who firmly established it in the dramaturgy of Bunraku.

Quite coincidentally, the form of development is comparable to Aristotle's in *Poetics*: "complete in itself" or "having a commencement, a central portion, and a conclusion." It is also the same as that of the classic five-act plays that originated in Rome and were revived during the Renaissance and established in seventeenth-century France. And it is essentially the same idea as that presented by Gustav Freytag (1816–95) in *Die Technik des Drama,* of five parts and three points. This, however, can be said only in relation to the framework of the plays. In actuality the mood and themes of each scene must be said to be anticlassic or even baroque rather than conforming to classic principles.

The Dramatic Elements of Jōruri in Sewamono

What must be given attention at this point is the common essential quality of all these plays—that is, the greatest theme that appears in Bunraku or in Tokugawa drama. In brief, it is the pride and the grief of people at the brink of death, people who have had their natural desires suppressed, people wrapped in complications as a result of the social contradictions brought on by Tokugawa feudalism.

This basic motif appears in its most classic form in *jidaimono* plays, in scenes wherein the hero sacrifices his own relatives, including children, for the sake of his loyalty to his lord. Archetypical of this motif in *sewamono* plays are double suicides committed because of obligations to a master or a father-in-law or caused by matters related to monetary debts. In all such scenes, the affection of parent and child or the tragedy befalling the pure love of a man and a woman is underscored in "lamentation" scenes. These are climaxes in those plays. (Note that this is true for Bunraku and Kabuki versions of *jōruri* plays; in Kabuki proper these are paralleled by more enjoyable and appealing elements of merry-making.)

Here is an example of this taken from a *sewamono* play, Chikamatsu's *Sonezaki Shinjū*.

Tokubei, a shop clerk of an Osaka soy sauce merchant, is a hard worker and a handsome young man. Recognizing the young man's abilities, the merchant decides to marry him to his wife's niece, but instead of telling Tokubei of his intention, he approaches Tokubei's elderly mother, who lives in the country. Here are the first misconceptions: namely the hypotheses that it will be sufficient to obtain parental consent to carry out the wedding and that the young man will have no objection to the niece of his master. Herein one may observe the general concepts of feudal society such as loyalty to one's master and subordination to one's parents, which take precedence over one's own sanctity as a human being.

Tokubei's mother is avaricious through and through. Thinking of the benefits and the considerable dowry that will accrue, she gives her consent—this too without a word to Tokubei. And to seal the agreement, she accepts a handsome dowry from the shop owner.

When he hears of this, Tokubei is shocked. Not only is he displeased with his master and his mother for making the agreement without speaking to him, but he has his own love besides. Her name is Ohatsu, and she is a courtesan at the Temmanya house. Since she is a courtesan, it would take a large sum of money before she could be free to marry. Here lies the second obstacle.

As human traffic, courtesans were sold to the bordellos where they were kept. They had to make their bodies available to even the most disagreeable visitor, provided he could pay for it. They were not to fall in love even if there were those whom they liked. Thus, the heroine, Ohatsu, existed in a society that did not permit normal human living. To free her from the chains of this society to marry her, Tokubei would need a great amount of money. Tokubei is a young novice drawing a low salary. He has no way to amass such a large sum. And, being honest, he cannot swindle or steal to get the money. Therefore, all he can do is to save his money, little by little, for the time in the future when he will be able to free Ohatsu and marry her, having exchanged vows of love with her.

Naturally, Tokubei refuses to marry his master's niece. His master becomes angry and retorts, "If you want a harlot instead of my niece, all right. Do just as you like. But on the seventh day of the fourth month, pay back the money I gave to your mother."

Tokubei returns to the country and takes back the money from his avaricious mother. But a malicious friend, insisting that it is a matter of life or death, implores Tokubei to lend the money to him. Naively, Tokubei gives him the money.

It is the day before Tokubei is supposed to repay the money, but his friend has shown no sign of giving him back the loan. When Tokubei gets excited and asks him to return the money, showing him the signed and sealed bond of debt, his friend retorts that the seal was the one he had lost a long time ago and that Tokubei might have forged this bond with the seal he had picked up, to blackmail him. Thereupon this man beats and kicks poor Tokubei. Without that money, Tokubei must give up his dream of buying Ohatsu's freedom and is forced to be expelled or to agree to marry his master's niece. To make matters worse, a wealthy patron is interested in buying Ohatsu's freedom, to have her for himself. There seems to be no chance that Tokubei will be able to marry Ohatsu. That night, Tokubei and Ohatsu slip away from the Temmanya to the wood in the Tenjin Shrine at Sonezaki to commit double suicide.

This drama is not a fictional tale. Just a month before it was written there was a double suicide at Sonezaki by two persons with the same names and social status of Tokubei and Ohatsu. While the government would not permit events involving samurai to be dramatized, it was more lenient toward dramatization of events related to the life of the common folk.

Such was the oppression imposed by the link of feudal obligations, and the way life often turned on matters of money. The time was the Genroku era. A century had passed since the civil wars had ended and peace had been brought to the land. A cash economy had made tremendous development, and merchants, especially in Osaka, flourished. It was a time invigorated by the feeling that as long as one had the money, anything could be accomplished. The spectacular clothing of wealthy merchants dazzled the eyes, and the gay quarters were at their peak. There was also the liberty to love the person one pleased. There are thus many reasons why the Genroku era is called the Renaissance of Japan.

However, the feudal thinking aimed at maintaining order in a military society—based on Neo-Confucianism—came to permeate society in general and to influence every family. Thereupon the natural order in human relationships was overturned. That is to say, the relationships of subject to master were considered to span three worlds: the past, present, and future; the relationships of husband and wife to span two worlds: the present and the future; and that of parent and child to span one world: that of the present. This concept of social order spread through samurai society as well as that of the townsmen.

Natural human relationships do not conform to this, however, and there was stiff opposition. The lovers in *Sonezaki Shinjū* opposed this order and, as a result, were led to suicide. Rather than live on in a world without love, where this unnatural order was imposed on people, they chose to die and make their love eternal. Rather than being a defeat of the two by the social order, to make this decision was the only way of accomplishing one's life in that feudal society.

In such decisions, we may see the influence of Buddhism, particularly in their belief that after death they would be reborn in the Pure Land paradise of Buddhism. Further, their spirits were buoyed by the belief that the relationship of husband and wife spans the two worlds of the present and the future. This differed, however, from the Middle Ages' religious belief (as evidenced in Noh plays and elsewhere) in espousing Buddhism to be one with Buddha. Their choice was one of expediency, as their primary concern was a happier life in this world, namely that of the present. And this philosophy was, in their case, materialized in the form of double suicide.

Chikamatsu expressed their way of living on through their love as he eulogized their act in his passage of *michiyuki* (lovers' suicide trip) in verse. It is a song of the couple hurrying to the shrine to commit suicide.

Narrator:
Farewell to this world, and to the night farewell.
We who walk the road to death, to what should we
   be likened?
To the frost by the road that leads to the graveyard,
Vanishing with each step we take ahead:
How sad is this dream of a dream!

Tokubei:
Ah, did you count the bell? Of the seven strokes
That mark the dawn, six have sounded.
The remaining one will be the last echo
We shall hear in this life.

Ohatsu:
It will echo the bliss of nirvana.

(Translated by Donald Keene, in his *Major Plays of Chikamatsu,* published by Columbia University Press in 1961. Used by the permission of the translator.)

In this, the love and devotion of the two as they stand in the dark forest of Sonezaki is remarkably well depicted. Chikamatsu's verse is, moreover, written in the seven-five meter. This is a rhythm of Japanese poetry that has survived throughout the years since antiquity. The seven-five metrical arrangement is to be found in various Japanese poetic forms: in *jôruri,* in Kabuki dialogue, in the *naniwa-bushi* songs, and in the popular songs of today. In Bunraku as well as in Kabuki, this meter is invariably used in climactic, highly emotional scenes and thus forms a musical and lyrical characteristic of Tokugawa-period drama.

Depicting love triangles, tragedies of adultery, double suicides of husbands and wives due to friction with fathers-in-law or mothers-in-law, suicides as a result of two women's compromising, the *sewamono* plays are full of diversity and variety. Despite the complexity of the situation, if, as in the case of *Sonezaki Shinjû,* the play is seen as a conflict between obligations, money, and natural human desires, all may be understood. This, then, may truly be said to be the drama of the society of the Tokugawa-period townsmen. The tragedies that embodied these themes were perfected at the hands of Chikamatsu.

The Dramatic Elements of Jôruri in Jidaimono

As an example of a *jidaimono* play, let us take up *Terakoya,* which constitutes one act of the long play *Sugawara Denju Tenarai Kagami.*

Among the retainers of Sugawara no Michizane are the triplets Umeô (or Umeômaru), Matsuô (or Matsuômaru), and Sakuramaru. The wicked minister Fujiwara Jihei had Sugawara banished to Kyushu, where he died. The triplets protect Sugawara's wife and son, Kan Shûsai, from their enemies as they plan to obtain revenge.

One of the triplets, Matsuô, becomes a retainer of the despised Jihei. He is castigated for this by others, as he appears to be oblivious of his obligations and disloyal. Actually, however, Matsuô has gone over to the enemy's side with the secret intention of wreaking vengeance at the right time. The basis for this tragedy is the concept that for the samurai there is no way to live without being loyal—fulfilling one's obligations—to one's master. Matsuô's chance comes. The young Kan Shûsai is hidden at a rural school (*terakoya*). News of this reaches the enemy, and the owner of the school, Takebe Genzô, is ordered to hand over the head of Kan Shûsai. The loyal Genzô returns to his school and tries to find out if there is anyone who can be sacrificed to substitute for the boy. Among the sons of the local peasants is one noble lad who could pass for the aristocratic Kan Shûsai. Genzô is told by his wife that this pupil has just entered the school, and Genzô, shedding tears, nevertheless resolves that this boy will be sacrificed.

Then the man assigned to bring back the head of the executed arrives. Matsuô has accompanied him, with the task of certifying the head as that of Kan Shûsai, because he is the only person in the enemy camp who has seen the young master and can identify his face.

Genzô shows the head to Matsuô in perhaps the most famous scene of this play. It is not the head of Kan Shûsai, however, but that of Matsuô's own son. Matsuô has taken advantage of his assignment with the thought that it would afford a chance to prove his loyalty to sacrifice his son to save Kan Shûsai. So he sent his son in advance to enter this school. If Genzô and his wife had not been faithful and had beheaded

Kan Shûsai as they had been commanded to do, Matsuô would have been spared his grief. But Genzô acted out of loyalty, and, not knowing that the child was Matsuô's son, he sacrificed the child. Matsuô had foreseen that his son would be killed. The tragedies of this play are thus the products of feudal vassalage and obligations. This is the main characteristic of the tragedies in *jidaimono* plays.

Matsuô examines the head and testifies falsely that it is that of Kan Shûsai. Genzô and his wife are surprised at Matsuô's statement and relieved from their fear by having saved Kan Shûsai. The inspecting officials depart. As the play draws to a close, Matsuô returns to the scene, now with his wife, and reveals that it was his own son who was beheaded. When Genzô tells them that their son died smiling and showing no signs of regret, knowing that he was going to save the life of Kan Shûsai, Matsuô and his wife burst into tears.

This scene is, of course, the high point of the play. The theme becomes clear only in the latter portion. That is, this play does not have praise for the callous substitution of one person for another, nor does it emphasize feudal loyalty. On the contrary, it should be said that the sacrifice of the child and the separation of husband and wife were used as the means of depicting the destiny of the samurai under feudal vassalage—the samurai who bears up even under the grief of the death of his own son.

Genzô, when he is about to kill the substitute for Kan Shûsai, tells his wife, "It is truly terrible to be in vassalage!" This is the theme of this play. Then, as the curtain is drawn, there is a poetic narration, in seven-five meter, in consolation for the death of the child:

Meido no tabi e	To journey to the shades
Terairi no,	The child entered the school.
Shishô wa Midabutsu	The teacher was Amida Buddha,
Shakamunibutsu.	Sâkyamuni Buddha.
Rokudônôge no	The boy became Jizô's disciple,
Deshi to nari,	To be protected in Hades,
Sai no Kawara de	And now learns how to write
Sunadehon.	On the sands of the Children's Limbo.
Iroha kaku ko wa	But the child who practiced the alphabet
Aenakumo	Unfortunately
Chirinuru inochi	Lost his life,
Zehimonaya!	Would he or not.

Further, let us examine *Kumagai Jinya*, one part of *Ichinotani Futaba Gunki*.

The hero, Kumagai Naozane, appears in *The Tale of the Heike*, and this play is set against the background of the Gempei wars. Kumagai is a person who actually existed, and there are also Noh songs (*utai*) that tell of him. By comparing the treatment of him in Noh and in Tokugawa-period works, we may obtain a good idea of how the same historical incident has been dramatized at different times and in different forms of Japanese theater.

The original *Tale of the Heike* has the following. The Heike have been defeated at the battle of Ichinotani and escape by sea. One young warrior, however, was late in escaping. Kumagai Naozane, a commander of the Genji forces, starts to chase him. The young warrior bravely returns to the shore and stands ready to face Kumagai in battle, only to be held down by him. When Kumagai sees that the warrior is a young man of high birth and about the same age, sixteen or seventeen, as his own son, Kojirô, he hesitates to kill him. As a father himself, he cannot bear to see this young man's father bereaved. However, since he is surrounded by his own men, he must cut the young man down. Kumagai, in tears, kills him. From the armor of the slain man, a flute (famous enough to have been accorded a name, the Green-Leaf Flute) falls out. Remembering the sound of a flute that came from the enemy's camp the night before, Kumagai feels deep sympathy for the refined character of the man he has killed. The young warrior is identified as the nobleman Atsumori, son of Taira no Tsunemori. Kumagai, realizing the meaninglessness of the life of a warrior who is obliged to kill even such a fine young man, renounces the world and spends the rest of his days as a priest, offering solace to the spirit of Atsumori. Thus the evil and tragedy of war, as well as the Buddhist concept of the transience of life, is presented in this story.

Zeami adapted this in a Noh play, *Atsumori*. In his version, Kumagai visits the old battlefield, a long time after the battle, as a monk. Accompanied by the music of a flute, a man dressed as a grasscutter arrives on the scene and, taking on the appearance of Atsumori, tells Kumagai of his suffering in the shades. He then dances to a narration of the battle. By the power of Kumagai's prayers, Atsumori finally enters nirvana. This is a masterpiece of Noh in which the elegance of the flute music is used as the motif in describing the grief of a man.

But the *jôruri* version of the same story is entirely different. In *Ichinotani Futaba Gunki* there is a beheading in one scene. However, it is not Atsumori who is slain, but Kumagai's son, Kojirô. The reason why Kumagai was required to kill his own son was that it was ordered by his master, Minamoto no Yoshitsune. Before the battle, Yoshitsune had ordered that a captured enemy commander, if a blood relative of the emperor, was not to be killed and that if the necessity arose, one should even sacrifice one's own relatives to save such a person's life.

Unfortunately Kumagai was the one who had to assume the task of killing Atsumori, but in the *jôruri* version Atsumori is assumed to be an unofficial son of the retired emperor, Goshirakawa. Kumagai therefore substituted his own son for Atsumori, who had been injured in battle. This marks the end of Kumagai's tragedy. Rather than losing his child, Kumagai had to kill him, with his son's understanding, in order to obey his master. I call this a "tragedy of implicit understanding."

The *Jinya* scene comes next. Everyone, including the audience, thinks that Atsumori has met his doom at the hands of Kumagai. Atsumori's mother, seeking revenge, approaches Kumagai with a sword. He calls on her to desist and begins to recount the battle, before his wife and Atsumori's mother. Then he shows the head of the person he has killed to Yoshitsune, who immediately understands all that has happened. But the two women are shocked, and it is Kumagai's wife, rather than Atsumori's mother, who has lost a loved one. Kumagai calls on his wife, who has broken into tears, to stop. He cuts off his topknot, symbol of a warrior, and dons a black robe, becoming a monk. Then he leaves on a journey that is meant to assuage the spirit of his slain son.

No further explanation is needed. The Noh playwrights created numerous works emphasizing the tragedies and the sense of transience in men confronted by the terrors of battle, accompanied by the elegant strain of the flute. They described in their plays the general cultural spirit of the pre-Tokugawa period.

Bunraku playwrights instead placed heavy emphasis on the tender feeling of parents for their children, which is also to be found in the original textual sources. An outstanding result of this emphasis is the *Kumagai Jinya* scene in *Ichinotani Futaba Gunki*. Kumagai is depicted far less as a man following his master's orders in joining the battle, or a warrior with feudal obligations, than as a father, and his wife is depicted as a mother rather than as the wife of a warrior. The climax is then made the parting of the man and his wife, and the play is, more than anything else, a story of the tragedy afflicting a family.

Even though the plays utilize actual historical incidents and feature historical heroes in the chief roles, at the climax a hero becomes nothing more than an ordinary father, having, like anyone, the emotional makeup of a parent. In this, the fact that Kabuki and Bunraku are popular forms of drama at their core is evident. Thus, even though we may speak of *jidaimono* plays as "historical drama," they are really family tragedies, with scenes such as the parting of grief-stricken parents from their children at the heart of the action.

When the fundamental motivation for this is found to be dependence upon one's lord and master, and it is seen that this relationship was held to span the past, present, and future, to take precedence over the weaker relationship of parent and child, which spanned but one of these periods, the unnatural human relations that were enforced by feudalism stand out in glaring form. The Edo-period masses who went to performances of such tragedies as *Terakoya* and *Kumagai* could feel empathy toward the dramatic characters of family tragedy and shed tears of sympathy for them.

Although *jidaimono* plays such as *Chūshingura, Sembonzakura, Imoseyama, Kokusenya Kassen,* and many others each have their own unique world and a wide variety of tragic events, at their core are such motifs and moods as have been explained above.

Having taken up the stylization, dramatic content, and beauty of Bunraku, with this in mind we may now turn to the history and development of Bunraku, as well as its present condition.

CHAPTER SEVENTEEN

THE HISTORY OF BUNRAKU

An Orderly Development

We have already seen that one of the characteristics of Bunraku is that the puppets may be described as being "superhuman" and "super-puppets," while the plays yet have a reality close to that of plays presented by living actors, and that Bunraku is a puppet theater for adults. In the history and development of Bunraku, also, a pattern similar to that of ordinary stage plays is evident, and the plays are orderly in nature.

The fundamental pattern of development of the drama is the gradual progress from early sacred performances to plays in respect to both content and form. Greek tragedies, for example, began as sacred performances associated with the god having power over agriculture and harvests. The rituals, called *dithyrambos,* were paeans for the virtues of Dionysus, the god of wine, telling of his overcoming difficulties and his rebirth and using a circular stage (orchestra) and *choros* dancers. In the latter half of the sixth century B.C., these performances were transformed by Thespis (c. 534 B.C.) into plays. There was no change in the societal function of making offerings to the gods, but the heroes of the plays (in many cases) were not all gods but, rather, heroic warriors belonging to the aristocracy. In the age of Pericles, this development crystallized in the tragedies of Aeschylus, Sophocles, and Euripides. The embryo of Greek drama had already been formed in the eighth century B.C. in the literature that included histories, poetry, and the works attributed to Homer.

To the sacred performances that originated in simple prayers was added a body of then established literature: epic and lyric poems. And through their coalescence, these different elements were put together to produce a great theatrical genre that in time divested itself of sacred functions and proceeded to acquire the secular characteristics of a form of entertainment and of a form of art: the drama. A similar process may also be seen in the case of Noh, which has as its root origins the primitive Sarugaku and Dengaku, to which were added the contents of *The Tale of Genji, The Tale of the Heike, waka* poetry, and the court diaries. Furthermore, there is also the process of transformation of folk dramas, performed in the rural communities, which were introduced to the cities, where they developed into urban dramatic forms.

It may be said that the pattern of Bunraku's development followed that outlined above. Bunraku began with "sacred dolls" (see below) and was in time elevated to the plane of human drama.

The Three Elements

The three elements fused to form Bunraku—the *jôruri* narration, the samisen music, and the manipulation of puppets—originated and developed independently of one another.

First, it was about the year 1480 that the *jôruri* recitation accompanied by the *biwa* and *ôgi-byôshi*—in the latter the fingers were used to make a sound by striking the ribs of a fan (*ôgi*)—was originated. Then, around 1560, the Japanese-made samisen, a modification of the *jabisen* introduced from Okinawa, came into use to provide the musical accompaniment. Around 1600 the primitive puppet drama was combined with these to form so-called Ningyô Jôruri, or puppet recitation.

Among these three elements, the element of religious performance that corresponds to the circular stage and chorus dedicated to Dionysus, or to the early Sarugaku and Dengaku, was the simple manipulation of puppets by operators called *kairaishi* or *kugutsu-mawashi*.

The Origin and Development of Puppeteering

Puppeteering originated in remote antiquity. There is no doubt that it had developed even before the performing arts of the Sui and T'ang dynasties were introduced from the Chinese continent to Japan (c. A.D. 600). Even today, in rural Japan, there remain several manipulators of old puppets related to primitive folk beliefs. The puppets are simple dolls used to represent gods, or the messengers of gods, who descend to earth to rid it of blights or dangers, or those of the god Ebisu that are used at New Year's and other times and, carried from one house to another, are made to dance while felicitous words are spoken.

As may be supposed from the above, in ancient Japan the use of puppets—manipulated by virgin girls and others in attendance at shrines—served for religious purposes in close link with the gods and folk beliefs, and there was virtually no thought of considering puppeteering as an independent performing art.

But then, in the Asuka-Nara period (seventh and eighth centuries), among the performing arts called Sangaku (the name later came to be pronounced Sarugaku), which, like Gigaku and Bugaku, were introduced to Japan via the Korean peninsula, there appeared a continental form of puppetry that became a popular performing art. A group of puppeteers, *kairaishi,* became naturalized Japanese *en masse.* Although they had settled in Japan, they had no fixed place of residence but traveled about in units of a family or a small troupe, the men putting on puppet shows by day and the women, as prostitutes, accepting callers by night. Accounts of their manner of living are to be found in a late eleventh-century document, *Kairaishi-ki,* or *Kugutsu-mawashi no Ki* (*An Essay on Kairai Puppeteers*), written by Ôe no Masafusa.

As they traveled from place to place, they imparted something of their art to the use of sacred dolls, which had been employed in connection with folk beliefs since ages before, and thus the art was assimilated in many places. In other words, while these puppeteers at first had the social function of presenting sacred performances, they gradually came to secularize their performing arts as a doll theater for amusement.

Since no written record of their performances is extant, we cannot determine just what the content was. Nevertheless, we may assume that there was considerable use of folk tales and tales of marvels as well as accounts of the virtues of the Shinto and Buddhist deities. (Similarly, in the West, as the word marionette—little figure of Mary—signifies, medieval puppet plays dealt mostly with religious tales or marvels.) With the addition of folk songs and popular songs, the puppet plays were welcomed as a form of entertainment by the public in various places in Japan.

In time, this rudimentary form of puppetry acquired, in terms of its content, the form of epic literature known as *jôruri,* and in its transition period—that is, from the Middle Ages through the early part of the Tokugawa period—Noh and Kyôgen were utilized in the preparation of texts. On many occasions command performances were given at the imperial court, and it is recorded that during the years from 1580 to 1600 as many as fifteen performances were held in the presence of the emperor. It was about this time that stringed marionettes (*ayatsuri*) as well as mechanical dolls were devised, and, as indicated in the writing of an aristocrat of the time, performances of plays like *Ichinotani no Kassen* (*The Battle of Ichinotani*) by such puppets were found to be remarkable because of their lifelike action.

Thus the puppet theater, having originated in simple sacred dolls and then fully assimilating techniques introduced from abroad, even while continuing to fulfill its early purpose of presenting sacred performances, with the addition of materials from Noh, Kyôgen, and military epics, as well as mechanical developments, acquired the capability of utilizing any kind of content whatsoever at the turn from pre-Tokugawa to Tokugawa times. Having assimilated such influences, the puppet theater then went on to develop further as a narrative art form—that is, *jôruri.*

Jôruri and the Samisen

The style of narrative recitation known as Heikyoku, or the Heike-*biwa* style of narration, which itself has a long history, is said to have been the precursor of *jôruri.*

The minstrel-like recitation or singing of a story was already very popular by the end of the Heian period (eleventh to twelfth century) as a performing art that was primarily the province of blind itinerant monks. Most popular among the presentations were those that were accompanied by *biwa* or *ôgi-byôshi* and told of the origin of temples and shrines, related Buddhist tales, or transmitted legends. The melody was based upon a method of reciting Buddhist scriptures called *tendai shômyô,* which had been introduced from China around the ninth century.

Later, with the termination of the war between the Minamoto and Taira clans, vivid documentaries of incidents during the war were created in large number. Recounting the defeat of the Taira, as in *The Tale of the Heike,* was perfectly suited to the pathos that the *biwa* could produce, and it struck a responsive chord among the masses. This was how the Heike-*biwa* narratives were created.

Around the beginning of the sixteenth century, however, as the Middle Ages were coming to a close, the Heikyoku performances deteriorated into manneristic repetition, and the desire for a new form of narration arose. It was *jôruri* that appeared in response to this need.

The name *jôruri* was taken from a twelve-part composition for *biwa* performance titled *Jôruri-hime Monogatari* (*The Tale of Princess Jôruri; jôruri* means lapis lazuli, the semiprecious gem). The tale was that of the love of the pure-hearted Princess Jôruri for the young man Ushiwakamaru, who later came to be known as Yoshitsune. The princess was the daughter of a wealthy man who lived in the vicinity of modern-day Nagoya. Actually, she was not an ordinary girl but was born as a result of her father's ardent prayer to an image of the Buddhist deity Yakushi Nyorai. She was thus a divine woman. Ushiwakamaru, who was traveling at that time, was invited to the princess' house, where he spent a passionate night with her, before continuing on his way. After journeying some distance further, he fell ill, and by means of the ministrations of the princess and the power of Buddha he recovered. He thanked the princess for her help and continued on his way.

The tale is one of a simple and naive belief. And the purity of love serves to create a warm, agreeable mood. It conveys the free romantic atmosphere of the Heian court and is in clear contrast with the pessimistic mood of inescapable doom that marked the military epics popular at that time. Thus it made a strong appeal to the people.

The tale of Princess Jôruri became the favorite of generations, and her name entered the language as a common noun, for all the new narrative recitations came to be called *jôruri*. Since there is a record in a travel diary written by a poet named Sôchô, dated 1531, that when he stopped at an inn "a priest sang *jôruri*," we may surmise that the tale had originated some time earlier than that date.

During the Eiroku era (1558–69), a revolutionary event occurred, one that determined the fundamental nature of premodern music, drama, and dance. In the port of Sakai, to the south of Osaka, the snake-skin-covered *jabisen* was introduced from Okinawa. This instrument, lighter than the *biwa* in terms of weight, appearance, and music, became popular among the people at the expense of the *biwa* and *ôgi-byôshi*, and new narrative songs similar to *jôruri*, performed with the aid of the *jabisen*, spread among the people. However, since snakeskins large enough to cover the body of the instrument were not available in Japan proper, the use of cat skin was adopted. Thus the *jabisen* was "naturalized" as a Japanese musical instrument, the samisen, and there was an accompanying change in the sounds produced.

The first person to use a samisen and recite *jôruri* was Sawazumi Kengyô of Kyoto. That all *gidayû* musicians today have "sawa" or "zawa" as part of their artist's names (such as Toyozawa, Tsuruzawa, Takezawa, and Nozawa) indicates their acknowledgment of their debt to Sawazumi. Although there are some who ascribe this first performance to another man, Takino Kôtô, in either case both were blind monks who had been reciters in the Heike-*biwa* tradition.

It was the disciples of these pioneers who amalgamated the samisen music, *jôruri* narrative, and puppetry. Sawazumi's disciple, Menukiya Chôzaburô, joined a puppeteer from Awaji Island, and Takino's disciple, Kemmotsu, worked with a puppeteer named Jirobei from Nishinomiya, on the shore of the Inland Sea. On Awaji Island, in the Inland Sea, and in Nishinomiya the tradition of the early puppet theater is still alive in the regions that were its cradle.

By this means, sacred performances, narrative literature, and music were combined into one. But what further deserves mention here is that Chôzaburô was also a master of the craft of making hilt ornaments for swords and, unlike the aforementioned blind monks, was an ordinary townsman. That is, by now it was already the townsmen who controlled the dominant dramatic form of the times rather than the aristocrats, who had controlled performances in the preceding period. Further, this is a sign that the puppet theater had left its tales of marvels and enactments of Buddhist myths behind and had developed to the level of humanity, treating everyday life in a realistic manner.

That is to say, the theatrical form known as Ningyô Jôruri had been created by the townsmen. It was only ten years before the time when Okuni danced on the Kyoto river banks to begin what developed into Kabuki. This was about the same time that public performances of

Shakespeare's plays were being presented on the banks of the Thames on the other side of the world.

The Age of Old Jôruri

Soon after the puppet plays became popular in the Kansai district, they were introduced to the newer, vigorously growing city of Edo. The success attained in Edo was due to the popularity of two men, Satsuma Jôun and Sugiyama Tangonojô.

Jôun was a great narrator, and his style matched the brusque, frontier-town character of the audiences he found in Edo. His disciple, Sakurai Tambanojô (or Izumi-dayû), also attained popularity as the creator of the *kimpira-bushi* style. There are such legends as *The Subjugation of Devils in the Ôe Mountains* and *Kintoki's Wrestling with a Bear*. The hero is called Sakata no Kintoki (or Kintarô). The author of *kimpira-bushi* invented a man of superhuman power, Kimpira, and called him the son of the above Sakata no Kintoki.

The famous Edo actor who created the Kabuki *aragoto* style, Ichikawa Danjûrô I, is said to have gotten a hint from *kimpira-bushi* in his making *aragoto* stand for superhuman powers—such was the popularity and influence of *kimpira-bushi*.

On the other hand, it was a more gentle style that became the area of interest of Sugiyama Tangonojô, who created many works accordingly. The *katô-bushi* piece included in performances of *Sukeroku* even today is the creation of Masumi Katô, a disciple of Sugiyama.

In 1657 a great conflagration laid waste to Edo, and among the many buildings that burned to the ground were the theaters. Performers, except those of the *kimpira-bushi* and some other styles, had no choice but to turn their backs on the ashes of Edo and head for the Kansai district to continue working. After a while, among the Kansai performers, two masters appeared: Inoue Harimanojô and Uji Kaganojô. Then a disciple of Harimanojô whose name also figures prominently in the history of Bunraku came to the fore. He was Takemoto Gidayû (1651–1714).

Harimanojô's style was vigorous and colorful and not quite in keeping with the refined, graceful style that had become the standard in

Kyoto over the centuries when it was the capital. In contrast, the style of Kaganojô was that of Kansai. Kaganojô had first studied the Noh narrative (Yôkyoku), but, finding that the art was monopolized by certain outstanding schools, he changed to *jôruri*. He used his background to add elements of the Noh and Kyôgen to the style of *harima-bushi* in forging his own somewhat melancholic style of beauty.

Development and Decline of Gidayû Jôruri

Takemoto Gidayû had been a farmer in Osaka, but his voice was so excellent that he became a disciple of Kiyomizu Rihei, who had been a disciple of Harimanojô, and thereupon he took the name Ridayû. He created his own style by adopting that of Harimanojô, adding to it something of Kaganojô as well as influences of the *sekkyô-bushi* and new songs that were popular at the time. He became adept enough to rival Kaganojô and eventually surpassed him. After this artistic triumph, he moved to Osaka, opened the Takemotoza theater in the Dôtombori section, and changed his name to Takemoto Gidayû.

Prior to this, Chikamatsu Monzaemon had already established his own reputation by writing *jôruri* for Kaganojô and Kabuki pieces for Sakata Tôjûrô. Takemoto Gidayû invited Chikamatsu to become the Takemotoza's star writer. The time was 1685, a year after the Takemotoza was opened. The first work by Chikamatsu for his new employer was *Shusse Kagekiyo*. This was a turning point in the history of Bunraku; works before it are termed old *jôruri,* and those created after it are called new *jôruri* or *gidayû jôruri*.

The important question is: Why was *Shusse Kagekiyo* an epoch-making work? The answer is not simply that it was the first joint work of Gidayû and Chikamatsu but also that in terms of form and content it marked the discarding of the Middle Ages style of narration for the distinctively Tokugawa-period style.

The nature of old *jôruri* covering the ninety years from *Jôruri-hime Monogatari* to *Shusse Kagekiyo* may be summarized as follows. Among the subjects, military epics about the heroes of the Gempei wars and stories of Buddhist- and Shinto-related marvels were common. *Jôruri-hime Monogatari* was a love story, but its background, from start to finish, was the superhuman powers of Yakushi Nyorai. There were many works that dealt with marvels and miracles, and as it was a common custom for these plays to be presented on the occasion of temple and shrine festivals, many of them dramatized the event or events that led to the establishment of the religion or of the temple or shrine.

There were, of course, many types and varieties of plays occupied with love stories, family feuds, and human traffic, but all relied heavily on mystic elements, stressed the spectacular, and were filled with action. It may be said that there were hardly any that dealt with the character or psychology of human beings. Even though they were on a human plane and were nearly human dramas, in terms of their subjects and the thought that figured in their creation they were still rooted in the Middle Ages. In terms of their style, they were in either six or twelve parts, were deficient in dramatic content, and were little more than the monotonous presentation of narrative verse.

Just a short while before the appearance of Chikamatsu, new plays were being written in five acts and were thereby closer to having a theatrical composition. Chikamatsu brought the development to perfection, and the basic form of the Tokugawa tragedy was established with the presentation of *Shusse Kagekiyo*.

Shusse Kagekiyo is a *jidaimono* play consisting of five acts. Its most important characteristic is that, instead of presenting a hero out of the legends of old, it depicts the suffering of a rather ordinary man who fell into the dilemma of choosing between his fiancée and a courtesan named Akoya. Being neither a military epic nor an account of a hero of the past, the play, in its emphasis on universal human nature, marks a turning point in the theater.

Moreover, Chikamatsu, with his *Sonezaki Shinjû,* created the first social tragedy of Tokugawa theater. In *Kokusenya Kassen* he presented the character of Kinshôjô, a woman who sacrificed herself because of her master and her obligations to others, and thereby established a central concept of *jidaimono* plays. But an even greater achievement of Chikamatsu was his most realistic handling of human character and psychology, his distinct expression of the complications arising from the confrontation of reason and emotions, and his embodiment of these in lyrical, poetic compositions.

Thus, through the work of Chikamatsu and Gidayû, the puppet theater was made into a truly popular theater that reflected Tokugawa society in its form as well as in its content.

In 1703, when *Sonezaki Shinjū* was first presented, Gidayū's disciple Takemoto Uneme left the Takemotoza and established the Toyotakeza, adopting the name Toyotake Wakadayū. The two theaters then entered a period of rivalry during which many masterpieces were presented.

Then, just ten years after Chikamatsu's death, in 1724, the master puppeteer Yoshida Bunzaburō (?–1760) perfected the system of using three men to manipulate a single puppet. Not only was he outstanding as a puppeteer, but he was also gifted with the ability to make such innovations as this and was at the same time a great producer. For the next two decades, Bunraku was so popular that Kabuki, in comparison, seemed not to exist. It was the golden age of Bunraku, during which Kabuki was obscured in the shadow of the puppet theater. The method of using three men to handle a puppet, as has been explained, was adopted about the time that the puppets came to have powers of expression resembling those of actual people. Also, the dramatic content of the plays was becoming more and more realistic. That is, the lyrical description of scenery, which had figured prominently in the works of Chikamatsu, was remarkably reduced, while the portions of the dialogue were increased. The reason was that it had become possible for the puppets to be used to present plays just like those presented by actors. It was at this juncture in Bunraku's history that the three masterpieces, *Sugawara Denju Tenarai Kagami* (1746), *Yoshitsune Sembonzakura* (1747), and *Kanadehon Chūshingura* (1748), were created.

These plays represented the combined efforts of Takeda Izumo (1691–1756), Namiki Sōsuke (also known as Senryū; 1695–1751), and Miyoshi Shōraku (1696–1775). Joint composition had become common after the latter days of Chikamatsu's career. Among these three writers, it seems that the most powerful was Namiki Sōsuke. Prior to those three plays, he wrote a stirring drama of a midsummer murder, in *Natsu Matsuri Naniwa Kagami*. In this play, Yoshida Bunzaburō attired the leading character, a fishmonger named Danshichi Kurobei, in a close-fitting summer kimono and used real water and mud to reconstruct the murder scene on stage, thereby achieving a truly realistic production. Up until then, even for summertime settings the puppets were dressed in heavy kimonos. The play is considered to be of signal importance as the source of the realistic *kizewamono* type of Kabuki plays that later (in the nineteenth century) became the rage of Edo. *Chūshingura* and the other two plays noted above, in which Namiki's realism and Yoshida's skills as a producer were combined, are still frequently performed, as both Bunraku and Kabuki plays.

This age marked the apogee in Bunraku's history. In 1751 Namiki wrote *Kumagai Jinya*, but it proved to be his last work, as he died before the year was out. His passing symbolized the decline of Bunraku itself. Meanwhile, Kabuki was assimilating and adapting Bunraku plays, making them more powerful and thereby rising in popularity. When Bunzaburô introduced the three-man system, Bunraku attained its peak with regard to realism and rose no higher. And at the moment when Bunraku went beyond the limitations of the puppet theater to become a creation unique in all the world and an equal to the theater of human action, it came to lose in popularity to the attraction of real actors and their individual talents.

The death of Namiki marks the transition from the golden age of Bunraku to the revival of Kabuki. Two years after Namiki died, his disciple, Namiki Shôzô, gave up writing for puppets and turned his attention to writing Kabuki plays. He brought with him to his work in Kabuki drama his talent in writing and in the production of puppet plays. He succeeded in enlarging the field occupied by *gidayû kyôgen* plays (also called *maruhon* plays: Kabuki plays using *gidayû* narration and taken over from Bunraku, of which *Chûshingura* was the first) and securing their position in Kabuki. He is also to be remembered as the person who created the revolving stage.

Bunraku declined rapidly. Although Chikamatsu Hanji (1725–83) wrote outstanding plays, including *Honchô Nijûshikô*, *Moritsuna Jinya*, and *Imoseyama*, this turned out to be a last stand, and the plays failed to win popular acclaim. In 1764 the Toyotakeza and in 1772 the Takemotoza were forced to close their doors for the last time because of lack of interest in the puppets' performances. It had been but eighty-seven years since *Shusse Kagekiyo*.

After that, several smaller puppet theaters were built, but all failed. Plays such as *Hadesugata Onna Maiginu* and *Igagoe Dôchû Sugoroku* (*The Vendetta at Iga*) were written and presented, but they were not up to the standards of old, and after *Ehon Taikôki* (1799) no new works were written.

Six years later, in 1805, the small theater of Uemura Bunrakuken, whose name is the source of the word Bunraku used today, was opened. By this time Bunraku had ceased to produce new works and had fallen back on reviving the old plays. In other words, it became a conservative theater, devoted to preserving its past.

Present Conditions of the Bunrakuza

The only theater devoted exclusively to Bunraku performances since the Meiji era and through the present is the Bunrakuza, more recently renamed the Asahiza, in Osaka. During the Meiji period, *Tsubosaka Reigenki* (*The Miracle at the Tsubosaka Temple*), a new play, was written and performed, and since the end of World War II, Bunraku versions of *Hamlet* and *Madame Butterfly* have been staged. But these have not brought about any change in Bunraku or had much influence on it.

For a while after the war Bunraku was split into two factions, and there was even fear that it would disappear. In 1963, however, these two factions united, and management of the Bunrakuza was taken away from the Shôchiku Company, a motion picture and entertainment company that had emerged in the theater world after Meiji times. After this, through the cooperation of the Japanese government, the Osaka prefectural government, and the Japan Broadcasting Corporation, the Bunraku Association was established and entrusted with the management of the theater and the troupe.

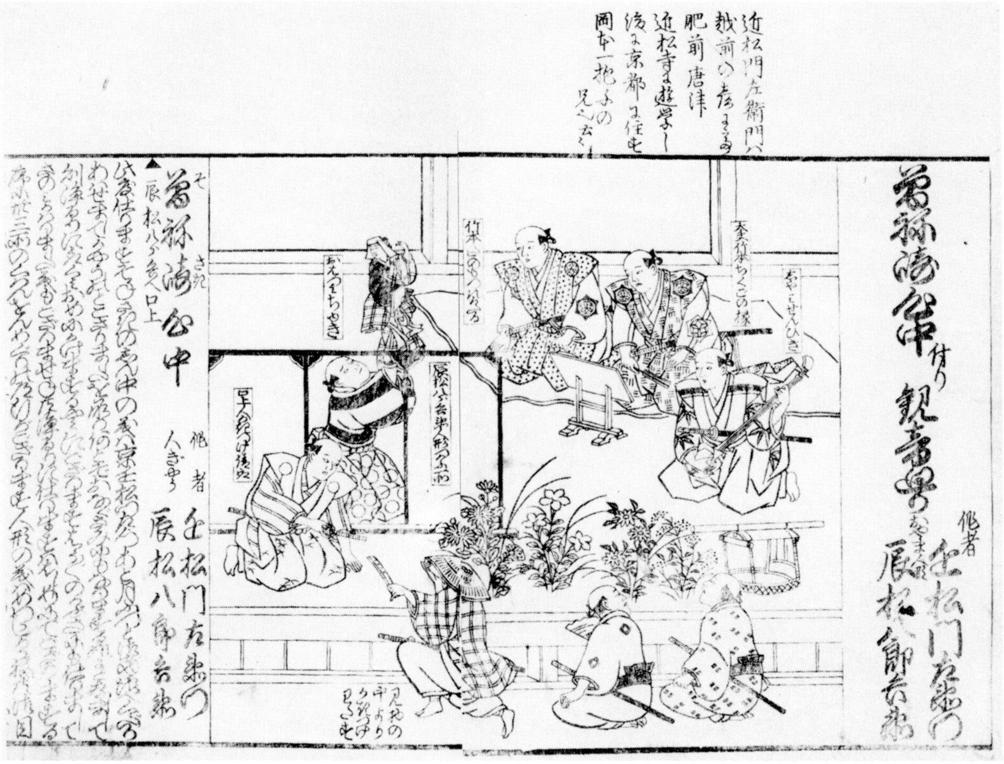

Pages from text of Chikamatsu's *Sonezaki Shinjū*, 1703.

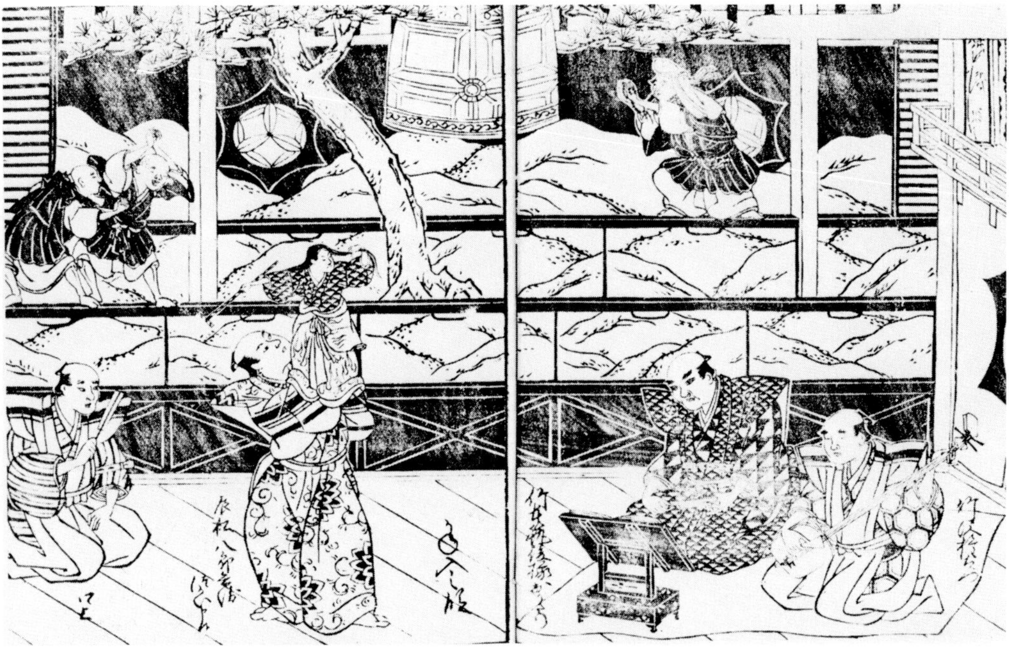

Pre-Bunraku puppet performance. Illustration from *Konjaku Ayatsuri Nendaiki,* a record of old and new puppet plays, 1727.

Scene from *Ichinotani Futaba Gunki*, Kabuki version.

Scene from *Ichinotani Futaba Gunki*, Bunraku version.

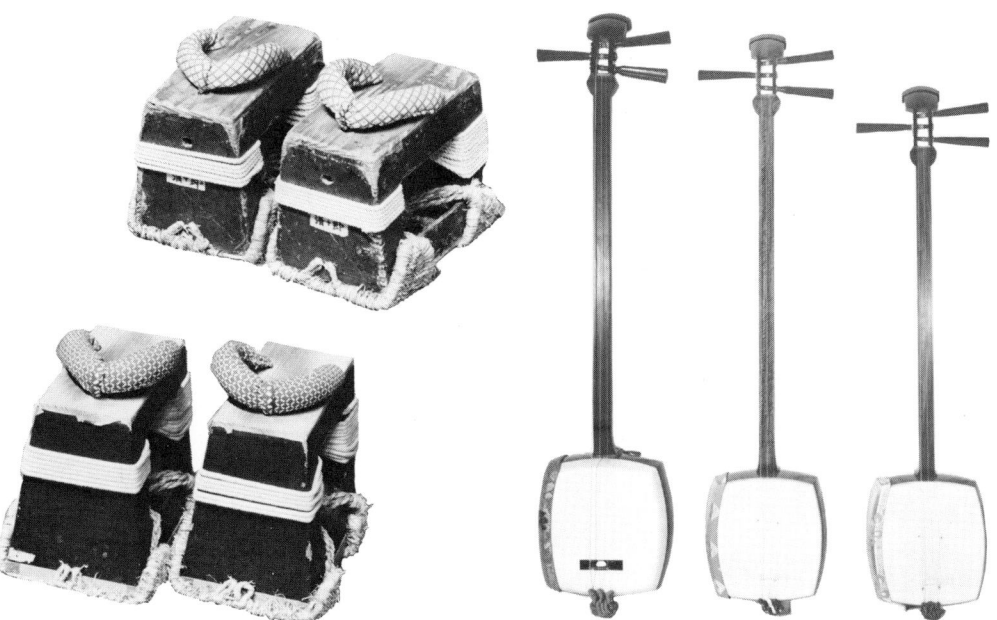

Footgear for puppeteers.

Gidayû samisen (left) compared with other types of *samisen*.

Funazoko and puppeteers.

Heads of Bunraku puppets.

Michiyuki from Bunraku version of *Yoshitsune Sembonzakura.*

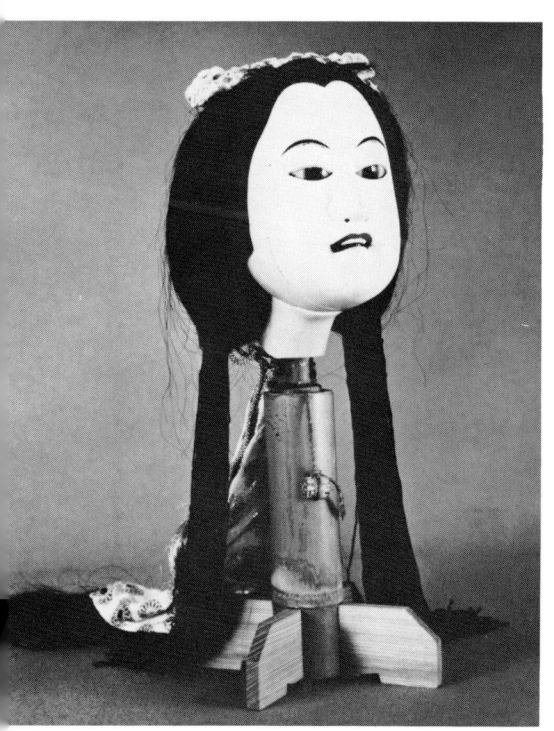 

Bunraku puppet with mouth closed and mouth open.

Instruments for *geza* music of Kabuki.

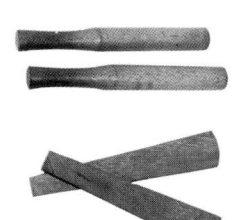
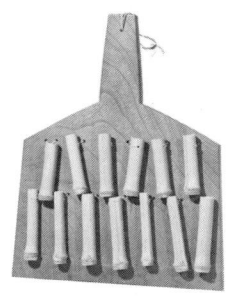
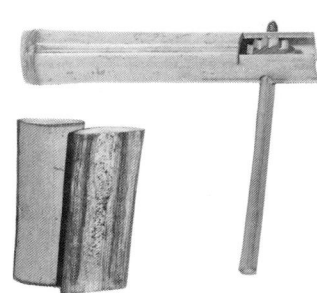

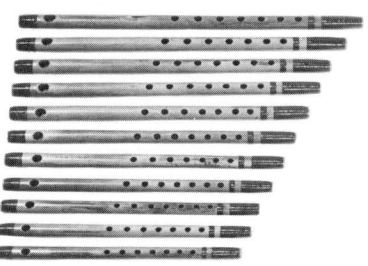
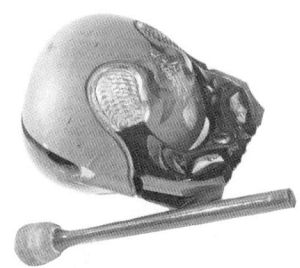
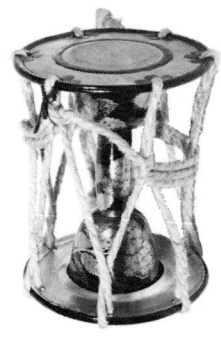

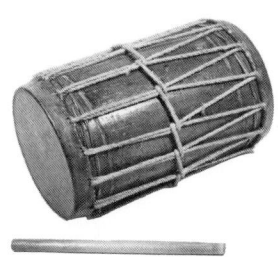

Double *hanamichi* in *Iro Moyô Chotto Karimame* (commonly called *Kasane*).

Seriage of *kozeri* type (lift for actors) in *Suma no Utsushie*.

◀ *Seriage* of *ôzeri* type (great lift; two views) in *Nansô Satomi Hakkenden*.

Tombogaeri somersault in *Rampei Monogurui* act of *Yamatogana Ariwara Keizu*.

Mie pose in *Kotobuki Soga no Taimen*.

Mie pose of Narukami Shônin in *Narukami Fudô Kitayamazakura*.

Mie pose of Benkei in *Kanjinchô*.

Mie pose in *Kusazuribiki*.

Mie pose in *Omatsuri*.

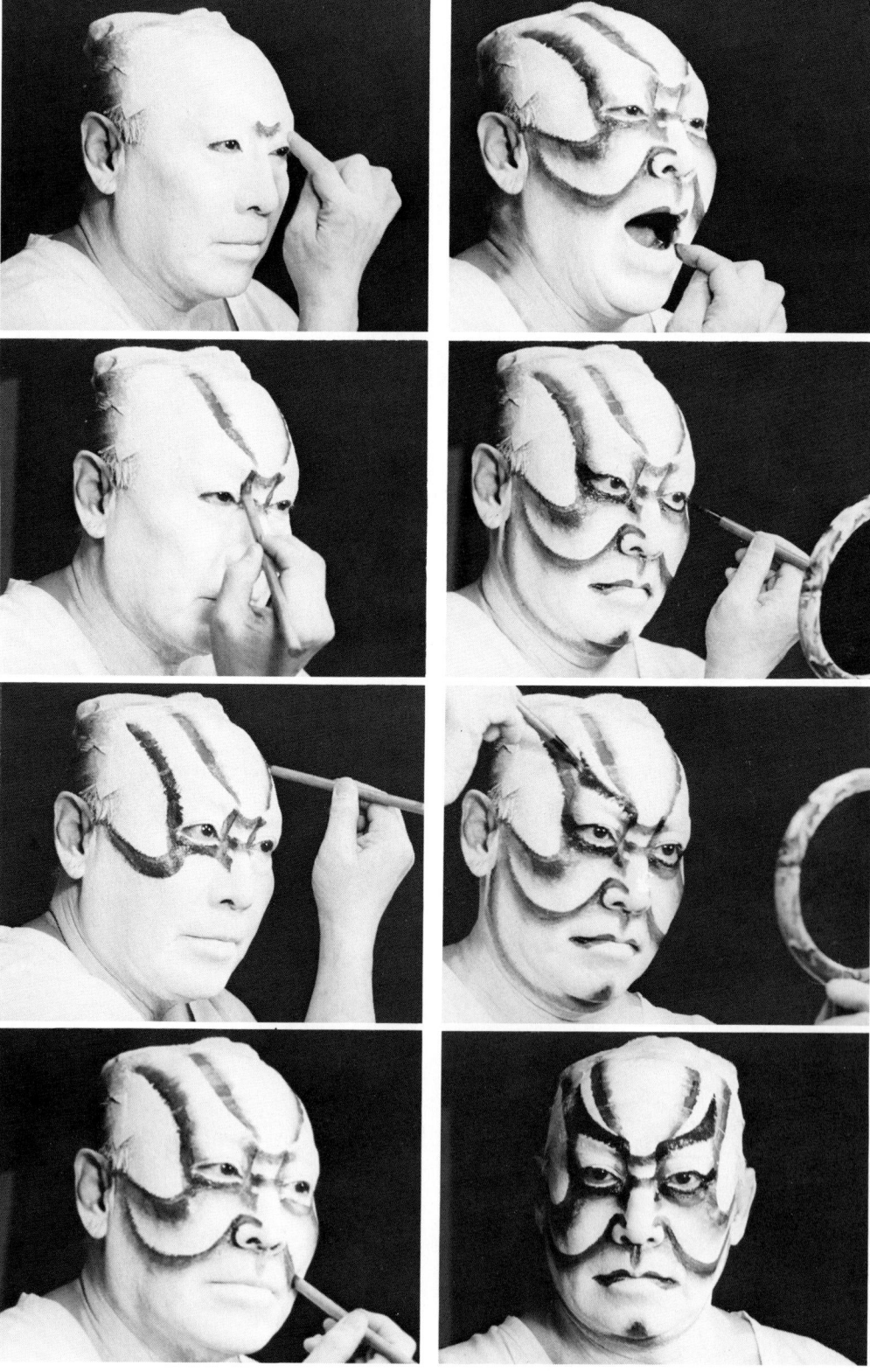

Finished makeup of Kamakura Gongorô in *Shibaraku*.

Process of *kumadori* makeup.

Aragoto in *Sukeroku*.

Aragoto in *Kanjinchô*.

Jidaimono: scene from *Terakoya* act of *Sugawara Denju Tenarai Kagami*.

Jidaimono: scene from third act of *Kanadehon Chûshingura*.

Jidaimono: scene from *Daimotsu no Ura* act of *Yoshitsune Sembonzakura* showing Tomomori and the anchor.

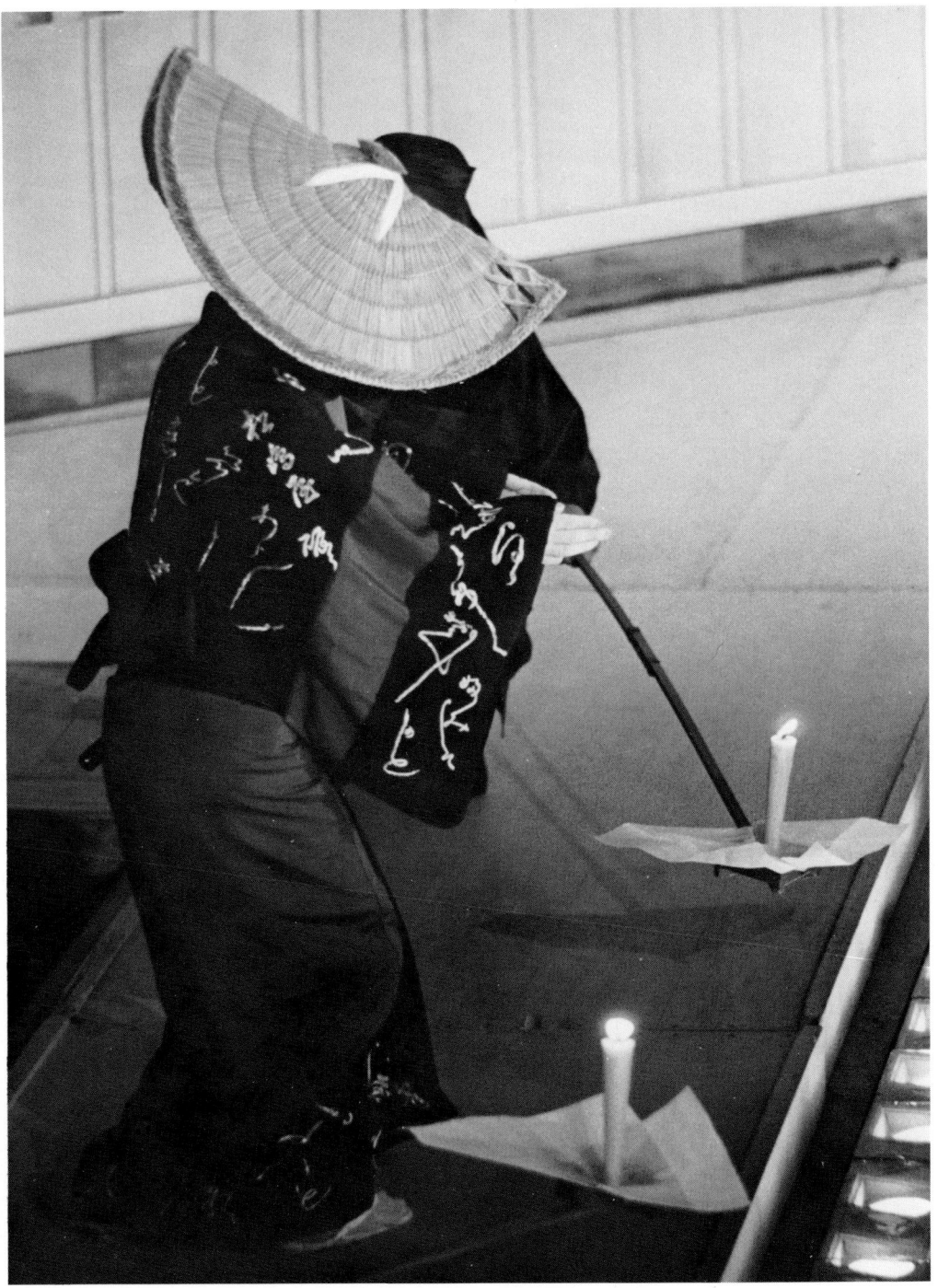

Wagoto in *Kuruwa Bunshô*.

◀ *Wagoto* in *Kawashô* act of *Shinjû Ten no Amijima*.

The poisoned Oiwa in *Tôkaidô Yotsuya Kaidan*.

Yusuriba in *Hamamatsuya no Ba* act of *Benten Kozô* (*Aotozôshi Hana no Nishikie*).

Scene from Ôkawabata act of *Sannin Kichiza Tomoe no Shiranami*.

Kabuki dance: *Renjishi*.

Kabuki dance: *Kyôganoko Musume Dôjôji*.

Kabuki dance: *Tsumoru Koi Yuki no Seki no To*.

Kabuki dance: *Kagamijishi*.

Kabuki dance: *Sagi Musume*.

CHAPTER EIGHTEEN

THE STYLE AND BEAUTY OF KABUKI

An Introductory Note

As has been noted earlier, Kabuki and Bunraku are sister arts. Both were born of, and nurtured by, the general populace, particularly the townsfolk, of the Edo period and accordingly have a number of characteristics in common.

Earlier in the book the mutual influences between Kabuki and Bunraku were taken up, and, in particular concerning the *jôruri* works that are an important genre within Kabuki, relationships with respect to dramaturgy, subjects, society of the times, and ethos were presented in detail.

Therefore in the present chapter only a few passages will be spared for these matters to the extent that they may be placed in proper perspective within Kabuki, and matters specifically proper to the latter will be presented. These points do not follow an orderly course of historical development as is true for Bunraku, however, and contain extremely complex factors. The primary reason for this is undoubtedly that for Kabuki the essence of its very being lay in the actors and in the sensual appeal of their art. For example, the oppression by the *bakufu* government, the complicated distortions, the accommodations, and the greatly entangled development, as well as the result of all this, summarily defined as a perplexing diversification of form and content, as will be explained in the section on history, all have as their cause Kabuki's being drama wherein actors are foremost.

Here I would like to begin by looking at a certain many-faceted style of expression of Kabuki today and identify the locus of beauty therein. Later I will show how Kabuki grew and developed in response to the desires of Kabuki enthusiasts over a long span of time. In other words, I will consider the history of Kabuki.

The Stage and the Theater

The Essential Nature of the Theater First of all, let us take up the Kabuki stage and theater. As will be noted later, these began as an imitation of those of the Noh, developed and changed through several stages in accordance with the evolution of the form and content of the plays, and, at the end of the eighteenth century, left the influence of the Noh precedents behind and attained their own form and construction.

The most outstanding characteristics of the stage are the *hanamichi* (literally, flower road or flower runway) and the revolving stage proper.

The *hanamichi* passes between the audience's seats (modern theaters all have chairs; originally the audience sat on a tatami-mat floor) on the left side of the theater. This runway extends from the rear of the theater onto the stage and is made of wooden boards. Ordinarily it is the only one used, but for some plays a somewhat narrower *hanamichi* on the right side of the theater is also used. The *hanamichi* on the left, which is a fixture in Kabuki theaters, is called the main *hanamichi* (*hon hanamichi*) and is 1.7 meters wide as compared with the 1.0-meter-wide temporary *hanamichi* (*kari hanamichi*) on the right.

The *hanamichi* is said to be so named because originally it was a passageway for presenting *hana* to the actors. Actually the word *hana* referred not to flowers (*hana*) but was a homonym for the gifts the patrons bestowed upon their favorite actors. Long ago, it was the custom for a representative of the common folk in the theater to stand in the wooden aisle that separated the tatami-mat "boxes," in the middle of the audience seats, and proffer a gift to the actor. The actor would descend from the stage to accept it and pay his respects by way of thanking the donor. The central aisle was called "footpath" (*ayumimichi*), but it later came to be used by the actors for their entrance to and exit from the stage. Moreover, we may look upon the development of the left and right *hanamichi* from the viewpoint of their being important spaces on which to act.

What is most important is that the *hanamichi* is not merely a passageway for entrances and exits but is also space for performing, which permits the closest relationships and rapport between performers and the audience. Never does the leading actor make his appearance at the extreme end of the *hanamichi* when the curtain is raised and then move briskly on to the stage proper. Without fail, he stops at the point on the *hanamichi* called "seven-three," three-tenths of the distance from the stage. There he turns to face the spectators, perhaps speaks a few lines of his role, and strikes one of the classic *mie* poses of Kabuki—the better to serve the spectators. At this juncture the spectators call out the actor's nickname, and cries such as "Naritaya!" or "Otowaya!" fill the theater. Sometimes they also clap their approval. Thus, by means of the existence and use of the *hanamichi*, any gap separating the stage and those watching the play performed on it is bridged, and empathy linking the spectators and the actors is made possible. This is the essence of Kabuki as a form of popular drama. We may say that completely unlike the aristocratic Noh, and unlike modern realistic Western drama, the essential characteristic of Kabuki, wherein the actor is foremost, is symbolized by the *hanamichi*. (In recent years, a similar construction or technique has often been used in the antirealism movement in the theater, both in Japan and abroad. Two examples are Thornton Wilder's *The Skin of Our Teeth* and *Hair*.)

The *hanamichi* is a standard fixture in Kabuki theaters today. As has been suggested above, all Kabuki plays are written and performed on the basis of the supposition of the presence and use of the *hanamichi*; without the *hanamichi* there would be no Kabuki. Therefore, even on the occasion of Kabuki performances overseas, a *hanamichi* is constructed in the theater.

Concerning the audience seats, in Japan today there are only a very few theaters that still have tatami-mat boxes to the left and right side of the parterre. Other than the Kabukiza and Shimbashi Embujô in Tokyo and the Minamiza in Kyoto, there are hardly any. But even in those theaters, the majority of the playgoers sit in chairs as they would in any theater in the West. This is one manifestation of the changes in life styles in Japan, which have become quite westernized. Originally, Kabuki playgoers sat, four or six people together, on cushions on the tatami-mat floors of square boxes called *masu,* surrounding braziers, and during the performance they would leisurely smoke, drink, and in general enjoy themselves. Moreover, they could send out to the theater's shop for cakes or lunch or charcoal for the brazier, or even go to the shop to have something to eat and drink during the intermission. From this the expression "to enjoy *kabesu*" arose, referring to partaking of *ka* (*kashi* or cakes), *be* (*bentô* or box lunch), and *su* (*sushi* or the popular raw-fish-and-rice combination).

Thus the Kabuki theater differs from today's theaters in general by being a place to establish a rapport with the actors and a place to enjoy a party. The Kabuki theater was a place where the townsmen, after diligently working at their job or trade and feeling the weight of the oppression of the *bakufu* officials and the samurai, could, without prejudice concerning sex, social standing, or occupation, enjoy their lives. In addition to the Kabuki theater there were gay quarters represented by the Yoshiwara district in Edo. The *bakufu* officials designated the two as places of vice and brought pressure upon them, in view of the fact that they were the sources of the luxurious mood of the public and, at the same time, the centers of the liberal spirit of the time.

A part of the audience space was replaced by chairs after the influx of westernization in the Meiji era. It was entirely converted into chairs of the present system from 1923, shortly after the Great Earthquake in Tokyo.

The Revolving Stage and Other Details Besides being a device permitting a portion of the stage and sets to be turned, the revolving stage possesses considerable significance in that it facilitates scene changes without closing the curtain and in that it may be used to emphasize the contrast between the earlier and later scenes. For example, in the famous spine-chiller *Yotsuya Kaidan* (*The Ghost Story of Yotsuya*) there is a scene wherein Oiwa, tormented wife of a wicked warrior named Iemon (she appears later as a ghost), meets her death in agony. Iemon's house is ashen-colored and desolate in appearance, and there Oiwa, tortured by poison and bearing a grudge against her husband, dies. At the same time, in the luxurious mansion of a wealthy lord, in sharp contrast to the pathetic death of Oiwa, her husband is wallowing in food and drink in a bright room, making an engagement with his young and beautiful wife-to-be. By use of the revolving stage, the switch is made from the tragedy-filled interior to the gay one, and back, several times, with the curtain open all the while. By the use of the revolving stage, the death of Oiwa and her deep resentment are etched in even sharper relief.

That Germany's Max Reinhardt (1873–1943) and Russia's Vsevolod E. Meyerhold (1874–1942), producers who were forerunners of the antinaturalism movement, were impressed by Kabuki's revolving stage and introduced it into Western theater was a natural outcome. Now there are a number of theaters in the West equipped with revolving stages.

In this way, the existence of the *hanamichi* and the revolving stage made possible the manifestation of theatricalism based on a baroque spirit, while of entirely different origin than the mainstream of drama that had developed since Grecian times in the theater of the West.

Moreover, we can identify, as another important characteristic of Kabuki as a musical drama form, the existence to the left and right of the stage of the musical-effects room and the platform for the narrators and samisen players. To the right of the audience is a slightly elevated dais, called the *chobo yuka* or simply *yuka*, where the *tayū* (narrators of *gidayū*) and samisen players sit. Although it is not true for every single Kabuki play, in those plays adapted from Bunraku, while the actors speak their lines, additional lines, comprising descriptions of the surroundings and of the psychological state of the characters, are spoken by the *tayū* in terms of the third person. For this reason, the dais is required. The text (*maruhon*) placed in front of the *tayū* is dappled with ink spots (in onomatopoeic Japanese expression, they are called *chobo-chobo*), which signify the accents and pitch and give the dais its name.

To the left, long, narrow windows have been cut into the wall. This arrangement is called the *kuromisu*. Beyond the windows is a small room, about four meters square, where we find the musical instruments used in Kabuki. They include large drums, flutes, samisens, small hand drums, gongs, and a variety of other metal percussion instruments. There is even a bell to be rung in the event a fire breaks out. This, the musical-effects room, is called *ohayashi-beya*.

In addition, concerning the construction of the stage, other than the sets, there are several large and small lifts built into the stage proper, and on the *hanamichi* there is a small lift, the *suppon*. For plays featuring dancing, a temporary dais for samisen accompanists and the narrators (called *hinadan* or *yamadai*) may be constructed. There are also complicated devices for spectacular uses, such as the revolving cart, on which an actor may ride, which is used on such occasions as when the appearance of a spirit is required.

Just by considering the complexity of its stage construction, the extent to which Kabuki differs from Noh may be understood. While Kabuki is firmly rooted in reality, this reality is not the same as that of modern Western drama and represents a quality that is Kabuki's very own.

Another difference from Noh is the presence of the curtain. Today, in plays featuring dancing or contemporary Kabuki plays, a Western-style curtain (*donchô*), which is raised, is used. But in the Edo period the *hikimaku* type of curtain, which was opened by drawing it from left to right, was used in large theaters such as the Nakamuraza, Ichimuraza, and Moritaza in Edo. It had alternating vertical stripes of black, dark green, and red-brown, three colors still connected with Kabuki and often used in program covers and other applications. This curtain is called *jôshikimaku* and is still used when classic Kabuki plays are presented. It is drawn aside while the wooden *hyôshigi* (clappers) are sounded. Formerly curtains were used only in the low-class theaters other than the officially permitted ones. Accordingly, the term *donchô* theater or *donchô* actors had some pejorative nuances.

Actors and Their Art

Their Low Social Status and Popularity The importance of actors is particularly great in Kabuki. The etymology of the Japanese word for performer, *yakusha,* indicates those who play some roles in the festivals dedicated to Shinto or Buddhist deities. Then gradually the persons performing dances and plays in festivals came to be called *yakusha,* and in time the word became synonymous with "actor."

Kabuki actors, for historical reasons that will be explained below, were called *kawaramono* or *kawarakojiki* (riverbed people or beggars) and, during the Edo period, were at the very bottom of the social stratification made up principally of warriors, farmers, craftsmen, and merchants. However, in actuality, the Edo masses liked and appreciated these people, who originated many of the fads that were popular among the masses. They corresponded to the television and motion-picture stars of today and were the sources of popular fashion and trends, even in manners and customs, language, and the like.

Among Kabuki actors today, there is one type that knows no parallel elsewhere: the female impersonator, called *onnagata* or *oyama*. Although they are men, they act beautifully and are even more womanlike than women on stage. In the current of modernization, Japanese women, like those of many other countries, have become westernized in manner and dress, and it can therefore be said that the *onnagata* are the ideal models of traditional Japanese femininity. The *onnagata* stars like Nakamura Utaemon, Onoe Baikô, Nakamura Shikan, Nakamura Senjaku, Nakamura Jakuemon, Ichikawa Monnosuke, Kataoka Gadô, and Onoe Kikunosuke may be called the most symbolic figures of today's Kabuki theater.

At present, however, some *onnagata*, like Baikô, Kikunosuke, and Senjaku, occasionally take male roles. On the other hand there are actors like Nakamura Kanzaburô and Ichikawa Ennosuke who, although they primarily take male roles, also sometimes appear as women. But in the past *onnagata* played exclusively the roles of women. For the other types of roles, such as the good Samaritan, the villain, or the fool, there were actors who specialized in those roles. This system of specialization was also to be seen in the Italian commedia dell'arte, which may be thought to be the successor of the impromptu *mimos* of Greece and Rome, and is common in transitional periods from actor-centric impromptu theater to professional dramatic troupes. With the progress of history, at times actors performed in roles outside their specialties, and this practice has continued through the present day.

While Kabuki has many types of roles, it is at least important to consider the three basic styles of Kabuki acting, established about the time of the Genroku era (1688–1703), namely, *aragoto*, *wagoto*, and *onnagata gei*.

Aragoto   *Aragoto* is a style of acting that is considered to have been devised by Ichikawa Danjûrô I in Edo. As has been mentioned before, he conceived of this style under the influence of the *kimpira-bushi* of old *jôruri*. In a word, *aragoto* is sparkling and simple, and its gallant and heroic movements, which always bring on thunderous applause, may be said to reflect the spirit of the Edo townsmen.

Aragoto, which literally means "rough stuff," is just that. The hero of

Shibaraku, which is included in Kabuki's Eighteen Favorites as one of the plays most representative of Danjûrô's art, furnishes a typical example of *aragoto*. The scene is in front of a shrine facing a vermilion *torii* gate at the rear center of the stage. An evil minister who aspires to overthrow the emperor has captured several innocent subjects and is about to have them executed by his retainers. The evil minister's face has been painted white, and lines have been drawn around his eyes and across his cheeks in dark-blue makeup. At one glance he may be identified as the villain. When a sword is about to be brought down on the victims' necks by one of the retainers, a cry of "Wait!" (*shibaraku*) is heard from the other side of the curtain at the end of the *hanamichi*. The voice must reverberate and still have plenty of reserve. This is the primary requirement of *aragoto*. Upon hearing the voice, the retainers become tense with anxiety. Who has spoken? The sword does not fall. An imposing actor appears on the *hanamichi,* shouting "Wait! Wait!" He is the hero of the play.

On the basic white pigment that covers his face have been painted bold red lines around his eyes and on his cheeks. This makeup indicates the great indignation of this honest hero toward the deeds of the villain; it is a theatrical representation of a man's veins standing out as anger wells up within. Called *kumadori,* it is often seen in woodblock prints and photographs and is inseparably linked with and representative of Kabuki. *Kumadori,* not realistic but representing great strength and superhuman power, is a major characteristic of *aragoto.*

The hero stops at the seven-three point on the *hanamichi,* and in a loud voice, drawing out his words, he speaks his lines, introducing himself. In the past, there was a small platform (*nanoridai*) extending from the *hanamichi* toward the center of the audience where actors would stand when introducing themselves (*tsurane*). This presentation of the role by the actor pleases the audiences. He must deliver his lines in a sonorous voice.

Then the hero moves to the stage proper, there to relentlessly mete out punishment to the villain minister, rescue the captives, and display a number of poses called *mie.* These poses make the hero appear all the larger than he actually is. When he finally unsheathes his great sword, he decapitates the wicked retainers at one swoop. But this is not performed in realistic fashion. Instead, the retainers fall to the ground, and a stage assistant, clad in the formal *kamishimo* garments, lets imitation heads tumble across the stage to represent decapitations. Childish, perhaps, but the act has a wholesome, direct quality that lends it interest. The heart of *aragoto* is this surpassing of naturalistic and rationalistic thinking in boldly exaggerated expressions of strength and righteousness.

The hero treats the villain minister disdainfully, holding his sword on his shoulder, and struts down the *hanamichi*. The spectators respond to this demonstration by calling out the actor's name, their voices rising in volume above the clapping of hands.

Such devices and actions as *kumadori*, *mie*, and the sonorous declamation of the actor's role (*tsurane*), which exaggeratedly indicate superhuman powers, constitute *aragoto*.

Ichikawa Danjûrô is said to have taught that "*aragoto* should be performed as if one were a five- or six-year-old child." In *aragoto* one can find the naive greatness of Kabuki as a popular performing art and enjoy its striking brilliance, which is also found in the woodblock prints of ukiyoe.

Wagoto In sharp contrast to the rough *aragoto* style of Edo, *wagoto*, which was created in the Kansai region (Osaka and Kyoto) is characterized by softness and gentleness in actions and gracefulness in mood. In the case of *wagoto*, this gracefulness is not that to be seen in Noh, where the term indicates an extremely refined and reduced expression of abstract beauty. In Kabuki, it is expressed in the realistic acting representing the everyday life and customs of the townsmen.

Sakata Tôjûrô is known as the man who perfected *wagoto*. To briefly describe his technique of *wagoto*, it may be likened to the expression of the emotions of a man in the gay quarters. For example, there is the impoverished young man, Izaemon, who, clad in a kimono offering as much protection as paper against the midwinter cold, paces the gay quarters in the hope of meeting his beloved Yûgiri. Izaemon has been disinherited by his father because of his cavorting in the gay quarters. This play, *Kuruwa Bunshô* (or *Yoshidaya*), is a *sewamono* play of Kabuki (not of Bunraku) written by Chikamatsu in 1712 for the actor Tôjûrô, and although the version we may see today has been somewhat rearranged, it is still an excellent summation of *wagoto*.

Like *Kuruwa Bunshô*, plays featuring *wagoto*, since they originally depicted the customs and passions of the gay quarters, are known as *keiseikai kyôgen*, which signifies a comedy of manners depicting a man visiting a courtesan (*keisei*) in the gay quarters. Among these plays, plots often feature a samurai who, although having had high social status, has left his mansion because of the familial squabbles of his lord and, acting like a townsman, frequents the gay quarters, attempts to trick his enemies, and awaits his chance for a return to his previous status.

In addition to the plays in which *wagoto* technique is utilized, the same style may be seen in many plays taken from Bunraku, as in the role of Tokubei in *Sonezaki Shinjū*, that of Chūbei in *Meido no Hikyaku*, and that of Jihei in *Shinjū Ten no Amijima*. All are works that were created in the Kansai region, and even today actors from that region, such as Nakamura Ganjirô and Nakamura Senjaku (father and son), Kataoka Nizaemon, and Jitsukawa Enjaku are considered to be among the best actors of *wagoto,* but even such Tokyo actors as Nakamura Kanzaburô, Ichikawa Ennosuke, and Morita Kanya also perform in *wagoto* style.

The following two remarks are to be cited from the book written by Tôjûrô, *Yakusha Rongo* (*The Actors' Analects*). He said, "On opening day, forget about the lines and get out on the stage." This was his reply when an actor asked why Tôjûrô's performance sounded on the first day as if it were the tenth day. In other words, if an actor has not memorized the lines correctly, he will be so much occupied in recollecting them the first day that he may falter and become unnatural. Accordingly, the lines must be perfectly mastered during rehearsals, so that on opening day, when one hears another actor deliver his lines and the cue, the answer just comes naturally.

Second, Tôjûrô said, "Forgetful of the audience, act the play [*kyôgen*] as if it is a reality." Both remarks show how he esteemed highly real and natural acting. These words remind us of the theory revolutionized by Konstantin S. A. Stanislavsky (1863–1938). Although there are many people who consider Kabuki in the patterns of *aragoto* and take it for something actor-centric without meaningful context, only the stylistic forms of which should be appreciated, there are many other elements in it, including those dramas that are to be performed in realistic fashion. One should not forget these factors of Kabuki.

The Art of the Onnagata The art of the *onnagata* developed in the Kansai region just as *wagoto* did. In the case of Noh and Kyôgen and in the West until the close of the Middle Ages, primarily for religious reasons, actresses were barred, and in authorized performances of plays actors took the roles of women. Even at the beginning of the modern age, in Shakespearean drama, for example, boys performed in the roles of women. Thus in olden days it was not a particularly extraordinary thing for actors to take the roles of women.

The special nature of Kabuki's *onnagata*, however, is that the custom had its origin as a performing art for women, who had been freed of religious restrictions and who were subsequently banned for a different reason, after which the roles were taken by actors. Spectators, who had become familiar with and accustomed to the reality and the sensual charms of women performers, had, so to speak, tasted of forbidden fruit. So the Edo spectators, while accepting actors taking women's roles, nonetheless demanded feminine reality of them. Thus there was a necessity for the lifelike charm and beauty that can be seen in the performances of *onnagata*. For this reason, the men who created and perfected the art of the *onnagata* made it a condition that women be presented in that art as if they had stepped out of actual life and onto the stage. This can be verified by passages from the writing of Yoshizawa Ayame (1673–1729), an excellent *onnagata* actor together with Tôjûrô, the master of *wagoto*. In his "Ayamegusa" (a chapter from *Yakusha Rongo*, published in 1776), Yoshizawa writes:

"If an *onnagata* is concealing the fact that he is married and finds people talking about his wife, he should feel like blushing. Otherwise he should not be performing *onnagata* roles and will not make his way in the profession. The *onnagata* should continue to have the feelings of an *onnagata* even when in the dressing room. When taking refreshment, too, he should turn away so that people cannot see him. To be alongside a *tachiyaku* playing the lover's part and chew away at one's food without charm and then go straight out on the stage and play a love scene with the same man will lead to failure on both sides, for the *tachiyaku's* heart will not in reality be ready to fall in love."

The Varieties of Roles There are various other types of roles in Kabuki. Even within the category of the villains, there are the real villain (*jitsuaku*), who is a terrible rogue to the core; the sensual villain (*iroaku*), a kind of Don Juan who is somewhat handsome but malicious in nature; the love-rival villain (*irogataki*), who is a rival of the good-natured lover of a girl; and minor villains (*hagataki*), who play secondary roles as the tools of a real villain. There is also a group of roles called *jitsugoto* that portray not only valorous heroes and their deeds but also men bearing a burden of pathos while still replete with human warmth and reason. Such are the roles of the hero of *Chûshingura,* Yuranosuke; the hero of *Kumagai Jinya,* Kumagai Naozane; the hero of *Terakoya,* Matsuô; and others. Also, while not necessarily related to *wagoto* style, the roles of handsome young men are described as *nimaime* (second-place roles), not in the sense of their being inferior but because they are listed second on Kabuki programs. Roles of fools, being listed third, are called *sammaime* (third-place roles).

What is most important of all is that while most of these roles originated independently of one another, during the process of their development there was mutual interchange, and even while the individuality of each was preserved, gradually they came to be remarkably harmonized for performance together on one stage. For example, this may be seen in the play *Soga no Taimen,* frequently given during the New Year's season. It is historical fact dating from the Kamakura period (1180–1331) that the Soga brothers, Jûrô and Gorô, after perfecting their prowess in martial arts over eighteen years, set out to confront Kudô Suketsune, the man who had killed their father. This tale was familiar to the general populace and has been made into many plays, of which *Soga no Taimen* is one. The brothers go to meet Kudô at his residence in order to identify their enemy. Gorô, a hot-tempered young man, is about to make a bold move but is restrained by Jûrô. At this time, Gorô acts in *aragoto* style and Jûrô in *wagoto* style. Although apparently Kudô assumes the role of their enemy, in reality he is ready to be killed by the brothers once he has completed his official duties. He plays the role of a man of feeling, a *jitsugoto* role. This involved role of *jitsugoto* has been influenced by Bunraku, which gave birth to such tense forms of literary drama, and Kabuki itself is furnished with such many-faceted roles, which make for complicated and diversified plays.

Actors' Lineage and Nicknames In the art of Kabuki there is a strong tendency for vertical transmission from one generation to the next, and therefore the actors often pass their names on from generation to generation. Today the oldest stage names are those of Nakamura

Kanzaburô and Ichimura Uzaemon, now being used by seventeenth-generation actors.

In addition to their legal and stage names, actors have nicknames (*yagô*). For example, Danjûrô is nicknamed Naritaya; Onoe Kikugorô, Baikô, and Shôroku are called Otowaya; Uzaemon is nicknamed Tachibanaya; Utaemon and Senjaku are called Narikomaya; and so on. The reasons actors have nicknames is thought to be as related below. In olden days, only men of warrior class or higher could introduce themselves by giving surnames, and the ordinary citizen used only his given name, although for business purposes he utilized the name of his commercial house, such as *Fujiya* Izaemon or *Mikawaya* Giheiji. At the outset, actors used their surnames, since they were also used in the signs of the theaters. But since this was considered an affront to the warrior class, in the sense of acknowledging that they, the actors, were common folk, they utilized their professional nicknames (*yagô*). Spectators acquired the custom of calling out their nicknames during performances, as an equivalent of the bravos of the West.

Since this tradition of vertical transmission of the art is strongly entrenched, when disciples of famous actors, even if immature, are given good parts, out of commercial motivations, particularly elaborate introductory ceremonies are held to announce the succession to an actor's name by a new actor. In contrast to this, the opportunities for success for a competent actor who is not of good lineage are limited, and many such actors never get further than supporting roles or the legs of the horses (a horse is played by two men in Kabuki). However, since the number of actors who will accept this preordained destiny traditional to Kabuki actors is decreasing year by year, what is now most necessary for Kabuki is to recruit these supporting actors, who are at the very base of Kabuki.

In this respect, it is desired that the National Theater in Tokyo soon initiate activities in the proper direction for the training and development of actors.

Style and Aesthetics

What Is Kabuki's Stylistic Beauty? The style of performance varies according to the program. The *gidayû* plays of Bunraku origin (these plays are also called *maruhon* or *denden* plays, the latter term suggestive of the heavier sound produced by the Bunraku samisen) feature narrative recitations set to music. *Aragoto* plays are characterized by supernatural exaggeration, while *sewamono* feature words and gestures close to those in actual use and are thus much more realistic. But even in the category of *sewamono* plays there is a great difference in mood between plays of Edo and Kansai that depict the emotions and lives of the people of those two places.

As has been mentioned above, it is characteristic of Kabuki performances to surpass these individual expressions or styles of beauty. This may be called "stylization" based on the reality of daily life. It is not the naturalistic realism of the modern West; it is a quasi-musical dramatic composite art form, which may also be called a kind of expressionism consisting of visual beauty that lays great stress on sensual use of color and pictorial composition and the complicated and versatile musicality of the samisen. The most extreme examples may be a scene from a long dramatic piece such as the suicide trip of a pair of lovers, like Okaru and Kampei in *Chûshingura,* and such one-act dance plays as *Musume Dôjôji*. Musicality and dance are the essential elements ever present in the art of Kabuki since its prototype dance of Okuni. Therefore, even in the most realistic pieces, these musical or dance techniques (including that of *mie*) inevitably constitute an integral part of the pieces.

Musicality Let us consider Kabuki's musicality in more concrete terms. First, there is always the sound of the *hyôshigi* clappers. These two pieces of wood are struck by a man who stands in the right wing, as the curtain is opened or closed. It is by no means a simple thing to do. First of all, the clapping technique varies according to the play being presented. When the curtain opens on *Chûshingura,* the *hyôshigi* are clapped forty-seven times, once each for all of the forty-seven loyal warriors. In the case of the closing of historical plays, they are clapped first heavily at long intervals and then in gradually accelerating tempo, an ever quicker rhythm resembling a fusillade. The curtain is also drawn in keeping with the tempo of the clapping, slowly at first and faster and faster until it is fully closed. In the case of *sewamono,* there is just a single clapping, followed by a line of statement, and then the clapping goes first in the manner of a fusillade to end in slow tempo at the last. Since it is difficult to properly master the intervals, considerable practice is required. Thus the penetrating sound of *hyôshigi* can be said to be the real symbol of the auditory qualities of Kabuki.

There are also the *tsuke,* which resemble the *hyôshigi*. When an actor strikes a *mie* pose in an *aragoto* piece, or when there is to be a fighting scene or a murder, a man clad in a black kimono and wearing a black hood sits down on the right wing of the stage. He has square pieces of wood in his hands and fiercely beats them against the floorboards. This serves as punctuation for the action and strongly emphasizes it.

Next, there are the special sound effects produced behind the *kuromisu* at the left of the stage. The music is called *geza* music (literally, beneath or outside the stage music) because it is performed outside of the stage proper. In addition to samisen, there is a large drum, one meter across, and other instruments, including xylophone, *kokyû* (four-stringed fiddle), and even wooden temple drums called *mokugyo*.

Besides the instrumental music, *geza* music may include singing to samisen accompaniment. The purpose is to intensify the mood of the pertinent scene, such as the singing of romantic songs (*meriyasu*) at the time of a love scene or tender songs when a woman is in a pensive mood while combing out her hair or the naive folk songs (*zaigôuta*) sung for a farmyard scene with a landscape of field and river. A variety of melodies are available for use to match the general setting and mood of the scene. Since the main function is to heighten the effect, the first task of *geza* music is to provide an appropriate mood for each scene. There are also some instrumental pieces that accompany the respective scenes performed, such as *Matsuri-bayashi* for a festival scene, *Kabuki* and *Tôri Kagura* for lively street scenes in Edo, and so on.

The second task of *geza* music is to create sound effects. The great drum alone can be beaten in more than thirty different ways. Heavily resounding drumbeats are used to depict the opening of battle scenes. Then there are sounds of nature, such as the pitter-patter of rain, which can be imitated on the drum hit lightly by the sticks. Although in modern pieces fans with dried beans attached to them are used to create the sound of rain, in classic pieces the big drum is used for the same purpose. The sounds of the wind, thunder, a babbling brook or swiftly flowing river, the roar of waves in the sea, and the echoes of mountain valleys (*yamaoroshi*) can all be reproduced on the drum. While the effects are not exactly the same as the sounds they imitate, they do represent yet another aspect of Kabuki's concern for reality.

The great drum is not used for sound effects alone. It is also used to create atmosphere. Snow, for example, may be represented by use of the drum. There is no intention here of imitating sound—for example, that of wind-driven snow or sleet—since falling snow ordinarily makes no sound. A special short and stout drumstick wrapped in cotton is used to softly rap the great drum. The resultant sound is symbolically suggestive of falling snow. At the same time, thousands of small triangular bits of white paper are released from a bamboo basket suspended over the stage and out of sight. At this moment, in a number of plays (such as *Meido no Hikyaku* and *Yaoya Oshichi*), a beautiful woman dressed in a crimson-red kimono appears amid the snow-white scene, thus appealing to the visual as well as to the auditory sense. The great drum also adds psychologically to the total effect, as in the case of the entry of a spirit or ghost, when a series of drumbeats, combined with music played on the flute, lends a haunting and foreboding air.

Music—especially samisen music—is exploited the most in the case of the dance plays. When plays such as *Kanjinchô* and *Musume Dôjôji* are performed, a two-tiered platform, covered with red cloth, spans the width of the stage, at the rear, and the upper level is filled with musicians and singers of the *nagauta,* while the lower level is filled with *hayashi* musicians (*ohayashi renjû*) similar to those in Noh plays: the flutists and drummers (players of the large and small *tsuzumi* and the *taiko*). The platform in red is called *hinadan* because it resembles that of the dolls' festival in March. When *tokiwazu* or *kiyomoto* musicians are required, they are seated to the left and right of the stage, as in *Momijigari* and other plays. At such times, the background scenery often consists of mountains, and a mountain motif is also used to decorate the dais on which the singers and musicians sit. This dais is called *yamadai*. Performances in which the narrators, singers, and instrumentalists play on the stage proper, not inside the *kuromisu,* showing themselves to the audience, are called *degatari* (disclosed narration) or *debayashi* (disclosed accompaniment).

Kabuki is thus given musical expression through a diversity of instruments and of samisen music. Compared with Noh, where only four instruments are used, or Kyôgen, where use of music is but rarely made, there is a world of difference. The samisen, in particular, was not in use in dramatic forms prior to Kabuki of the Edo period. And it may be said that in samisen music the sensuality of the Edo townsman's culture was most clearly symbolized.

A word may be added here about the rhythm of the seven-and-five-syllable meter, which has already been noted in the section on Bunraku in connection with the *michiyuki*. The musicality of this rhythm is also one of the very important factors in Kabuki. For example, in the play *Benten Kozô*, when a thief disguised in the costume of a woman slips into a clothing shop, it is discovered that the thief is actually a man, as is made clear by his tattoo. This is the hero of the play, Benten Kozô. Suddenly, he takes on a decidedly masculine air and strikes a *mie* pose, knocking the ashes out of his pipe. He then starts to deliver his lines in the above rhythm:

Shi-ra-za-a-i-t-te (7)	If you know me not,
Ki-ka-se-ya-shô (5)	I shall let you know.
Ha-ma-no-ma-sa-go-to (7)	Like the grains of sand on the shore,
Go-e-mo-n-ga (5)	So [the famous thief] Goemon
U-ta-ni-no-ko-se-shi (7)	Left in his song,
Nu-su-t-to-no (5)	"The thieves'
Ka-zu-wa-tsu-ki-ne-e (7)	Number is countless
Shi-chi-ri-ga-ha-ma (6)	As the sands of the shore of Shichirigahama. . . ."

In brief this is a self-introduction and belongs to the category of *tsurane*, similar to the one in *Shibaraku*. In the case of *Benten Kozô*, however, the action is not a fully stylized *aragoto* performance, and a very realistic clothing shop is created on the stage, to the extent that the clerks, the apprentices, and the customers are just as might actually have been around that time. The hero, who up to that moment has acted in a most realistic manner, suddenly begins to act in an unrealistic manner. His trick of disguising himself as a woman having been seen through, he identifies himself at the climax of the play. Facing the audience, he declaims his lines in seven-and-five-syllable rhythm. The situation is typical of Kabuki, and since it is what the spectators have been waiting to see, this is the time when they shout the nicknames of the actors such as Naritaya or Otowaya and bravos such as *"Mattemashita"* (a compact equivalent of "That's what I was waiting for!" and "*Tappuri*" ("Excellent!").

The primary charm of Kabuki may be the ample musicality, including this agreeable effect of the rhythms of lines, which is found in almost all the pieces.

Visual Appeal The beauty of Kabuki is not confined to the backdrops, sets, costumes, and makeup, the careful use of color or pictorial composition. It includes temporal movement (at times, including that of stage sets and backdrop decorations) and thus may be regarded as a beauty of kinetic formation.

At its heart is the beauty of the actors and their performances. This quality has already been noted in relation to *aragoto* and *onnagata*. In general it is observed not simply in the momentary pause when an actor performs a *mie*. In any motion whatsoever there should be an element of dance-like elegance, and in any pause the actors should stand still in a balanced form of beauty. For example, at the moment just before the curtain is closed, the entire stage must constitute a picture. After the curtain is closed, as the hero makes his exit alone on the *hanamichi* to the accompaniment of *geza* music, perfect kinetic forms should be created. As an example of this, we have the exit of the hero of *Shibaraku*, who, carrying a sword on his shoulder, retires in a pompous fashion. Another example is Benkei in *Kanjinchô*, who exits in bold gesticulation along the *hanamichi* holding a banner on his back and a staff in his left hand and waving his right hand about in an exaggerated manner. The villain of *Sendai Hagi*, Nikki Danjô, magically changing himself into a rat with the loot of a family treasure in his teeth, scurries from the stage as if he floats in air. Since he is supposed to vanish into the darkness, a stage assistant dressed in black holds out a candle at the end of a long stick, to light Nikki's face, and effects what would be a close-up in a motion picture. This candle is called *tsura-akari* (lighting of the face).

In this traditional art form, what are known as *kata* (set forms) have been transmitted from generation to generation. The skipping gesture of Benkei and the scurrying of Nikki are such examples. In the West also, as in the first act of *Hamlet*, when Hamlet moves toward the ghost while holding a sword, we may find any number of acting forms. But in Western drama the vertical transmission of the art by certain actors' families is not present, and each generation of actors is free to act as it wishes. In Kabuki (and Japanese drama in general, in this respect) the traditional factors in the art of acting are strongly maintained, and the set musical rhythms provide guidelines or a framework, so that there is little room for innovation.

Nevertheless, concerning details, it must be said that there are variations that may be used according to the individual discretion of the actors. In *Terakoya,* for example, when Matsuô identifies the head of the executed child, the actor may use the *kata* wherein he lightly puts his hands on both sides of the container for the head while peering into it, or the *kata* wherein he shades his eyes with his hand, or the one wherein he unsheathes his sword toward Genzô and looks into his face, and so on. In these variations one can observe individual interpretations and characteristics of the actors that are to be appreciated. However, taking for example *Hamlet,* in some productions of the West the ghost may not be actually performed, or the actors may play either in modern costumes or in Renaissance style or in the fashion of eleventh-century Denmark, or Hamlet may assume a melancholy look of contemporary youth or a wild manner in the style of the Beatles. But Kabuki's production can never be so flexible as that of Western plays and is bound by certain set patterns inherited in its history. In recent years the actors of modern plays have performed Kabuki plays in realistic style or rearranged them in film versions. These are, however, modern performances based on Kabuki and not Kabuki proper.

Among classic forms of the *kata* there is what is known as *tachimawari.* These are the scenes when one strong hero (who may be a woman) confronts a single adversary or a crowd for a fight. The acting is not as realistic as in similar scenes in motion pictures or television but is dance-like and accompanied by *geza* music. There are several basic forms of *kata* that may be combined in various fashions to create a scene of complicated fighting action. They may be likened to stylized forms of fencing postures and maneuvers. Among them is the *tombogaeri* somersault, which, like dancing, unless practiced from an early age, cannot be mastered.

Various props such as ladders, ropes, and even rooftops are used in the *tachimawari.* The effect is so spectacular that in some plays (like *Rampei Monogurui*) a particular scene is entirely dedicated to it.

Another form of visual beauty is that of the quick change of the actors' costumes. One form of this, *hikinuki* (stripping off), calls for the actor to wear several costumes, one on top of another, and strip them off one by one with the aid of a stage assistant. The outer costumes are not sewed in ordinary fashion but are held together by hidden cords. These are swiftly pulled out to allow each costume to fall from the actor's body and reveal the one underneath. Swift changes can thus be made, from a red to a green costume, or to white, pink, or other colors, to delight the spectators. Another method, *bukkaeri* (falling off), is the use of a completely independent upper half of a costume. By a quick turn of just the upper portion, a new color combination of the lining may be had.

Next, let us take up some examples of spectacular productions through the use of the special structure of the Kabuki stage.

In addition to the revolving stage, the lifts (*seriage*) are particularly valuable for attaining visual effects. For example, in the play *Sammon Gosan no Kiri*, when the curtain is pulled open, a broad expanse of flowering cherry trees, all at their peak, is seen in the background. The foreground is occupied by the roof of a large temple, where a single robber is admiring the scenery while enjoying a puff on his pipe. This set is modeled after the great gate of the Nanzenji, a temple in Kyoto. With the man seated on it, the entire gate is lifted, revealing the structure of an even larger gate. Then a man in the garb of a priest is lifted up from beneath the stage to confront the robber.

A technique called *aorigaeshi* is used when a great fight takes place on the roof of a temple. While the fighting is going on, the entire roof rotates about ninety degrees to disclose the side of the temple, where a vermilion railing and a corridor occupied by actors appear. The last scene of *Benten Kozô* is one of such examples.

There are even techniques for quickly collapsing an entire building (*yataikuzushi*) set up on the stage.

A special small lift built into the *hanamichi* at the seven-three point also provides special effects. It is called the *suppon* (soft-shelled turtle). It is not used for entrances or exits of ordinary characters but only for those with superhuman or supernatural powers. For example, Nikki Danjô changes himself into a rat and flees away by this lift with the treasure scroll in his mouth or reappears in his real person on the same lift. A fox that has transformed itself into a samurai (Satô Tadanobu) in *Yoshitsune Sembonzakura* and appears to the beating of a drum by

Shizuka Gozen also utilizes this lift. *Ninja* (practitioners of the martial art of invisibility), disguised animals, apparitions, and ghosts that must appear unexpectedly on the stage use this lift.

Other than these techniques, a wire rope is occasionally also used in Kabuki, so that an actor may fly through the air.

For all of these visual effects, accompaniment is provided by appropriate *geza* music. That is to say, the beauty of Kabuki fuses visual and auditory effects. This may be said to be the stylistic beauty of Kabuki production.

Various Aspects of Kabuki's Attractions Kabuki thus has any number of attractions that have over the years been refined by stylized performances and are amalgamated with the plots of the plays. There are a number of types or patterns of these attractions.

Love scenes (*nureba*) are common. Typical scenes of passion are those of Izaemon and the courtesan Yûgiri in *Yoshidaya,* the secret meeting of Yosaburô and Otomi in *Kirare Yosa,* and the stealthy rendezvous scene of Naozamurai (Naojirô) and the courtesan Michitose in *Kôchiyama to Naozamurai.*

Murder scenes (*koroshiba*) are to be found in the act where Danshichi Kurobei kills his father-in-law in *Natsu Matsuri Naniwa Kagami;* in *Tsuta Momiji Utsunoya Tôge,* in which a masseur is killed; in *Onnagoroshi Abura no Jigoku,* where a woman, writhing in agony in pools of oil, is killed; and in many other plays. In these scenes are observed stylizations according to the *kata* utilized for *tachimawari.*

Torture scenes (*semeba*) may be seen in such plays as *Hibariyama,* where Princess Chûjô is tormented; in *Akegarasu,* in which a beautiful woman, Urazato, is tortured in the snow; and in *Dannoura Kabuto Gunki,* in which the courtesan Akoya is cruelly treated. In such scenes are combined elements of sadism and eroticism.

There are also scenes of extortion by intimidation (*yusuriba*), wherein a villain takes advantage of someone's weakness to extort money. In *Benten Kozô* (on the pretext of the scar made on his forehead) and *Kirare Yosa* such scenes are included. In the latter, the money is taken from Otomi, now married to a wealthy man, by Yosaburô, her former husband. Also in *Tsuta Momiji Utsunoya Tôge* a traveling thief, Nisa, extorts money from an innkeeper, Jûbei, availing himself of the tobacco case he collected.

Another type that often appears in Kabuki is the scene of parting (*enkiriba*). Often in these scenes the woman, hiding her real love, assumes a stony attitude toward her lover for some reason or other and asks him not to see her again. The reason may sometimes be that she wants to save her lover by securing a great treasure for him, so that she is obliged to give herself to the owner of that treasure, or motivation may be derived from a similar situation. Often the woman's lover is so shaken by this turnabout that he kills her. This may be seen in *Godairiki Koi no Fūjime, Kagotsurube, Ise Ondo,* and *Chijimiya Shinsuke.*

At other times, parents must part from their children (*kowakare*). One example is the scene in *Sakura Gimin Den* in which a village master, Sôgorô, knowing that he will be executed, leaves his children to make a direct appeal to the shogun to save the lives of his villagers. The parting scene of a nurse, Shigenoi, and her son, Sankichi, in *Koinyôbô Somewake Tazuna* is another example of this.

A *shūtamba,* or scene of pathos, occurs when suppressed sorrow bursts forth into a series of tragic lamentations—for example, the sorrow of those who have lost one of their family members for the sake of their lord or of those who have sacrificed their child. Such are the cases of Matsuô and his wife in *Terakoya;* Kumagai's wife, Sagami, in *Kumagai Jinya;* and the nurse, Masaoka, in *Sendai Hagi,* in which her son dies in behalf of her young master.

CHAPTER NINETEEN

THE DRAMA OF KABUKI

Classification

As has been pointed out, Kabuki plays that have been adapted from Bunraku are called *gidayû kyôgen* or *maruhon kabuki* (*maruhon mono*) or *denden mono*. In addition, there are plays taken from Noh and Kyôgen, mainly dance plays. We may therefore roughly classify Kabuki plays into *gidayû kyôgen*, *noh-torimono* (versions of Noh and Kyôgen plays), and plays properly of Kabuki. The more famous plays are as follows:

GIDAYÛ KYÔGEN
Hadesugata Onna Maiginu, or *Sakaya* (*The Love of Hanshichi and Sankatsu,* 1772). By Takemoto Saburobei.
Heike Nyogo ga Shima, or *Shunkan* (*The Exile of Shunkan,* 1719). By Chikamatsu Monzaemon.
Ichinotani Futaba Gunki (*The Chronicle of the Battle of Ichinotani,* 1751). By Namiki Sôsuke and his assistants.
Imoseyama Onna Teikin, or *Imoseyama* (*An Example of Noble Womanhood,* 1771). By Chikamatsu Hanji and his assistants.
Kanadehon Chûshingura, or *Chûshingura* (*The Treasury of Loyal Retainers,* 1748). By Takeda Izumo, Miyoshi Shôraku, and Namiki Senryû.
Meido no Hikyaku, or *Fûinkiri* (*The Messenger from Hell,* 1711). By Chikamatsu Monzaemon.
Ômi Genji Senjin Yakata (*Strife at Uji,* 1769). By Chikamatsu Hanji.

Shimpan Utazaimon, or *Nozakimura* (*The Village of Nozaki*, or *Osome and Hisamatsu*, 1780). By Chikamatsu Hanji.

Shinjû Ten no Amijima (*The Love Suicide at Amijima*, 1715). By Chikamatsu Monzaemon.

Sonezaki Shinjû (*The Love Suicide at Sonezaki*, 1703). By Chikamatsu Monzaemon.

Sugawara Denju Tenarai Kagami (*The Secret of Sugawara's Calligraphy*, 1746). By Takeda Izumo, Namiki Senryû, and Miyoshi Shôraku.

NOH–TORIMONO
Taken from Noh plays

Kagamijishi (*The Dancing Lion*, 1893). Adapted by Fukuchi Ôchi from *Makura Jishi*.

Kanjinchô (*The Subscription List*, 1840). Adapted by Namiki Gohei III from *Ataka*.

Kyôganoko Musume Dôjôji, or *Musume Dôjôji* (*The Maiden at the Dôjôji Temple*, 1753). Adapted by Fujimoto Tobun from *Dôjôji*.

Momijigari (*The Maple Viewing*, 1887). Adapted by Kawatake Mokuami from a Noh piece of the same title.

Sumidagawa-mono, or those plays belonging to the *Sumidagawa* cycle adapted from the Noh play of the same title.

Taken from Kyôgen plays

Bôshibari (*Pinioned*, 1916). Adapted by Okamura Shikô.

Migawari Zazen (*The Substitute Meditator*, 1910). Adapted by Okamura Shikô.

Sannin Katawa (*Three Deformed Persons*, 1898). Adapted by Takeshiba Kisui.

Tachinusubito (*The Sword Thief*, 1917). Adapted by Okamura Shikô.

PLAYS PROPERLY WRITTEN FOR KABUKI

Aotozôshi Hana no Nishikie, or *Benten Kozô*, 1862. By Kawatake Mokuami.

Godairiki Koi no Fûjime, or *Godairiki*, 1794. By Namiki Gohei.

Kanzen Chôaku Nozoki Karakuri, or *Murai Chôan* (*The Physician Chôan*, 1862). By Kawatake Mokuami.

Kosode Soga Azami no Ironui, or *Izayoi Seishin* (*Novice Seishin and Courtesan Izayoi,* 1895). By Kawatake Mokuami.
Narukami Fudô Kitayamazakura, or *Narukami* (*Abbot Narukami,* 1684). By Tsuda Hanjûrô.
Nezumi Kozô Haru no Shingata, or *Nezumi Kozô* (*The Thief Nezumi Kozô,* 1857). By Kawatake Mokuami.
Sannin Kichiza Kuruwa no Hatsukai, or *Sannin Kichiza* (*Three Rascals Called Kichiza,* 1860). By Kawatake Mokuami.
Shibaraku (*Wait a Moment,* 1697). By Ichikawa Danjûrô I.
Soga no Taimen (*The Meeting of the Soga Brothers,* 1697). By Ichikawa Danjûrô I.
Sukeroku Yukari no Edozakura, or *Sukeroku,* 1713. By Tsuuchi Jihei.
Tôkaidô Yotsuya Kaidan, or *Yotsuya Kaidan* (*The Ghost Story of Yotsuya,* 1825). By Tsuruya Namboku IV.
Tsumoru Koi Yuki no Seki no To, or *Seki no To* (*The Barrier Gate,* 1784). By Takarada Jurai.
Yowa Nasake Ukina no Yokogushi, or *Kirare Yosa* (*Wound-scarred Yosa,* 1853). By Segawa Jokô III.

Of course the plays can also be classified into *jidaimono* and *sewamono* as in the case of Bunraku pieces. This classification is more commonly used and has already been explained in detail in the section devoted to Bunraku. Here I would like to confine the discussion to the plays taken from Noh and Kyôgen and to the pieces that are properly of Kabuki. Their main characteristics and dramaturgy are discussed below.

The Eighteen Favorites

Among the plays of Kabuki proper, those clearly characterized by their uniqueness vis-à-vis *gidayû kyôgen* are the *aragoto* pieces and *kizewamono* plays, a group of *sewamono* plays, and a third group consisting of Edo *jôruri* and *nagauta* dance plays.

The artistry of *aragoto* is a distinctly Edo form of Kabuki, perfected at about the time of the Genroku era (1688–1703). It is associated in particular with Ichikawa Danjûrô I and his successors. The characteristics of this style and its relation to the religious beliefs prevalent at the time have been mentioned elsewhere, and in this section attention is given to the larger picture, or the so-called Kabuki Eighteen Favorites, which comprise the core of *aragoto* plays.

These eighteen plays were selected by Ichikawa Danjûrô VII, in 1840, from among the outstanding plays performed by his predecessors. The use of the number eighteen has a Buddhist origin, which was familiar to the people through a variety of Buddhist tales and such expressions as "even a devil can be eighteen years old" or "eighteen dandies" or again "eighteen vows of Amida."

While many people think that the Eighteen Favorites are Kabuki's eighteen masterpieces, this is not true. Strictly speaking, they are the eighteen specialties of the Danjûrô line of actors, and in terms of content they are purely *aragoto* pieces of Edo style.

In Kabuki the actors and their artistry are foremost, and form and tradition are accorded a high level of importance. The existence of the Eighteen Favorites is the most striking example.

The eighteen plays are *Fudô, Fuwa, Gedatsu, Jayanagi, Kagekiyo, Kamahige, Kanjinchô, Kan'u, Kenuki, Nanatsu Men, Narukami, Oshimodoshi, Shibaraku, Sukeroku, Uirôuri, Uwanari, Ya no Ne,* and *Zôhiki*.

Kanjinchô, an adaption of Noh's *Ataka*, was first performed by Danjûrô VII. As it is strongly tinged by dancing elements with the accompaniment of *nagauta* singing, it is also considered one of the finest pieces by *nagauta* musicians and is a typical modern Kabuki play. As such, it has been performed overseas on a number of occasions.

Here Minamoto no Yoshitsune, vilified by his older brother Yoritomo, seeks to escape, in the disguise of an itinerant monk, accompanied by Benkei and five other retainers. They arrive at a guard station. Benkei explains that they are monks who collect money for the reconstruction of the Tôdaiji temple. The guard, Togashi, being suspicious, orders Benkei to read out the subscription list of donors as a means of checking Benkei's story. Benkei then "reads" the text of the list from a scroll of paper on which actually nothing is written. Togashi then poses a number of questions dealing with Buddhism, and Benkei marvelously gives correct answers to all. They are therefore given permission to pass the guard station. But then a sentry notices that the man wearing a straw hat resembles Yoshitsune, and Togashi orders them to halt. There being no other way to effect an escape, Benkei seizes a stick and begins to beat the man (Yoshitsune, his master). Since it is unthinkable for a retainer to beat his master, the guard and sentry, satisfied that the man cannot be Yoshitsune, let them pass. Actually, Togashi has seen through the plot and recognized Yoshitsune, but his heart goes out to Benkei, deeply troubled because the latter has had to beat his own master, and out of sympathy he allows them to go. Benkei, now drunk on sakè, follows the group, dancing as he goes.

Benkei's craft and valor, the guard's human feeling—these are depicted in a superb drama. In its combination of such *aragoto* acts as the reading of the list of donors and the heroic beating of Yoshitsune as well as the musical rhythms of the *nagauta* and samisen accompaniment, dances, and then the final exit, this is a masterpiece replete with dignity and thrills.

Sukeroku is about the most famous dandy of Edo and the hero of the Edo townsmen. It is a one-act play in which Sukeroku and an evil samurai, the bearded Ikyû, contend in the Yoshiwara gay quarters over its leading courtesan, Agemaki. The scenes and the mood that pervades the entire play are more or less in *sewamono* spirit and suggest the life and times of the masses, but in the acting of Sukeroku there are many elements of *aragoto*. Sukeroku is a handsome young man, remarkably brave and quite able to roundly put down his evil opponent with his defiance and to win the impassioned applause of the Edo masses. Rich in comic taste and most dazzling and luxurious among Edo Kabuki plays, *Sukeroku* is a masterpiece, full of simple but human sentiment.

Narukami and *Shibaraku* have already been discussed in detail. The other fourteen plays present dramatic situations to which are added the style and eloquence of *aragoto*, but most of them are not frequently presented.

KIZEWAMONO

The *ki* of *kizewamono* means "pure" and "unadulterated." These plays are *sewamono* pieces depicting the lives and mores of the lowest class of Edo society in realistic style. Their origin is thought to be a Bunraku work by Namiki Sôsuke, *Natsu Matsuri Naniwa Kagami*. Development of this type of play into a genre took place after Bunraku ceased its growth, in the early-to-middle part of the nineteenth century. The genre belongs to pure Edo Kabuki.

Typical of early plays of the genre is one of the greatest *sewamono* pieces of all, *Yotsuya Kaidan,* by Tsuruya Namboku IV. Through the literary version by Lafcadio Hearn and the recent film version of his story, this play has become familiar to many outside Japan. The story is based on such actual tales as that of a samurai wife who dies of madness brought on by jealousy, after which her spirit haunts a family, and that of a man and a woman who had enjoyed illicit relations until they were discovered and killed and nailed to both sides of a plank that had been set adrift in a stream. But what is foremost in the play is the scene in which Oiwa, wife of the masterless samurai Tamiya Iemon, has been tormented by her husband and given poison by a scheming neighbor, whereupon her face becomes transformed into something monstrous, and she meets an agonizing death. As background to this, there is the realistic depiction of the slum area of Edo, showing the plight of Iemon, who mends broken umbrellas for his living, and the masseur who also appears in the scene. There is again the bloodcurdling transformation of Oiwa's face from a normal one to the poison-ravaged one she has at her death. Then, after she dies, there is a rapid and frightening procession of specters and spirits. Second, there is the scene set on the bank of the river Ombôbori, where the decomposing corpse of Oiwa rises to confront Iemon. Third, there is the scene in which Iemon, by now neurotic, is mercilessly tormented by the spirit of Oiwa in the room of a temple where he is hiding. Further, although it is somewhat of a digression from the main story, there is a scene in which, directly after Oiwa's younger sister marries a villain, the two are discovered to be long-lost brother and sister and commit suicide. The scene takes place in a house of assignation.

Another *kizewamono* play is Kawatake Mokuami's *Sannin Kichiza.* It presents three robbers, all with the name Kichiza—Oshô Kichiza, Ojô Kichiza, and Obô Kichiza—who unexpectedly meet beside the Sumida River in the middle of the night and, after introducing themselves, swear to be brothers. This kind of realistic drama with robbers as main characters is called *shiranamimono,* or picaresque story. One of the robbers pushes a streetwalker into the river to rob her of a hundred *ryô* in cash, then puts his leg on a stake on the riverbank and speaks the following lines, rendered here in the approximate manner of their delivery by the actor:

Tsukimo oboroni shirauono	A hazy white moon hangs dimly aloft.
Kagarimo kasumu haruno sora	Watch fires are lit in a hazy air of spring.
Tsumetee kazeni horoyoino	In the cold breeze I became tipsy with wine.
Kokoromochiyoku ukaukato	In good humor, I, absent-mindedly
Ukare garasuno tada ichiwa	Like a happy crow, all by myself,
Negurae kaeru kawabatade	Was going home. But on a riverside,
Saono shizukuka nuretede awa	Probably my fingers being wet by the dripping of the punt pole, I chanced to find
Omoigakenaku teniiru hyakuryô.	Unexpectedly a hundred ryô in my hands.

Spoken in seven-five meter, this rhythm is familiar to every Japanese. One cold evening, when a misty moon can be seen, moonlight dances on the ripplets of the stream.... Real, yet not real, this feeling of stylized beauty is wonderfully exploited in *sewamono*.

There are other examples, such as the previously mentioned *Benten Kozô* (*Shiranami Gonin Otoko*), but, looking at the whole of *sewamono* in addition to its depiction of the lives, customs, and mores of the masses of Edo's downtown district, there are many depictions of lust and bloody atrocities, and beneath it all is the throbbing of a nihilistic philosophy, of hedonism and individualistic views.

This is quite different from the situation we find in the case of heroes of *jôruri* of the early Edo period, who sacrificed blood relatives for the sake of their feudal obligations or committed suicide, hoping to find happiness in the world to come because they could not face the contradictions of this world.

For an illustration of this, we may take up *Izayoi Seishin*. Izayoi is a harlot; Seishin is a temple monk. Seishin has been thrown out of his temple because he transgressed Buddhist prescriptions by having relations with Izayoi. He is about to cast himself into a river when Izayoi, who has run away from the gay quarters, catches up with him and offers to die with him. They have set their hearts on dying together. Up to this point, the story is the same as Chikamatsu's tales of the pure love of men and women. But from this point on, the story is entirely different from one that Chikamatsu would have written. Seishin can swim, and he paddles about on the surface of the water. Izayoi is carried downstream to a fisherman's boat and is rescued. Although they had hoped to die together, both are alive. Seishin tries leaping into the river again and again but still fails to kill himself. During this time, pleasure boats pass by and the sounds of geishas' samisen and *nagauta* singing and of wealthy guests enjoying themselves come over the water to Seishin, who now changes his view of life. He decides that since life is short it is best to have a good deal of money and enjoy oneself, a down-to-earth view that next finds him murdering a passing store clerk in order to rob him before disappearing into the shadows of the night. Much later, in the Hakone Mountains, he once again meets Izayoi, who has become the wife of a bigtime thief, and together they attempt to extort money from her husband. Later, when they discover that a young man they have killed is Izayoi's younger brother, the two decide once more to commit suicide. But unlike Chikamatsu's Ohatsu and Tokubei of *Sonezaki Shinjû,* who sought respite and happiness in the next world, Izayoi and Seishin only sought to balance the books for their hedonism and degeneracy.

The *kizewamono* plays thus depict various aspects of the lives of the masses, at the same time portraying with stylistic beauty the desperate situations that arise when characters blindly follow their instincts.

Dance Pieces

There are many dance pieces in Kabuki, and therefore there is no simple means of classifying them. For example, they may be classified as to their origin, the type of samisen music used, or the subjects they take up, to name a few ways.

Classification of the dance pieces according to their origin is as follows. First, there are the dance scenes taken from longer dramatic pieces (called *keigoto* in Bunraku) and used as independent Kabuki dance pieces. For example, from *Chûshingura,* there is *Ochiudo* (*The Suicide Trip of Okaru and Kampei*); from *Yoshitsune Sembonzakura* there is *Chûshin* (*The Suicide Trip of Lady Shizuka and Kitsune Tadanobu*); and from *Kôchiyama to Naozamurai* there is *Michitose.*

Second, there are dance pieces taken from Noh and Kyôgen plays. These are called *noh-torimono*. Examples are *Musume Dôjôji, Tsuchigumo, Kagamijishi, Momijigari,* and *Sumidagawa* from Noh, and *Bôshibari, Sannin Katawa,* and *Migawari Zazen* from Kyôgen. Among these, the plays that go so far as to make use of the old pine backdrop of the Noh stage and follow the original closely are *Tsuchigumo* and *Bôshibari.* Such plays are called *matsubamemono,* after the pine backdrop (*matsubame*). *Kanjinchô* may also be considered to belong to this subgroup of dance pieces. However, as has been indicated above, in the case of Kabuki there is an important and fundamental difference in that the samisen is used for accompaniment.

In Kabuki proper, there are many dance plays like *Seki no To* and *Modori Kago.* It is the genre of the transformation dances (*henge buyô*), however, that is typical of pure Kabuki dances. In these, one actor (dancer) in a single play, or rather in a single scene, dances the separate parts of a number of different characters.

As an example of a historically famous incident, there is the appearance of Bandô Mitsugorô III in *Yamatogana Iroha Nana Moji.* By rapid onstage changes of costume, he danced the seven roles of a courtier, a trained monkey, a country girl, an old woman, Genda (a virile young man), Momotarô (of the ancient Japanese fairy tale), and Sambasô (an old traditional role danced on felicitous occasions).

These transformation dances originated in the Genroku era (1688–1703) and are seen in Kansai Kabuki plays. Since Kabuki originally placed great stress on music, dance, and a performance that would appeal to and delight the spectators, dance pieces with many transformation scenes are considered to be most Kabuki-like. It was not until the late Edo period, however, that these became very popular. What made them popular was the play mentioned above, *Yamatogana Iroha Nana Moji.* At the peak of their popularity even one dance might include as many as twelve transformations. They are not performed today in their entirety, but many popular scenes of the transformation dances are still performed as independent dances.

The reason that transformation dances were so popular at the end of the Edo period was not only that the audience loved spectacular productions but also that they had grown weary of ordinary plays and dances and could not be satisfied unless there was a wealth of thrills and variety in what they saw. It seems that this was eventually the same as what we have seen in the origin and growth of *kizewamono*, in which the quick-change technique, love scenes, murder scenes, and the appearance of ghosts quickly shift from one to another.

One more characteristic that must be added to Kabuki proper is the choreographing of the actual life of the late-Edo townspeople. The various peddlers, the customs and activities of the Yoshiwara gay quarters, and the gaiety of festivals were the main subjects of the dances.

In classifying the plays according to the type of samisen music used, there are *nagauta* plays (for example, *Musume Dôjôji*) and *jôruri* plays. The latter may be further classified into *tokiwazu* plays (for example, *Seki no To*), *kiyomoto* plays (for example, *Ochiudo*), and *takemoto* or *gidayû* plays (for example, *Rokkasen*).

If the plays are to be classified according to their content, there are the *Musume Dôjôji* group (for example, *Musume Dôjôji, Yakko Dôjôji, Keisei Dôjôji, Ninin Dôjôji*), *shakkyômono* (for example, *Shûchakujishi, Aioijishi, Kagamijishi, Renjishi*), *asamamono* (for example, *Takao Sange, Futaomote*), *sogamono* (for example, *Kusazuribiki, Ame no Gorô*), *matsukazemono* (for example, *Shiokumi, Suma no Utsushie*), and other subclassifications.

KABUKI AND THE LIFE OF THE PEOPLE

We have seen the various categories of Kabuki plays classified from various angles. Here I would like to explain the arrangement and production of the plays in relation to the practice of theatrical enterprise in Japan, because a knowledge of the show techniques and the arrangement of program is also necessary to an understanding of Kabuki's role in the society of the Edo townsman—indeed, of its essence as including its spectators.

We are concerned here predominantly with the theaters in Edo. In Edo, such theaters as the Nakamuraza, Ichimuraza, and Moritaza were the only officially licensed theaters. Each theater consisted of the owner-manager (*zamoto*), chief actor (*zagashira*), other actors, chief playwright (*tatesakusha*), and other playwrights. At that time the period of employment for actors was one year. If they were successful, a long-run performance could be given, while at the same time, if a play was not well received, it could be replaced in a matter of days by some other play, using the members of the same group of actors. But the contract of the one-year period was observed, and, seasonal factors being taken into account, it was common for the major part of a year's schedule to be blocked out.

The year-long season opened in November of the lunar calendar. In October each theater (including those in the Kansai region) announced the new casts of the year's plays through mutual agreements with actors. Because the start of the season was vital in regard to business performance throughout the year, the first presentation was also used to introduce the actors, including the new actors who had just joined. This initial performance was termed *kaomise* (introduction) *kyôgen*. Today, similar presentations are given at Kyoto's Minamiza and other theaters in December (November of the lunar calendar), but since the one-year basis of operation is no longer in practice, the word does not have its original meaning.

In the *kaomise* of Edo, there was the custom of presenting an *aragoto* piece—*Shibaraku* in a theater where Ichikawa Danjûrô was employed. The reason was that the play was not only best suited to exploit the drawing power of the *zagashira* but also afforded the opportunity to introduce the entire troupe through different characteristics of the actors specializing in villains' roles, oafs' roles, *onnagata*, and lovers' roles.

Then the *hatsuharu kyôgen*, or New Year's plays, were presented. For this, felicitous plays such as *Kotobuki Soga no Taimen* were chosen.

These were followed by *yayoi kyôgen*, or March plays. Since this month corresponded to the season of cherry blossoms, "flowery" productions were given, such as *Sukeroku Yukari no Edozakura* (or *Sukeroku*), which is set in the gay quarters of Yoshiwara at the peak of the cherry blossoms, or *Yoshinoyama Michiyuki*. Further, since ladies-in-waiting and house servants of the residences of feudal lords and samurai had their vacations during this month, *oiemono* plays having such residences as their setting were very popular.

During the summer months from May to August the major performances were suspended, and the time was used to repair the theaters. However, this afforded the chance to present "summer plays," or plays meant to help "enjoy the cool of the evening." The most experienced, top-flight actors vacationed, and their places were taken by secondary and supporting actors. This equivalent of America's "summer stock" season also afforded new playwrights opportunities to have their works performed. Also, entrance prices were reduced. Lest spectators become bored with plays, there were many presentations of *sewamono*, particularly ghost stories, with numerous transformational costume changes, as well as plays that utilized summertime festivals as their setting and plays in which real water was used on the stage. During the *obon* season, when people's thoughts turn to their ancestors and when Buddhist services are performed for the souls of the departed, plays in which spirits appear were presented and are referred to as *bon kyôgen*.

September was the time of "autumn plays." As this marked the end of the year's performances, plays given at this time were considered "farewell plays" and included many tragic plays concentrating on the complications of social obligations. Thus, for example, tragedies including scenes of parents' parting from their children were common at this time.

In this way, Kabuki maintained close contact with the seasons and the events of the seasons, including simple folk customs, festivals, and rites. Playwrights had to work so as to make the most of the roles and special abilities of the leading actors, while writing within the guidelines indicated by the seasons and the year-long method of management. Success in this, of course, pleased the spectators all the more. Rather than offer the playwright a chance to express his own artistic theories or his opinions on social problems as is common in modern theater, Kabuki thus had the nature of being a kind of cocktail party with theatrical entertainment as a portion of the lives of the masses.

Chikamatsu Monzaemon said that theater was a "comfort" of the masses, and Kawatake Mokuami said the playwright should be kind (1) to the actor, (2) to the audience, and (3) to the troupe's manager. Completely different from Noh's refined aristocratic aloofness, Kabuki was created in keeping with more concrete, real, colorful, and diversified characteristics of the masses.

CHAPTER TWENTY

THE HISTORY OF KABUKI

The history of Kabuki may be thought of as spanning five periods: (1) origin and early development (early to mid-seventeenth century); (2) establishment of genuine drama with spoken dialogue (late seventeenth through first half of eighteenth century); (3) expansion through adaptations from Bunraku (mid-eighteenth to late eighteenth century); (4) maturation of Edo Kabuki (late eighteenth century to Meiji Restoration of 1868); and (5) modernization (Meiji Restoration to present). A brief discussion of these periods follows.

Origin and Early Development

The origin of Kabuki is in the songs and dances of a woman called Okuni, a priestess of the Izumo Shrine, which were performed in 1603, in Kyoto. The sources were probably those songs and dances, collectively called Furyû, that had become popular among the masses in the nihilistic decay left in the wake of the Ônin Rebellion during the latter half of the fifteenth century. Furyû were dynamic dances accompanied by the singing of popular songs and were performed in colorful costumes at the time of festivals and other auspicious events. Among them were dances by women. As women had been prohibited by Buddhist precepts from appearing on the stage, a number of them traveled around the country, mixing prostitution with their work as performers. At the end of the sixteenth century, these performers often appeared in the area of the capital. Okuni is thought to have been one of them. Through his victory in the Battle of Sekigahara in 1600, Tokugawa Ieyasu (first of the Tokugawa shoguns) gained command of the entire country, and peace was restored to the land. An atmosphere of freedom prevailed, and this afforded an opportunity for Okuni and her troupe to appear openly before the masses of the capital.

Okuni, in male attire, performed the role of a man frequenting the teahouses, which had just come into vogue (forerunners of the gay quarters), and dallied with the women there or danced a version of the Buddhist *nembutsu* chant clad in the manner of the newly arrived Christian fathers, wearing a rosary and cross around her neck. These completely new presentations, her popular songs, and her dances took the spectators by storm.

Okuni's dances then came to be called *kabuki* dances, the word being an adjective describing the *avant-garde:* new things that went beyond the normal range of life. Writing the word with three Sino-Japanese characters meaning song (*ka*), dance (*bu*), and skill (*ki*), as is done today, did not come until later.

Okuni, on a stage as simple as that of Noh, also attracted attention with short sketches presented between her novel dances (these may have been popularized forms of Kyôgen), and thereafter many troupes of women performers were established. However, since these women continued to practice prostitution and their performances stressed their physical charms, their art came to be called the Kabuki of the women of pleasure. The Tokugawa shogunate, regarding the performances as a social evil, finally banned them in 1629.

In their place, young men's Kabuki—Kabuki performed by good-looking boys—became popular. But because this also relied on sensual beauty for the appeal of its dances and was associated with homosexuality, the shogunate saw it too as a social evil, and in 1651 it was banned. Kabuki did, however, win official approval a year later, with two conditions: first, the young men appearing on stage had to cut off their forelocks, thus appearing as men rather than boys, and second, their performances had to exclude sensual singing and dancing and were to be limited to nonsensational mimes (*monomane kyôgen*). In this way, Kabuki started again toward development as a true dramatic form.

The Establishment of Real Drama with Dialogue

The two restrictions imposed by the shogunate necessarily had the effect of advancing and enlarging the drama of Kabuki and fostering the development of realistic performance, production, and stage properties. In 1664, plays in several acts were presented for the first time, and the sidewise-drawn curtain was devised. Stage devices became more complex and were improved. In 1666 the forerunner of the *hanamichi* was invented—the "walking plank" (*fumiita*) in the midst of the spectators' boxes—and soon after that the stage was enlarged. In 1717 the semi-open theater, which had been only partially roofed in the manner of the Noh theater, was completely roofed, and with the development of the interior of the Kabuki theater, all ties to the Noh stage and theater were severed and a stage proper to Kabuki was created.

In relation to drama, whereas previously the chief actor had determined the principal story line and the other actors had improvised in keeping with it, at the close of the seventeenth century entire plays were written for the first time and were more complex than earlier plays. In the Kansai region, the great Chikamatsu Monzaemon appeared, and, through the performances of Sakata Tôjûrô, *wagoto* was established. Similarly, through those of Yoshizawa Ayame, the art of the *onnagata* attained a set pattern. In Edo, the spirited *jôruri* piece *kimpira-bushi* provided the hint that led to the establishment of *aragoto* by Ichikawa Danjûrô I. In other words, the basic techniques of acting and producing, and their styles, were established. It was also during this period that Kabuki roles were differentiated and developed.

Expansion Through Adaptations from Bunraku

Around the beginning of the third period, Kabuki was subordinate to Bunraku, which was at its peak (masterpieces such as *Chûshingura* were being performed by the puppets). But in the meantime the composed drama and production of Bunraku, as well as its musicality, were fully absorbed by Kabuki, which was fortified by the creation, thereby, of the major genre of *gidayû kyôgen*. As the latter half of the eighteenth century began, Kabuki displaced Bunraku as the leading dramatic form. The revolving stage was perfected in 1758 by Namiki Shôzô, and in the 1770s the dual *hanamichi* became established. The Kabuki stage had reached its ultimate form. *Sewamono* plays reflecting Edo's own life were brought to the stage by Namiki Gohei, a disciple of Shôzô, through his *Godairiki* and other plays, and by Sakurada Jisuke through his *Gohiiki Kanjinchô* and other plays. Jisuke also wrote dance pieces like *Modori Kago* and *Yoshiwara Suzume*. The development of dance pieces of course paralleled the development of samisen music, and in that regard Miyakoji Bungonojô, who developed the *bungo-bushi* style, has the distinction of having made a great contribution. His compositions, which utilized double suicides as subject matter and were deeply imbued with pathos, struck a responsive chord among the Edo masses, especially among young people, to the extent that double love suicides increased rapidly. For that reason in 1739 the *bakufu* prohibited his compositions from being presented, but his disciples formed new groups, with the result that there was further development of theatrical music. They formed the three schools of *tokiwazu*, *tomimoto* (which has almost died out today), and *kiyomoto*. *Tokiwazu* and *kiyomoto*, in particular, together with *nagauta*, have formed the basis of traditional Japanese dancing, which is popular even today.

The Maturation of Edo Kabuki

During this period, Edo *kizewamono* and transformational dances were created and enjoyed great popularity. Historically, the period may be divided into two, the first being the Bunka and Bunsei eras (circa 1804–30) and the second being the period from the Tempô Reforms (1841–43) to the Meiji Restoration, the latter corresponding to the close of the Edo period, or *bakumatsu*.

Yotsuya Kaidan, written by Tsuruya Namboku IV, is the representative work of the first period. The important actors included Danjûrô VII, Onoe Kikugorô III, Bandô Mitsugorô III, and Matsumoto Kôshirô V. In this period, greatest emphasis was placed on such characteristics of *kizewamono* as variety and the spectacular, in plays that featured torture, eroticism, incest, prostitution, depictions of the dismal world of the lower class of society, ghosts, and transformations.

But the Tempô Reforms, which were carried out to firm up the economy, also had the effect of greatly suppressing Kabuki. Danjûrô, the most famous actor in Edo, was banished from the stage, the three main theaters were ordered to relocate in desolate settlements, and erotic and grotesque aspects of the plays were rigorously policed. As a result, while *kizewamono* and transformational dances were still popular, Kabuki became considerably more lighthearted and (through the music and the pictorial aspects) stylistically more beautiful. Kawatake Mokuami's *Benten Kozô* and *Sannin Kichiza* were representative works of this period that reflected the changing times.

Modernization

With Japan's entry into its modern age, Western customs, culture, arts, and theater were introduced to the country, engendering changes in Kabuki. In brief, a tendency toward westernization of Kabuki became apparent. This tendency, however, was particularly strong during the first twenty years of Japan's modern age (1868–88). At that time, Kabuki was Japan's only living dramatic form, continuing to evolve and change with the times, and therefore responded to the new trend then prevalent.

It was the Kabuki theater that most smoothly absorbed Western influences. In 1872 some Western-style seats were installed. The theater was also enlarged. Then electric lights replaced gas lamps, and the stage devices came to be mechanized.

But since the drama, acting, and production of Kabuki plays had already been firmly stylized in set patterns, change in these areas was exceedingly difficult. Of course plays that accorded with rationalistic principles and historical truths were written and produced, as well as plays that included Western elements. There was also experimentation in acting styles that closely imitated life, and opinions were voiced to the effect that the *onnagata* should be dropped in favor of actresses. In the end, however, these changes proved impossible for the actors and writers who had become accustomed to following the traditions of the Edo period, and the Kabuki fans did not favor the innovations.

Then, in 1888, a completely new form of contemporary theater, Shimpa, was born in Japan for the performance of plays depicting the life of modern society. It led to a rather forceful movement called Shingeki, which arose in 1909, taking as its basis the concepts and styles of contemporary Western theater, with the incidental result that Kabuki was made into a "classic" dramatic form. This change was also a result of the death of playwright Kawatake Mokuami in 1893 and those of Ichikawa Danjûrô IX and Onoe Kikugorô V in 1903. During World War II, Kabuki continued to exist as classic drama. For one or two years during the postwar Occupation, plays dealing with revenge and torture, and particularly plays in which women and children were sacrificed, were considered to be inappropriate, and such performances were prohibited or restricted. But since it was understood that this form of classic drama had few peers in the world, in no time at all restrictions were removed, and Kabuki has prospered since then.

With the improvement and development of transportation and communications since the end of the war, the potential of drama in relation to cultural exchange has been accorded high value, and there have been many instances of Kabuki performances overseas. In particular, in 1960, to commemorate the Centennial of Japanese-American Amity, the Kokusai Bunka Shinkôkai (Japan Cultural Society, now the Japan Foundation), with the cooperation of the Shôchiku Company, Ltd., which owns the Kabukiza theater in Tokyo, Kabuki performances were presented in New York, Los Angeles, and San Francisco, drew rave reviews, and filled the theaters in each city. The following year Kabuki went to the Soviet Union and in 1965 to West Germany, France, and Portugal, so that Japanese drama was presented in more Western cities. The author accompanied the troupes on these three occasions and can vouch for the fact that the favorable reception given to Kabuki was not due so much to its exotic appeal as to the high evaluation as drama placed upon it by Western audiences and critics.

In 1966 the National Theater was constructed on a site just across from the moat that encircles the Imperial Palace, in central Tokyo. Kabuki, through the National Theater and the privately owned Kabukiza, has a firm foundation for its continued existence as a Japanese dramatic form.

Appendices and Index

APPENDIX ONE

THE REPERTOIRE OF BUGAKU DANCES

Samai

The Samai or Left dances are those introduced from China proper and old Indochina and those composed in Japan on the same lines. They include many historical curiosities such as those belonging to the ancient Indian opera, to the Tibetan dance music, or to the drama of Central Asia. They are generally of slow and gentle movement but full of elegant forms. Those preserved are:

Ichikotsuchô pieces:	Ama, Hokuteiraku, Karyôbin, Katen, Konju, Ninomai, Ryôô, Shôwaraku, Shunnôden
Hyôjô pieces:	Bairo, Goshôraku, Kanshû, Katôraku, Manzairaku, Sandaien
Sôjô piece:	Shundeiraku
Ojikichô pieces:	Kanseiraku, Kishunraku, Sekihakutôrika, Yôgûraku
Banshikichô pieces:	Manjuraku, Rintai, Saisôrô, Seigaiha, Shûfûraku, Sogôkô, Somakusha
Taishikichô pieces:	Batô, Genjôraku, Keihairaku, Sanju, Tagyûraku, Taiheiraku

Umai

The classical dances imported from Korea and the country dances of P'ohai (the region of the ancient Mo-ho tribes inhabiting Manchuria and northern Korea) and all those composed on the model of Korean and P'ohai pieces are named Umai or Right dances and are mostly of humorous and spirited movement. They are:

Koma Ichikotsuchô pieces:	Ayakiri, Chôbôraku, Engiraku, Hannari, Kansuiraku, Kitoku, Kochô, Komaboko, Konron-hassen (Korobase or Hassen), Kotokuraku, Kotoriso, Nasori, Ninnaraku, Ônintei, Shikite, Shin-maka, Shin-shôtoku, Shin-soriko (or Soriko), Shin-toriso, Tai-shotoku
Koma Hyôjô piece:	Ringa
Koma Sôjô pieces:	Chikyû, Hôhin, Soshimari, Tôtenraku

APPENDIX TWO

THE REPERTOIRE OF NOH PIECES

The numbers indicate the categories to which individual pieces belong:
  I. Kami Noh or Kami Mono (divine pieces) or Waki Noh (opening pieces)
  II. Shura Noh or Shura Mono (battle pieces)
  III. Katsura Noh or Katsura Mono (woman or wig pieces)
  IV. Genzai Noh or Genzai Mono (present-life or earthly pieces); Kyôran Mono or Kurui Mono (lunatic pieces); Shushin Mono or Onryô Mono (obsession pieces); Yûkyô Mono (enthusiasm pieces). Group IV is also called Zatsu Noh (miscellaneous pieces).
  V. Kichiku Noh (demon and animal pieces) or Kiri Noh Mono (final pieces)

Title	Category	Translation
Adachigahara	V	The Black Mound of the Adachi Plain
Akogi	IV	The Ghost of a Fisherman
Ama	V	The Fisherwoman
Aoi no Ue	IV	Lady Aoi Possessed
Arashiyama	I	The God of Mount Arashi
Ashikari	IV	The Reed Mower Hunted Out
Ataka	IV	Benkei at the Barrier of Ataka
Atsumori	II	A Young Flute Player of the Heike
Aya no Tsuzumi	IV	The Damask Drum
Bashô	III	The Spirit of the Plantain Tree
Chikubushima	I	The God of the Isle of Chikubu
Chôryô	V	Chang-liang, the Great Tactician of the Han

Title	Category	Translation
Daibutsu Kuyô	IV	Kagekiyo at the Enshrining of the Daibutsu
Daie	V	The Great Meeting Before the Buddha
Dampû	IV, V	The Divine Wind
Dôjôji	IV	The Temple Dôjôji
Ebira	II	A Plum Branch in the Quiver
Eboshi-ori	IV, V	The Hatmaker
Eguchi	III	The Courtesans of Eguchi
Ema	I	The Votive Offering
Fuji	III	The Spirit of the Wisteria
Fuji Taiko	IV	Court Musician Fuji's Drum
Fujito	IV	A Poor Young Fisherman of Fujito
Funabashi	IV	The Lovers on the Broken Boat Bridge
Funa Benkei	V	Benkei in the Boat
Futari Shizuka	III	Two Dancing Girls Named Shizuka
Gekkyûden	I	See Tsurukame
Gembuku Soga	IV	The Soga Brothers at the Ceremony of Coming of Age
Genji Kuyô	III	The Mass for Genji
Hachinoki	IV	Pot Plants
Hagoromo	III	The Robe of Feathers
Hajitomi	III	The Woman at the Wicket
Hakurakuten	I	The Poet Pai-lo T'ien
Hanagatami	IV	The Flower Basket, a Keepsake of Love
Hanjo	IV	The Courtesan's Fan
Hashi Benkei	IV	Benkei on the Bridge
Hibariyama	IV	Princess Chûjô's Nurse on Mount Hibari
Higaki	III	The Woman Within the Cypress Fence
Himuro	I	The Sacred Ice House
Hiun	V	Cloud-Drift the Monster
Hôjôgawa	I	Ceremony of Setting Fish Free at the River Hôjô
Hôkazô	IV	The Player Monks
Hyakuman	IV	The Insane Mother Hyakuman at Saga
Ikkaku Sennin	IV	The One-horned Hermit
Ikuta Atsumori	II	Atsumori at Ikuta
Iwafune	I	The Stone Boat
Izutsu	III	A Woman and a Well Curb
Jinen Koji	IV	Lay Priest Jinen
Kagekiyo	IV	Kagekiyo the Blind Man in Hyûga
Kagetsu	IV	Priest Kagetsu

Title	Category	Translation
Kakitsubata	III	The Spirit of the Iris
Kamo	I	The Thunder God of Kamo
Kamo Monogurui	IV	A Madwoman at Kamo
Kanawa	IV	The Metal Crown
Kanehira	II	A Brave Warrior of the Kiso Genji
Kantan	IV	A Dream at Han-tang
Kan'yô-kyû	IV, V	The Palace Hsien-yang
Kashiwazaki	IV	The Lady of Kashiwazaki
Kasuga Ryûjin	V	The Dragon God at Kasuga
Kayoi Komachi	IV	Nightly Visits to Poetess Komachi
Kazuraki	III, IV	An Itinerant Monk and the God of Mount Kazuraki
Kazuraki Tengu	V	The Goblin of Mount Kazuraki
Kenjô	V	Kenjô, the Finest Lute
Kikaigashima	IV	*See* Shunkan
Kikujidô	IV	*See* Makurajidô
Kinsatsu	I	The Gold Charm (*shûgen* or felicitation piece)
Kinuta	IV	Beating the Fulling Block
Kiyotsune	II	Kiyotsune and His Love
Kochô	III	The Butterfly
Kogô	IV	Lady Kogô
Koi no Omoni	IV	The Burden of Love
Kokaji	V	The Swordsmith and the Fox God
Kosode Soga	IV	The Soga Brothers and Their Mother
Kôu	V	Hsiang-yu the Defeated
Kôya Monogurui	IV	The Madman at Kôya
Kumasaka	V	Kumasaka the Chief Robber
Kurama Tengu	V	The Hobgoblin of Mount Kurama
Kureha	I	Kurehatori the Weaver (*shûgen* or felicitation piece)
Kurozuka	V	*See* Adachigahara
Kurumazô	V	The Monk in a Carriage
Kuzu	V	The Sweetfish of Kuzu
Makiginu	IV	The Rolls of Silk and a Priestess Possessed by a God
Makurajidô	IV	The Sacred Pillow and the Eternal Youth
Manju	IV	*See* Nakamitsu
Matsukaze	III	The Sisters of the Seashore
Matsumushi	IV	The Cries of Insects and the Sadness of Friendship

Title	Category	Translation
Matsuno-o	I	The Story of Matsuno-o Myôjin Shrine
Matsuyama Kagami	V	The Mirror of Matsuyama
Mekari	I	Offering of Sea Tangle
Michimori	II	A Noble Warrior of the Heike
Miidera	IV	The Insane Mother at the Mii Temple
Miwa	IV	The Goddess of Miwa
Mochizuki	IV, V	Mochizuki Revenged
Momijigari	V	The Maple Viewing
Morihisa	IV	Morihisa Saved
Motomezuka	IV	The Tomb of a Maiden
Mutsura	III	The Spirit of the Maple Tree
Nakamitsu	IV	The Loyalty of Nakamitsu
Naniwa	I	The Flowery Capital of the Emperor Nintoku
Nishikido	IV	Izumi no Saburô and His Brothers
Nishikigi	IV	Courtship by Piling up the Twigs of Nishikigi
Nomori	V	The Field-keeping Demon
Nonomiya	III	The Princess of the Provisional Palace
Nue	IV, V	The Monkey-headed Monster
Obasute	III	The Old Woman Abandoned on the Mountain
Ôeyama	V	The Demon of Mount Ôe
Ôhara Gokô	III	The Imperial Visit to Ôhara
Oimatsu	I	The Ancient Pine Tree
Ominaeshi	IV	The Spirit of the Mountain Flower
Ômu Komachi	III	Komachi Replying in an Ode to the Emperor
Orochi	IV, V	The Eight-headed Serpent
Oshio	III, IV	Narihira at Oshio
Rashômon	V	Rashômon, the Southern Gate of Kyôto
Rôdaiko	IV	The Prison Drum and the Woman
Sagi	IV	A Heron and the Emperor
Saigyôzakura	III, IV	The Cherry Tree of Saigyô the Hermit
Sakuragawa	IV	The Mother on the River Sakura
Sanemori	II	Saitô Bettô Sanemori, a Brave Veteran of the Heike
Sanshô	IV	The Three Laughing Hermits
Seiganji	III	Abbot Ippen and Lady Izumi Shikibu's Spirit
Seiôbo	I	Seiôbo the Fairy Queen
Sekidera Komachi	III	Komachi at the Seki Temple
Semimaru	IV	The Blind Prince and His Sister
Senju	III	Senju no Mae and Shigehira

Title	Category	Translation
Sesshô Seki	IV, V	The Killing Stone of the Nasu Plain
Shakkyô	V	The Dancing of the Lion on the Stone Bridge
Shari	V	The Sarira, or the Sacred Ashes of Buddha
Shichiki-ochi	IV	The Escape of the Seven Warriors
Shiga	I	The Poet-God of Shiga
Shirahige	I	The Revelation of Shirahige Myôjin
Shôjô	V	Shôjô and an Obedient Son
Shôki	V	The Minister Chung-k'uei
Shôkun	V	Wan Chao-chun Sacrificed
Shôzon	IV, V	Shôzon Attacks Yoshitsune
Shun'ei	IV	Shun'ei-maru Saved
Shunkan	IV	Shunkan in Exile
Shunzei Tadanori	II	Court Poet Shunzei and Tadanori
Sôshi Arai Komachi	III	Komachi Washing the Poem Book
Sotoba Komachi	III	Old Komachi at the Stupa
Suma Genji	V	Hikaru Genji at the Seashore of Suma
Sumidagawa	IV	The Mad Mother at the River Sumida
Sumiyoshi Môde	III, IV	Lady Akashi and Hikaru Genji at Sumiyoshi
Tadanobu	IV	Tadanobu at Yoshino
Tadanori	II	Warrior-Poet of the Heike
Taema	IV, V	The Temple of Taema
Taihei Shôjô	V	A Big Jar of Wine and Shôjô
Takasago	I	The Pine Tree of Takasago
Tamakazura	IV	Lady Tamakazura
Tamura	II	Sakanoue no Tamuramaro
Tanikô	IV, V	The Sanction Against Throwing into a Valley
Tatsuta	III, IV	The Goddess Tatsuta
Teika	III	The Princess Shokushi, Teika's Love
Tenko	IV	The Rare Drum
Tôboku	III	A Plum Tree of the Tôboku-in
Tôbôsaku	I	Tung-fang-shuo the Hermit
Tôei	IV	The Succession of Tôei
Tôgan Koji	IV	Lay Priest Tôgan
Tokusa	IV	An Old Rush Cutter
Tomoe	II	The Woman Warrior, Wife of Kiso Yoshinaka
Tomonaga	II	The Death of Tomonaga, Young Prince of the Genji
Tôru	V	The Ghost of Tôru, the Minister of the Left
Tôsen	IV	Homeward Bound for China

Title	Category	Translation
Tsuchigumo	V	The Cave Monster
Tsuchiguruma	IV	A Mad Cartman
Tsunemasa	II	A Noble Biwa Player of the Heike
Tsurukame	I	The Crane and the Tortoise
Ugetsu	IV	Rain or Moon
Ukai	V	A Cormorant Fisherman
Ukifune	IV	Princess Ukifune
Umegae	IV	A Musician's Wife
Uneme	III	The Drowned Court Lady
Unrin-in or Urin-in	III, IV	Narihara at the Temple Unrin
Utaura	IV, V	A Missing Father and a Diviner
Utô	IV	The Ghost of a Hunter
Yamamba	V	The Mountain Demoness
Yashima	II	Hôgan Yoshitsune at Yashima
Yôkihi	III	Yang Kuei-fei
Yorimasa	II	Minamoto Yorimasa at Uji
Yôrô	I	The Care of the Aged
Yoroboshi	IV	A Blind Weakling
Yoshino Shizuka	III	Shizuka at Yoshino
Youchi Soga	IV	The Soga Brothers' Night Attack
Yûgao	III	The Ghost of Lady Yûgao
Yugyô Yanagi	III	The Itinerant Monk and the Willow Tree
Yumiyawata	I	The Bow and the God of Yawata
Yuya	III	The Mistress of Munemori
Zegai	V	The Hobgoblin of China

APPENDIX THREE

THE REPERTOIRE OF KYÔGEN PIECES

Abbreviations of schools: I. Izumi school
　　　　　　　　　　　　O. Ôkura school
　　　　　　　　　　　　M. Mibu Kyôgen

Title	School	Translation	Translator
Aiai Eboshi		Headgear for Two Peasants	
Akagari	I., O.	Chapped Feet	
Akubo	I., O.	The Priest and the Knave	Honda, Masujirô & Williams, Frank Backus
Akutagawa	I., O.	Two Cripples on the River Akuta	
Akutarô	I., O.	Akutarô	Sadler, A. L.
Asaina	I., O.	Asaina	Sadler, A. L.
Asau	I., O.	The Headgear of the Lord	
Awasegaki	I., O.	Persimmon Vendor	
Awataguchi	I., O.	Sword Contest	
Bakuchi Jûô	I., O.	A Gambler in Hell	
Bakurô	I., O.	Horse Riding in Hell	
Bishamon Renga	I.	A Godsend	
Bikusada	I., O.	A Nun and Her Godchild	
Bôbôgashira	O.	See Kiku no Hana	
Bonsan	I., O.	Miniature Landscape	
Bonsan Nusubito		See Bonsan	
Bôshibari	I., O.	Pinioned	
		Tied to a Pole	McKinnon, Richard N.
		Attachés au bâton	Renondeau, G.

234 • APPENDICES

Title	School	Translation	Translator
Buaku	I., O.	Buaku	Sakanishi, Shio
Bunzô	I., O.	Bunzô	
Busshi	I., O.	The Buddha Maker	Sadler, A. L.
Busu	I., O.	Somebody-Nothing	Itô, Michio & Ledoux, Louis V.
		Around the Hibachi	Lombard, Frank A.
		Busu	Keene, Donald
		Sweet Poison	McKinnon, Richard N.
		Le poison	Péri, Noël
Chakagi Zatô	I., O.	Pepper in a Bowl of Tea	
Chasambai	I.	A Woman and Her Chinese Husband	
Chatsubo	I., O.	A Tea Caddy	
		Vaso di thè	Shiomi, Harukichi & Vingiani, Rodolfo
Chidori	I., O.	Embezzling of the Sakè Barrel	
Chigirigi	I., O.	All Are Brave When the Enemy Flees	
Chigo Yabusame	I.	A Substitute Child	
Chikubushima Mairi	I.	Mimicry	
Daihannya	I., O.	The Prayer Contest	
Daikoku Renga	I., O.	The Revelation of Daikoku	
Dobu-katchiri	I., O.	The Two Blind Men	Noguchi, Yone
		Plop! Clip!	Sakanishi, Shio
Dochihagure	I.	Two Chances	
Dogonsô	I., O.	A Sermon to a Fool	
Domori	I., O.	A Stammerer's Quarrel	
Dontarô	I., O.	Mr. Dumb Tarô	Sadler, A. L.
Ebisu Bishamon	I., O.	Ebisu and Bishamon	
Ebisu Daikoku	I., O.	Ebisu and Daikoku	Sadler, A. L.
Echigo Muko	I., O.	The Dancing Bridegroom	
Esashi Jûô	I.	The Bird Catcher in Hades	Keene, Donald
		The Bird Catcher in Hades	Sakanishi, Shio
		The Bird Catcher in Hell	Waley, Arthur
		The Fowler	Sadler, A. L.
Fujimatsu	I., O.	A Pine Tree of Fuji	
Fukitori	I., O.	A Piper Hired	
Fukube no Shin	I., O.	The Mendicants' Prayer	

Title	School	Translation	Translator
Fuku no Kami	I., O.	The God of Wealth	
Fukurô	O.	See Fukuro Yamabushi	
Fukurô Yamabushi	I.	The Yamabushi and the Owl	
Fumi Ninai	I., O.	The Love-Letter Deliverers	
Fumi Yamadachi	I., O.	Testaments of Two Bandits	
Funawatashi Muko	I., O.	The Boatman's Son-in-Law	
Fune Funa	I., O.	Fune or Funa?	
Fusenai	I., O.	No Offering	
		Pas d'aumône	Péri, Noël
Fusenaikyô	I., O.	See Fusenai	
Futaribakama	I., O.	One Hakama for Two Men	
Futari Daimyô	I., O.	The Two Daimyo	McKinnon, Richard N.
		Two Lords	Hori, Eishirô
Fuzumô	I., O.	Wrestling by Instruction	
Gan Daimyô	I., O.	Goose-stealing Daimyo	
Gan Karigane	I., O.	Two Words for Goose	
Gan Tsubute	I., O.	See Kari Tsubute	
Gyûba	I.	See Ushi Uma	
Hachiku Renga	I., O.	Poems Solve a Debt	
Hachitataki		See Fukube no Shin	
Hagi Daimyô	I., O.	Bush-Clover Daimyo	
		Hagi Daimyô	Florenz, Karl A.
		A Man and His Wife	Clements, Colin Campbell
Hakuyô	I., O.	Competition for a Lute	
Hana Arasoi	I., O.	Argument over a Flower	
Hanago	I., O.	Hanako	Sadler, A. L.
		Mademoiselle Hana	Péri, Noël
		Die Busse	Gersdorf, Wolfgang von
Hana Nusubito	I., O.	Flower Thief	
Hana Ori	O.	See Hana Ori Shimbochi	
Hana Ori Shimbochi	I.	A Novice Breaks a Flower	
Hanatorizumô	I., O.	Nose-pulling Sumô	
Hansen	I., O.	A Priest and A Horse Dealer in Hades	
Haratatezu	I., O.	The Priest Who Would Not Get Angry	
Haridako	I., O.	Dried Octopus	

236 · APPENDICES

Title	School	Translation	Translator
Hige Yagura	I., O.	The Fortifield Beard	
Hikkukuri	I., O.	What a Divorced Wife Wants	
Hikuzu	I., O.	Tea Dust and a Devil	
Hi no Sake	I., O.	A Pipe of Sakè	
Hisshiki Muko	I., O.	The Groom's Trousers	
Hito ka Kui ka		See Kui ka Hito ka	
Hito Uma	I., O.	A Man-Horse	
Hôchô Muko	I., O.	Bridegroom' Manual	
Hôjô no Tane	I., O.	Seed of Hôjô	
Honekawa	I., O.	The Ribs and the Cover	Sakanishi, Shio
		Ribs and Skin	Chamberlain, Basil Hall
		Les os et la peau	Péri, Noël
Hôrokuwari	M.	The Breaking of the Plates	
Hôshi ga Haha	I., O.	The Reunited Couple	
Igui	I., O.	The Disappearing Boy	
Imajimmei	I.	A Teahouse in Front of Ima Shrine	
Ima Mairi	I., O.	The New Servant	
"I" Moji	I., O.	The Letter "I"	
In'abadô	I., O.	The Oracle of In'abadô Shrine	
Inu Yamabushi	I., O.	A Fierce Dog and an Itinerant Monk	
Iori no Ume	I., O.	Poems on the Plum Tree	
Iroha	I., O.	A-B-C	Shiomi, Harukichi
Irumagawa	I., O.	The River Iruma	
Ishigami	I., O.	The Stone God	Sadler, A. L.
Itoma no Fukuro		The Bag of Leave-taking	Sadler, A. L.
		The Bag of Parting	Sakanishi, Shio
Iwahashi	I., O.	Song of Iwahashi	
Jisenseki	I., O.	The Chanting of Jisenseki	
Jishaku	I., O.	The Magnet	
Jizômai	I., O.	The Dance of Jizô	
Jûki	I., O.	Jûki and Tonsure	
Kachiguri	I., O.	Dried Chestnuts as Land Tax	
Kagami Otoko	I., O.	The Man and the Mirror	
Kagyû	I., O.	The Snail	

Title	School	Translation	Translator
Kaichû Muko	I., O.	Souvenirs for a Bridegroom	
Kakiuri		The Persimmon Seller	Sadler, A. L.
Kaki Yamabushi	I., O.	The Persimmon Priest	
		Le yamabushi et les kaki	Renondeau, G.
Kakushi-danuki	I., O.	The Selling of a Badger	
Kakusui	I.	Poetry Contest of Prospective Bridegrooms	
Kakusui Muko		See Kakusui	
Kamabara	I., O.	The Sickle and Injured Pride	McKinnon, Richard N.
		Un coup de serpe dans le ventre	Péri, Noël
Kamappara		See Kamabara	
Kaminari	I., O.	Thunder God	
		Dieu du tonnerre	Tuck, Oswald G.
Kanaoka	I., O.	Painter Kanaoka and His Wife	
Kanazu		See Kanazu Jizô	
Kanazu Jizô	I.	The Child's Guardian Deity Alive	
Kane no Ne	I., O.	The Price of Gold or the Sound of Bells	
Kani Yamabushi	I., O.	The Crab and the Yamabushi	McKinnon, Richard N.
Kari Daimyô		See Gan Daimyô	
Kari Tsubute	I., O.	A Stoned Wild Goose	
Kasa no Shita		Under the Hat	Sadler, A. L.
Kasen	I., O.	The Master Poets	
Kawakami Jizô		See Kawakami Zatô	
Kawakami Zatô		The Blind Man and Jizô	
		Il Jizô sul fiume	Shiomi, Harukichi
Kawara no Tarô	I., O.	The Request for Rice Wine	
Kazumô	I., O.	The Mosquito Wrestler	
		La lutte avec le moustique	Renondeau, G.
Keimyô	I., O.	Father's Life and a Cat	
Keiryû	I., O.	Does a Cock Sing or Crow?	
Kembutsuzaemon	I., O.	Mr. Sightseer	
Kikazu Zatô	J., O.	The Blind and the Deaf	
Kiku no Hana	I.	The Chrysanthemum	

238 · APPENDICES

Title	School	Translation	Translator
Kikusui Ôji		*See* Yakusui	
Kintôzaemon	I., O.	A Bandit Menaced by a Woman	
Kinya	I., O.	The Virtue of Silence	
Kirokuda	I., O.	Six Loads of Wood	
Kitsunetsuki		Possessed by Foxes	
		La possession par les renards	Bénaget, Alexandre
Kitsunezuka	I., O.	The Fox's Grave	Itô, Michio & Ledoux, Louis V.
		Fox Hill	Noguchi, Yone
Kiyomizu Zatô	I., O.	The Blind Get Married	
Kobugaki	I.	Sea Tangle and Persimmons	
Kogarakasa	I., O.	The Feigned Priest	
Kôji	I., O.	Three Tangerines	
Kôjidawara	I., O.	A Bag of Tangerines	
Kombuuri	I., O.	Vendor of Seaweed	
Konkai		*See* Tsurigitsune	
Konomi Arasoi	I., O.	The Battle of Fruits	
Ko Nusubito	I., O.	The Thief and the Child	Sadler, A. L.
Koppi		*See* Honekawa	
Koshi Inori	I., O.	The Back-straightening Prayer	
Kôyaku Neri	I., O.	The Ointment Vendor	Sadler, A. L.
Kubihiki	I., O.	The Tug of War	McKinnon, Richard N.
Kuchimane	I., O.	Mimicry	
Kuchimane Muko	I.	The Mimic Bridegroom	
Kui ka Hito ka	I.	Stake or Man?	
Kuji Zainin	I., O.	Criminal by Lot	
Kumo Nusubito	I., O.	Thief in a Spider's Web	
Kurama Mairi	I., O.	A Pilgrimage to Mount Kurama	
Kurama Muko	I., O.	The Bridegroom from Kurama	
Kurikono Shimmei		*See* Imajimmei	
Kurikuma Jimmei		*See* Imajimmei	
Kuriyaki	I., O.	Chestnut Roasting	
Kusabira	O.	Mushrooms	McKinnon, Richard N.
Magomuko	I., O.	The Grandson Bridegroom	
Makura Monogurui	I., O.	The Old Man's Love	

APPENDICES • 239

Title	School	Translation	Translator
Mari Zatô	I., O.	Blind Men's Football	
Matsubayashi	I., O.	Felicity Dance	
Matsuyani	I., O.	The Spirit of Pine Resin	
Matsu Yuzuriha	I., O.	One Hat for Two	
Mechika		See Mejika Komebone	
Mejika Komebone	I., O.	Two Kinds of Fan	
Mikazuki	I., O.	The Winnow-Basket Hat	
Miyage no Kagami		The Gift Mirror	Noguchi, Yone
Mizukake Muko	I., O.	The Family Quarrel	Sakanishi, Shio
Mizukikazu		See Kikazu Zatô	
Mizukumi		See Mizukumi Shimbochi	
Mizukumi Shimbochi	I., O.	The Acolyte's Water-drawing	Sadler, A. L.
Mochizake	I., O.	Rice Cake and Wine	
Monomane		See Chikubushima Mairi	
Moraimuko	I., O.	The Repentant Hubsand	
Munetsuki	I., O.	A Punch in the Chest	
Nabeyatsubachi	I., O.	Pots and Drums	
Nagamitsu	I., O.	Nagamitsu	Velenziani, Carlo
		The Sword Nagamitsu	
Naginata Ashirai	I., O.	Reception by Halberd	
Nakiama	I., O.	The Crying Nun	
Nakimuko		See Moraimuko	
Namagusamono	I., O.	Fishy Sword	
Nariagari	I., O.	Evolution of A Sword	
Narihira Mochi	I., O.	Narihira and the Rice Cakes	
Naruko	I., O.	The Clapper Guards	
Naruko Yaruko	I., O.	Naruko or Yaruko?	
Natorigawa	I., O.	Name-stealing River	
Nawanai	I., O.	Twisting a Rope	
Negi Yamabushi	I., O.	The Shinto Priest and the Yamabushi	
Neongyoku	I., O.	The Recumbent Singer	
Nikujûhachi	I., O.	Two Nines Make Eighteen	
Niô	I., O.	The Deva King	Noguchi, Yone
		Le nio	Péri, Noël
Niwatori Muko	I., O.	The Bridegroom Imitates a Cock	
Nukegara	I., O.	The Demon's Shell	Noguchi, Yone

Title	School	Translation	Translator
Nurishi		See Nushi Heiroku	
Nuritsuke	I.	Lacquered While You Wait	
Nushi		See Nushi Heiroku	
Nushi Heiroku	I., O.	Heiroku the Lacquerer	
Nyakuichi	I., O.	The Nun Nyakuichi's Revenge	
Oba ga Sake	I., O.	Aunty's Sakè	Noguchi, Yone
		Le saké de la tante	Bénazet, Alexandre
Ocha no Mizu		See Mizukumi Shimbochi	
Ohiyashi	I., O.	A Cup of Water	
Okadayû	I., O.	A Forgetful Husband	
Okosako		See Uchizata	
Onda	O.	Rice Planting	
Ongyoku Muko	I., O.	Musical Bridegroom	
Onigawara	I., O.	The Demon Tile	Noguchi, Yone
		The Gargoyle	Sadler, A. L.
Onimaru	I., O.	The Thief Onimaru	
Oni no Mamako	I., O.	The Devil's Stepchild	
Oni no Tsuchi		The Demon's Mallet	Noguchi, Yone
		The Magic Mallet of the Devil	Sakanishi Shio
Origami Muko	I., O.	The Bridegroom and the Dowry	
Ôtônai	I., O.	Priest Ôtônai	
Rakuami	I., O.	The Ghost of Rakuami	Sadler, A. L.
Renga Jittoku	I., O.	A Poetry Instructor	
Renga Nusubito	I., O.	Poem-chanting Robbers	
Renjaku	I., O.	The Silk Dealer Beaten by a Woman	
Roku Jizô	I., O.	The Six Jizô	
Rokuninsô	I., O.	The Six Priests	
		Tous religieux	Péri, Noël
		The Six Shavelings	Sadler, A. L.
		Drei Tonsuren	Langegg, F. A. Junker von
		The Six Who Became Priests	
Rômusha	I., O.	The Excluded Old Man	
Roren	I., O.	A Converted Innkeeper	

Title	School	Translation	Translator
Sadogitsune	I., O.	The Fox of Sado Island	
Saihô	I., O.	Old Man Saihô	
Sai no Kawara	I., O.	The River of Fate	
Sai no Me	I., O.	Counting Dice Spots	
Sai no Me Muko		See Sai no Me	
Sakekô no Shiki	I., O.	The Sake Sermon	
Sakka	I., O.	Sakka the Rascal	
Sako no Samurô	I., O.	Samurô the Hunter	
Sambonbashira	I., O.	Three Logs	
Sannimpu	I., O.	Three Peasants	
Sannin Chôja	I., O.	Three Millionaires	
Sannin Katawa	I., O.	The Three Cripples	Brinkley, Frank
		Sannin Katawa	Hori, Eishirô
		The Three Deformed Men	Tsuda, Umeko
		Les trois estropiats	Revon, Michel
Saru Kôtô		The Second-Class Master	
		An Unfair Exchange	
Saru Muko	I., O.	The Monkey Bridegroom	
		The Blind Man and the Monkey	
Saru Zatô	I., O.	The Blind Man's Wife	
Satsumanokami	I., O.	A Free Ride	
Sazae		The Wreath Shell	
Seirai	I., O.	See Esashi Jûô	
Semi	I., O.	The Cicada	
Senjimono	I., O.	The Tea Vendor	
Setsubun	I., O.	The Eve of Spring	
Shatei	I., O.	Brother Thief	
Shibiri	I., O.	Pins and Needles	Sadler, A. L.
Shidôhôgaku	I., O.	The Horse Shidôhôgaku	
		Ubicumque domate	Shiomi, Harukichi
Shikagari		The Stag Hunter	Sadler, A. L.
Shimbai	I., O.	Pine Branch and Sword	Tsuda, Umeko
Shimizu	I., O.	Spring Water	
Shujô	I., O.	The Priest's Staff	Sadler, A. L.
Shûku Karakasa	I., O.	Poems and Umbrellas	
Shûron	I., O.	Religious Competition	
Sôhachi	I., O.	Sôhachi	Hori, Eishirô
		Sôhachi	Péri, Noël

242 • APPENDICES

Title	School	Translation	Translator
Soraude	I., O.	The Blusterer	
Suehiro		See Suehirogari	
Suehirogari	I., O.	An Old Umbrella for a Fan	
		Allargapunta	Shimoi, Harukichi
Sugoroku	I., O.	Backgammon	
Su Hajikami	I., O.	Vendors of Vinegar and Ginger	
Suminuri		See Suminuri Onna	
Suminuri Onna	I., O.	The Ink Smear	Hori, Eishirô
		The Ink-smeared Lady	Sakanishi, Shio
		Ink-stained	
		The Ink Woman	Noguchi, Yone
		La femme barbouillée d'encre	Péri, Noël
		Tinten Blecken	Langegg, F.A. Junker von
		La donna d'inchiostro	
Suô Otoshi	I., O.	The Lost Dress Coat	
Surukae Kôtô		See Saru Kôtô	
Suzuki Bôchô	I., O.	An Uneaten Fish	
Tachi Ubai	I., O.	Sword Stealing	
Taiko Oi	I.	The Drum Carrier	
Taishi no Teboko	I., O.	The Halberd of Prince Shôtoku	
Takara no Kasa	I., O.	The Magic Straw Hat	
Takara no Tsuchi	I., O.	A Mallet of Treasure	
Takenoko	I., O.	Bamboo Shoots	
Tako	I., O.	The Cuttle-Fish	Sadler, A. L.
Tanuki no Hara Tzuzumi	I., O.	A Badger's Drum	
Taru Muko	I., O.	The Bridegroom's Barrel	
Taue	I.	See Onda	
Teoi Yamadachi		The Wounded Highwayman	Sakanishi, Shio
Tobikoe	I., O.	A Novice Fallen in the River	
Tobikoe Shimbochi	I.	See Tobikoe	
Tôjin Kodakara	I., O.	A Chinese and His Son	
Tôjin-zumô	I.	See Tôzumô	

APPENDICES • 243

Title	School	Translation	Translator
Tokoro	I., O.	The Mountain Potato	
Tôzumô	O.	Chinese Sumô	
Tsûen	I., O.	Tsûen	Sadler, A. L.
Tsukimi Zatô	O.	The Moon-viewing Blind Man	
Tsukushi	O.	See Uta Arasoi	
Tsukushi no Oku	I., O.	Laughing Peasants	
Tsuribari	I., O.	A Fishhook	
Tsurigitsune	I., O.	The Fox and the Trapper	McKinnon, Richard N.
		Le renard pris au piège	Péri, Noël
Tsuri Onna		She Who Was Fished	Ito, Michio & Ledoux, Louis V.
Tsuto Yamabushi	I., O.	The Stolen Lunch	
Tsutsu Sasae	I., O.	Tsutsu or Sasae?	
Uchizata	I.	Causa Privata	Shimoi, Harukichi
Uguisu	I., O.	A Bush Warbler	
Uozeppô	I., O.	A Sermon on Fish	
Uri Nusubito	I., O.	The Melon Thief	Noguchi, Yone
		The Melon Thief	Tsuda, Umeko
Urusashi	I.	Don't Be Nosy	
Ushi Nusubito	I.	The Cow Thief	Obata, Shigeyoshi
Ushi Uma	I., O.	Cow and Horse	
Uta Arasoi	I., O.	Poetry Contest	
Utsubozaru	I., O.	The Quiver Monkey	Hall, M. E.
		The Quiver and the Monkey	McKinnon, Richard N.
		Scimmia per faretra	Hori, Eishirô
Wakame		Seaweed or Young Woman?	
Wakana	I., O.	The Flower Girls	
Yao	I., O.	A Man from Yao in Hades	
		Le Jizô de Yao	Péri, Noël
Yao Jizô		See Yao	
Yakusui	I.	The Water of Longevity	
Yasematsu		See Kintôzaemon	
Yawata no Mae	I., O.	The Would-Be Bridegroom	
Yobigoe	O.	Irresistible Rhythm	
Yokoza	I., O.	A Cow Named Yokoza	

Title	School	Translation	Translator
Yoneichi	I.	A Bale of Rice and a Kimono	
Yoroi	O.	A Suit of Armor	
Yoroi Haramaki	I.	*See* Yoroi	
Yukiuchi	I., O.	Snow Battle	
Yumiya	I., O.	Bow and Arrow	
Yumiya Tarô	I., O.	A Coward with a Devil's Mask	
Yûzen	I., O.	Umbrella Maker Yûzen	
Zazen		*See* Hanago	

INDEX

Abe, 34
Abe Suehisa, 31
Account of the New Sarugaku, see *Shin Sarugaku Ki*
Achime, 21
actors' lineage, 194-95
ado, 122
Aeschylus, 171
Agemaki, 209
Ai Kyôgen, 88, 113
Akechi Mitsuhide, 159
Akegarasu, 203
Akoya, 179, 203
Akoya no Kotozeme, see *Dannoura Kabuto Gunki*
Amabe, 17, 22
Ama no Iwato, 6, 19
Ame no Gorô, 214
Ame no Uzume, 19, 20
Aoi no Ue, 118
aorigaeshi, 202
Aotozôshi Hana no Nishikie, 206
aragoto, 141, 177, 189-91, 194, 199, 200, 207-8, 215, 219
aramai, see *Bushimai*
Arashiyama, 119
Aristotle, 149, 161
Ariwara no Narihira, 157
asamamono, 214

Asano Takuminokami Naganori, 142-43
Ashikaga Takauji, 70
Ashikaga Yoshimasa, 73, 99, 102
Ashikaga Yoshimi, 73
Ashikaga Yoshimitsu, 84, 90-91
Ashikaga Yoshinori, 93, 96
ashirai, 120
ashirai-ai, 119
Ataka, 117, 119, 206, 208
Atsumori, 115, 158, 168-69
Atsumori, 74, 116, 137, 168
Atsuta no Shunkô-mon, 73
aware, 8
Ayai, 74
Ayakiri, 35, 37
ayatsuri, 174
ayumimichi, 184
Azumi, 22

Bandô Mitsugorô III, 213, 220
Bangaku, 77
Baramon, 25
baroque, 142, 161, 187
Bashô, 99, 116, 118
Batô, 38, 61
Benkei, 140, 208-9
Benten Kozô, see *Shiranami Gonin Otoko*
Benzaiten, 60

245

Binzasara, 73
binzasara, 71, 73
Bishamon, 48, 124
Bishaô Gonnokami, 64–65
biwa, 14, 43, 54, 172, 176
Biwa Hôshi, 54
Bodai Senna, 32
bokufu, 96
Bôshibari, 120, 123, 206, 213
Bugaku, 3, 6, 8, 9, 11, 31–39, 127, 144–45, 173
bukkaeri, 202
Bun'an Dengaku Noh, 73–74
Bun'an Noh Ki, 73
bungo-bushi, 220
Bunno, 34
Bunnomai, 36, 37, 38
Bunomai, 36, 37
Bunraku Association, 182
Bunrakuza, 146, 182
bunya-bushi, 148
Bunzô, 114
Bushimai, 76, 79
busshôe, 26–27
Buttetsu, 32
Byôbu, 73

Chichi-no-jô, 115
Chidô, 25
chidô, 28
Chien-ch'i K'un-t'uo, 41
chigo, 52, 53, 56
Chigo Sarugaku, 99
Chigusa, 114
Chijimiya Shinsuke, 204
Chikamatsu Monzaemon, 135, 156, 178, 179, 191, 205, 206, 211, 212, 216, 219
Chikubushima, 116
Chisô (Chih-tung), 24
chobochobo, 187
chobo yuka, 187
Chôjû Giga, 129
chokushi-mai, 56
Chôkyô (Ch'ang-kung), 37
Chôtengaku, 32

Chronicles of Japan, see *Nihon Shoki*
Chuang-tzu (*Sôshi*), 60
Chûbei, 192
Chûjô, 115
Chûmonguchi, 71, 73
chû no mai, 113
Chûshin, 212
Chûshingura, see *Kanadehon Chûshingura*
commedia dell'arte, 141, 189
Craig, E. Gordon, 154

Daifuryû, 54, 56, 57, 60–61
Daijô Kagura, 77
Daikagura, 18
Daikoku Renga, 120
daishû, 52, 53
Daitô Monju-te, 48
Dannoura Kabuto Gunki, 159, 203
Danshichi Kurobei, 180, 203
debayashi, 198
degatari, 198
Dengaku, 9, 12, 62, 172
Dengaku, 43
Dengaku Hôshi Yurai no Koto, 71
Dengaku Noh, 12, 13, 69–74, 83
Densho, 120
Dionysus, 171, 172
Dôa, 70, 83, 87, 91
dobyôshi, 27
Dôjôji, 79, 117; see also *Kyôganoko Musume Dôjôji*
Dôkemai, 76, 79
donchô, 188
Dôren, 70
double-suicide plays, see *sewamono*

Ebina Nan'ami, 84
Ebisu, 173
Echi, 114
Echizen Deme, 115
Eguchi, 93, 116
Ehon Taikôki, 159, 181
ei, 37
Eighteen Favorites (*jûhachiban*), 139, 207–9

Ei'in, 55
Embu, 39
Emmai Za, 63, 65, 82
enkiriba, 204
Enkyoku, 12, 14
Ennen Noh, 11, 13, 15, 52-61, 87, 128-29
En no Ozunu, 75
Enoshima, 119
Entairyaku, 69
Enya Hangan, 136, 143
Etenraku, 59
Euripides, 171

Faithful, The, 135
folk dramas, 172
Freytag, Gustav, 161
Fudô, 208
Fudoki, 6
fue, 113
Fûinkiri, see *Meido no Hikyaku*
Fujimoto Tobun, 206
Fujiwara Jihei, 166
Fujiwara no Akihira, 42, 44, 45
Fujiwara no Teibin, 72
Fujiwara no Yorimichi, 33
Fuji Yasha, 70
Fukai, 115
Fukuchi Ôchi, 206
fukumatsu kaiwa (fumo k'aiho), 130
Fuku no Kami, 120, 122; mask, 124
Fukuô school, 108
Fukurai, 114
Fûkyokushû, 92
fumiita, 219
Fumyô-ô Kyô, 72
Funa Benkei, 100, 119, 139-40
funazoko, 147
Furihoko, 39
Furugôri, 74
Furu no Noh, 93
Furyû, 46-47, 53, 54, 55, 57, 119, 217
furyû-goe, 59
Fûshi Kaden (Kadensho), 89-90, 91, 92, 104

Fushizuke, 92
Futaomote, 214
futozao, 149
Fuwa, 208
Fuzokumai, 17

Gafu Zatsuroku (Yüehfu Tsalu), 127
Gagaku, 32, 33; *see also* Bugaku
Gagakuryô, 32
Gakkaroku, 31
Gappo, 71, 74
Gedatsu, 208
geinô, 4, 17
Gempei Seisuiki, 116, 157
Gen'e, 88
Gengorô, 102
Genji, 74
Genji and Heike cycle, 157
Genji Monogatari (The Tale of Genji), 8, 35, 111, 116
Genjô, 73
Genjôraku, 37-38
Genkyoku (Yüan-ch'ü), 129
Gesamtkunstwerk, 134
geza music, 197
ghost stories, 216; see also *Tôkaidô Yotsuya Kaidan*
gidayû, gidayû-bushi, 147, 148-49, 176, 181, 195-96
gidayû jôruri (new jôruri), 148, 157, 178
gidayû kyôgen, 181, 205-6, 207, 219
Gidô Shûshin, 90
Gigaku, 6, 8, 9, 11, 24-30, 126-27, 173
Gikeiki, 157
Gireimai, 78
Go, 46, 63
Godairiki Koi no Fûjime, 204, 206, 220
Goethe, Johann Wolfgang von, 154
Gohiiki Kanjinchô, 220
Gojo, 25, 28
Gokô, 25, 28
Gokomatsu, emperor, 91
Gômin Sarugaku, 63
Gongen, 76
Gongen-mai, 76, 78

gôsei, 128
Goshirakawa, emperor, 169
Greek drama, 149, 171, 189
gyôdo, 26
Gyokuyô, 47

Hachiman, 17
Hadesugata Onna Maiginu, 160, 181, 205
hagataki, 194
Hagoromo, 116, 118, 137
Hajitomi, 116
haka-jishi, 78
Hakozaki, 74
Hakushiki-jô, 115
Hamlet, 141, 159, 182, 200, 201
Hamuro Tokinaga, 157
hana, 13, 39, 85, 94, 184
Hana Matsuri, 12, 76
hanamichi, 147, 184–85, 187, 190, 219
Hana-ori, 56
Hana Yasha, 70
haniwa, 5
han noh, 97
Hannya, 115
Hanzoku Taishi, 71, 72
Harada Kai, 160
Haraka, 74
harima-bushi, 178
hashi-gakari, 71, 108
hashiride, 37, 48
Hashirimai (Hashirimono), 37
Hashirimono (Hashirimai), 34, 37
hashirimono (running things), 61, 128, 129
Hata no Kôkatsu, 34
hataraki, 113
hatsuharu kyôgen, 215
hayashi, 22, 47, 66, 106
Hayashi family, 34
hayashi-kata, 107
hayashi-uta, 22
hayato, 20
haya-uchi-ai, 119
Haya-uta, 21

Hearn, Lafcadio, 210
Heike-*biwa* narration, 174–75
Heike Monogatari (*The Tale of the Heike*), 14, 72, 111, 116, 168, 172, 175
Heike Nyogo ga Shima, 159, 205
Heikyoku, 14, 174, 175
Heikyoku, 57
henge buyô, 213
Hibariyama, 203
hibuse, 76
hichiriki, 36, 54
Hi Chôbô (Fei Ch'ang-fang), 60
Hidakagawa Iriaizakura, 150
Hidensho, 93
Hie family, 101
Hie Yahei, 89
Hikihito no Mai, 43, 128
hikimaku, 188
hikinuki, 202
Hikorokuza, 146
Himi, 114
Himuro, 119
hinadan, 187, 198
Hiramai, 36
hiramono, 122
Hisamatsu, 160
Hitori Sugoroku, 43
Hitori Sumai, 43
hitotsu-ashi, 50
Hitsuji, 74
Hiyama, 77
Hôbutsushû, 72
hogaibito, 88
hôgatame, 66, 78
Hoho Hikodemi, 20
Hôin Kagura, 77
Hôjôji Za, 63
Hôjô Takatoki, 69
Homer, 171
Honchô Nijûshikô, 135, 159, 181
Hônen Shônin, 73
hon hanamichi, 184
Honjo no Monjaku, 46, 47, 54
Hon Kyôgen, 119
hô-noronji, 48

Hono Susori, 20
Honza, 62, 63, 70
hôraku, 50
Horikawa, emperor, 33
Horikawa Nami no Tsuzumi, 160
Hôryûji temple, 24, 55
ho-sheng, see *gôsei*
Hoshi, 21
Hôshô Kurô, 106
Hôshô Za, 99, 103
hôsôshi, 127
Hyakki Yakô Zu, 129
Hyakuman, 85, 117, 118
hyôshigi, 188, 196, 197
Hyûgajima, 159

Ibojirimai, 43
I-chien-chih, see *I-ken-shi*
Ichikawa Danjûrô I, 177, 189, 191, 207, 215, 219
Ichikawa Danjûrô VII, 208, 220
Ichikawa Danjûrô IX, 222
Ichikawa Ennosuke, 189, 192
Ichikawa Monnosuke, 189
Ichikawa Sadanji II, 139
Ichimura Uzaemon, 195
Ichimuraza, 188, 214
Ichinotani Futaba Gunki, 135, 159, 168, 169, 181, 194, 205
Ichinotani no Kassen, 174
Iemon, 186, 210
Igagoe Dôchû Sugoroku, 181
i-guse, 86
I-ken-shi, 128
Ikkaku Sennin, 119
Ikko-shû, 11
Ikkyû, 98
Ikyû, 209
imayô, 58
Imoseyama Onna Teikin, 158, 170, 181, 205
Inanomi no Okina, 50
Inoue Harimanojô, 177
Inquest in the Court of the Local Governor, see *Honjo no Monjaku*

Inuô Dôa, see Dôa
iroaku, 193
irogataki, 193
Ise cycle, 157
Ise Monogatari, 111, 116
Ise Ondo, 204
Ise Sarugaku Za, 63
Ishiô-hyôe, 114
Isora, 21, 22, 61
issei, 112
Isso school, 108
Itchû, 70, 83, 87, 91
itchû-bushi, 148
Iwato Kagura, *see* Kagura of the Heavenly Cave
Izaemon, 191, 203
Izayoi Seishin, see *Kosode Soga Azami no Ironui*
Izumi school, 102, 106, 120-21
Izumi Shikibu, 67
Izutsu, 116, 118

jabisen, 172, 176
Jayanagi, 208
ji, 149
jidaimono, 157, 158-60, 161-62, 166-70
Jiga Yozaemon Kunihiro, 104
Jihei, 192
jimai, 78
Jindai Kagura, 20
Jinen Koji, 85, 118
Jingû, empress, 22
Jisei, 71, 74
Ji-shû, 11, 94
jitsuaku, 193
jitsugoto, 194
Jitsukawa Enjaku, 192
ji-utai, ji-utai-kata, 56, 107
Jôdo-shû, 11
jo-ha-kyû, 38, 111, 117, 161
Jômon culture, 5
jo-no-mai, 113
jôruri, 16, 148, 156-70, 172, 174-81
Jôruri-hime Monogatari, 175, 178
jôshikimaku, 188

250 · INDEX

jûhachiban, see Eighteen Favorites
jushi (noronji), 9, 48, 63, 76, 79, 128
jushi-hashiri, 48, 78

kabesu, 186
kabuki dances, 218
Kabukiza, 185
Kabu Zuinôki, 65, 98
Kadensho, see *Fûshi Kaden*
Kadono school, 108
Kagamijishi, 206, 213, 214
kagami-no-ma, 108
Kagamiyama Kokyô no Nishikie, 160
Kagekiyo, 208; see also *Shusse Kagekiyo*
Kagotsurube, 204
Kagura, 6, 7, 11, 12, 17–23
Kagura of the Heavenly Cave, 19–20
Kagura of Luck of the Sea and Luck of the Mountain, 20–21
Kaiken Gedô to Rongi, 61
kaikô, 53, 56, 57, 128, 129
kairaishi, 173
Kairaishi-ki, 173
kakeri, 113
Kakyô, 92
Kamahige, 208
Kamakura Gozan, 90
Kamakura-period Sarugaku, 65
Kamigakari Za, 103
kamimai, 113
Kami Noh, 110, 116
Kamishima Kagemori, 83
kamishimo, 148, 152
Kampei, 196
Kanadehon Chûshingura, 134–35, 142–43, 148, 155, 170, 180, 181, 194, 196, 205, 219
Kan'ami, see Kanze Kan'ami Kiyotsugu
Kanampo, 38
Kanemaki, 79
Kanjinchô, 198, 200, 206, 208–9, 213
Kanjin Noh, 73, 97
Kanju Manju Ryôka no Koto, 61
Kansho (Hanshu), 57
Kan Shûsai, 166–67

Kan'u, 208
Kanze Kan'ami Kiyotsugu, 13, 82–89, 91
Kanze Kiyokado, 106
Kanze Kokusetsu, 103
Kanze Motomasa, 93, 118
Kanze Motoyoshi, 93
Kanze Nagatoshi, 15, 118, 119
Kanzen Chôaku Nozoki Karakuri, 206
Kanze Nobumitsu, 15, 100, 118, 119
Kanze On'ami Motoshige, 13, 95–96, 97, 100
Kanzeonji, 25
Kanze Shôemon Motonobu, 104
Kanze Sôsetsu, 101
Kanze Yajirô Nagatoshi, 101
Kanze Zeami Motokiyo, 13, 39, 82, 84, 85, 89–95, 111, 118
kaomise kyôgen, 215
Karakami, 21, 61
kari hanamichi, 184
Karora, 25
Karora, 28
Karura, see Karora
Kashima, 17
Kashiwa, 74
Kasuga Miko Sarugaku Noh, 66–68
Kasuga Ômiya Wakamiya Gosairei no Zu, 74
Kasuga Shrine, 71
Kasuga Wakamiya Shrine, 22, 27
kata, 200–201
Katana-dama, 73
Kataoka Gadô, 189
Kataoka Nizaemon, 192
katô-bushi, 148, 177
Katen, 36
Kawachi, 115
Kawatake Mokuami, 206, 207, 210, 216, 221, 222
Kayoi Komachi, 85
Kechimyaku, 31
kegon'e, 55
keigoto, 212
keisei, 192

INDEX · 251

Keisei Dôjôji, 214
keiseikai kyôgen, 191–92
kendai, 148
Kendaraku, 38
Kenkikodatsu, 41
ken-te, 48, 79
Kenuki, 208
Kia, 70, 87, 91
Kiji (Ch'iu-tzu), 25
Kiku, 87
Kikusui, 71, 74
Kimpira, 177
kimpira-bushi, 177, 189, 219
Kindai Shiza Yakusha Mokuroku, 104
Kinkafu, 7
Kinshôjô, 179
Kintarô, 177
Kintoki's Wrestling with a Bear, 177
Kira Kôzukenosuke Yoshinaka, 143
Kirare Yosa, see *Yowa Nasake Ukina no Yokogushi*
Kitano Monogurui, 73
Kita school, 108
Kitoku, 38
Kitômai, 76, 79
Kiyohime, 150
Kiyomizu Rihei, 178
kiyomoto (*kiyomoto-bushi*), 148, 149, 198, 214, 220
kizewamono, 180, 209–12, 220
Kôchiyama to Naozamurai, 203, 212
Kochô, 37
Kôfukuji temple, 52, 53, 55, 61, 63, 71
Koguryô music, see Komagaku
Kô houses, 108
Koi no Omoni, 117, 118
Koinyôbô Somewake Tazuna, 204
Kojiki (*Record of Ancient Matters*), 6, 19, 57
Kojirô, 169
Kokusenya Kassen, 148, 159, 170, 179
Kokushiki-jô, 115, 124
Komaboko, 61
komabue, 36
Komachi, 56

Koma Chikazane, 27, 31
Komagaku (Kôraigaku, Koguryô music), 32, 36, 127
Koma Moroyuki, 32
Koma Tomokazu, 31
Komparu Gonnokami, 65, 87
Komparu Mitsutarô, 87
Komparu Shirojirô, 101, 120
Komparu Za, 99, 101
Komparu Zempô Motoyasu, 101, 119
Komparu Zenchiku Ujinobu, 65, 95, 96, 98–99, 103, 118
Kongô, 25
Kongô, 28
Kongô school of *shite-kata*, 108
Kongô Za, 99, 103
Konjaku Monogatari, 57
Konju, 38
Kôno Moronao, 143
Konron, 25, 28–29, 126, 127
Ko Omote, 115
Kôraigaku, see Komagaku
Kôren, 70
Korohase, 38
koroshiba, 203
Ko Sarugaku (Old Sarugaku), 40, 41, 43
Kosode Soga, 117, 119
Kosode Soga Azami no Ironui, 207
koto, 5, 7
Kotobuki Soga no Taimen, 194, 207, 215
Kotokuraku, 38
kotsuzumi, 66, 108, 113
kotsuzumi-kata, 108
Koushi-jô, 115
Kouta, 64, 86
kouta, 14
Kouta-bushi Kusemai, 86
Kôwakamai, 16, 76–77
kowakare, 204
Kubo, 34
kuchiake-ai, 119
kuchidate, 105
Kudaragaku, 32
Kudô Suketsune, 194
Kugutsu (Sarugaku piece), 43

kugutsu (puppet show), 128
kugutsu-mawashi, 172
Kugutsu-mawashi no Ki, 173
kumadori, 190
Kumagai Jinya, see *Ichinotani Futaba Gunki*
Kumagai Naozane, 158, 168–69, 194
Kumanomai, 77
kurai, 94, 113
Kurama Tengu, 100, 119
Kuregaku, 24
kure no tsuzumi, 24–25
kuromisu, 187, 198
Kuromu, see *Konron*
Kuruwa Bunshô, 191, 203
kusabana-awase, 46
Kusazuribiki, 214
kuse, 111
Kusemai, 12, 14, 16, 64, 86
Kyôganoko Musume Dôjôji, 137, 196, 198, 206, 214
Kyôgen, 10, 11, 13, 14, 15, 87–89, 101–2, 103, 105–6, 119–25, 133, 137, 145, 174, 178, 205, 213
Kyôgenki, 105
Kyôkunshô, 27, 31, 37, 38, 41
Kyûi Shidai, 92, 94, 98
Kyûi Shûdô Shidai, see *Kyûi Shidai*
Kyû Tôsho (*Chiu T'ang-shu*), 127
Kyûzô, 118, 119

Lien Ch'eng-wu (Ren Shôbu), 61, 72
Lin-i (Rin'yû), 32

Macbeth, 159
Machi-iri Noh, 104
Madame Butterfly, 182
mae-jite, 111, 119
Magojirô, 115
mai, 14, 112
mai-guse, 86
mai-kata, 107, 112
mai no fu, 38
makude, 78
Makura Jishi, 206

Man'yôshû, 7
marafurimai, 29
marakata, 29
maruhon, 147
maruhon kabuki, 205
maruhon mono (*maruhon* plays), 181, 196, 205
maruhon plays, see *maruhon mono*
Masaoka, 204
Masefield, John, 134–35
masks, 22, 25–26, 27, 35, 57, 77, 114–15, 124, 137
massha-ai, 119, 124
masu, 185
Masumi Katô, 177
matsubamemono, 213
Matsudomoe, 74
Matsukaze, 116
Matsumoto Kôshirô V, 220
Matsuô, 158, 166–67, 194, 201, 204
Matsuômaru, see Matsuô
Matsura no Noh, 93
Matsutake Furyû, 88
Meiboku Sendai Hagi, 135, 159, 204
Meido no Hikyaku, 160, 192, 198, 205
Mekura Hôshi, 53, 54
Menukiya Chôzaburô, 176
meriyasu, 197
Meyerhold, Vsevolod E., 187
Michitose, 203
Michitose, 212
michiyuki, 57, 58, 59, 112, 129, 164, 199
mie, 185, 191, 197, 199
Migawari Zazen, 206, 213
Miidera, 117, 118
Mikagura, 7, 9, 17–18, 21–22
miko, 20, 44, 66
Miko Sarugaku Noh, 66–68
Mimashi, 24, 26
mimos, 189
Minamiza, 185
Minamoto, 158, 175
Minamoto no Yoshitsune, 140, 169, 175, 208–9
Miroku, 114

INDEX · 253

Mitsuteru, 115
Miyakoji Bungonojô, 220
Miyoshi Shôraku, 180, 205, 206
Mizukumi, 74
modoki, 20, 21, 28, 48, 50, 78, 102, 119
Modori Kago, 213, 220
mokugyo, 197
Mokyû, 57
Momijigari, 100, 117, 119, 198, 206, 213
Momijiyama Gakusho, 34
Momotarô, 213
mondô, 58, 59, 87
monomane, 83, 84, 85
"Monomane Jôjô," 90
monomane kyôgen, 218
Morita Kanya, 192
Morita school, 108
Moritaza, 188, 214
Moritsuna Jinya, 181
Môtsuji temple, 15, 56, 87
moutari, 78
Mukotsu and *Ukotsu*, 43
Murakami, emperor, 33
Murasaki Shikibu, 67
Muromachi-dono On-moteasobi Ennen, 55
musha-te, 48
Musume Dôjôji, see *Kyôganoko Musume Dôjôji*
Musume Kagekiyo Yashima Nikki, 159
myôka-fû, 94
Myôrakuji temple, 15, 55

nagauta, 198, 208, 209, 212, 214, 220
Naikyôbô, 35
Nakamura Ganjirô, 192
Nakamura Jakuemon, 189
Nakamura Kanzaburô, 189, 192, 194–95
Nakamura Senjaku, 189, 192
Nakamura Shikan, 189
Nakamura Utaemon, 189
Nakamuraza, 188, 214
Nambu Kagura, 77
Namiki Gohei, 206, 220
Namiki Gohei III, 206
Namiki Senryû, 205, 206

Namiki Shôzô, 181, 220
Namiki Sôsuke, 180–81, 209
Nanatsu Men, 208
nanoridai, 190
Nanto Negiryû, 106
Naozamurai (Naojirô), 203
Narikomaya, 195
Naritaya, 185, 195, 199
Narukami (*Narukami Fudô Kitayamazakura*), 139, 207, 208
Nasori, 38, 61
Nasu no Yoichi, 121
Natsu Matsuri Naniwa Kagami, 160, 180, 203, 209
nembutsu chant, 218
"Nenrai Keiko Jôjô," 90
netori, 28
New Sarugaku, 9, 40–45, 128
Nezumi Kozô Haru no Shingata, 207
Nichiren-shû, 11
Nihon Shoki, 6, 19
Nikki Danjô, 160, 200, 202
Nikkô, 114
Nikyoku Santai Ezu, 92, 94
nimaime, 194
Nimmyô, emperor, 32, 33
Nimpeiji temple, 87
Ningyô Jôruri, 16, 146, 172, 176
Ninin Dôjôji, 214
ninja, 203
Ninnô Kyô, 72
Ninomai, 35
Nishigawara Kakuzaemon, 157
Niwabi, 21
Nobumitsu, see Kanze Nobumitsu
nochi-jite, 111, 119
Nohgaku, 10, 13, 14, 39, 82
Nohmai, 77
Noh Sakusho, 92, 111
noh-torimono, 205, 206, 213
Nonomiya, 116, 118
Norikiyo, 66–67
norito, 7
noronji, see *jushi*
Nozakimura, see *Shimpan Utazaimon*

254 • INDEX

Nozawa, 176
nureba, 203
Nyôbô Kyôgen, 99
Nyôbô Sarugaku, 99

Obasute-yama, 56
Obo ga Mukashi, 56
Obô Kichiza, 210
Ôboshi Yuranosuke, 143, 152, 194
Ochiudo, 212
ôchômono, 158, 160
Oda Nobunaga, 158
Ôe no Masafusa, 69
Oga, 34
ôgi-byôshi, 172, 176
Ohatsu, 162–63
ohayashi-beya, 187
ohayashi renjû, 198
oiemono, 158, 159–60, 215
Ôishi Kuranosuke, 143
Oiwa, 186–87, 210
Ojô Kichiza, 210
Oka, 34
Okamura Shikô, 206
Okaru, 136, 196
okashi, 8
Okina, 18, 49, 50, 65, 66, 76, 88, 110
okotsuri, 57, 58
Oku, 34
Okuni, 141, 176, 196, 217–18
Ôkura school, 88, 101, 108, 120, 122
Ôkura Toraakira, 105, 120
Ôkura Torakiyo, 105
Ôkura Torazumi, 120
Old Sarugaku, *see* Ko Sarugaku
Ômi Genji Senjin Yakata, 205
Ômi Izeki, 115
Ominaeshi, 56
Ômi Sarugaku, 70, 83, 89
omo, 122
omote (mask), 114
omozukai, 150
On'ami, *see* Kanze On'ami Motoshige
Onda, 49
Ongyoku Kowadashi Kuden, 92

onnagata, 136, 142, 189, 193, 219, 221
Onnagoroshi Abura no Jigoku, 160, 203
Onna no Adauchi, 74
Onna-zata, 73
Ono, 34
Ôno Deme, 115
Onoe Baikô, 189, 195
Onoe Kikugorô, 195
Onoe Kikugorô III, 220
Onoe Kikugorô V, 222
Onoe Kikunosuke, 189
Onoe Shôroku, 195
Ono no Komachi, 73
Oshimodoshi, 208
Oshô Kichiza, 210
Osome, 160
Oto, 124
Otomi, 203
Ôto no Kiyokami, 32, 33
Otowaya, 185, 195, 199
Otozuru, 86
ôtsuzumi, 100, 113
Owari no Hamanushi, 32
Oze Hoan, 157
Ozuchi, 87

Paekche music, *see* Kudaragaku
Pai-hsi, 40
Pedu, king, 38
Poetics (Aristotle), 149, 161
Princess Chûjô, 203
Princess Kumo no Taema, 139

Rakuyô Dengaku Ki, 69
Rambyôshi, 53, 56, 57, 58, 66
Rampei Monogurui, 201
Record of Ancient Matters, *see* Kojiki
Reinhardt, Max, 187
Renaissance drama, 141
Renji, 53–54, 55, 57, 58–59, 128
Renjishi, 214
Ren Shôbu Biwa-kyoku no Koto, 61, 71, 72, 73
Ressenden (*Lieh-hsien-chuan*), 57
revolving stage, 181, 184, 186–87, 220

rikidô style, 65
Rikugi, 121
Rikurin Ichiro, 98
Ringo, 43
Rin'yû, 32, 35
Rin'yûgaku, 127
Rin'yû Hachigaku, 32
Roami, 89, 101
Rodayû, 102
Rokkasen, 214
Romeo and Juliet, 158
rongi, 56
Ryôjin Hishô, 18
Ryôô, 37, 39, 127
ryûgo, 128
ryûjin no mai, 113
ryûteki, 36

Saga Monogurui, 85
Sagami, 204
Saibari, 21
saidô style, 65
Saigyô, 67
Saigyô Monogatari, 67
Saisôrô, 38
Sakammai, 44
Sakata no Kintoki, 177
Sakata Tôjûrô, 135, 156, 178, 191, 192, 219
Sakaya, see *Hadesugata Onna Maiginu*
Sakôdo Za, 63
Sakurada Jisuke, 220
Sakura Gimin Den, 204
Sakurai Tambanojô, 177
Sakurama Bamba, 106
Sakuramaru, 158, 166
samadate, 78
Sambasô, 88, 124
Sambasô, 213
Sambon-ken, 79
samisen, 147, 148, 149, 172, 176, 197, 198, 213
sammaime, 194
Sammon Gosan no Kiri, 202
Sampô Gakusho, 34

Samurai Sarugaku, 64
San'e Jôitsuki, 53
Sanekata, 73
Sanemori, 118
Sangaku, 40, 41
sangyô, 148
Sanjônishi Sanetaka, 101
Sanju, 38
Sannin Katawa, 124, 206, 213
Sannin Kichiza Kuruwa no Hatsukai, 207, 210, 221
sannoko, 36
Sannô Shrine, 70
Sanyüeh, see Sangaku
Sarasvatī, see *Benzaiten*
Sarugaku, 9, 40–45, 54, 65, 128, 172, 173; see also Sarugaku Noh
Sarugaku Dangi, 65, 87, 93, 101, 114
Sarugaku Noh, 11, 13, 27, 62–68, 81; see also Sarugaku
Sarugô, 40
Sarume no Kimi, 20
Sasaki Gakurakuken, 102
Satokagura, 18
Satô Tadanobu, 202
Satsuma Jôun, 177
Sawazumi Kengyô, 176
Segawa Jokô III, 207
Seigaiha, 35
Seinô, 22, 27
Seinô dance, 17
Seinô Kagura, 9
Seishi Rokujû Igo Sarugaku Dangi, see *Sarugaku Dangi*
Seizatsugeki (Ch'eng-tsa-chü), 130
Sekidera Komachi, 116, 118
Sekihara Yoichi, 74
Seki no To, see *Tsumoru Koi Yuki no Seki no To*
sekkyô, 16
sekkyô-bushi, 178
semeba, 203
Semmin Sarugaku, 63
Sendai Hagi, see *Meiboku Sendai Hagi*
Senzai, 21

seriage, 202
serifu, 149
sewa jōruri, see *sewamono*
sewamono, 157, 160, 161–66, 207, 209–12, 220
Shakespearean drama, 141, 159, 182, 200, 201
shakkyōmono, 214
Shakuhachi, 73
Shakuzuru, 114
shamanism, 21
shang-mi, see *shōmei*
Shiba, 34
Shibaraku, 190–91, 199, 207, 209, 215
shidai, 112
Shidō Yōshō, 98
Shigenoi, 204
Shihiki no Oni, 73
Shii no Sōshō, 85
Shijin Senka no Sake o Nomu Koto, 60
Shikadō, 92
shikigaku, 144
Shimbashi Embujō, 185
Shimogakari Hōshō, 108
Shimogakari Za, 103
Shimotsuki Matsuri, 12
Shimotsuma Shōshin, 101, 103
Shimpa, 133
Shimpan Utazaimon, 160, 206
Shinadama, 43
shinadama, 128
shin-butsu shūgō, 12
Shindō school, 108
Shingeki, 133
Shinjū Ten no Amijima, 160, 192, 206
shinki-geki (shen-kuei), 126–27
Shinnō Hajin Raku, 37
Shinobu, 74, 79
Shin Sarugaku, see New Sarugaku
Shin Sarugaku Ki, 40, 42
Shin Tōsho (Hsin T'angshu), 128
Shinza, 62, 63, 70, 87
Shinzei Kogaku Zu, 41, 128
Shiokumi, 214
Shirabyōshi, 53, 56, 58, 60, 62

Shiragigaku, 32
Shirahige, 86
Shiranami Gonin Otoko (Benten Kozō or Aotōzoshi Hana no Nishikie), 197, 202, 203, 206, 211, 221
shiranamimono, 210
Shishimai, 77
shite, *shite-kata*, 107, 108, 111, 112, 122
shiza ichiryū, 103
Shiza Yakusha Mokuroku, 104
Shizuka ga Mai no Noh, 85
shō, 36, 54
Shōfuryū, 54, 57, 59–60
shōko, 36
shōmei, 128
shōmonji, 99
shōmyō, 56
Shōmyōshi Shōryōzan ni Mōzuru Koto, 59
Shosha, 73
Shōtoku, prince, 7, 24
Shōzan no Shikō, 58
Shōzon, 119
Shūchakujishi, 214
Shūdōsho, 87, 92
Shugendō, 12, 49, 75, 76, 79
Shugen Noh, 12, 14, 75–80
Shundō school, 108
Shunkan, see *Heike Nyogo ga Shima*
Shunnōden, 35
Shūō no Fune ni Iru Hakugyo no Koto, 60
shurai, 46
shushi, see *jushi*
Shusse Kagekiyo, 156, 178, 179
shūtamba, 204
Silla music, see Shiragigaku
Sōchō, 175
Soga brothers, 194
Soga Kyōdai, 79
Soga no Taimen, see *Kotobuki Soga no Taimen*
Sōgorō, 204
Son'ei, 55
Sonezaki Shinjū, 135, 162–65, 180, 192, 206, 212

INDEX · 257

sonohachi-bushi, 148
Sophocles, 171
Sôshi, 60
Sotoba Komachi, 118
Stanislavsky, Konstantin S. A., 192
Subjugation of Devils in the Ôe Mountains, The, 177
Sugawara cycle, 157
Sugawara Denju Tenarai Kagami, 135, 148, 155, 158, 161, 166–67, 170, 180, 194, 206
Sugawara no Michizane, 157, 158, 166
Sugiyama Tangonojô, 177
Suiko, empress, 7
Suiko-ju, 25
Suiko-ô, 25
Sukeroku Yukari no Edozakura, 177, 207, 208, 209, 215
Sumai no Sechie, 41
Sumidagawa, 117, 118, 213
Sumidagawa-mono, 206
Sumiyoshi, 17
super-puppets, 154, 171
suppon, 187, 202
Susano-o, 19, 61
Susano-o no Mikoto Daija o Shitagaeru Koto, 61
Suzuka Monjo, 66
Suzuki no Saburô, 79

Taasobi, 49
Tachiai, 72, 73
Tachibanaya, 195
tachimawari, 201, 203
Tachinusubito, 206
tachiyaku, 193
Taigenshô, 31
Taiheiki, 70, 143, 157
Taiheiraku, 36, 61
Taiko, 29
taiko, 36, 114
Taikô cycle, 157
Taikofu, 25
Taikôki, 157
Taira, 158, 159, 175

Taira no Atsumori, 158, 168, 169
Taira no Kagekiyo, 159
Taira no Kiyomori, 159
Taira no Tomomori, 140
Taira no Tsunemori, 168
Taira no Yasuyori, 72
taka-ashi, 50, 71
Takao Sange, 214
Takarada Jurai, 207
Takayasu school, 108
Takebe Genzô, 166–67
Takeda Izumo, 180, 205
Takemoto Gidayû I, 148, 156, 177, 178, 179
Takemoto Saburobei, 205
Takemoto Uneme, 180
Takemotoza, 148, 156, 178, 180, 181
Takeshiba Kisui, 206
Takezawa, 176
Takino Kôtô, 176
Tale of Genji, The, see Genji Monogatari
Tale of the Heike, The, see Heike Monogatari
Tamakuzura, 117, 118
Tamatsushima, 74
Tamiya Iemon, see Iemon
Tamura, 118
T'ang music, see Tôgaku
Tarô-kaja, 122, 123
tatesakusha, 214
Tatsuemon, 114
tayû, 148, 187
Tazunuru Tsuki no Kazura Renji, 59
Teatro Farnese, 141
Teatro Olimpico, 141
Technik des Drama, Die, 161
ten, 37
tendai shômyô, 174
Tenjinki, 157
Tenjinsama, 158
Tennôji temple, 24, 34
Tenri, 79
Tenshôbon Kyôgen Shû, 105
Terakoya, see Sugawara Denju Tenarai Kagami

Te Sarugaku, 99
tesuri, 147
Thespis, 171
tôben, 56, 128, 129
Tôbushô, 101
Tôdaiji temple, 26, 52, 54, 55, 62
Tôgaku, 32, 127
Tôgi, 34
Tôin Kinkata, 69
Tôjutsu (T'ang tricks), 43
tôjutsu (jugglery), 128
Tôka, 7, 8
Tôkaidô Yotsuya Kaidan, 186, 207, 210, 220
tokiwazu, 148, 198, 214, 220
tokiwazu-bushi, 148
tokiwazu plays, 214
Tokubei, 162–63, 165, 192
tombogaeri, 201
tomimoto, 220
Tomoe, 79
Tôri Kagura, 197
Torimono (dance), 21
torimono (accessories), 36
Tô Sangaku (T'ang Sanyüeh), 41
Toyohara, 34
Toyohara Muneaki, 31
Toyotake Wakadayû, 180
Toyotakeza, 180, 181
Toyotama-hime, 22
Toyotomi Hideyoshi, 103, 157
Tsapan, see Zappun
Tsubosaka Reigenki, 182
Tsuchidayû, 87
Tsuchigumo, 213
Tsuda Hanjûrô, 207
Tsugaimai, 38
Tsuina Festival, 48
tsuke, 197
tsume ningyô, 151
Tsumoru Koi Yuki no Seki no To, 207, 213
Tsunemasa, 74
tsura-akari, 200
tsurane, 190, 191, 199

Tsurukame Furyû, 88
Tsuruzawa, 176
Tsuta Momiji Utsunoya Tôge, 203
Tsuuchi Jihei, 207
tsuzumi, 198

Ubusuna-gami, 68
Ue, 34
Uemura Bunrakuken, 146, 181
Ugetsu, 99, 118
Uirôuri, 208
Uji Kaganojô, 177
Uji Yatarô, 120
Uma no Shirô, 65
Umeô, 158, 166
Umeômaru, see Umeô
Umewaka Minoru, 106
Umewaka school, 108
Umi-sachi Yama-sachi, 6, 17, 20
Unshû Shôsoko, 42
Urazato, 203
Usa Hachiman Shrine, 22
Ushiwakamaru, 175
Usobuki, 124
uta-awase, 46
Utaryô, see Gagakuryô
Utsubozaru, 123
Uwanari, 208
Uzumasa-dera temple, 24

Wagner, Richard, 134
wagato, 191–92, 219
waka, 7, 57, 59, 111, 172
Wakamizu, 74
Wakan Rôeishû, 57
waki, waki-shi, 100, 111, 115
warabemai, 53
Warabiori, 79–80
Warambegusa, 105
Watônai, 159
wazaogi, 19, 20
Wilder, Thornton, 185

yagô, 195
Yakko Dôjôji, 214

yakusha, 188
Yakusha Rongo, 192, 193
Yakushi Nyorai, 178
yamabushi, 12, 75
Yamabushi Kagura, 77
Yamabushi Seppô, 87
yamadai, 198
Yamanoi, 34
yamaoroshi, 198
Yamashina Tokitsugu, 101
Yamatogana Iroha Nana Moji, 213
Yamatomai, 7-8
Yamato Sarugaku, 70, 86
Ya no Ne, 208
Yaoya Oshichi, 198
Yasha, 114
Yashima, 79, 116, 118
yataikuzushi, 202
Yatsudama (jugglery), 43
yatsudama (knucklebones), 128
Yayoi culture, 5
yayoi kyôgen, 215
Yôkyoku, 101, 110, 111-12, 178
Yonembutsu, 74
Yoritomo, 208
Yoroboshi, 93, 117, 118
Yoroboshi mask, 115
Yosaburô, 203
yosei, 8
Yoshida Bunzaburô, 180, 181
Yoshida Shinto, 94
Yoshidaya, see *Kuruwa Bunshô*
Yoshino Shizuka, 85
Yoshinoyama Michiyuki, see *Yoshitsune Sembonzakura*
Yoshitsune, see Minamoto no Yoshitsune
Yoshitsune Sembonzakura, 135, 139, 158, 161, 170, 180, 202, 212, 215

Yoshiwara, 186, 214, 215
Yoshiwara Suzume, 220
Yoshizawa Ayame, 193, 219
Yotsuya Kaidan, see *Tôkaidô Yotsuya Kaidan*
Youchi Soga, 100
Yowa Nasake Ukina no Yokogushi, 203, 207
yudate, 76
yûgen, 13, 84, 85, 91, 94, 95, 104, 111, 117, 130
Yûgiri, 191, 203
yuimae, 53, 55
yuka, 148
Yuki Matsuri, 12
Yuki Oni, 74
Yuranosuke, see Ôboshi Yuranosuke
yusuriba, 203
yusô, 54, 56
Yusôbyôshi, 56

zae no onoko, 18, 21, 46
zagashira, 214, 215
zaigôuta, 197
Zappun (Tsapan), 130
zamoto, 214
Zatsugeki (Tsa-chü), 129
Zazen'in, 114
Zeami, see Kanze Zeami Motokiyo
Zekan, 115
Zempô, see Komparu Zempô Motoyasu
Zenchiku, see Komparu Zenchiku Ujinobu
Zôa, 70, 91
Zôami, 114
Zôhiki, 208
Zoku Kyôkunshô, 31
zômen, 22, 35
Zô Onna mask, 115

The "weathermark" identifies this book as a production of John Weatherhill, Inc., publishers of fine books on Asia and the Pacific. Book design and typography: Miriam F. Yamaguchi and Meredith Weatherby. Composition of the text: Kwangmyong Printing, Seoul. Printing of the text: Kenkyusha Printing, Tokyo. Engraving and printing of the plates, in offset: Kinmei Printing, Tokyo. Binding: Makoto Binderies, Tokyo. The typeface used is Monotype Bembo.